MW00581378

BY FRANCES MAYES

A Great Marriage

A Place in the World

See You in the Piazza

Women in Sunlight

Bella Tuscany

Every Day in Tuscany

Under the Tuscan Sun

Swan

In Tuscany (with Edward Mayes)

A Year in the World

Bringing Tuscany Home (with Edward Mayes)

The Tuscan Sun Cookbook (with Edward Mayes)

Always Italy (with Ondine Cohane)

Pasta Veloce (with Susan Wyler)

The Discovery of Poetry

Sunday in Another Country

After Such Pleasures

Hours

The Arts of Fire

Ex Voto

A GREAT MARRIAGE

BALLANTINE BOOKS
NEW YORK

a great marriage

A NOVEL

frances mayes

A Great Marriage is a work of fiction. Names, characters, places, and incidents are the products of the author's imagination or are used fictitiously. Any resemblance to actual events, locales, or persons, living or dead, is entirely coincidental.

Published in the United States by Ballantine Books, an imprint of Random House, a division of Penguin Random House LLC, New York.

Ballantine Books & colophon are registered trademarks of Penguin Random House LLC.

LIBRARY OF CONGRESS CATALOGING-IN-PUBLICATION DATA
Names: Mayes, Frances, author.
Title: A great marriage: a novel / Frances Mayes.
Description: First edition. | New York: Ballantine Books, 2024.
Identifiers: LCCN 2024006257 (print) | LCCN 2024006258 (ebook) |
ISBN 9780593498989 (hardback; acid-free paper) | ISBN 9780593498996 (ebook)
Subjects: LCSH: Marriage—Fiction. | LCGFT: Romance fiction. | Novels.
Classification: LCC PS3563.A956 G74 2024 (print) | LCC PS3563.A956 (ebook) |
DDC 813/.54—dc23/eng/20240216
LC record available at https://lccn.loc.gov/2024006257
LC ebook record available at https://lccn.loc.gov/2024006258

Printed in the United States of America on acid-free paper

randomhousebooks.com

2 4 6 8 9 7 5 3 1

First Edition

For Edoardo

A GREAT MARRIAGE

April 1995

When spring came, even the false spring, there were no problems except where to be happiest.

—ERNEST HEMINGWAY

1

THE WINE SPILLED. As I reached across the table, my sleeve grazed Austin's glass and the big globe fell over, quickly spreading a circle of carmine red on the white tablecloth. Austin shot up fast, chair tipping backwards. He grabbed his napkin and spread it over the stain. I glanced at my daughter, bride-to-be Dara, her eyes widened, the slight quiver of her thin nostrils, a response Rich says she must have learned from her horse. She shot me a look—she knew I'd spent the afternoon lavishing my attention on every place card and dessert spoon. Rocco woke up from his nap by the door, barking and circling the table.

"Oh, no. Sorry!" I pressed my napkin into the dark stain, too, and moved the flowers and water carafe to cover it. Rich shooed Rocco out the door.

Austin dabbed at his tie with a cloth I grabbed from the kitchen. "Doesn't matter, Lee—good as new," he said. Austin's unusual eyes—hazel, yes, but it's the way he looks at you rather than their river-water color, as if he's surprised to find you in front of him. But glad. (I've had the odd thought that he might say, *I see you. Do you see me?*) I rinsed his glass in the kitchen and Rich refilled. Austin raised it: "To Rich and Lee and Charlotte! I'm a lucky guy. Thank you for this feast, and thank you, Amit and Luke, for making the trip. And everyone," he slightly bowed toward our friends, "I will be privileged to get to know you. Dara, you have my heart." Nothing broke but the glasses all around clinked hard.

All solved, except not. Damn, the spilled wine seeped into the napkins.

For some moments, I just want perfection. Tonight was one, the intimate celebration—family and best friends—of my Dara's imminent wedding to Austin. Dara, finally. After all her are-you-kidding-me romances—don't think of the waiter with big buttons distending his ears, the modern dancer always slipping out of recovery, the too-blond scuba diver that time in Key West. Mama always said she's glad of her granddaughter's high spirits, but she's one to overlook consequences. If we expressed misgivings, Dara always snapped, "Quit! Leave me alone. I've grown up in Hillston! And it's not Thrillston here. I need life." Many brief disasters, my bright bird, all soars and plunges. Now this opening into an exhilarating future. I was blessed, as they say around here, with meeting Rich, someone special. And now that's her great fortune, too.

Her menu, my table—white linens monogrammed with Mama's and her mother's initials. The Waterford candlesticks we brought home from our honeymoon in Ireland, and two silver champagne urns (one borrowed from the florist) filled with apricot roses. Rich's welcome-to-the-family toast, Mama on good behavior, for god's sake, and Dara and Austin's best friends, along with our dearest neighbors, Fawn and Charles, Elizabeth and Eric. Long and sparkling, two tables abutted, and the seam didn't even show. Her intimate party: now marred. The night of the first photographs for the wedding albums—Jerry, our photographer friend, came for half an hour—to be pored over decades later, when I'm up floating in the clouds and they're still walking the beach, paying taxes, and figuring out the great mystery ride that is marriage.

. . .

A small blip. No explosive political rants. As a state senator, Fawn can get going at times, and Eric, the town mayor, is often drawn into inflammatory discussions. Thankfully no oversharing or boring childhood anecdotes. A wine stain is not important. Rich is probably just mourning the waste of good Brunello.

Why am I careening in the sheets? Life right now seems a sweet unfolding. Dara's radiance—her eyes, the aqua blue of the inside of a glacier, the only genetic gift from Rich's overwound father. When she was small, I sometimes looked at her and wondered if she were an alien. Well, my cranky father-in-law did have those same eyes, but his were shaded by a burly monobrow, and his jaw was like the side of a meat cleaver, so you didn't really notice the sublime aquamarine. Tonight, luminous, she looked at everyone with a vibrancy and joy I'll never forget. We love Austin. Son we never got to raise? (My stillborn son when Dara was five. In thousands of moments I imagine our boy, Hawthorn Willcox, at six on a pony, at ten on the swim team, awkward at fourteen with peach fuzz. After all these years, I can barely say his name.) Is Austin my projection, is that why I attached to him from the start? The only solace for that lost oval face with faint blue-veined eyebrows and a fringe of eyelashes? I never saw his eyes but imagine them the color in that astronaut photo of Earth taken from space, swirling dark blue orbs.

Beside me, Rich sleeps like the newly dead. I almost laugh because his mouth in an O looks as if he's about to blow a bubble. Just before he went to bed, he threw a few things in his bag for—where is he going? Investigating an environmental disaster in Alaska, I think he said. Oil. A spill. At least better than the last trip into Somalia, where the engine stalled and a gang of bandits tried to overtake the boat he and the photographer hired. Every night, as his head touches the pillow, he conks out for dreamless hours. I don't envy him that—there's something primitive about it—though my insomnia is crazy-making and something equally primitive lurks there, too. His snoring does make me laugh. Alpha bear guarding the cave entrance?

❧

RICH HEARS THE BEDROOM DOOR CREAK, THEN CLICK SHUT. SHE'S WANdering, as usual. Lee often doesn't know what sleep is. I left her a melatonin by her toothbrush before I signed off. This day lasted a week. I think the kids would have preferred to throw steaks on the grill, but I was told this had to be an occasion. Lee damned made sure it was. Dinner was memorable, those quail from our shoot down in Thomasville, near where Charlotte comes from. Odd to think of Lee's mother as a South Georgia girl once upon some godforsaken time down in the pineys. At least the old bird behaved tonight. Unlike at Big Mann's wake. Lord, when she stood by the casket at the funeral home and burst out with "The Night They Drove Old Dixie Down." Flabbergasted the visitors who were there to offer condolences. And not only. She'd arranged for church bells to ring all over town after the service. Nothing grand enough for Big Mann. Rich smiled in the dark. A mother-in-law for the books. Someone should write a book. Her breed is disappearing—or never was. Who could write, Lee? Not me, no way. Being son-in-law is enough. Tomorrow—three flight changes to get to Fairbanks. A four-wheel waiting, the map in my backpack already marked. Lee will be alone, as much as she ever is, with Dara and Austin on their uncharted way and her mama heading south to her eagle's nest at Indigo Island. Too damn bad Big Mann croaked. He was a right SOB, bigger than life.

Rich closes his eyes and lets himself travel around the table, looking at every guest, pegging each into the picture of Dara's future. Best and brightest? Some of them. Moira, maybe not anymore. A future here in town writing for the *Regulator News*? So much for the Vanderbilt summa cum laude. Married to poker-face, frizzy-hair, what's his name? Ear specialist in Lee's dad's old practice. Carleton, that's it. Moira might turn into one of those who suck lemons for a living. He flashed on her and Dara bonding at nine over horse madness. Camps. Overwrought thoroughbreds snorting fog on winter mornings. Dara's mess in the kitchen when she concocted grain and cereal mixes for the stable horses' Christmas breakfast. Those tedious dressage shows. Hauling the horse in a wobbly trailer over to Winston and Charlotte. Dara, small on that beast Chelsea, sailing over jumps, trotting off with a big smile. Except when she didn't. Two falls. Dislocated shoulder and jammed knee. Those gone days, thank you, Jesus. That horse we bought off the racetrack out to pasture somewhere. Mei Hwang, fragile. Thin as a straw. When I dropped off the dry cleaning, she was always there, little thing cutting out paper patterns, her parents taking in the shirts. Now she designs. Even making Dara's wedding dress. Rich smiled again, remembering Dara telling him Mei used to try on the dresses and sweaters women brought in to be cleaned. Daringly wore some to high school games. Spunky girl. The two guys, Austin's friends, arriving today, out tomorrow early. Big lives under way. Luke something, the American one, from Florida somehow got himself to Cambridge. Architect, too. All architects wear black and those thin glasses? Big smiles to match big lives, especially the Indian guy, Amit something. Luke seemed to lean toward the Hwang girl. Humble family, but this girl emerged with a cool natural dignity and poise.

Austin strikes me as quite a particular guy. I get the feeling of rumbling currents under smooth water. What does he have that draws Dara? Well, looks. He's a match for her there. Probably Fairfield Porter would have liked to paint his type, the casual, lanky poise made to hang a good linen suit on. Bony, maybe. A cut above the creeps Dara brought around previously. Man, she could pick them. Rich paused and let an image of Austin frame itself in his mind's eye. His face looks sculptural. Molded lips. High cheekbones. Those squared shoulders more elegant than strong. Tennis player, no doubt, not a hard-core athlete. He closes his eyes and feels a whoosh of excitement from his own early fame, the crack of the bat, the flat-out run to first. Dust swirling in the field lights. The Purple Hurricanes, jersey number 15.

But Austin . . . Wide mouth, and Dad would admire the rare, slightly rounded and slightly spaced teeth. Easy to floss. What a legacy from Dad: I can't help but notice people's teeth. Whatever else he was, he was a damned good dentist. Full of rage at parents who wouldn't pay to have their kids' teeth straightened. Full of rage, period. Austin is about as blond as they come—he's constantly tossing back that big shock of straight hair falling in his face. True blonds, what, 5 percent of people? What is a *shock* of hair? What's even a *hank* of hair? Big dreamer like Dara. Maybe that's the connection. Maybe she likes the posh-sounding accent. The dad owns a bookstore, antiquarian, which Lee finds marvelous. Dara said his mother died young. Where's Lee? Are we going to hear Dara tiptoe down the hall to the guest room, or he to hers? I certainly don't care, and you'd think on such a night . . . And they seem like lightning in a jar.

Earlier, as Lee got into bed, we were remembering that first visit to my family's house—creaking steps and latched door and some quick and desperate lovemaking, with my parents in the next room. At one moment that night, we started laughing. Dad called out, "Barbarians!" At breakfast he glared but Lee kept smiling at him with all her perfect teeth.

Rich shifts to his side, tosses off the duvet, and plumps the pillow. He imagines tomorrow, sitting beside the pilot of the small charter plane that shimmies, bumping through cloud layers, aiming toward a short runway, first spotting the oil spill, arcing down, drifting, rising toward him, the shining black oil oozing over boundless snow.

❧

DOWNSTAIRS, LEE FEELS THE HOUSE GONE STILL. I LOVE THE SOLITUDE, she thinks, of stove light in the kitchen, dishes done, faint lingering aromas of bacon and citrus cleanser. Even as a child I liked to creep in after everyone was asleep and find a cold biscuit, robe pulled tight, that low hum of the fridge. Not really wanting anything but wanting something, I pour a splash of grapefruit juice and step outside to the terrace. The setting moon throws silvery light across the old mother gardenias and the lawn splotched with shadows that fold into darkness under the boxwood hedge. A sheen of dew glazes the downslope to the meadow. Looking up, I expect a starry swath over the house, but the sky is obscured, as if a veil has been tossed across the constellations. Bridal veil; the one I wore has moth holes. And Dara thinks veils are creepy.

Oh, Austin—there, just beyond the circle of the last lantern. No one blew out the candles. I have the crabby thought that if I don't do it no one does. And then the corrective: Well, no one asks you to, so the fault is yours.

Chair tipped back, feet up on the railing, and the meadow winking with fireflies, he's silhouetted, a cutout of himself. "Oh, you're awake, too!" A wine bottle stands in the pebbles beside him.

"Lee, you're up late. The quail was delicious, so rich—those juniper berries and thyme. What a woodsy combination. And the cake—roulade—I could roll in it. Everything was superb." He lifts his glass to me.

"That's sweet. It's the cognac and slow roasting that make the meat just fall off the bones. Why are you out here all by yourself? Getting spooked about marrying into this nutty family?" I sit down beside him on a slightly damp chaise longue.

"Oh, no. Aren't all families crackers? Oops, not that yours is. Your mom's the only loose cannon, Dara said. Right?" He smiles. "I think I'm safe. Too bad about the wine spill, and good wine, too. Dara told me you expected perfection."

"Yes—'Perfection of the life or of the work.'" I quote from Yeats, and it isn't lost on him. I'm guessing very little is lost on him. "My side of that has always fallen toward the life part. I hope yours falls toward the work. Much better in the long run. Yes, wackos abound. Mama's who she is, just never had any filter. But she was lovely tonight. Mostly. I thought her toast was sweet—calling you a darling boy and Dara a fairy grandchild."

"But then she said that we're celebrating a suitable first marriage." Austin throws back his head and laughs a big laugh. You want to laugh, too, hearing him roar.

"That's my mama. I'm sorry."

"No problem. She had only two marriages, right? I've seen the photos of your dad, Dr. Stark. And then the next one in line—Senator Mann, big-time guy, Dara's hero. Maybe your mama only speaks the truth no one else will—the Greek chorus function."

"At times, maybe, but she's a born romantic, and that often turns to cynicism in old age. No need to mention her various interim candidates such as the Mexican bullfighter in San Miguel, a head shorter than she and married, that summer of her divorce from my dad, when she and I went to Mexico to study Spanish. How could she? I'd feared Dara was following her example." Maybe I shouldn't have said that.

Austin laughed. His laugh! Wake the dead! What a raucous, abundant laugh. And we will get to hear it forever! The juice tastes bitter and a shooting pain hits above my right eye. Too much Brunello? From the end of the meadow, coyotes start up their mournful yapping. That's the females announcing they're in heat. I can't see them but imagine a passel cavorting and leaping in pursuit of some hapless vole or rabbit. They sound rather endearing.

"What a wild sound. And it's close. I heard owls conversing back and forth—spooky to the ears of a London boy. And that insane croaking. They sync!" He beats out a rhythm on the arm of the chair. "And suddenly stop. Then start up like they're obeying a conductor. My god, they're loud."

"Oh, our tree frogs, my favorite symphony. Fireflies sync, too." We sit facing the palest moon setting into the sycamores along the river. Quiet. Has he fallen asleep—his head tipped back, a slight frown and his eyes closed? I take the glass out of his hand and set it on the table beside him. Let him wake later in this deep southern night in spring, a night to remember. Do I see on his cheek (there's only candlelight) a shiny tear like a snail track? Why not, it's an emotional time.

I walk along the terrace wall blowing out the lanterns. Our farmhouse looms behind me, rectangular ingots of light from the hall windows stretching like doorways across the shadowed lawn. Mysterious, as houses often are, as in that painting by Magritte, *Evening*, where the house in deep twilight is seen by the viewer and you feel the hidden life beyond the lighted windows, all golden and shadow.

What is it like, I wonder, to be him, to walk into all this because you love a girl. There's the girl, Dara, on her own—center stage. She's compelling. She's all you ever wanted. Now a floppy velvet curtain jerks aside, and behind her stand all of us. Ready to bring to bear whatever we bring. I feel a pang of sympathy and hope he didn't feel assaulted by Rich offering to take him out duck hunting on the river, by Mama questioning him about what his father does and where do his parents live (only to hear that his mother is dead), Moira (she's looking pinched) sizing him up. How cutting she can be to those who don't live here. And by me fussing over the way the napkins are folded, and generally "driving everything into the ground," as Rich sometimes fumes at me.

Two owls start their back and forth calls to each other. Could be worse, Austin, honey, I would like to say. Could be a lot worse. As in Rich's family when I went to visit them in Pensacola for the first time. His mother, Deb, was agoraphobic, though no one knew the word then. She couldn't cross the threshold of the front door. She lit one cigarette with the end of another, all windows closed. We were fumigated. Rich's father, Cooper Willcox—I privately referred to him as Coo-Coo—a dentist originally from New Jersey, lost a leg in Vietnam but suffered even more from a terminal case of arrogance. I was helping Deb set the table. From the dining room, I overheard him in the kitchen say to Rich, "Pretty, I'll grant, but with that southern accent how do you know if she's as dumb as she sounds?" His mother's eyes squinted, then she smiled rather conspiratorially at me. I knew we would not be friends. Later, at dinner, he asked—joking, I thought—to see my teeth. Rich said, "Dad!" but I bared my gums. "Nice," he said. "Some good genes somewhere." Any compliment from him meant a quick cut, too. My mother, Charlotte Lee Pomerance Stark now Mann, would have risen on her haunches and hissed a withering comment. But I just smiled. What a miracle that Rich, nicest person on Earth, came out of that viper pit.

Little do you notice all that background noise at the beginning of a romance; not in your ken to know how seemingly ancillary people are in reality appendages who will ruin or enrich or bog down or amuse your life. Or bore you silly. Austin doesn't know what's in store, and flipping that, neither do I. He's stepping over our threshold as well. What joy and despair will he bring to the damp jigsaw puzzle at the beach, the handing around of gifts on Christmas morning, the fender bender in the parking lot, and worse, much worse, the various early onsets and faulty valves and, who knows, breakdowns. I am just feeling taut. Or weepy, though I'm not prone to that.

I feel my way up the stairs. A slab of light shines under Mama's door. As a child I'd wake up at two or three and wander to my parents' room. Seems she was always crouched on her side, the low lamp glowing enough for her to read, my father hunched on his side, back turned away like a boulder.

Rich, sleeping. His strong shoulders where I can always press my face. All in all, a fine evening, intimate and relaxed. Shining Dara. Carol, who helped serve the dinner, placed the strawberry roulade in front of her and she cut big pieces for everyone, remembering to say something particular to Austin's two friends who'd traveled to get here, and to thank her family. "Luke gets the biggest piece because he drove all the way from Sarasota." "To the best daddy on the planet." "For Austin, because we're two peas in a pod!" She's a pleaser, instinctively, a gentle presence sometimes exposing a formidable stubbornness. "Mom and Mimi, my everythings," she said. Austin, that wing of blond hair always falling over his right eye, and the constant gesturing with his hands, those fine hands that look cloned from a marble statue. Head cocked, eyes wide, smile always about to start but sometimes turning to a slight pucker. Did the wine spill onto his lap? His tie is ruined.

"Soul mate" is bandied about. She's found him and he her. Anyone could feel the hot wire sizzling back and forth between them. They are young but old enough to recognize when water turns to wine. Stand in a field your whole life, Mama maintains, and you'll get only one lightning jolt, though wasn't she hit a few more times than that? How was she such a successful psychologist when much of her handed-down wisdom is outrageously idealistic or drastic? Maybe that's why. And I think people just feel her zest strongly enough that it transfers to them. I underestimate her. How rare it is for her psychology books to sell all over the world? Growing up, I felt my response to anything—winning debates, swim club ribbons, seeing the Grand Canyon, opening birthday presents—was inadequate compared with her outsized enthusiasm. Thank god, as we cleared the glasses from the living room, no one else heard her say that Amit, Austin's friend from Delhi, "could benefit from having his ears pinned back." And wasn't Carleton knocking back a good bit of wine? She'd noted, as she passed me in the hall earlier, that the way Dara's friend Moira slumps, she'll develop osteoporosis by fifty, and that the crimped hem of my romantic blue dress looks chewed by hounds. When challenged about such comments, she replies that observing foibles makes life remarkable.

❧

AUSTIN FEELS THE GLASS LIFTING FROM HIS FINGERS BUT KEEPS HIS eyes closed. Lee, what an incredible mother. She might want to talk more, though, and he can't. He's done for, slipping onto that floating platform on the shimmering lake between dream and sleep. Then he jerks awake, seeing Lee wandering away along the terrace wall, blowing out candles. Poof. Poof, then her white robe going ghostly against the boxwoods.

And here it comes at him. Ball of fire.

Just before he left New York to go south for the party, he dashed into his apartment. He had to pack in a hurry. His presentation had gone overtime. All good. Flying high. The project a GO. The scale model and specs only completed at two the night before, then a round of drinks with the team. Running on fumes but exalted. Sleep on the plane, all forty-five minutes? Dara, Dara. I will get to say *my wife*!

The big boss from London was all smiles and congratulations except for two rather major "suggestions." Two hours till the flight out of LaGuardia for DC, where Dara surely has packed her yellow Mini with enough clothes for a week instead of this flying overnight trip. As carefully as he can, he rolled his suit and poked it into his duffel. Almost out the door, he sees the message light blinking.

"Austin, Shelley calling. Can you please ring me back asap? We should talk right away."

A wash of guilt traveled from his throat down to his shoes. He's told her. Told her. I'm long done. Those pointy pink lacquer nails of hers always seem about to dig into his flesh. "I'm a damned fool idiot," he said aloud. He slipped up in November when he traveled back to London to pitch his project.

He grabbed his bag. At university, she attracted him—someone so unfamiliar—those giant hoops swaying from her ears, sometimes even a bangle (worn ironically) around her ankle? Black waves of hair rippling down to her waist. Oh, she was mysterious and fresh, like nothing he'd ever seen before. Amit had known her in Delhi and vaguely thought there were complicated family stories, a mother who was an Irish nun or something. To Austin, she never said more than "It's too baroque to unravel." Shelley, with that eyeliner, thick like on mummy lids. What is it? Kohl? Something fatalistic about her. Shelley, smart enough to get herself to Cambridge and to stand out among the intellectual English girls.

This nagging fear ever since that message. I should have grabbed my stuff and left the red light blinking.

Austin ran the film of when, since junior year and for six months before he took the job in New York, he and Shelley were sometime lovers. He'd definitively broken off contact but sometimes saw her at parties. A friendly wave, a how-are-you, that's all. A relief.

At Cambridge they'd had the same maths class, Austin suffering through the course and taking pass-fail to maintain his first-class honors goal. She sailed through, maths being instinctive to her. They ended up in an on/off relationship, on for her, mostly on/off for him.

Pass. Fail. Her flowery scent and haunting inky eyes. Teakettle whistling in her bedsit, hanging lampshades made of pleated Indian fabric, strumming of sitar music in the background. "A bit of home," she explained, "for comfort. I need my props, although my mother would be shocked. Our house in Delhi is all flokati rugs, white sofas, and Eames chairs." A word she used often: *need*. That's what she projected. Dara, the opposite—her spiky independence and take-charge energy. Hard to pin Shelley down—clingy? Not exactly, but more that some voracious open space in her threatened him . . . Threatened what? He was glad for the work assignment in New York. A total break, finally.

In October 1994, a week after he arrived in New York, Austin met Dara. They were both staring at an incomprehensible construction at a Mary Boone Gallery opening. They looked at the contorted, deflated gray balloons glued to a manhole cover for a full minute, then at each other. They started laughing. Amid all the girls in black, she wore a red dress with big black buttons. She was slender; "trim" came to mind. Her skin, peachy with a few scattered freckles, her azure eyes like the clear waters of Greece on school break when he was in secondary school. Usually not prone to pick-up intros, he found himself turning to her. "Is this cool or not? I'm Austin. What's your name?" he'd asked. "Can I get you a plastic glass of something?"

"Well, I'm Dara Amelia Willcox. I'm from Hillston, North Carolina, a long way from where you're from, and yes. Then I wouldn't mind getting out of here asap." Whoa, who's picking up whom?

Those eyes, almost shocking, but mesmerizing. She might have been less stunning without that color, he thought (thin nose), but she was not without it; and obviously she was ballsy, cheeky, up for it, whatever "it" might mean. "Are you an artist? This kind of artist?" She waved her hand around the room of flocked garbage bags.

"Not at all, unfortunately. I rather like the sticky garbage bags." He told her about working at Calvert & Marlowe Architects, what luck to be picked by that firm. "Oh, not luck," she said, "they liked your confidence and your—what do you call it—your bespoke shoes."

"What about you?"

"I'm thinking of moving up here because Washington is a one-subject town. But I like the subject, that's the problem. I graduated three years ago from Georgetown, and I'm probably going to law school there this fall, but I also applied to NYU and Columbia. I want it to be fun as well as, you know, rigorous." She raised her eyebrows. "I volunteer at HUD—that's Housing and Urban Development. And my paid job is minor speechwriter for the administration. I try to slip in quotes from Yeats."

"Yeats?"

"My mom's a Yeats scholar. My dad's a journalist. Whereas I may or may not be floundering a bit right now."

That's my girl, Austin found himself thinking. Smart, too. They wandered the gallery, both galvanized by, if not love at first sight, a totally unexpected recognition of each other.

"A spark in dry kindling," she later said. "Blow softly and you have a flame."

Then they were out into the rainy SoHo night, ending up at Raoul's with wine in real glasses, and talk, talk, talk. Easy.

Stepping out of the intimate bistro, he took her arm and she leaned into his shoulder. "Please don't say the Taj Mahal or the Acropolis, but what are your favorite buildings in the world?" No one had asked that, ever. "Your favorite place, the place you feel is you? You *can* say the Pantheon." He loved her zany side. "If you could pick any single thing in this window, what would it be? I would choose the angora mittens." (Now he sees it comes from her Mimi, Charlotte, that quirky grandmother.) She picked up a penny from the sidewalk and dropped it in his coat pocket. "That's good luck forever."

When the light rain turned hard and he started to steer them into a doorway, she said, "Let's just get wet." She'd surprised the hell out him with her credible imitation of Janis Joplin's "Summertime." This is new, he thought later that night, and felt a surge of confusing, electric joy. Dara, her bright and forceful energy, the surge that drives bulbs to flower. Her tawny, blowsy hair fit just under his chin. Her clear optimism and wit matched who Austin felt he wanted to be. They rhymed, laughed in the same places, shared a love for Woolf, Chekhov, Lorca. "Heresy, I know, but I don't go for Sylvia Plath," she confessed. He said the same about Ted Hughes. She said as a child she dreamed of galloping across the moors to find Heathcliff. He told her that at ten he practically memorized *The Swiss Family Robinson.* They both dreamed of Morocco and Sevilla. "Have you read about the Serengeti? Laurens van der Post?" They exchanged numbers. As she got in the taxi, she rolled down the window and called out, "And what about a train from Moscow to Novosibirsk, reading Dostoyevsky, eating potatoes and drinking vodka out of the bottle!"

He closes his eyes, remembering that their relationship began with laughter.

I should bag it, he thinks. But staying out with the fireflies and tree frogs keeps tomorrow at bay. I go to bed, and tomorrow will come sooner.

In late October, early in their romance, their timing snagged. Austin needed to go back to London for the presentation and meetings for his first major project. He was chosen for this chance, miracle chance, to be the right-hand assistant to the lead architect on the design of an endowed library at Bowdoin College. He started clocking seventy hours a week. Impossible to get down to DC. No way out of the crush. He had to come through. If not, they might not readily toss him another juicy bone. First at the door every morning, last to leave. Then, semi-finished drawings completed, he went back to Calvert & Marlowe headquarters in London for the presentation and subsequent meetings. He then was wedged in last-minute for another super project out of the American office, this a possible bayfront headquarters for a suddenly successful start-up in Redwood City, California. He would be in on the initial proposal from London, and after that, maybe extended time in the United States. His firm was onto securing his green card. With that he could stay in the States. Without it, he's available for ninety-day spurts twice a year.

Though they were dizzy in new love, over the weeks back in London, a fissure opened and transatlantic drift set in. When he called, Dara seemed always to be with Shepley Roth, someone she used to date early on at Georgetown. "He's a pal," Dara insisted. "He's working with me at HUD."

They weren't yet exclusive. Austin grabbed dinner with colleagues. His boss invited him to dinner to meet his sister. Awkward, as all Austin could think was *not Dara.*

In London, Austin ran into Shelley at a party. Amit was also back, and all their Cambridge mates gathered for a night out, everyone flying high to be together. When would it ever happen again? There was Shelley Suri with her *hello stranger,* steering him with her hands on his shoulders to Reggie's cleared-out dining-room-turned-dance-floor. Shelley, tall as he, slinking her glass around his neck for him to sip. Then she drank and they fell into a group, swaying and singing, arms linked, him edging away from her. After, they hit a pub with Reggie, Amit, and Angie Thomas, one of Shelley's old suite mates at Cambridge. He hardly remembers how, and nothing of why they all ended up, smashed, back at Shelley's flat. More drinks. He remembers saying he was knackered, then the others were gone and she was pulling him up, laughing. And he woke up in the early hours amid squishy quilts and Shelley, her hair a fan around her head. He kicked off the covers, stunned at the lurid sight of his own naked body and unbelieving that he'd been so fucking bloody stupid. How sick, the fleeting memory of his cock standing up like a glow stick, her reared above him, dragging her hair across his chest, his murmur *I've not got a . . .* and her tongue on his nipples, *not to worry.* The act gone dark, gone to some nether region of his brain, some special coil for ape-shit drunk betrayers. She must have been drunk, too. In her kitchen alcove, he found a pad. *Shelley, I'm sorry but this never should have happened. I hope we can remain amicable, but this is over, whatever* this *is. I am on another path, and as I've said, this relationship was never my future. You deserve someone who will appreciate fully your many great qualities, as well as your smarts and beauty. I wish you everything good. Austin.* As he left, she still slept.

He vomited in the street as he headed for his dad's house.

He did not return Shelley's call. He packed quickly and, almost out the door, recorded a new message: "This is Austin Clarke. I'm away. Leave word after the beep beeps. Catch you later."

He instantly thought what he can't think. She was always on the pill. Deep breaths, he's counting. October, it was. If it's true: almost seven months along. If it's true, there's someone with a beating heart, fingernails, someone who could now survive, someone coming quickly out of the abyss to meet him. But goddammit, surely not true. She would have been in touch sooner. Way sooner. It seemed to him then that she must have some news to share. But what? Maybe she's coming to New York. She'd dropped out of architecture school. "Such sexist swill," she said. And she wasn't wrong. The men got all the prizes. She switched to art classes, then dropped out and got in with an interior design group. No idea what she does there. Her boho taste is hip but not for everyone.

❦

CHARLOTTE STACKS THREE SOFT PILLOWS IN THE MIDDLE AND CRAWLS into bed. Even this late, she surrounds herself with books. But the evening is still swirling. She moves three to the bedside table, keeping her finger in one to hold her place. I know men, she thinks, that I do, regardless of what my lovely Lee would say. My daughter persists in thinking that I was simply *profligate, promiscuous,* with several other pejorative adjectives, and she would think so even more if she knew that I—outrageous age of seventy—am "seeing" someone down at Indigo Island, someone who mixes a fine piña colada to match the sunset, whose shirt is unbuttoned, and hairless legs tanned and taut. Wouldn't she be *confirmed* if she knew that her mother was making out on a sailboat, and with a sailor to boot? Oh, more than making out. But I was never *flighty*, another of her words for me, I just know sooner than most when enough is enough. There's always someone who answers the call just as static comes on the line. Other words she might use I could accept. *Flinty*. Also, definitely, *resilient*. As I know from hundreds of patients, divorce scars are permanent. You might as well have a big D tattooed on your back. The children—victims—yes, victims, create fantasies of their parents' betrayal because the parents' betrayal of each other is incomparable to the betrayal of the child left to wonder and invent and mistrust both parents. I am this or that, her father was this or that, all paper chains and costumes, and painted backdrop scenes enabling the child to exist in a new context. Long after she was old enough to understand how impossible her father was for me, Lee kept seeing ways we would reunite the holy family because that is what is *supposed* to be. That's a book I haven't written because I've never discovered a cure for betrayal. Well, back to my instinct.

Austin I recognize as one of those who holds out a hand just as you need to rise from the low sports car. He always will be there for you. Carl Jung had a theory. A positive one: When you're ready for transformation, the one you need will appear and help you cross the abyss. Lee should understand. She fell for Rich Willcox when they were practically infants. Her last year at Hopkins, a dance at Georgetown—bang, there he was, long-boned and tousled—come to think of it, not built that differently than Austin, a bit more robust. (Hmm, are there more paternal connections? I'll have to think about that.) He was a senior foreign service major, and already a stringer at the *Post*, waiting for my pretty Lee Stark to teach him the dance moves, to drink scotch neat like a southern girl, and more than he thought he wanted to know about the English poets. Third dance, she claims, and they'd melded into one. What was playing then, she told me, was "At Last," Etta James. If it had been something less primordial, would they have connected? Music, as Shakespeare noticed, is the fruit of love. Play on!

Is Austin that man for Dara? Austin, of the shapely lips and single charming dimple. His spirit animal, a wild horse? Not very English, but what animal is? Surely not those pesky dogs the queen has. Umm, Austin. Will have to think on this. Dara, of course, a young tigress. Rich, a St. Ber . . . no, more refined, not an Afghan to be combed, maybe a stag, yes, proud one with a mossy rack of antlers? Oh, Lee probably would call me some kind of slinking cat and she'd be wrong. She loves me and is always wrong about me. I'm avian, maybe a quetzal? (Each of my patients I typecast and forever visualize seated on my curved blue sofa—elephants, rabbits, foxes, seals.) At dinner, I saw how Austin looks at and into each person, as if he must form a judgment right now. Leap the gap with his steady hand held out to you, and soon another wanderer in the mist might reach out. What would Jung say about that? Are there serial transformers? I could discuss this with Lee. She would be interested. She's head-over-heels for Austin, raving about him as she unloaded the dishwasher. (Insight: She's determined that Dara's marriage will be like hers, *not* like mine to her father.) Lee went to her room, and I know she cried. She's a crier. I envy that. People who can cry are close to themselves. I didn't and don't, except at sentimental movies. They'll be back for the wedding, soon enough to cry then.

If sailor-boy Bing Blake, my retired U.S. Navy admiral, tipped over in his sloop and disappeared, I would miss our picnics on his boat. His memories of Japanese gardens, and citrus groves on Cyprus, his dead wife, Jenny, now a photo in the boat's shelf of books. He smells fresh—I want to say frangipani, but I have no idea what that smells like. The military habit appeals: neat, spotless, polished, smooth. Every morning he cleans—even the soles—and buffs his shoes, and he even uses those wooden things that keep them in shape. A bit much. He reads the sailing novels, who are they by, Patrick someone, that endless series; he gives money to his twin sons and grandchildren. (I loathe stingy men, especially those uptight punishers who think their children should work as hard as they did. Oh, learn the value of a dollar. Better to learn the value of a generous gesture. Whatever the foibles of my family, even my father, who didn't have that much, not one was mean with money.) The accumulation of it as a virtue is much overrated. Better to acquire knowledge of something that will enrich your life. Music. Literature. Building houses for those in need. Planting dahlias. Bing raises a window box of herbs in the stern of his boat, and when he cooks on the cantilevered grill, my only job is to pick sprigs of thyme, mint, rosemary, and oregano. There is nothing sexier than a man who cooks.

Lee bonded for life like a swan, and Rich, too. When one comes into the room, the other lights up, feet paddling underwater toward the other. After all these years, that is very sweet. When I left her father, she was fifteen. I can hear her shout, "You have a character flaw," and I shot back, I'm sorry to say, "I'm inhumanly bored, that's what." "Heal thyself, physician," she stung back at me. I had my psychology practice, my plaque, Charlotte Pomerance Stark, Ph.D., on the door across the hall from my husband's eye, ear, nose, throat suite, or, as I called it, the Hear No, See No, Smell No, Say No practice. The year I gave him a telescope for Christmas, he gave me a floor waxer. I slammed out of the house one night after he persisted in talking about a malpractice insurance policy at dinner. One more blasted evening of my precious life.

A year on, the scandal finally died down. I understood later that my doctor man was a victim of his time, same as I. I meant to talk to him—apologize for my part, always sizzling, but he'd cast me as evil personified and I bowed out, since he'd found a more compliant new partner and then in two years was dead of pancreatic cancer. If I'd held on, Lee would have been spared the divorce—the primordial betrayal. *If* is a lonesome word.

My lucky night—when I met Senator Stephen Mann at a Habitat for Humanity dinner. Rich volunteers and drags us to the fundraisers. Stephen was the keynote, and after he spoke, I told him that fair housing was the least we should expect from our elected officials. I was prepared to flounce off into the night, but he took my elbow and said, "Let's just have a drink and talk about this."

I enjoyed the imbroglio with Stephen Mann of political life in Washington much more than I did my role of suspended-in-amber wife of Craig Stark, sainted father of Lee, now defunct at Evergreen Cemetery. Seventeen years of my life. Heroic of him, I'd say, to peer into ears for decades, and always the joke to each patient: cleanest ears I've seen all day. Not funny. Not funny a bit. So, I didn't mate for life. Though I might have if I had met Stephen when I was young. He scooped me into his big life, and I brought him into mine. I wonder about Austin. Dara no doubt is the rosy apple that didn't fall far from the tree. She told me she's having the inside of his ring engraved with the word *forever.* I couldn't help but say, "That's a very long time."

Although I would miss my Bing—quite virile at sixty-eight—if he fell into a riptide, at my stage of life I know that water closes over any splash. I've never seen him take those potency pills. But surely . . . How sharp those instant deaths, impossibly sharp, but soon you're tossing the salad, setting the table for another great meal.

Austin loves Dara, that's clear. His lip trembles after he speaks to her. He can't believe his good luck. Was that a sketchy explanation when I asked what his family does, just a blunt "I lost my mother. My father has a bookstore, antiquarian and fine editions"? Nothing more but maybe I was inappropriate at the table. I didn't ask anything else, so his la MaMa is unaccounted for. A madwoman pacing the moors? Maybe drunk in a London studio apartment? Rich's mother, what an end she came to. Smoked dry like a cod. My next book, the inflictions of parents, their Strum und Drang, angst, all those descriptive Germanic nouns, which often boil down to selfishness. But no. No more books. More sunsets! And I have never been to Egypt. Bing can guide us down the Nile on a felucca, or dahabiya—or is that some garment?

Anyway, something flat to the water so we can be eye to eye with crocodiles.

Best, my dear Dara, if your boyfriends love their mothers. Otherwise, ugly, twisted feelings can turn on them. I know that's why women are hard to elect. (I have honed political instincts from my great years with the intrepid Stephen Mann.) Any Son Junior who holds Mama grudges spills them over on anyone with boobs. Lee's totem animal? Funny I never considered one for her. Maybe dolphin. I swam with the dolphins once. All they did was poop. Lee? Gazelle?

❧

DARA FLUFFS HER PILLOWS AND TOSSES BACK THE SILKY LAVENDER coverlet. The tester bed still seems high, she thinks, as she leaps up. If we could stay, Austin would love to take the canoe downriver to my—now our—favorite spot on the Eno, that bend with a crescent of sandy beach. The willow tree branches trail into the water, glittering, tessellating—I love the word *tessellating*—and reflecting. When I was little, I called it Willowbend. She glances at the organdy curtains, window seat, the bookcases crammed full of everything from Pooh to Proust, and her closet door still studded with tatty ribbons from hunter-jumper competitions. This room stays caught in its time warp. The only current item being her diploma from Georgetown.

Rocco noses in the door and leaps onto the bed, scrambling to keep from slipping down. At fourteen, he barely can make the jump. "Sweetheart, you're my sweetheart." Dara scoots him up beside her, just where he slept all through high school. She rubs his ears, backing off from his swamp breath, and reaches to turn off the light. Where is sleep? Always an insomniac, she conjures the river as a way to drift, the brown river lazing along, the spot to wade in and catch tadpoles in jars. On the bank, she imagines, my lean-to shaped out of branches, where Mei, Moira, and I roasted marshmallows over stick fires. I read there, with only the gurgle of water parting around fallen trees, the quick plop of a sunning turtle rolling off a half-submerged limb. I always hoped to find Mole, Rat, Toad, and Badger having tea on a log.

When Austin first came down to meet Mom and Dad, he and I took sandwiches, chips, and iced tea there for a picnic. My spot. I couldn't wait to show him. I shouldn't even have been surprised when Austin stepped up on a stump and called across the water, "Where are you, Mole?" Always, it's like that with us. When we're old, we'll finish each other's sentences. ("What imbeciles," Mimi says when she hears someone do that.) That day, it was warm enough to wade out to the flat rocks. Tomorrow we could again, if only we didn't have to get back. We made such sweet love, there on Dad's scratchy stadium blanket. He laughed. I laughed. He cried. Through the branches, I looked into the bluest sky, Carolina blue they say here, roiling with cottony clouds. He said, "I get to make love to you for the rest of my life." I said, "Can we try that again now?" We lay back, finding dragons and angels and Santa Claus in the shifting clouds. How defined the images, how quickly they shifted. A perfect afternoon of false spring, balmy hints of May in early March. We left only when we heard the old farm bell, summoning us home.

How many times did I run along the river on an Occaneechi trading path, trying to net butterflies. Now I feel like the butterfly. Am I pursuing myself? With the wedding, and Austin's big break—he's so lucky—we've no time. He seems distracted, and who wouldn't be after the intense work on the library, the even more stressful work now of getting every pipe and light switch in place. As soon as he came home from London, our love seemed to explode. In a few intense weeks, we suddenly seemed to seal. What we had before might have been a wild infatuation but now it was as though we had no choice. DC and New York, what a commute. London. What would I do in London! How will we ever work this out? Am I really going to law school? But our connection just is, and our separate trajectories will have to accommodate.

From my front window, I can see Mom putting out the lanterns.

She looks . . . mythic. White robed in wan light—mythic to me, she is. Why is she out so late? Maybe after we're married, I can sleep with Austin in this bed. Right now, it still belongs to me.

She falls into sleep, netting butterflies and letting them go.

CHARLOTTE LOVES A QUIET SUNDAY MORNING AT REDBUD. THE FRIENDS left early, right after they stopped over for goodbye and Amit headed off to RDU and the other boy to the interstate. The *Times*, blueberry scones, a walk along the river, all the way to that bend where Dara used to play. I'll leave early tomorrow for my cottage, she thinks, and my dalliance with the admiral. I can't be away from my books for long. What a fine word, *dalliance*. Redbud is Lee's house now, where I grew up after age ten when my daddy moved us "north" from Georgia. The first day here I traced my finger around "1806" chiseled into the brick chimney. I drank cold water from the spring and that was a kind of baptism. I was home. Through two marriages, I held on to Redbud, and long after that, always lucky to have Lee and Rich live with me during many years of travel, travel for work and travel for the sake of it, and then I was gone to hold court for Stephen in DC and write my books. I still keep my private bedroom and its alcove study overlooking the meadow. My space is papered with fanciful William Morris lily patterns but mostly with memories. Nice to visit. At this point, nice to leave. I never will be one of those old biddies living on the past. Rich is heating the leftovers. Just the three of us in the rambling old place. Time to go. What's the Scandinavian proverb, stir your soul with a stick every day or you freeze over?

Tomorrow, back to Indigo Island, my own airy cottage, and what a relief to have it, instead of acres to tend to and unending upkeep on this ramous house. Back to my one big room with a mezzanine bed. Maybe Austin the architect would approve. I had a huge round window cut where I can wake up and see the sunrise, orange and wobbling out of the ocean in Creamsicle suffusions of gold and pink. This happens every day, the gobsmacking same miracle. Sacred moments, I should write a book of sacred moments.

At three, the car service picks up Rich for his flight and Charlotte takes another walk in spring mist. This watery air pierced with light—she feels as if she's inside a lush aquarium. When the rain surges, she runs inside, lured to her room for a rest. She's propped in bed reading Flannery O'Connor but dropping the book constantly to think about Dara. Dara happy. Not thrashing around with all that energy going in a thousand directions. She's back in Washington, Charlotte thinks, right now turning the key in the green door to my town house, left to me in Stephen Mann's last will and testament. I'm happy for Dara to live there while she decides what's next. She's drawn to politics. No doubt the influence of her step-grandfather, the charming blowhard, brilliant, hard-living, indefatigable (until he wasn't) great senator from North Carolina. When he was felled on the front porch of Redbud—massive heart attack—it sounded as if a great beech tree had hit the house. He was thrilled with Dara, a teenager interested in the workings of the Senate, asking astute questions and seeing through bullshit. They had no blood ties, but he was a doting grandfather.

Austin, wasn't he riding back and then catching a flight to New York? I'm in charge of salad tonight and I'll make that vinaigrette with a splash of cream. The potatoes dauphinois will be even better reheated. What's Rich's trip? Some oil pipeline article. Ah, I remember Bing's writer; it's Patrick O'Brian, those sailing adventures he reads late at night in that hard bed angling into the bow. Cozy, but lying there can feel like being buried alive. God knows a glass of the leftover Brunello would be nice. Lee, lovely Lee, all to myself. So much to say, always. This Austin, Dara's great dream.

2

As Austin drives us back to Washington, I fall asleep and have a vivid dream of crystals forming, grouping, and faceting in cold spring water. Something complex coming together, but it feels uncomfortable, this shifting, geometric dream. I wake up suddenly when we hit roadwork around Richmond. Why are they working on Sunday? Austin has a whistle habit, not blowing through his lips but a higher sound, coming through his teeth. He's heard the tale about Mimi singing out at Big Mann's funeral home viewing—it was exhilarating, like a bolt of lightning hitting the casket. Austin thought that was splendid, so now he has "The Night They Drove Old Dixie Down" stuck in his ear. His knowledge of what Dixie means is minimal. He says my grandmother is a one-off. I am happy that he gets her. Mama maybe felt the brunt of some of her whims, and certainly the divorce from her sweet father, but for me she shines as a woman who took the course preordained for a girl of her time, the dark ages, and bent the hell out of it. If she ever dies—that could not happen—maybe I'll copy her at the funeral and sing out "Let's twist again, like we did last summer," which she performed on the beach at Indigo one night. I'm eternally glad my grandmother taught me to twist on the beach under the moon.

I wave to the six guys leaning against their massive yellow equipment and smoking. Richmond behind us, I ask Austin if he's okay.

"For all your high spirits at the table and that quick maneuver when Mom spilled the wine, you seem a bit, um, what—preoccupied. Are you okay? Do you want me to drive now?"

"No, I'm fine. It's fun for me to drive. Not to worry, babe. Maybe a slight case of the jitters? You know I really love your old home. Your family, too. Lucky girl!"

How right he is.

I don't ask, but I saw him out my window very late last night, looking toward the meadow from the terrace. When I met Michael, Austin's quite reserved father, I tried to imagine him young, dancing with Austin's mother, playing rugby at Cambridge. I was determined to make him laugh and did. But maybe my crew is overwhelming. Not that my family is difficult, but with the old friends there, and . . . But Austin is gregarious, loves new people.

"Sure?"

"A few things have stacked up. I may have to nip back to London but let's see. I should know next week."

"You remember we're supposed to go to Amit's major dinner Saturday. Isn't his whole family coming in from Delhi? He'll be cooking for this feast all week."

"I truly would hate to miss that. We'll see. Fingers crossed that it's a false alarm." His stomach flips. If only you knew . . . He hates this prevaricating.

The town house. We pull into my parking space, Mimi's place. Years gone and she had not even cleared out Big Mann's baggy suits, his stash of Cuban cigars, or his files crammed with papers that need to go to the Duke archive. What luck for me—she waved her arms and said, "Just move right in. You are doing me a favor because I can't deal with selling it. Water my begonias on the windowsill and throw out what obviously needs throwing out. Oh, hell, throw out the begonias, too." I did. Gobs of expired flours and crackers and cans of drinks in the pantry. Spices, freezer-burned meat. I moved their clothes under the guest room bed so I could have the spacious bedroom with the nice bathroom and soaking tub. Over it, a large window looks out into a spot of woods where sometimes I see a startled deer peering back at me. Beyond those scraggly pines, the fairyland Kalorama neighborhood of looming houses where diplomats live. We often walk there. Austin likes to analyze/criticize the architecture of the grandiose houses. I fancy moving into one, that Italianate beauty with the tiered garden, when I am the senator from the great state of North Carolina. Dream on!

We unload my bag and the carton of papers I've brought from Big Mann's study (now Dad's) at home. Mom packed a Little Red Riding Hood basket of dinner leftovers, the wild rice and quail, some fruit, chocolate bars with hazelnuts, my favorites, and a bottle of the champagne from last night's toasts. I brought back a bunch of yellow hyacinths in a jar that Mei dropped off, and they brighten the kitchen table. "Can you switch your flight? Look at all this. Are you hungry? I'm starving."

"Maybe a bite but I'd better ring a taxi in about an hour. This was a smashing trip. Dara, I hate having pressure interfere. A week here together would be super. You're lucky the old couple didn't have frumpy taste." He walks around looking at the southern folk art on the fireplace wall, smiling at the wild colors and flat perspective of a man on a horse that could have been a camel or donkey, the flat disc of sun overhead. Dara takes two glasses of iced tea out the doors opening onto the oval patio where a slender urn spills water into a fern-lined pool. They put up their feet on the stone ledge and sink back into the cushy chaise longues. Momentary, he knows, but Austin feels suddenly relaxed. He runs his finger around the rim of the glass, making it zing. Everything is going to be fine.

Dara heats the leftovers and takes their plates upstairs to the living room. "Oh, sweets, we didn't get any time together . . ." She slips off her shoes and flops onto Mimi's long coral sofa. "Aren't you overwhelmed? There are a million things to do and less than a month to do them."

Austin kicks off his loafers, pops the cork, and they clink glasses. Lips wet, they kiss, a long kiss that turns to desire, desire for desire, and the body surge of *I love him*. She doesn't know words for the elation filling her, the river of it, the plunges and waves. "My body becomes your body," she whispers.

He nuzzles her neck and blows a raspberry, then disentangles and looks at his watch. "Oh, dammit. Twelve hours from now I'll be in a snake-pit meeting about the library."

"Do you want a quick shower?"

"No way I'm rinsing you off."

A few quick bites, then he's gone. Along with pangs of missing him already Dara feels exuberant, a surging joy. After twin-bed dorm sex, after TGIF encounters, sex like a tennis match, oh, after all that, here's Austin, she thinks, my boy. We go far. It's nothing like before, with the body merely playing. He's mine, he's for me, he loves with his body, and I love back.

Time to run a bath and throw in a bunch of Mimi's bath salts and lavender liquid soap and then some lemon oil, too. She takes Austin's photograph—he's by the ocean, smile that could launch a thousand ships, hands on hips, all the lovely length of him in his bathing suit patterned with fish—and sets it on a stack of towels at the end of the tub. She remembered the three wild horses pacing along the tideline. He'd said that day, *We will always come here*. She dozes in the warm water, waking to find it has gone tepid. She wraps in a big towel and runs to bed, shimmying down, and falling immediately asleep.

❧

THE FRONT WINDOWS OF MEI'S STUDIO OVER THE DRY CLEANER'S LOOK out on King Street, where a long-ago garden club lined the street with pink dogwood trees. Not the best choice, maybe, but briefly enchanting on a spring Sunday. Along the intersecting Queen Street, they planted ginkgoes, which have a burst of glory in fall, then the awful smell of rotting fruit. Every year debates erupt at town hall meetings, but no one dares raise an ax. The view includes a row of turn-of-the-century brick buildings, now cafés with outdoor tables, a chocolate shop, and a gallery for local artists. A good light all morning falls across her cutting table and machines. I can't believe my luck, she's thinking, alone on Sunday with the whole day to sketch and pore over art books.

The dress could be finished this week, Mei calculates. Of course, Dara would not want the traditional white extravaganza, train and lace and minute pearl buttons down the back. She sketched this willowy sheath, pale buttercream silk. Intense and risky, I'd say. That's Dara, though. It's chic but romantic, and I insisted that her hair is piled up, with a few tendrils for softness. Part of the credit goes to Rich. He brought five yards of thin, slubby silk home from one of his trips to Thailand. Almost always he brings home gifts to Lee and Dara. Chocolates, kilims, ceramic pitchers, a pygmy helmet once, and we all laughed when Lee said, "Oh, how fascinating. I always wanted one of these." Finding a surprise for them might be challenging on this trip to oil spills.

She pores over the details of historic paintings, the subject wearing her finest dress for her portrait, but finds equal inspiration from a favorite book on ancient Egypt, and photographs of rice field workers, old movie stars, maids, uniforms of all sorts.

The skeins of thread looped on wall hooks look as beautiful as any artwork, every color she can name and shades of each. Mei scans the workshop/loft. A room of one's own, yes, but this is more. She flashes through all the years of growing up here, above the store, until her parents moved out when she finished her design degree at State and started to work. They love their cottage on Margaret Lane, especially the back porch and yard that slopes down to the Eno. She brings her tea to the window seat, feeling the contentment of *all this space is mine!* She had the flimsy partitions for the former bedrooms removed, the heart-pine floors refinished to a honey glow, the brick walls whitewashed, and then scraped and painted the window frames apple green. This is heaven to me, Mei is thinking. Dara says I should move at least to Raleigh, better, to New York. No and no. Here I can do what I want. Anywhere else, I would be eating soup and waiting tables or, I don't know, doing too much other than what I want to do. I wish she lived here but no chance of that ever happening again. I miss her.

I'm thinking hard about Dara, after that beautiful party last night. In such a small town and not much to do, Dara had her horse. I had my sewing. She taught beginners on Saturdays, and I worked on my drawings. Every Sunday, it seems, we used to drive around (she drove before she had a license) in the country taking pictures of tobacco barns and cabins, stopping to wade in streams, picking plums and cattails along the roads, pushing into abandoned farmhouse doors and feeling spooked by what was left behind—a rusted blue enamel pot, newspapers stuck on the walls as if they were wallpaper, a Bible torn in half. She drove fast. Yakking about what we would someday do, where we would go. Paris atelier for me, Italy for her, always Italy.

Without rent, I'm good here. I want to work with linen and I'm getting into embroidery on my designs—words on cuffs, blocks of alternating color squares around hems, white-on-white flowers twining along the edges of linen curtains. But Dara's dress will be simple, ankle length, knee-high slit on each side, cap sleeves with tiny pleats, and a scooped low neck also with a pleated border. She will walk out the front door as buoyant as a bride can be, Rich beaming on one side of her, Lee on the other. Down the steps to the terrace and into the perennial garden, where surely the roses will cooperate. On out to all of us waiting in the meadow. My pale blue linen, Moira's, too, the friends of Austin I've just met, Reverend Wilson, the crowd turning to see her . . . Oh, and Austin standing there, maybe hair combed back for once. For him, the purest joy. Tears brimming? But that break-out smile. You hear "English teeth," but not his; I imagine people say whatever they can to make him smile.

Lee has long had her chapel made of hog wire. In summer, gourds and morning glories climb the structure, but for the big day, Lee will go all out. All the morning before the wedding at four, Blossoms Florist will be threading the wire walls and roof with jasmine and Dara's favorite pink hydrangeas and white roses. Three weeks away. I see it as if it already has happened.

3

AUSTIN CHECKS HIS WATCH. Midnight when he exits LaGuardia, a hassle for a taxi, then finally back at his apartment at one. First thing to notice: no message light blinking. He sighs. She was just touching base. Call her tomorrow? She. Could. Not. Spring something this horrific on me. Let it slide. And see if she calls back? After the Willcox farmhouse and the venerable trees and gardens, the four walls of the studio feel oppressive, the undercounter neon casting a hard glow onto the generic counter. Standard contractor's granite. But the studio was a lucky find, a month-to-month so he can mostly move down to DC after the wedding and train it to the city and stay at Amit's. Just until Dara knows where she will be going to law school. Georgetown or NYU or Columbia, what a girl. Even without a recommendation from Senator Mann and with an art history minor. She killed the LSAT.

The Thai takeout in the fridge is only two days old and heats up fine but afterward, his stomach feels sour and acidic. He drinks a large glass of water, showers, and throws himself across the bed. Dara, my love, must be a sleeping beauty by now. He jams his fists under the pillow. *Let me have my life.*

IN THE MORNING, DARA UNPACKS, LUGS STACKS OF FOLDERS TO BIG Mann's office, just off the living room (second floor in these narrow town houses). She arranges them on the partner's desk, which takes up most of the room. Just to sit there must generate testosterone, she thinks. What luck to land this new job for the biography Bill Dellinger is writing. His publisher is paying for an assistant because thirty years in the Senate generated a boatload of records. By midafternoon, she has squeezed onto the shelves the rest of the files she brought and will be organizing. Oh, tedious, Dara thinks, but I can work here and keep my own schedule. Thanks, big guy, thanks, Mimi.

One more raid of the leftovers, and Dara climbs upstairs and sinks into the huge bed with an array of downy pillows. Ah, princess and the pea, she remembers. (Mei saw the sleepless princess as spoiled. I saw her as sensitive.) What's hovering? She pounds the pillow to fluff it. Something, a mental version of those maddening floaters that sometimes pop up in my vision. Drifting but trying to focus, she launches into *Marking Time*, one in a series of five connected novels she reads in every spare moment. She jerks the pillows against the headboard, sitting up properly. If he needs to go to London, am I going all the way to New York to meet Amit's family? she wonders. The book's characters living their complex lives in Sussex suddenly seem to come from Mars. She pictures Austin in his "snake pit" meeting, everyone hunched over drawings and stabbing pointers at arches and doorways. "Focus, Dara," she says aloud. I need to work. I want to. But the crystals are forming in cold water. At Willowbend, among the pebbles, sometimes I found quartz crystals. Once a bird arrowhead delicately carved from flint by the Occaneechi tribe. Tomorrow, I will . . . What will I do tomorrow? Austin, already turning the key to his studio now, what will he dream tonight . . . The river . . . her book thumps onto the floor.

❦

AUSTIN WALKS OUT EARLY FOR COFFEE AT POD'S. THE DARK AROMA whooshes out as he opens the door, and he sees several of the regulars hunched over their newspapers and books. He takes his cappuccino to a table and reads the *Times* that someone left. On the way out, he stops at the pay phone and calls Amit. “Hey, I know it’s early but knew you’d be up.”

“Yeah. I am picking up my parents today so I’m cleaning like crazy. My mom is antiseptic, and I saw a roach by the trash yesterday.”

“I wanted to run something by you, and it’s not a great wake-up call.”

“Shoot.”

“You know that party at Reggie Forsyth’s last October when we were back? Well, I did the dumbest thing ever in the history of dumb things. Remember we all went back to Shelley’s place after we left the pub?”

“Sure.”

“I got sloshed. I honestly barely remember, but short story shorter, I slept with her. No excuse, but we kept drinking and I don’t even remember what happened.”

“My god. My god, Austin. Unbelievable.”

“I think I’ve got a problem.”

Long pause. “That was months ago. October. It’s almost May. No way. Is she on the pill?”

“The one thing I do remember is that I told her I didn’t have a condom and she said ‘no worries’ so I assumed . . .”

“She can be a kook but surely she wouldn’t . . .”

“I’m having this hovering sense of foreboding. She left a clipped message that didn’t sound like she was calling to announce her engagement or an upcoming trip to New York.”

“Oh, Christ, I’m buggered, Austin. Are you calling back?”

For a moment, Austin smiles, remembering Dara’s down-home expression *Christ on a tire swing*. “That’s what I’m calling about. Should I, do I have to?”

“I guess I’d assume the best. If it’s serious, she’ll call back. How fucked that a quick, idiotic choice can come down over you like an avalanche. Which way is up? Out?”

"Right, but I would prefer an avalanche to this. Blinded by the light . . . what is that song? I'm blinded by reverting to uni bad behavior. And worse, I'd already met Dara. It was so complicated with our separate orbits that we hadn't committed, but I knew, and she did, too. I'll keep you posted. Thanks, my friend."

Austin glances at the mirror above the bar where his normal reflection stares back at him. The man about to marry his soul mate.

No calls. Monday, Tuesday, Wednesday. Austin wakes up with resolution to dial London. Seven here, noon there. But then he doesn't. He lies in bed feeling like a fox gnawing off its own foot to escape the trap. Work is immersive. Later, back at his studio with his curry takeaway, he calls Dara. "How was your meeting at HUD?"

"Wait. I have to get my soup so we can have dinner together." He hears a cabinet bang, cutlery. "It feels good to work on urban housing bills. You know Big Mann laid a lot of rails to ride. I did well, considering that my mind is somewhere else entirely. Important things like shoes. I don't have the right shoes for my dress, and I'll have to cross half the meadow in whatever I find." She chattered on about wedding presents pouring in and that Mimi announced she'll be bringing her "man friend" and they'll be staying at the inn downtown to be away from the fray. "I haven't had a chance to get my ticket up there for the Amit extravaganza. I'll do that first thing tomorrow. Austin, you there?"

"Yes. I'm here." He wants to say *I'll always be here*. "I feel scattered, too. Lots to juggle." They settle on the noon flight for her on Saturday. Plenty of time for lunch at the Japanese place they've wanted to try. A slow Sunday, surely, after Amit's feast.

"Then we'll have the whole weekend. I can get back here early enough on Monday to get some work done. Oh, this is fantastic—in those papers I brought back I found a notebook with copies of sixty letters he wrote to presidents. Bill Dellinger is going to sail naked over the moon. I haven't told him yet."

"That's incredible. You know, you should be writing this biography."

"I don't have the credentials. Random House never would have signed me on."

Austin imagines serious Bill Dellinger waving his arms as he sails naked over the moon. "Dara, you are what's incredible. I miss you, miss you."

On Thursday, Austin knew he could not go through the weekend without knowing if his fears were justified or irrational and guilt induced. Coming out of the subway, he decides he will call Shelley during lunch. But at work, he finds on his desk a fat registered letter addressed to him in the loopy handwriting of Shelley Suri. So now, he thinks, this is definitely not a card congratulating me on my upcoming marriage, if she even knows about it. Until her cryptic message, they've had no contact since he left the note on her kitchen counter.

He hangs his satchel on the cubicle door, picks up the envelope, and walks back outside. His stomach feels like he's stepped onto a lift in free fall. He crosses over and finds a bench in Washington Square.

Blue paper, thin as tissue. No doubt it would have a lingering scent, but he refrained. Austin is not quite shaking but feels his hair bristling and shoulders rising. As he slides the letter from the envelope, three pressed white flowers fall on his knees. He brushes them to the ground and grinds them into the dirt with his heel. Here we go.

Dearest Austin,

Forgive me. Out of so much to say let me start and end there. I must tell you that I am pregnant, and I know you can do the addition. I have been near no one but you. You will think I had an additional motive in keeping this secret, and I did, but not what you imagine.

When I realized I was pregnant, I never intended for you to know. I had your last note and respected your clear message. That this delay is unbelievable from your point of view, I understand. But Austin, I'm not cold-blooded or scheming, I'm not crazy. I made a clear, deeply personal choice.

When I heard about the party and that you and Amit would be there, I fantasized that we would make love. I haven't been on the pill since you broke off with me last time, as I didn't need protection. I have not and won't ever know love except for you.

This goes back to when we studied together. While you concentrated on the problems, I found myself strangely almost projecting into you. Given that, Austin, I will always try to have you. Because I'd heard of your romance from Amit, I sensed that night would be my last chance to be one with you, if I could make it happen. I freely admit, I kept the drinks coming for everyone. When they left and you flopped on the daybed, I was lucky. When I woke up the next morning and you were gone, I almost went to the clinic for a pill. To be transparent, I knew the time of the month was vulnerable, but I thought that if I did fall pregnant, it would be glorious. My private achievement. I see now from anyone's vantage point that this was wrong, but the idea hit me as right. Something deeply intimate of you would always be mine. I can hear you groaning at that but I'm affirming my choice. (My power.) Your note was unequivocal and from the moment I read it, I accepted that we would never communicate again, no matter if I was pregnant or not.

Then the stars misaligned.

Here's my explanation for telling you now, not that I expect you to be sympathetic, or anything but outraged. I know you had every right to be told. Now something unforeseen has come up, and I must protect this child who is no longer a flutter like moth wings but a presence that rakes a foot or elbow across my sides.

The child is a boy. The sonograms are normal, and I can attest that he is an energetic surfer of amniotic waves.

Rage cramps his hands. He crumples the letter then smooths it on his knee. Spare me the poetics. Ever heard of sperm donors? Of consent? You are unhinged. I have "every right"??? Thanks for granting me that, you, god, you patronizing . . .

Suffer with me this background.
Here's why I am writing to you now.

That surge of *Get Me Out* that I remember, then very little. A glass breaking, Amit leaning over me, his eyes looking bulged and his smile like a clown's. Let's go, let's go, he's saying. But I'm wasted and Shelley's sloshing scotch and I stumble over a rug. Their exit, someone singing "Freak Like Me."

When we were dating, I never told you much about my family. Now it's relevant. Briefly, my father was a brahmin, an only child, who enraged his Hindu family by marrying the Irish au pair of English neighbors, my lovely mother, going against the family's arrangement for him to marry a young woman of their echelon. All my childhood, my mother Fiona Williams, has lived in thrall to my father, unaccepted by his family, seething in their spacious house, where we had the third floor and were seldom invited to the lower floors, kitchen courtyard, and garden. But we had our own roof terrace, which my mother cultivated. It was our sanctuary and hideout. She read to my two older brothers and me in an alcove of vines, all the English novels of Dickens, the Irish fairy tales and poems of her childhood, and taught us Catholic prayers. We created sets, made up plays and performed. We raised radishes and carrots in my sandbox, and thrived in this private paradise. My grandparents never came to the third floor. They hardly acknowledged us children and our mother if we crossed paths in the stairways, but my father continued to dine with them several times a week. They never spoke the foreign names my mother gave us. Summers we spent in Ireland at my mother's family home. I never knew, as a child, the awful balancing act my parents performed every day. Were they happy? Only in our private world, a small slice of a big, steamy pie. All this to say that my mother wrested the situation enough to get me into the good international school. Amit was, as you know, my classmate and became the impetus for me to study abroad. My father took my mother's side and saw that I got out of the toxic house and into Cambridge.

The tyrant grandparents are dead, and my father quite reduced with early Parkinson's. Where I come into this story now is that my surviving grandmother changed her will in the months before she died, and who knows what gods she was supplicating. Revenge against my grandfather seems the obvious explanation. She left the family compound to me and my two brothers, with the stipulation that our parents could live out their lives there. My third-floor childhood home now belongs to me. My brother Billy and his family live on the bottom floor, where the big kitchen is, and my parents live where my grandparents did. My other brother, Ollie, works and lives in Manchester, as you may recall, and has no plans to return to Delhi, although he could move into the grandest part of the house, the second floor, when our parents pass on.

During my mother's visit late in the fall, I told her about our romance. I told her that you came into my life like a holy visitation, and at that she shook her head, just aghast. (How many of our friends have told me to let go, move on.) But as soon as I met you in that maths class you struggled through, I was certain. You were the person I needed to spend my life with, and I know that sounds overly romantic, but being with you was as if I had stepped into my real life, not the imbroglio of my family. Like seeing a light out of that labyrinth into something open and possible. I adored your ambition and talent. With you I would flourish, too. I know I'm as smart as you, but you have this capacity for life that is rare. Beside you, I always felt that I was shining. You once knew this; I confessed it all during the few months we were a couple. You were stunned, and I freely admit that you said I should do this and that for myself and should not expect anything from someone who was not geared for a commitment, years of study coming up, etc., etc. For me, this didn't apply. My love never changed. It was not as if we'd met but as if we were reunited. I was crushed as I gradually realized that for you, I was a friend, a date with an interesting cultural background, a pleasant stop on a long voyage that would continue without me.

From this, you can probably predict the rest. My mother, although appalled at my choice to keep my condition secret from you, wants me home. She was alarmed over my news, and went home dreading my father's reaction. But I have heard from her, and they both expect me back there, even under the circumstances. For women, possibilities are beginning to open more in India, and for the upper classes, women's opportunities never have been as limited as for others. I can finish my long-lost architecture degree there, get out of expensive London, and make a fresh start. I apologize again. I know you will hate this: I am thirty-one and have ever since we met wanted your baby.

At the party, you were exuberant to see all the old friends, even happy, I thought, to see me. I insisted that we all go back to my flat—it now seems to me my fate. Me, in charge of my fate. I knew you were in love with Scarlett O'Hara from the South, and Amit described that affair as "colossal." As you were always averse to commitment, I did not expect that marriage was on your mind.

Later, looking at the pregnancy test, I thought that if I cannot have you as my own, I could have the most intimate sharing, something for a lifetime. Your child. At first, I saw a girl, with fair hair like yours and my mother's. I saw her arranging paper

> dolls in the grass. A bright being to raise on the enchanting rooftop in Delhi, with my doting mother, cousins to play with, my dad, me home for good now, sitting in a patch of sun and watching. We two will have a secure home where I can be independent, forge a career, and feel grounded in the culture I know best. I was never at home in England, with its prissy ways and beery pubs and toad-in-a-hole and whingeing men. (Not you, of course!) In my plan, you NEVER would have known about this child being yours, or maybe you would decades on, if I decided he needed to know. I would make up an MIA partner to explain to our mutual friends.

Fuck's sake, is this not insane? None of this makes sense, how can she invent this bubble scenario to star in?

> As I am writing this, it still is a viable option. But with best-laid plans, I've learned, as well as far-fetched plans, something can go awry. At the initial consultation with the ob-gyn, my lab tests were normal. In the third month, just as I was preparing to go back to Delhi and start my life over, I got the news that kept me in London and which now impels me to contact you. You probably see this as the scheme of a coldhearted trickster, but to reiterate, I had NO intention of involving you in my future. Now I am forced to face the facts. Please call me because I don't want this on paper.
>
> Always, Shelley

Always? No, *never*. You just A-bombed my life.

Austin walks the endless blocks to his apartment. He throws himself across the bed and cries as he had not cried since his mother died when he was eleven. The image of Dara in her red dress retreats.

Back, further back to the vanishing point, only a splash of red left, then nothing. He's falling, pushed from a plane, grasping for a cord to pull, the land spinning below. And oddly, face buried in a pillow, he remembers his mother vividly, when she has faded over the years. He's holding her hand as they walk to the ducks. He's clutching a bag of bread crusts in his other hand, and they start skipping. She's bringing broth when he had measles, her violet dress blurred by steam from the bowl, and then her soft hand on his forehead. *My darling sweet boy.* She's teaching me how to thread popcorn for the Christmas tree. She's only thirty-five. Her chestnut hair up in a big loop, busy, strong hands kneading, knitting, shelving books. And a soft presence. She read me all the Beatrix Potter stories. I think she loved them more than I did. Undiagnosed ovarian cancer swept through her body, and she was just gone, her life pulled out from under her, her husband broken, daughter and son stunned silent. What would she expect him to do? Shame. I'm shamed. I'm ashamed for my mother's sake. A stupid fool. I am not able to solve this, and I have to solve it. Fact is, it's not just me. A boy is coming to the light, to link to me forever. *Forever* is the word Dara chose to have engraved inside my wedding ring. I was on my way somewhere. I'm betrayed, I betrayed, and she is betrayed, and all of those around that table just four nights ago are betrayed. Only this boy will come forth in innocence. Or is this original sin? Shelley, flake. All the gross words I can say don't touch the situation. Legally, I will be responsible. Morally, too.

He rolls out of bed and looks out the window. Below, a boy on a bicycle whizzes by, a man pushes a dolly stacked with boxes toward the bodega, and a stooped woman overdressed in a bulky coat pauses for her dog to pee on the base of a cherry tree, which in this early and promising spring is about to break into blossom.

4

LIFE IS FILLED with impossible choices and we make them. Not sure if I read that somewhere or if that is just the cold truth dawning. I'm faced with this bizarre situation I could not imagine. I may have to hoard a handful of Dara memories to last me a lifetime. Austin peers into the fridge and finds nothing, but in the freezer there's Dara's butter pecan ice cream. He takes it to the sofa and sprawls his feet on the coffee table, the Noguchi-style coffee table that he and Dara picked up off the street, sanded down, and stained. He stabs the frozen ice cream with a fork, the memories unfurling faster than he can catch them.

That first night at the art opening. Stunning, meeting Dara. Later that weekend at Central Park Zoo, a giraffe leaned over the high fence and licked her hair. Most people would have shrieked, but Dara put both hands on its neck, smiled back at the huge yellow teeth dripping gobs of slobber, *oh, hello, sweet thang,* and rubbed her hair on its muzzle. Back at her room, I waited while she shampooed and came out in the hotel robe, way too big for her. She grabbed clothes and changed in the bathroom. All ready to go to lunch, then on to the next adventure. Will I be able to live up to her, what, her energy for life? Her gamut. The goofy times and the sublime. Sublime being the afternoon at her secret beach on the river, the limpid water, then the first time for us. The winter weekend on the Outer Banks, where we saw wild horses running along the ocean, and we ran with them into the heart-attack icy surf, and then we holed up in a B and B where our room had a fireplace and quilts and we read Neruda aloud to each other in between making love twelve times. That sealed it. I could never get enough of this remarkable, luscious woman, and miraculously, she of me. I've had plenty of sex but never have I cried as I came. Or laughed so much. The ten thousand things. How she continually comes as a surprise—how she swerves instead of turning and always orders the least likely thing on the menu. I would never be able to finish her sentences. Her gigantic sneeze, her neat ears she keeps covered because they point at the top like an elf's, her sweet singing voice that pings on the high notes, her photographic memory. Scary how she can quote whole passages she's read only once or twice. I once accused her of staying up at night memorizing paragraphs and lyrics to impress me. *I want to do with you what spring does to the cherry tree.* We loved that line.

I am spiraling because of my mother. Dara, this is my mother, Delia. Her name, as in the song "Delia's Gone." There must have been ten thousand gestures of hers, smiles, anger, words, acts, and I see how they have disappeared. I can't imagine forgetting Dara. I'm groaning because they say soldiers cry for their mothers as they lie dying. I slap each cheek in the bathroom mirror. Can't be that bad, can it?

5

Hey Mei, Hey Moira,

Dropping you a line about our girls' weekend up here. It will be just us home girls. My old roommates Courtney and Kat can only fly in from California the following weekend for the wedding. I'm planning our first night out at a cool Vietnamese restaurant you'll love (Austin and I go there all the time), Saturday the National Gallery, lunch at an Italian place near a great bookstore, some shopping—Mei, I want to show you a linen shop—and a late afternoon massage at a swanky salon. Hope it's not too dull but I really thought it would be fun to cook here at Mimi's Saturday night, just stay in, relax, and catch up. If you'd rather, we can get tickets to something at the Kennedy Center or go glam and out on the town. Not that DC has much nightlife. Let me know.

Meanwhile, I'm working so well with Bill Dellinger, the guy who is writing the bio of Big Mann. I'm assigned to go through the Giza pyramid of papers and sort them by date. That done, I'm to sort those files by subject. All he must do is write! Much to wade through but I'm learning a lot. Big Mann was a force of nature and what a will. Among other causes, he never wavered in trying to get the districts ungerrymandered, if that's the word, and to see that all got to vote. Vote! Is that too much to ask? Can you believe that is still at issue? I'm working like mad on the archive, mostly organizing right now, and still interning for the disorganized geek at HUD. He has smart plans but is so distractable that I wonder how he gets his pants on the right way in the mornings. I would love to have his job someday.

Austin is working—absorbed and overextended. Cannot believe that we will have a two-week honeymoon in Italy. (No rest for him there!) Remember, I had a semester abroad in Florence so I will dust off my Italian.

My oldest friends, I love you both and cannot wait to have solid time together, Dara

6

COUNTDOWN!!!

Check with Mei about tablecloths. Measure. Long enough for seating 60?

Remember to tell florist our peonies may have ants. Must rinse and shake.

D wants rosebuds for groomsmen and Rich. No carnations.

Reconfirm number of servers. 8 enough for 60? 10 including wine service?

Rich—ice—check wine openers and glasses & tell waiters to keep glasses half full.

Mei to show me her design for place cards.

Plenty of lanterns. Enough candles for later? Who will light?

A and D to deal with music selection.

Chair delivery to garage day before. Between 2 and 4. Who sets up?

Update list of wedding gifts.

D found shoes yet? Don't bug her.

Their flight out 10:05 RDU to Paris 2 hrs. to make connection to Rome. D to reconfirm.

Finalize menu TODAY. Thick asparagus available?

If heavy dew the day before, substitute lavender crème brûlée for the meringues w/ lemon curd.

Okay with caterer? Final cost?

Manicures for the girls day before. Same polish color TBD.

❧

WRITING ABOUT AN OIL SPILL IS EASIER THAN WRITING THE WEDDING toast for my only daughter. May she be as lucky as Lee and I—or is that too self-satisfied? Marriage, a great one, is partly a dice roll but mainly a dance of complements. Where Lee veers, I go straight; where I stumble, she leaps, where my sentence breaks, she continues, where she goes dark, I shine a light. Pick up the slack. Run with it. Charlotte may be writing the better toast. Only two times, but she's the marriage queen, after having written that book. God knows they're reading it in Nairobi. I saw it in the airport kiosk. I'm not handing Dara off to Austin—we're all joining arms and going forth together. The old saw, not losing a daughter but gaining a son. *Son,* loaded word. The babe we lost, small bundle gone blue. Took only a few breaths. His life force evaporated. I have never felt like such a failure. Off the edge of the meadow, a rusty wrought-iron square plot holds four of the souls who lived here once upon a time. Also, the graves of Charlotte's parents. That's where our Hawthorn lies. The lichen-covered stone angel spreads protective wings. Up come the daffodils as early as February, naturalized around the stones just outside the gate. No names on those, just grass-covered humps over the remains of three good dogs and two fine cats. Oh, that Sister was a feline queen! From where the wedding dinner will be set, I can glimpse the old cemetery. Okay, I guess, to have a memento mori in sight.

The toast. What to say? That I'm glad she's not marrying one of the bad boys she favored during high school and college? Or the Italian from her semester abroad. Who could feel relaxed around someone so well dressed? That Austin has intelligence in his eyes, perception, forthrightness. Above all, he's mad about my quirky daughter. The toast. Shall I list her qualities? Say she's fierce and honest and moral and may be confused about her career but she will work it out. The oil spill. Now to cut three hundred words. Wedding toast TK.

❧

MOIRA FOLDS THE THIRD LOAD OF LAUNDRY. THE TWINS ARE AT DAY-care, and she has two free hours before she's due at the paper. She's thinking of the Willcox crew, how they seem to really *live,* and how she can somehow recapture zest for her own life. She smiles to think that what got her into writing was not the greats, Eudora Welty or William Faulkner, but the accounts of southern weddings in local newspapers. What a cultural reveal—southern gothic but touching. "The train bearer wore black satin Lord Fauntleroy suit with white blouse." A whole narrative unfolds. The note that a groom's family's windshields had been broken in the church lot during the ceremony. A couple married on the stroke of midnight, and the post-ceremony guests enjoyed barbecue, cupcakes, and games of Scrabble, while dancing to the bluegrass band Buckeyed Rabbits. Makes her smile. She shifts the basket to her hip and heads upstairs to distribute the clean, still warm baby clothes. I'm drawn to what makes a place that place, she thinks. "The bride wore a trumpet gown of burgundy lace and her late mother's cowboy boots." A guest comments, "Her pants were so tight I could see her religion." What on earth does that even mean?

Dara's father should have been my inspiration. He's all over the globe with important dissections of drastically relevant subjects. God, he won a huge prize. He recommended me for Vanderbilt and even offered to help me get an internship at the *Washington Post* when I graduated. So I've let everyone down, settling for the local paper. Have I let myself down? Marrying the August after I got that BA, Carleton in the middle of med school, and the only job I could find was writing about grads' accolades for the alumni magazine. Then the twins came along, then, moving back home, life and my job at the *Eno News,* closer than I ever would have expected to the wedding write-ups I used to read aloud to Dara and Mei. I do get to cover Town Hall and Historic Review meetings. Meanwhile, Carleton . . . Oh, not going there. I'm going to be writing about Dara's wedding! I so wish her well and for the outdoor wedding to be sunny and perfect. Lee will see to that. She and Mei are my best friends. Who would envy Mei up there with all that sewing, but Dara is made of luck. Grandmother just hands her the keys to her town house. She flits around among interesting jobs and got into all those law schools. Now this English charmer swoops down like a wolf on the fold. (Who wrote that simile?) He is mesmerized by Dara. Envy, I do, and I don't. Afraid I have the occasional meow. Carleton . . . Carleton is stressed. I bet I can finish the crossword before I go.

7

BEFORE WORK ON FRIDAY, Austin calls London.

"Hell-ooo," Shelley answers.

"Austin here."

"I know. I could tell by the ring."

Oh, please. "Listen, Shelley, I'm getting married. I'm sure you know. I'm sure you know what an unbelievable blow your letter was. Is."

"You didn't call back. I had to write."

"Letter, call, whatever. You did something completely despicable. You've ruined my life. If you had let me know right away, there were alternatives, arrangements, solutions. You cut me out of a conversation that was vital."

"You don't know by halves . . ."

"What are you talking about?"

"As I wrote, Austin, please try to listen, as I wrote, something happened. I did NOT plan to involve you at all. Remember that."

"Yes, well, how is what you did not criminal? Don't men have rights? You are an intelligent person. How can you have told yourself this was in any possible universe acceptable? You played with my fate as well as yours."

"I didn't think of it like that. I saw another side."

"You saw something delusional."

"Be that as it may, I am pregnant with our child, and I have been ecstatic."

Austin holds the phone away from his ear, shaking it. He slides open the window for air. Her defiance makes him sick. "Well, what's the great mystery?" Down in the street, people are living their normal lives. A homeless woman spreads her cardboard carefully, as if making up a bed.

Big sigh and pause. "In my last appointment, I was diagnosed with ITP."

"And what is that?"

"Something that could be serious and life-threatening to the baby. And to me."

"WHAT is it?"

"Immune thrombocytopenia."

"English, please?"

"Early on, I had lower blood platelets than normal, but the doctor said that was not unusual. At every check, the count worsened. I may have always had this but never had any condition that ignited it. In pregnancy, he says some antibodies can start attacking the red blood. I'm on steroids now but there's not been much improvement."

"Still not following. Anemia? Low red blood cells—that means the blood won't clot? Hemophilia like the royals . . ."

"Exactly. This probably will stabilize but the doctor is concerned that the count is low this soon. It's not a good indicator."

"What's the prognosis if the count does continue to fall?"

"I hope to the gods that won't happen. In labor, they will be starting plasma transfusions, and if that helps, I may have a safe delivery. They probably won't be able to give me an epidural—that's the pain blocker, in case you don't know—and they can't use any forceps or vacuum stuff on the baby."

Austin hears her voice break. "Vacuum? What?"

"If these transfusions they're starting don't get me through, when the baby is about to be born, they will give me gobs of platelets by transfusion. That should work. Usually that works. Otherwise, I may bleed out. The baby . . . they don't know."

"What a shitstorm, Shelley. This can't be happening." On so many levels, he thinks. His rage sinks. She's facing weird odds. Sounds like the doctors have little control over this. Imagine her confusion and helplessness. "Who's there for you?"

"I've only told Ollie, my brother in Manchester, and my mother. Right now, it is a wait-and-see situation."

"Yeah. So is something else. My wedding."

"But, Austin, it's a child. A child's life. I'm only telling you because of this possibility, even if it is remote. I had to tell you. I must protect him. My mother can't raise a child without me. My dad has Parkinson's. She can't care for a child as well. My next appointment is in a week. I will call you afterwards. Please pick up."

No use berating her now. And the blood thing, he could hardly take in what she said. Maybe she's exaggerating, taking the worst-case scenario. But then, that's exactly what she'd laid out. The worst. But it could be just fine. She said usually it's fine. "Shelley, this shouldn't be happening to either of us."

"No. But it is."

Platelets. Tectonic plates, isn't that what causes earthquakes?

Not possible that I can tell Dara this on the phone. When's her flight? She's due here tomorrow at four. It's work, work today or else. Too much is percolating no matter what my problems are. I can't even call to say I'm coming. She'd be all over why. Catch the flight late this afternoon and be at her place by eight. If she's not home, I sit on the steps.

He books the 5:30 flight. Instead of his usual twenty-block walk to the office, Austin throws some clothes in his backpack and grabs a taxi. His group is already in conference, working on the client's requests for revision. The off-center entrance to the library had been his idea. Client wants symmetry. Wants to narrow the halls, which makes no sense, and to lower the ceiling in the main reading room. Where to begin with what's wrong with all this? The university had been enthusiastic, but the donor has his own bad ideas. What else can happen?

Delayed flight. Turbulence, and why not? A seatmate who manages three Bloody Marys in forty-five minutes of flying time. Austin tries to think what Dara will say. Surely not anything with a happy-ever-after solution, since there isn't one. Best hope, that she comes around to some workable acceptance. What would that look like? If Shelley and baby are okay, surely she will forgive and we move on together. But even with that, it's the blot of my mistake. And there's this newborn taken off to India, who must somehow be raised, accommodated, supported, ignored, or what? And Shelley with her obsession always on the margin of our new life.

Crowded taxi queue at National, traffic through Rock Creek Park, finally the turn into the shady driveway, porch light on and the dining room lamplight falling on the camellia bushes by the steps.

Dara is home. She opens the door and immediately says, "What's wrong, Austin? You're here! Are you okay? What is it?" She kisses him and pulls back. "Sweetie, you're scaring me. You look . . . Tell me, come in." She grabs his backpack and tosses it to the corner. "I was just taking some time off to read." She holds up a paperback and leads him back to the kitchen island, where her mug of tea and a half-eaten sandwich sit. "See my lonely little dinner?" She smiles and Austin grabs her close, burying his face in her neck, inhaling her clean scent, the lavender soap she likes.

"Something really terrible has happened. I have to tell you. It's not health or job. Let me try, try to explain."

"If it's not health, we're okay." She poured him a glass of cold white wine and pushed it across the island. Leaning forward on her elbows, a strand of hair grazed across her sandwich and Austin reached to tuck it behind her ear.

"Let's go up to the living room. The light is so bright in here it could be an operating room."

Austin told Dara. Everything. From the beginning maths class where he met Shelley and thought her sexy, even though he hardly knew what sexy meant. She was his first and exhilarating lovemaking, and with an older woman (three years). Right away, he began to feel claustrophobic around her when they weren't in her bed, roommate locked out. "There was always this needy part. The *why didn't you call* and the *are you attracted to Caroline,* and *you don't have more time for me?* I didn't like the way she hung on my arm when we were walking or held my hand. She puffed out her lips and stared if I danced with others or got into discussions. She could blow up and I was wary of that quality. Gradually, I pulled away, although I admit I phoned her and went over a few times when I needed someone. What an ass I was."

Dara does not interrupt. No understanding *oh, you were so young.* She just glares at the floor, the ceiling. Closes her eyes. Bites her lip. What the hell?

Austin spills everything. "I was drinking. We all were sloshed. I was dead drunk. That's my fault regardless of who was pouring. I blocked out—which I knew—that she still wanted me, just danced like a fool and slogged a few too many. Mea culpa, I was out of my head. She was, too, in a different way." He talks all the way to this morning's conversation and the bloody details about the platelets and the ominous possibility. He tries to read her reaction but when she turns to him her face looks open and blank, as though she is alone and looking out to sea. Finally, he stops. Of all possible reactions, he couldn't have predicted hers.

From the middle of the sofa, Dara shifts to face him. "I used to watch this old movie with Mimi when my parents went out for dinner, *A Place in the Sun*. She loved the book it was based on, a novel by Theodore Dreiser. And she thought Montgomery Clift was so handsome. He's married to a kind of crass, big-boned woman who gets pregnant. Meanwhile he has met Elizabeth Taylor. As one would, he falls hard for her and ends up pushing the wife he's outgrown off a rowboat, or she falls and he doesn't save her. She drowns. He looks quite beautifully tragic. Then things don't go well. I don't quite remember, but I think he winds up in jail. Shelley! The wife who drowns is played by Shelley Winters! My grandmother cried, but I felt sorry for the wife at the bottom of the lake. *A Place in the Sun,* what a great title. That's what we'd found, our place in the sun. Lucky us."

Austin stares. No idea what to answer. Her silence envelops the whole room.

"Austin, I'm sorry. That's all I have. I can't come up with a single thought or feeling that doesn't contradict another one."

"I know. I don't have any excuse for my idiotic behavior. And the ugly twist: It could have been a slipup that made no difference except to my own conscience. Now it's all there is. I was wishing I could jump out of the plane so I didn't have to tell you." He remembers the dizzy recurrent dream of being shoved out of a plane, tumbling fast and madly feeling for the rip cord.

Dara walks to the window and looks down at the shadowy garden. Is that a deer, nudging its antlers through the hedges? "Well, now I know. Now it's my world. My head feels like it could explode. I don't know if my heart can stand this. You sleep in the guest room and tomorrow we will have to talk again. Or do we? Seems like we may both have to figure out our own flight paths." She feels a rush of apocalyptic anger, but also stunned, as when she fell off her horse at a high jump and hit the turf hard.

"Dara, you're my life. If there is a way, I want to find it."

"It's after two. We're not going to find anything tonight."

Austin falls on the unmade bed's bare mattress pad under the blanket. He expected to churn but burrows into the pillows and is out almost immediately. His knocked-out sleep turns into dreams of the red car. He's had this red car nightmare before. It's heading off a cliff toward water and he's grabbing all the knobs, searching for the one to open wings. Just before hitting the sea, he wakes up gasping.

Maybe he is not surprised in the morning when he quickly showers, goes down to the kitchen, and Dara is not sitting at the island with coffee, ready to discuss. He races back upstairs and pushes open her bedroom door. The bed is made. Was it even slept in? He runs back down to the kitchen and finds a note by the cold coffee machine.

I'm going home. I'm sorry for you. Sorry for us. Don't call. Right now, I just can't. Won't. You had all my love, now where do I put that love? Beside the note, his mother's engagement ring he'd adored seeing on Dara's hand, a cluster of small diamonds set up on prongs like kitten's teeth.

8

Always first up, Rich lets Rocco out the back entrance. It rained during the night and the stone walkway gleams. Slow drops fall from the dangling white wisteria climbing over the trellis. Rocco bounds toward Dara's yellow car parked in the driveway. Rich follows in his slippers and looks in the window. He places his hand on the hood. Faintly warm.

He cracks open the door to her room. Dara, asleep in her jeans and sweatshirt on top of the bedspread, her raincoat on the floor in a heap. He quietly closes her door.

"Lee, Lee, are you awake?" She opens her eyes and for an instant looks at him without recognition, then smiles.

"Are you up earlier than usual? It's barely light." Rich stands over her, his hands on his hips.

"Did you know Dara's home?"

She sits up. "No. Really? She's here? Why?"

"She's asleep, came in without us hearing anything." She'd pulled that often during senior year when she was dating Marshall Long, sexy, gum-chewing Marshall, sweet and clueless as they come.

"Let's let her sleep. What could this be all about? She was supposed to be going to Amit's dinner. Maybe Austin got caught at work, maybe she just wants to revise the menu, seating, something."

"You want a coffee this early?"

"Sounds good. Thanks."

Lee. Always the optimist. The raincoat on the floor to me says otherwise.

❧

DARA NEVER WENT TO BED THE NIGHT BEFORE. SHE WENT BACK DOWN to the kitchen after Austin collapsed in the guest room. She thought of her mother's wee-hours habit of roaming downstairs at home, looking in the fridge for something to want, maybe a cold biscuit with cane syrup or a few spoons of her favorite lemon ice cream. But Dara didn't want anything at all. She felt flayed, long strips of flesh ripped off her back. She recalls a hideous slide from an art history class, a man—what is the word?—*écorché*. Skinned. She grabbed her keys and handbag. Raining! She threw her raincoat over her head and left through the side door. A raccoon poised on the garbage can lid gave her a wild look as she scooted by, but did not move or stop his inspection of a pineapple.

With hardly anyone on the road, she sped south. The roadwork was still in progress around Richmond, and she was thrown to think of passing only a few days that seem a lifetime ago, when she was happily facing north and a lucky future. She reached Redbud at dawn. How sweet the air felt and the wet grass smelled green-green and earthy. Mimi's right—living in a beautiful landscape makes you want beauty in your own life. She wanted to lie down in the grass and roll with abandon like the horses stabled nearby.

At the bottom of the meadow, mist drifted over the river and the earliest birds in the sycamores were already practicing their welcome to the day. *T-shirt, T-shirt,* one of them repeated. Dara had her key out, but the back door was unlocked. Her parents were bad about that. Too trusting. She crept upstairs and into her room. On the end of her bed, Rocco raised his head and looked at her with his old eyes that look like blue pearls. "Hey, boy," she whispered. "I'm home."

❧

WHEN DARA COMES DOWN AT NOON, HER PARENTS ARE OUT IN THE meadow, grooming every inch for the wedding. Dara makes tea and watches them from the kitchen window. Rocco sleeps under the pergola. Dad, lean and strong as ever, is grooming the stand of cedars, trimming off low branches. Mom crouched down to arrange Boston ferns on the grass floor of her hog-wire chapel, where the vows were to be exchanged. *Were,* Dara notes. Already, the wedding shifts into the distance. Lee sometimes quotes a line from Yeats that Dara remembers. About pity. Such a humiliating word, but the quote? "A pity beyond all telling is hid in the heart of love," she says aloud. That feels true. She hardly can think of how she pities Austin, even more than herself, but in the most private hurt, he had sex with that woman when we were already in love.

Rich piles branches into the back of the Gator. What they don't know, Dara thinks. What do they have to know? I don't want pity. I adamantly refuse to be stuck in a victim role. I can hear it, "Oh, poor Dara." No.

If I say I changed my mind, there will be no pity. There will be the upbeat *better now than later,* there will be the solace of *take your time and sort things out,* there may be anger, or *what are you thinking?* But I've changed course before, not like this, but enough minor ones to pave the way for a big one. I don't think I've ever lied to my family. Well, I don't have to lie to establish that I've changed my mind. Just omit the iceberg from the *Titanic* and let the ship spring a leak, founder, and go down. Dara feels a jolt of clarity, followed by hard thrusts of pure hurt. Austin, why in hell is this happening?

She showers and pulls off her closet shelves denim shorts and an old linen shirt Mei embroidered with random honeybees. Shall I tell Mei? I'm not telling Moira that I'm a shattered mess. They're my oldest and best, but Moira's got frustrations that spill onto me. Last thing

I need is her sympathy, which might show a glint of, well, not pleasure but maybe a bit of comfort for her own problems. Mei would just be sad for me. Courtney and Kat need to cancel their flights now. And Mimi. She's the one least likely to believe a bullshit story.

First, my parents. They adore Austin. I do, too. Did?

Dara steps barefoot out to the toolshed, where her parents are rinsing off their rakes and shovels, hanging them back on the wall in their appointed places. "Mom, Dad," and she begins to sob as Rich hugs her to him. He buries his bristly chin into her neck, breathing in her sun and flowery scent. What's wrong?

"Dara, we've been so worried all morning. Are you okay?" Lee throws her arms around both of them, and they stand without saying more for a long time. "Cry all you need to."

"Let's step outside. It smells like fertilizer in here," and Dara laughs, a short, choked laugh.

Around the edges of the peony bed, the outrageous, invasive Oriental poppies are opening their blatant red and mauve flowers to the sun. Though they've invaded all over Redbud land, Lee can't bear to control the spread. "Look, the peonies are going to bloom just in time," Lee says. "Right now, they're drooping from the rain but will be just perfect."

Rich already senses that this might not be the best thing to say. Dara drops her head. "Forget the flowers. Forget it all, Mom. Dad. There will not be a wedding."

Rich looks up at the sun and squints. "What happened? What's happening?"

Lee only frowns and stares.

"I'm sorry. So sorry. I can't. I cannot get married. Not now. Things have come up that make me see that this wedding can't . . . I can't. As of last night, we're estranged." She draws in a deep breath. *Estranged*, sounds like it has *strangle* trapped in it, and that's the way I feel, strangled. How many times will I be saying I'm sorry? "Austin, um, Austin may have to go back to England." That was true, dammit. "And his green card is in limbo. You know I've been working at HUD, and with Bill on the biography—am I going to shelve all that? I'm too young, you thought that at first, and maybe I am. I never wanted to marry early but Austin overwhelmed me, and I felt certain that getting married was perfect for us. I could go to New York for law school . . ." Where to go next? "He has issues. I can't go into all that but trust me, nothing is easy now. A week ago, life seemed, if not simple, at least clear and right. Careers, where to live, plans to juggle, but doable, with determination. Now it's all a mess."

"The cake layers are baked; they're in Elizabeth's freezer. What . . ." Lee falters at the end of her sentence. Rich looks at her, open-mouthed. What a terrible response, she realizes. "Oh, sweetie, I'm shocked, but whatever you know is best, we will be behind you all the way."

"Of course," Rich said, "but, darling, are you sure? You and Austin seem to have something rare." Tread carefully, he thought. There's more to this than she is saying.

"I know we do, but I am going to need time. I should tell Mimi and Mei and Moira. Oh, Mom, I know there are a hundred things to undo, and I promise I will do it all. I don't want to burden you and Dad." But as she knows, it's way too late for that. Tons of money spent, the roaring engine of a wedding already speeding down the runway for liftoff. Ribboned boxes of gifts not even opened yet, the vows we've written and rewritten, those Crane invitations, creamy, heavy paper and the calligraphed addresses . . . She sees the stacked cake layers, double-wrapped in plastic and foil; they seem to be whirring around in the freezer.

"Let's go in and have some lunch and start to sort out the situation." Rich puts his arm around Dara. The three of them without another word walk back toward the house.

Lee's mind starts to reel. Runaway bride, she thinks. Sounds frivolous and whimsical but runaway brides usually bolt for a powerful reason. *Estranged,* Dara had said; the word has *strange* in it.

9

AT NINE THIS morning Amit picks up a message from last night when he was out to dinner with his family. Austin calling from the airport, apologizing, saying they won't be coming to dinner tonight. Now he waits to hear more. He calls Austin every hour. No answer. Austin off the radar means bad news from the Shelley situation.

Back in Delhi, Shelley was a loner, pudgy, known to come from a weird extended family who lived in a big place with the grandparents holding court on two floors, and who didn't mingle with the top floor, where the children were confined, except when they exited the house. Amit was attracted to her (her brown eyes with a darker brown rim, the swath of her plump creamy side that showed between the wraps of her sari), but his mother cautioned never to get involved with someone from a drama-filled family. In their maths class at the international school, she did a presentation on the meaning of zero, and how it was the Hindu thinkers who really brought to the fore the concept. The faculty recognized that Shelley was uncommonly bright. Well, she was one of two out of eleven of us who applied who were accepted at St. John's. That bright. Once she got to Cambridge, she dumped the saris, lost weight, and morphed into a party girl. Amit remembers introducing her to his mate Austin when he and Shelley saw him at Parker's Tavern. Austin had been studying with a friend across the way in Downing College and stopped by to shake the chill of a dreary February day. He spotted Amit, and the girl, big smile, pouring from a teapot held high over the cup, the big windowpanes steaming and Parker's Piece a green swath behind her. Austin was intrigued at first. Those lips, and her smile made you smile back. She was knocked backwards by his sunny looks, his thick jumper tossed just so around his shoulder. Someone at ease in the world, she'd said later.

Amit tries again. Message machine. "Austin, I'm trying to reach you. I'll keep on, so please call back."

❧

AUSTIN, WITH SURGES OF FIGHT OR FLIGHT, MAY NOT BE THINKING clearly. He has no plan. He cleans his studio, straightening the books so they're all equidistant from the edge of the shelf, lining up his drawing pencils in his desk drawer, ordering the staple gun and envelopes, placing each paper clip in a box. He moves to his closet, refolding his T-shirts and stacking them perfectly on a shelf, rearranging his shirts by color, rehanging ties and belts, and zipping his sport coats into a garment bag.

He'd caught a morning flight back to New York and faces the rest of Saturday with nothing to do but obsess. *Nothing to do* isn't accurate. He could, should, and would go to the office and throw himself on the problems the client raised about the library project. Because he cannot imagine facing the evening, he calls Amit and says he'd like to come to the family dinner. "I'll tell you later what has happened. It isn't pretty."

10

In the afternoon, Lee calls her good friends Fawn and Elizabeth to break the news. She rings the wine shop and cancels the delivery that was supposed to come this afternoon. There's been a glitch . . . she explains over and over. Soon the grapevine will send tendrils all over Hillston, *Have you heard about the Willcox girl . . .* Probably the story will come back in a different form—she's in love with someone else, he's gay, she fancies someone, wasn't she always, what? Capricious. Willful. Blah, blah. That's life in a small town and Lee knows what to expect.

Mei and Moira come right over late in the afternoon. They're dumbfounded by the news but full of support and comfort for Dara, even if they don't understand at all what could have made strong-willed, clear-eyed Dara change her mind. Moira even seems especially sympathetic, without a hint of satisfaction. Mei keeps topping up the wineglasses.

When Lee and Rich leave for their usual Saturday night dinner with friends in town, Mei and Moira stay with Dara. Lee left a mac and cheese in the oven and had a feeling that the wine rack would be raided. Moira calls home to Carleton with instructions for the twins' dinner, ending with "don't wait up."

For Dara, there will be much to unravel but not tonight. She wants a reprieve, a time to be her normal self with her friends. After the initial halting explanation, the same she'd offered her parents, she says, "Let's move on right now. I would so like to forget all this for a while anyway." Like for the rest of my life.

They toast one another. Moira brings up embarrassing high school stunts, decking the history teacher's yard with toilet paper, each piece signed with a historical date, bumping across a cotton field in Rich's car, the class trip to Williamsburg and Mount Vernon, when they left the motel after hours, looking for a 7-Eleven to try out Dara's fake ID.

Eventually Dara plays some of their choice high school music, the old "Dance with Me," and "Take My Breath Away." If the fun feels forced, they don't admit it to themselves. They never eat the mac and cheese. At some point, it seems like a good idea to go to Randy's, the local bar with live music, mostly country, out near the barbecue place. Mei drives, as she likes to pour but not drink much. They know a lot of the regulars there. Dara's high school boyfriend Marshall asks her to dance. His girlfriend Kissy already has picked up the news. "Heard you're hightailing it out of marriage!" she shouts down the bar. "Here's to you—smart girl!" She smirks at Marshall. Dara just gives a thumbs-up and stands up to dance to "Purple Rain," a fav of hers. Everyone along the bar lit with candles in jelly jars starts to croon loud with "Like a Virgin." The girls dance solo to "Whip It" and "Celebration." They howl when Moira remembers that Lisa Stubbs walked down the aisle to "Sexual Healing." Kissy performs a Tina impersonation of "What's Love Got to Do with It."

When the lights dim at one, they drive off into the balmy night with far, clear stars, windows down for the scent of wet pines and plowed fields, singing "Time After Time." *If you fall, I will catch you . . .* Amazing how lyrics stick.

Dara hops out at home. "You be careful, Mei!"

Moira rolls down the back window. "Carleton is not going to be amused," she almost shouts. "Who cares? Screw Carleton."

Mei looks at Dara, mouth open with disbelief. Moira! "Bye. Call me . . ."

At the kitchen table, Lee has been rereading one poem for half an hour, snatches, lines, reading some verses backwards, the last two stanzas over and over:

We sat grown quiet at the name of love;
We saw the last embers of daylight die,
And in the trembling blue-green of the sky
A moon, worn as if it had been a shell
Washed by time's waters as they rose and fell
About the stars and broke in days and years.

I had a thought for no one's but your ears:
That you were beautiful, and that I strove
To love you in the old high way of love;
That it had all seemed happy, and yet we'd grown
As weary-hearted as that hollow moon.

The old high way of love. Two words. Students always thought that it was *highway.* She could see Austin sitting alone outside after the party, the moon going down. Her inkling that night that he was anxious. Or sad; it has something to do with this break. She closes the tattered Yeats. In all the wedding planning and excitement, she has neglected writing the last chapters of her book, the tome on William Butler Yeats. Her contract with the University of North Carolina Press states a September deadline. She must get back to work. Men's careers are seldom derailed by the crises in the love lives of their children, but she wonders how many women's are. What happens to your child is worse than if the same thing happens to you. As Mama knows, and says repeatedly, a child ransoms you to fate.

Dara leans down and kisses the top of her head. "I hope you're not waiting up for me like I'm in high school. But I must admit tonight we acted like we were—we totally reverted. We ended up at Randy's. Marshall was there. He is still knock-down gorgeous."

"I know. I see him when I get gas. That kilowatt smile. He always asks about you."

"Oh, he's got Kissy—and good for her." Dara opens the oven. The mac and cheese is still there. "Want some?"

"No, we had such a great dinner at the Bistro. They have a never-changing menu but still make the best roast chicken, and the strawberry shortcake is perfect." At dinner, Lee was so preoccupied she hardly tasted a thing.

Even lukewarm, the mac and cheese tastes savory and comforting. Dara has not eaten since last night, when the doorbell interrupted her sandwich at the kitchen counter and there was Austin. Hangdog face. Heartbreaking sweet face. His face.

Four bites and she drops her spoon into the sink, covers the casserole, and puts it in the fridge. "Mom, am I going to get through this? I can't even say how devastated I feel. A big part is guilt for all the trouble you and Dad have gone to."

"That's the least of this. And you know we don't do guilt. We're concerned and stunned, and, oh, totally worried. But as you'll hear a thousand times, better now than later, when you have children and mortgage and menopause! How about that for cheerful justification? I know you're scalded."

She didn't say, *I wish to hell you'd tell us what is going on*. Eventually we'll know why she's bolted, she thought.

"I'm going up. You staying down here with your Yeats?" The poet always has been a living presence in their house, him and all his coterie of Irish writers.

"For a bit." Lee doesn't say she couldn't sleep if she took a handful of melatonin.

"Tomorrow I am going to drive down to Indigo and tell Mimi. I feel like calling is too brutal. I'll come back on Monday then head back to DC on Tuesday. Bill has a key, so he can work on the archive, and I can get started again on Wednesday. Give me a list, please, please, of anything I can do to undo this fiasco."

"Mama wouldn't expect you to make a four-hour drive just to spare her the shock."

"Maybe she'll have some wisdom."

"Maybe you will be surprised at her reaction. She might seem stoic. You know, you never can predict her."

Exhaustion doesn't begin to describe how Dara feels as she throws back the covers. Right away, she begins to dream. She's in the back seat of a car. Someone is driving fast onto a frozen lake. A gigantic crack like lightning and the car is wobbling down, gurgling, filling with water, she's beating her fists on the window, screaming.

"Dara! Dara! You're having a nightmare. It's okay, wake up. Hey, I'm right here." Rich turns on the lamp and lies down beside her, as when she was small and wanted her bears lined up.

"Oh. That was so scary. I was sinking. I could see the ice up above. I couldn't let the window down . . ."

"Okay, okay." He strokes her hair. "You're fine. You're home. Everything will be just fine." Scared the bejesus out of me.

11

FACING A BAR SCENE or a TV night alone in his studio looms as punishment. Austin feels relieved that Amit's family will fill the evening. He stops at the flower stall on the corner and buys yellow tulips. He manages to appear at Amit's apartment as an extraordinarily well put-together, smiling friend. Amit's mother, regal in a gold silk sari printed with silver medallions, extends her hand. Austin is glad he's grabbed a blazer on his way out, even though it's over a black T-shirt. She's six feet, eye to eye with Austin, and the plump father in a shiny suit is a head shorter. Amit's brother, Jayesh, is just getting a black fuzz on his upper lip, and Anita, the sweet-faced sister, with pixie curls, rises up en pointe and practices smiles with a quick twirl.

Amit must have been all over New York gathering ingredients for this home-style welcome. Austin wonders if his family might have enjoyed an American evening—he's remembering Lee's quail—but is all too happy himself with the lamb biryani, the butter chicken, fluffy basmati, and that dynamite spinach-and-paneer curry. They're gregarious, talking nonstop, and super polite. The little brother is full of goofy riddles and questions about basketball and American football. Anita keeps teasing Amit about his baggy pinwale cords and slouchy jumper. "Baggy American," she taunts. "He looks splendid," the mother interjects. Amit must have warned them about the impending wedding because they only politely ask Austin about his work in architecture. The father inquires about what to do with their four more days in New York and what to expect from their trip to visit friends who've moved to Sedona, Arizona.

Austin is glad to think of Sedona, Arizona, which he's never heard of, happy to pass the chicken, happy to imagine Amit's majestic mother as the ruler Indira Gandhi, to hear of Anita's ballet classes, and to spend the evening away from his stabbing pain. Attentive as always, Austin raises toasts to Amit's skills, which he must have learned from the best, toasts again to his beautiful mother. As if he's watching from the doorway, he plays the part of himself. As he helps Amit clear away the plates, Amit has a chance to ask. "What happened in DC?"

"She said very little but was obviously stunned and freaked. Repulsed. She kept staring at me as though she'd never seen me before. She left late that night. I didn't hear her go—I was konked out in the guest room. I've been sleeping like someone drugged. She left a note saying do not call and I haven't. She headed south. I feel sorry, so damn sorry for her."

"She's not facing what you are, my friend. Relatively, you're facing the firing squad. She's got those great parents. She is in good hands, you know that. Do you think she told them the whole gory story?"

It had not occurred to Austin that she wouldn't. "Don't know. I guess so."

"The wedding is what, off? Postponed?"

"She did not leave a chink of light. Felt like the house collapsed."

Anita brought in a tray of glasses. "Mum would like tea. May I make it?"

12

I and this mystery here we stand.

—WALT WHITMAN

DARA LOVES INDIGO ISLAND. All her life, her family has popped down for long weekends, staying at Biba Harrison's old Palms, a rustic wooden hotel where the term *laid-back* might have been invented. The summer before college, Dara worked there as a waitress for three months of dances, a brief romance with one of the other waiters, who would be off to Davidson in the fall but then was all party, all for skinny-dips in the ocean at night and smuggling tequila out of the hotel storeroom. A summer of reading *Anna Karenina* under an umbrella while checking out the lifeguard, watching at dawn the loggerhead turtles make their way back to the ocean after burying their eggs in the warm sand, kayaking through the marshes at sunset, alert for alligators rising from the dark water, bulging eyeballs first, opening their ferocious jaws. Those sunsets, glorious and garish with blurred pink and saffron skies, dark purple streaks at the horizon, the sun wobbling down like a scoop of orange sherbet about to melt. And all the reflections rippling across patches of open water. Dara learned the pure pleasure of living where the tide and the motion of the sun and moon control the day.

She wonders what happened to the lovely Biba, who ran the inn with the help of two blond-braided teenage girls and her boy with spiky hair, who must have been thirteen and was already a painter?

Or that guy—Jamie—whose toenails she painted purple and whose penis bobbed like a fishing cork as he lay in the clear shallows.

Dara wonders if she imagined that she learned to know the exact moment the tide changed. If she was out on the marsh in open water, did she see a definite quiver in the water just as the lunar pull released or strengthened and the tide changed?

Driving south, she waits for the first sight of those supple marshes separating the barrier island from the South Carolina coast. Nothing on this earth, she thinks, compares with the play of light over this not-land, not-ocean, the grasses all in green, rust, golden motion undulating in the tidal waters, scattering light in sine waves. Wanting the scent, the balm, she lets down the windows and turns up the radio. Oldie playing—"Sha-la-la." She sings along.

When Charlotte decided to decamp from Washington to Indigo, Dara was at Georgetown but still managed to get down to the island now and then. Big Mann's death was fresh, and Charlotte was crazy with grief. Still, she always had suppers out on her deck, big piles of crab to crack and dip in lemon butter, a bowl of potato salad, and loaves of bread that she got in the village from a woman who also made caramel cakes. So, Indigo, always Indigo, landscape of the heart.

On the thin end of the island, Charlotte's cottage, "Banana Republic," faces the beach and backs up to a broad marsh view. What could be dreamier? Dara pulls into the lattice garage under the stilt-built house and beeps.

"Mimi, hey, Mimi, it's Dara!" She slings her backpack over her shoulder and clatters up the stairs. For the first time since Austin's secret fell on her, she feels a surge of exuberance from the spreading spruce and salt air, the thrilling slosh of waves breaking and retreating, dog roses blooming against all odds in the loose sand. What a good idea to come touch base with a place where she always has been happy.

Charlotte flings open the door and grabs Dara in a hug. Dara doesn't want to let go. "Oh, Mimi, I had to come."

"What a grand surprise. You must have left early. From Redbud? Why didn't your mama come?" She knows nothing. Dara had asked, and Lee had refrained from calling her.

Dara drops her backpack and rushes to the sliding doors, all open to the sea. "I never forget this view—the whole ocean right in your lap. Can we walk? I've got news. Not good news, I'm afraid."

"Oh, Jesus H. Christ, are you pregnant?"

Dara reeled, then half-laughed. "No. Not a chance." It hits her: But someone else is.

"Take this scarf. It's windier than it looks."

On the beach, Dara tells the same story she told her parents, Mei, and Moira. "There's more, Mimi, but not for now. I'm still sorting out what's happening to me."

"Happening to you? From what you said you are making this break. Is that right?" She looks hard at Dara, and Dara knows Mimi always goes around behind everything she's told and often makes outrageous conclusions but often comes out the other side with what's been unsaid. More than once, Dara has heard Mimi say, "A secret hides another secret, and that secret controls the narrative."

"Can we leave it there, Mimi?" Her throat seizes in a hard cough, and tears start stinging.

Charlotte slides her arm around Dara's shoulder, and they walk. She thinks she can feel Dara's bones vibrating. She lets go and Dara races to the water's edge, splashing. Close in, two dolphins throw their slick bodies in the air, twisting as they fall back into the water, repeating the leaps over and over for pure joy.

"That's John Harrison. Remember him?" Mimi gestures with her chin toward the dunes in front of the shuttered Palms where Dara once worked. A man stands in front of an easel, not turned toward the ocean but facing the top of the weathered hotel through the high dunes. Sand blowing around him, the same spiky hair.

"Oh, John—that's Biba's son? All grown." Dara remembers him, he must have been thirteen, drawing on the backs of menus, receipts, anything at hand. His sisters meanly called him "tadpole eyes" because of the limpid gray color. "Does he live here?"

"No, but he comes now and then and stays up in the employees' attic rooms. No one else lives here, except Biba now and then. She keeps trying to refinance but the place needs so much work. Dry rot. Mildew. Window putty, tile grout. He's finishing at RISD. Full ride there. They say he's quite talented with landscapes and portraits. Must be spooky in there at night. Shall we go say hello?"

"Let's don't. I'm just not feeling like I can make the effort."

They put their heads down into the wind and walk on. When they turn to walk back toward Mimi's, he's gone.

"Sorry the pickings for dinner are lean. If I'd known you were coming, I'd have shopped." Charlotte doesn't say she'd called Bing when Dara was in the bathroom and canceled her dinner with him. "My plan for tonight is grilled cheese-and-bacon sandwiches. Will that suit you? I do have a hunk of frozen pound cake we can toast over the coals for dessert. Or, if you'd like, we can go in town to the Shrimp Shack."

"Let's stay home. Sounds great, perfect, and I hope you have some wine."

"Well, of course. I have a cold sauvignon and plenty of red."

"I'll have both!"

"Curl up right there." Charlotte lights the fire. There is just enough chill, and she wants Dara to be cozy under the white mohair throw and for the primitive comfort of the crackling hearth to help sooth whatever in tarnation is going on with her.

"Mimi, all these books. And you wrote a lot of them." Books line either side of the fireplace, the thick white shelves neatly jammed. Charlotte's *The Good Marriage,* still in print, sold millions of copies and is still selling, one of those phenomenal books like *What to Expect When You're Expecting* and *What Color Is Your Parachute?* It was translated into so many other languages that Charlotte lost count. The foreign editions fill one whole bookcase. Three years on, she published *The Good Divorce: It's Never Too Late,* also a runaway bestseller. Those editions fill the bookcase flanking the other side of the fireplace. Her personal reference library and mystery novels, cookbooks, and fiction line the front wall of the house. Books everywhere, and big-paned windows along the back wall, where you can look out at the changing ocean and always be astonished. Charlotte takes that positioning seriously—the inquiring mind and the natural world.

Dara sips her wine and almost dozes in the comfort and security of Mimi's cottage. Built just as Mimi desired, the house seems an extension of her grandmother.

Charlotte sits by the coals long after the sun falls into the marsh behind them. Dara falls asleep on the sofa. Charlotte's mind picks over what Dara said about bailing out of the wedding. Nothing makes sense, of course, and she wonders what Lee and Rich feel about the story. She has a mind to ring Austin in New York and ask what in bloody hell is all this about? But would not, of course, disrespect Dara like that. One thing she recognizes: Dara is in shock.

Showered and changed, Dara helps with supper. Charlotte takes the wine to the hearth, and they settle again in front of the fire with their trays. If Dara is going to reveal more, surely it will be during this intimate, simple meal. But Dara is thumbing through *The Good Marriage.* "I read this so long ago. I need to read it again."

"It can wait until you're needing advice. I'm surprised that it still has currency. Seems like all my great wisdom should be commonplace by now."

"Your advice all came from working with your patients? All that group therapy you used to do?"

Charlotte laughs. "Oh, there are anecdotes, plenty of those, but mainly I told them what they needed to hear! Some of them followed my leads. The others, well, they inspired *The Good Divorce*."

"From your perspective now, as well as from when you wrote, what makes a good marriage, other than love and luck?"

"Love, yes. Luck hardly ever. There's good and there's great. Most, hell, all therapists tell you that a good marriage is about compromise. And isn't that dreary, a life of compromise, meaning that neither gets what they really need." She stands up and jostles the logs with a poker. "Many are okay with a good marriage. Learning to balance chores and taxes and such. And small things! You don't correct your partner in front of others. You can hammer out a good marriage.

"Great is a whole other thing. Boiled down, way down, a great marriage happens when two people are big enough to want more for the partner than they want for themselves. Not just as much. More. You fan the partner's sparks, make a blaze. You want for and value yourself but not more than you want for your partner. The partner is not ever sidelined while you work for yourself. You know their most hopeful vision for their lives and you are damn sure you help them stay in the light of that path. Otherwise, when life just happens and you wind up not knowing what became of your core desires, there's all hell to pay. And you always make each other shine. You take the partner's side when any argument comes up between the two of you. You don't insist on your side—this is crucial because it totally undercuts the argument when you both honor the other. I learned that from Stephen. He always insisted I was right. Knocks the fight right out."

"Sounds like Mom and Dad."

"You bet. They are big models for me. They have a rare connection. And they're smart. That helps because most marriages fail through lack of imagination. You can't see around what's happening now. You have to be able to imagine otherwise and find the way over and around the lump that is the present. Mostly I learned to identify all these dark mysteries when I was married to Lee's father. My career was okay by him, as long as it didn't interfere with his mighty medical career. Sorry to speak ill of the dearly departed. Any schedule problem that occurred, guess whose time was most easily sacrificed? That coming-in-second mode accumulates and becomes very quietly massively destructive. Some are too cowed ever to realize this. Women especially, with that long training to be accommodating, supportive, giving. I remember one patient saying, 'The night I, for once, slid that bigger pork chop onto my plate I knew that I was done.' She inspired the chapter 'The Bigger Pork Chop.'" She smiles, remembering her delight with that patient's revelation. "And for me, the great pretender, finally, a friend slyly said to me about Craig, 'Looks like big muscles your doctor man has; must come from all that air you blow up his sleeves.'"

Dara laughed at the image.

"I got my chance for the real thing with Stephen Mann. What a grand relief we found in a *great* marriage."

"Sounds tough to be so generous." I am not generous enough, Dara thinks.

"Sounds tough, but I know that's what the so-called lucky ones have. I know—sounds all Christian do-unto-others, but no way that I mean a tit-for-tat. I mean do unto the one you love as he or she, ideally, would most desire for themselves. Not at all 'as you would have them do unto you.' Lose yourself for your love and you find your great marriage."

Charlotte had let her sandwich sit. "Isn't this delish? Want another? And, oh, this must work both ways. Balance is all. If one person has the great love and the other is even slightly not up to it, then," Charlotte laughs, "then it's time to read *The Good Divorce,* or settle into one of those best-friend things."

"Let's split one more. Is this sharp cheddar you used? I'll fix it. You finish. You know, it sounds like you're talking about what a good parent does, without the 'you're grounded.' Let's have some of that pound cake, too. I have hardly eaten anything in how many days . . ." Only two endless days, she thinks, and I'm still in one piece, wanting cake.

Dara makes two and comes back to the fire with a tray of sandwiches and pound cake slices.

"That's all in the last chapter, called 'The Great Marriage.' It's not for everyone. Most of the book is about making a good marriage. Most people must settle, even if they don't know it, for the relationships, the partnerships, the companionships—all those have their merits and demerits, their checks and balances. A lot of those chapters come from my practice. I used to know half the marriages in Hillston and Chapel Hill, all those who rushed into marriage and woke to a long hangover, the open marriages, usually so sad, and those earnest couples who worked on their marriage like it was an old car, and those civilized *marriage blanc* arrangements. No sex but sometimes good roommates."

"White marriage? Why white?"

"*Blanc* can mean 'blank,' too. But maybe no blood on the sheet on the wedding night? If that's not too far-fetched. Basically—no sex."

Is Mimi distracting me? Dara wonders. Or am I to learn something? Knowing her, why am I even asking. I'll read the books again. I think I scanned them when I was twelve or so, but I don't remember all these nuances and levels of marriage.

Charlotte has no idea what Dara will make of the prism she's held up to the light, if out of all she's said, anything landed near whatever has caused her lovely granddaughter to drive all night to get home, to flee again to Indigo, and to be planning another drive back to a solitary place where she must see if there's a path of dropped crumbs to follow somewhere.

She brings sheets and pillows from the linen closet, and they make up the sofa bed.

Dara slides open the door enough to hear the sluice and slurp of tide. She stares blankly at the black ocean, the curls of breaking waves foamy and moonlit. She is too sated to parse the drastic ideas Mimi proposed. Millions have read her book. How many were able to be earth angels and make selfless commitments? But Mimi had not thought of her great marriage ideas as selfless, but as a creative way to find happiness. How am I to think of Austin's situation held up to the light of these propositions? Besides, we are not in a marriage and maybe I'm not a big enough person to leap right over and embrace someone else's newborn child, even if it gives me back my love. I don't want to and I won't. When I don't want children at all right now, where does that leave me? What about writing *The Good Engagement*? A chapter on Austin's betrayal with someone delusional? Or one on lying flat on the floor and letting circumstance stomp all over you. But Austin, I know who he is, in and out. His sweetness and his wanting me to bloom. Am I at fault? Should I just be all that's okay, we'll better-or-worse it. Maybe what Mimi was showing not telling is that I need to think about the great marriage, not the one with checks and balances like in the House and the Senate, or the one where marriage is tinkering with an old jalopy, or even the one where her patient's vows stressed that the bride and groom were best friends. Where's the electrical voltage there? Mimi has quietly carved the subject like she peels apples, never breaking apart the dangling skin and leaving the fruit whole.

With the chattering monkey on her back, with the looming elephant in the room, she wills her mind toward the ocean outside the door, its repetition of shush, shush.

She hears a faint humming, like a bee buzzing against a windowpane as if it could bore through glass. She remembers that Mimi chants her own night mantras before meditating, something part Buddha, part "Wonderful World," and a dose of Walt Whitman: "Out of the cradle, endlessly rocking . . ." But that is all Dara remembers.

Awake early, Dara hears nothing from Mimi's loft bed. She slips out the door for the sunrise on the beach, long a habit of the only child during summers here. Walking the empty beach in her bathing suit, sun performing its everyday miracle, picking up and dropping shells, making footprints for Robinson Crusoe to find, cartwheeling, running, kicking the surf . . . the deep pleasure returns, and she thinks, always this will be there for me. She imagines coming upon Austin. He rounds the high dune and runs to meet her. Dara wades in up to her knees and lets the waves slap her waist.

Mimi has coffee ready on the deck. "You always did that when you were little. Did you ever suspect that Rick was at the window, watching to see if you were okay and not going in far enough to catch the riptide?"

"I didn't." Dara knows they'll all be watching for her now. "I better take off soon. I need to spend some of the day at Redbud. Mimi, you have been so great to be with."

"You come here anytime. Tell Lee I have a good idea. Let's plan a late summer trip with your parents, ten days somewhere—Scotland? Spain?—then you can go off as you please, maybe meet Austin and talk by then . . ."

"Umm. Sounds good, the trip. About Austin, remains to be seen."

"When you're ready. When you're ready to talk to all of us. You're damming something up and there's pressure. That's okay for a while but remember Jung, or was it Freud, said secrets are 'psychic poison.' Jung it was."

13

May 1995

Back over the causeway, recrossing the marshes. Just yesterday, Dara thinks, only twenty-four hours, I was coming upon the coast. Something weird has happened to time since the apparition of Austin appearing at the town house door Friday night. That couldn't be real. It is real. It's only Monday and it seems like weeks have passed through my body. I can't talk straight. It's ghastly that I have this encroaching shadow above me and I'm acting the role of a frivolous runaway bride who doesn't know her own mind. His absence aches. Why isn't he here, exclaiming over the rippling colors of the grasses, the layer of aquamarine between slabs of pink clouds? Why can't I be fully truthful? Coffee, I'd like another. Is there a place? I don't want anyone to think badly of him. I know, I know they suspect complications and are kind enough not to press when they sense I don't want to say more. Mimi, Mimi, she knows, I'm sure, that something big is festering. Mimi, did I thank you enough for everything?

Dara turns into the main drag just on the mainland. Those books she wrote gave me my college fund, with plenty left for law school; those books provided our family trips to Mexico, Paris, Italy, years of riding lessons, big repairs for Redbud, generous checks for birthdays and Christmas. She sees that she should get gas. Lee's professor salary and Rich's journalism provided for us nicely, but Mimi's generosity makes our lives sweet. She practically single-handedly supports the shelter for domestically abused women in Chapel Hill.

She spots Pam's Cuppa & Donuts and pulls into a parking spot right in front. For Mimi herself, she's not so extravagant, although in Taormina one day she spotted an antique sapphire ring in the window of a jewelry store and promptly bought it. Thirty thousand dollars. Rich almost choked on his gelato. But normally she was all sticky over the price of aluminum foil and eggs and insistent that drugstore moisturizers are as good as Lancôme. I should turn around and thank her again. But I'll have to do that later.

Dara orders at the counter. Might as well have a hot glazed doughnut. As she turns toward a window seat, she recognizes just as he looks up John Harrison's beguiling stand-up hair. It looks like someone took the scissors to it with their eyes closed. He sees her and immediately stands up, shocked, looking hard with the gray eyes his sisters said were the color of tadpoles but are more like the color of storm clouds. "Is that really you, Dara Willcox?"

She's shocked, too. "Hey, Johnny boy! Mimi told me you're painting down here. So great to see you after . . . oh, no, how many years?"

She sits down at his table. She can still see the shy boy.

For an hour, they catch up: Georgetown, RISD, family, luck, his application for a fellowship in Rome, trips, books, exhibits, style, what-became-of . . .

Biba, John, and his sisters want The Palms to reopen. They're scheming and imagining but haven't found a feasible path. Influenced by Mimi, Dara says, "What about finding an unfeasible path?"

John looks startled but smiles. "I get that. Good thinking. We've been looking for investors. Maybe I should dream in another direction . . ."

She teases about him drawing on the inn's kitchen walls and on receipts. He teases back about her always tracking sand into the dining room and waiting tables barefoot. "Oh well, it's Indigo. It was a great summer. One of the best."

"Your Mimi likes it here. I've seen her with the good-looking Navy guy."

"Yes, we haven't had the pleasure. You know how private she is."

"I was a big fan of Senator Mann. Sorry he's gone."

Dara tells him about the biography in progress and her job organizing his papers. With that, she realizes she needs to hustle. Four hours of empty road ahead. But John says, "Hey, I know we haven't seen each other in an eon but is something wrong? Am I out of line asking? You seem, I don't know, it's nothing, I guess. Maybe a little sad to be leaving Mimi?" He thinks she looks haunted, seems hesitant, which is totally unlike the firecracker Dara he remembers. "Maybe it's just that I remember when you danced on the table at the Waffle House! Of all places, the damn Waffle House!"

Dara recalls that crazy morning and laughs. "Always hard to leave. But yes, something is wrong." She looks at the skinny palms flapping under the telephone wires. Looks back at John.

An hour later, gassed up, heading north, Dara speeds, needing to be home, needing to get today done with and for tomorrow to come, to return to DC, throw herself into work and the unimagined life ahead. Blank unfurling, ugly days. Bleak days. She has told John, almost a stranger, everything that she did not tell her parents, her grandmother, and her best friends. Yes, almost a stranger, John, but a connection to the summer she broke loose from her family and began to see herself independently.

He listened hard. And she could see the enormity of it all reflected in his eyes, his bewilderment and empathy.

All he'd managed to say was "That's stupefying. I'm sorry. You don't see any clear way forward but that's because there's not one. You're brokenhearted, Dara, but in terms of dilemma, your Austin's the one hanging in the wind. I know someone who wrote a math PhD dissertation proving that if a problem is insolvable, it is no longer a problem. I doubt that helps, but think about it. Dara, if I could help, I would, believe me. Just tell me. Keep in touch." He wrote his number on a torn-off piece of newspaper left on the table. "When you see some glimmer—or anytime—I'd like to hear how you are."

He walked her out to her car. "Okay if I take a photo? You know I'm into portraits. I could try to paint you. You're a mysterious beauty, not the conventional type, like my two blessèd blond and glowing sisters, but like someone in a story." He's picturing that Millais pre-Raphaelite painting, Ophelia floating face up in a clear stream, eyes and mouth open. She's clutching bright flowers. Singing, he recalls, before she drowns. He shakes away the image and pulls a camera out of his satchel. Dara stands still, head tilted back. The slightest smile, her eyes wide and stunned. She watches John click from one side of her face to the other, then straight on.

"Would it be okay if I took a stab at a portrait?"

"What would you call it? *The Betrayed?*"

"Not that! Look at those palms behind you. Maybe you're *Queen of Palms.*" The confused attraction he'd had as a thirteen-year-old boy came back. Something unattainable about Dara.

"Better than *Left in the Lurch Girl.*"

Shaken from the confession, Dara slows down from 80. Troopers lurk behind billboards just for drivers like her. You pay the fine on the spot and they go home happy. He would be about John's age, the lost little one. For long stretches of time she forgets Hawthorn, but now she thinks of her brother, whom she never saw. Rich hauling out of the car the empty bassinette. Lee, wan, crying, scooping Dara into her arms in the driveway. And John, kind, really listens, he seems familiar. Family familiar. She envisions The Palms, itself again but better. Her room there, shared with two other girls, had two narrow dormer windows always open to the breezes. She can still lie awake in that room, listening to the smack and sluicing of waves. A semi passes, cutting in close. Dara brakes and the trucker also slows, almost causing her to ram into him. She swerves into the left lane and presses the accelerator as far down as it goes, shooting out around the truck and blowing the horn. Flips the bird and speeds on.

❧

RICH WALKS NAKED ACROSS THE MEADOW. CERTAIN HABITS PRECEDE A new article, and his river soak, cool at this time of year, always gives him an opening, or at least a glimmer of direction. Besides, walking his own turf naked is an exhilarating pleasure of country living. The oddity, if you happened to see him, is the boots—rubber boots to the mid-calf, worn in defense of snakes and ticks. Otherwise bolt naked in the sunlight.

The Eno runs shallow and rocky, with occasional dips deep enough to swing over on a rope and drop. Four flat rocks, just around the bend from Dara's small beach, break the current, and onto the largest he hauls himself to dry on the sun-warmed stone. A political profile on Gingrich. What a prick. These pieces are always tense. Getting the balanced tone, winning the trust or, minimally, the tolerance of the subject, then presenting the obnoxious, the grandiloquent, the crusader, the idealist (only twice), the supernovas, without praise or blame. Raise the questions. Acutely. Let them bury themselves or win hearts and minds. He catches movement on the far stone and sees a skinny chartreuse snake slither up to warm itself on it. Rich splashes across to the shore and grasps a hanging muscadine vine to pull himself out. He grabs his towel, dries his feet, and heads for the house.

He hears a car turn into the driveway and knots his towel around his waist. Dara's yellow car. Home.

Mimi's call already has alerted Lee. They've expected Dara sooner. He sees Rocco attempting to leap on her as he always has, but now he can only lift his front paws briefly into the air before thudding down almost spread eagle. Dara bends to snuggle him and catches sight of Rich wrapped in a blue towel. He must be starting a new article.

❧

"CRAB CAKES! I AM LUCKY." DARA SETS DOWN THE BREAD AND LIGHTS the candles, even though it is still light. Rich mans the grill, gently browning the thick, breaded crab patties. These three at the table, where they have gathered thousands of times. The Dr. Van Fleet rose, older than Dara, clambers over the lattice top of the pergola, faint pink buds just beginning to open, and the woody honeysuckle already sending out a heady perfume.

"Just like always." Lee raises her glass of rosé and their glasses ring. She remembers the dark red spill staining the tablecloth, Austin leaping up. Not at all like always, why did I say that, wishful thinking, but maybe this will someday be just a story, and someone will say it was for the best, or how lucky that it all worked out the way it did in the end, or something unimaginable now will have happened instead of what we wanted to happen. "Right now, we're all in shock but pass the lemons, sweetie, and let's have a little feast. Never hurts." Rich brings over the platter of crispy crab cakes and some grilled zucchini.

They talk about everything but. Dara running into Johnny Harrison, Mimi's books, the baby zucchini, Indigo marshes, Rich's upcoming interview, and Lee's inching progress with Yeats. Rich gets up to switch on the overhead fan when the first mosquito of the season lights on Lee's hair.

Dara clears. Left at the table, Lee looks at Rich. "She's just not, not, not going to tell us what happened."

Rich poured more wine in her glass. "We'll know soon enough."

14

AUSTIN WAITS UNTIL ELEVEN—four o'clock in London—to call his dad. He's surprised when his sister answers. "Annsley! You're at Dad's—everything all right there?"

Annsley never comes to the city on Mondays, even though her home is only an hour away. She has her own First Edition Books in Cambridge. Like their father, she's wedded to folios and letterpress and signed copies and long-out-of-print books. She often has Michael to her place or she comes up to London on Sundays.

"Yes. Came for Dad's birthday. That's why you're calling? He'll be so pleased."

"Ah! Yes! That is today." God, another thing to be ashamed of. His dad's sixty-fifth birthday. "So glad I caught you. How are you? How's the book world?"

"Good. The shop is ticking along. I started a side specialty of early-twentieth-century children's books. They are so delightful. I just sit there reading all the time. I hate to sell them." After Annsley studied at Clare, she never left Cambridge. Said she wanted to stay in a place where cows sometimes wandered from the college Backs across the meadows and into town. That kind of place. "So lovely to hear your voice! But you want to speak to the birthday boy. Let's catch up soon. Not long until the wedding. I so wish I could come but . . ."

"No worries at all." This was not going well. He'd called to confess. "Yes, put him on. Love you. Talk soon?"

"Austin! I was worried about you. I had a dream that you were climbing up this tall, tottering ladder into the sky. It was swaying and you couldn't look down, just up and up." Something clattered in the background. "Annsley, the cups are still in the dishwasher. We're about to have a bit of tea here, my boy. I wish you were here." Austin could almost see his dad standing by his desk piled with books, the flickering green light from the square streaming through the long windows, and his sister arranging her cake and berries on the table by the deep red sofa, the crushed velvet long worn bare by everyone in the family plopping there to read book after book. Dad's cat, Boss, has limited her shredding to one arm. The whole gentle scene took him hurling back into a comfortable time before insanity gripped his life.

"Dad, it's a big day. I just want to say 'happy birthday.' Sixty-five years of there being a Michael Austin Clarke in the world—something to celebrate. I wish I could be with you. I don't want to interrupt your tea with Annsley. I bet she's brought her famous lemon drizzle cake."

"You guessed right. You should be here."

"Let's talk more later. I may be coming back sooner than I thought. Some things are up for grabs right now, but I'll explain later. You go! Hope you have something to toast with other than tea."

Austin sat on his bed, throbbing head in hands. "That was bloody awful. Forgotten my own father's milestone birthday." And now I'm talking to myself. He flopped backwards—fuckwit—and wished his body would melt into the coverlet and disappear.

But body and mind remained in overload, a shaky database about to crash. Options? Few. He reiterates them again.

1. Ignore the situation entirely, which is exactly what I want, but legal issues, as well as moral ones, loom.

2. I agree to support with no contact.

3. Agree to support with limited contact.

Boy has an MIA father, an object of fantasy and loss. For a child to have grudging parental involvement, when there is a perfectly healthy and sane parent, well, what's it going to be like to live with that? For him and for me? Too many of my Canterbury and Cambridge friends had families characterized by estrangement. Mine broken but not by choice, my mother ripped away—what a different sorrow. That Christmas I watched my father try to put the broken pieces (blame the cat) of a precious Japanese vase of his back together. The mend was clumsy and one jagged triangle just wouldn't fit, even though it looked as if it should. Mother's vase still sits in the bookcase, the hole turned to the back.

Rising from memory, the two trips to Greece he took at fifteen and sixteen with his mate Reggie, Reggie's mom, and her "friend." I was, he supposed, invited as a distraction for Reggie, whose dad was off with someone else skimming the Aegean waters in a sailboat but ringing at all hours from tavernas, screams and hysterics hurling across the patio, and Reggie pretending nothing was going on. Kept reading his Dostoyevsky, while I froze with alarm. With a shiver, he remembered Reggie saying, "Dad wants nothing to do with me. I'm not worth his time. Well, he's not worth mine. He can pay the fees at King's School, and he can go fuck his secretary till his dick falls off." We managed to laugh. Bad as that was, many of the other boys in our dorm had it worse. Art Simons-Smythe waiting near the cathedral, as he'd been told, and neither parent remembering to pick him up for hols. But that's not this boy, Shelley's boy. He'll have her extended family in Delhi. He'll have that extended family in Delhi unless . . . Unless Shelley doesn't make it. Please, please let her bounce back.

Option 4: Support and involvement. All summer with me. I fly out and take him to see the tigers and elephants and the holy river. Cliché? What the hell do I know? Send gifts. Call. This calms my mind in one dimension and upturns it in the other, the life I would have with Dara.

Option 5: The worst—I'm left with sole care for this infant, and I am well and truly screwed. At least I could work anywhere. But in London, I'd have Dad and Annsley to help me get through.

None of the above, thank you.

Austin heaves himself out of bed and stands under the cold shower until it turns scalding hot. Finally, the endless weekend is over. Other than dinner at Amit's, Austin hardly knows what he has done, other than pace. He walked all the way to Central Park, all new budding green and blooming. So many carriages and strollers he couldn't stop staring at, those tiny doll faces and little fists shaking at the air.

Now he plans to work. Amit sent him home with a shopping bag full of leftovers from the feast. He reheats mounds of rice and butter chicken and naan, spreads his drawings on the table, and opens a beer. A night I normally would relish, he thinks. Quiet. My big project waiting. He takes careful measurements of the façade and looks for a solution other than the one the library donor wants, the center door. Maybe there's another option. Maybe two doors instead of one. Maybe there's a window or a sculpture that goes between them. Sometimes a setback is an invitation to find a better solution than the one you thought was perfect. Sometimes not. He draws two doors onto the plan, dripping a bit of butter chicken.

Looking over at the armchair under the window, he puts Dara there, underlining sections of Big Mann's notes, twirling her pencil through her hair, looking up at him, her eyebrows raised in question.

Austin waited until the birthday aura faded to call his father again. Six o'clock in London and Michael is sautéing a chop for his dinner. "Dad, me again. I needed to call back and let you know about something that has thrown my plans into a major tailspin."

"Thought something was off. What's happened?" Michael turns off the gas and takes his sherry to the sofa.

Bluntly, Austin outlines the sequence of events and the medical problem and the evaporation of Dara from the scene.

"That's a hell of a lot to take in. Glad I'm sitting down. I suppose you don't know where to turn. I wouldn't."

"What do you think I should do?"

"Bloody hell, go run with the bulls in Pamplona."

Austin manages a laugh. "As good advice as any, I guess. But I'm already gored. Seriously, I'm left with few choices, but the best is that Shelley will be fine and take the kid to India and I send child support for eighteen years or whatever. And maybe Dara would eventually come back."

"That's best, but you have to brace yourself for the worst. Sorry to throw a match on the oil. All you can do now—stay put and lay down a couple of plans. I think it will seem like an eternity. Try to ignore the whole infra dig aspect and just pray to every god in the sky that the doctor knows what he's doing."

He does not bring up his rage over the appointments his Delia made to find out what was wrong with her; how many doctors said the twisting pains were only cramps, that she was young and healthy, probably prone to imagining problems.

Instead, they talk about how Austin will manage his job in this uncertainty, when he might return to London, his iffy finances, and if he should tell his sister now. Something else to dread, as Annsley will be shocked down to her socks. And who wouldn't be.

As they sign off, Michael says, "There's another story after this one, Austin, and I'll help you get to it in every way possible. And you know Annsley will, too. You are not a whit alone."

Austin feels an uplift after they talked. Not a whit alone, he'd said. Again, that twinge: Dara left me alone with this. She has every right, but still . . .

What's left for the moment is good work. In all the negativity, Austin's projects are saving him. And the college library project is 99 percent done, almost all changes approved, and, really, he thinks the client might have been right. The new library looks airy and contemporary but has also a classical formality that adds dignity. The

California possibility, still out in the ether, is taking a slow shape in his imagination. He needs to see the site. First, he needs (yesterday) to talk to Julian, his New York boss. Facing the consternation in the hierarchy of the firm is more dread, but Austin feels certain that his superiors won't skin him alive, as long as his work continues to please. The complication will be location. But that's not a problem, if Shelley is taking the child to India.

Austin begins to write letters. Three calls with plaintive messages left—can we talk, can I come down and try to work on some solution that keeps us together, I'll do anything you want—all unanswered. It hurts. Couldn't she have sympathy for me? Maybe not. It's still too raw and shocking. And ugly.

Dearest, dearest Dara, When we fell in love, my whole body snapped into being . . .

My sweet girl, I have to spend my life with your eyes . . .

Dara, you know, you know I have your touch all over my body . . .

Dara, do you dare, Dara, there's dare in your name, dare to love me again . . .

My love, I want to hear you singing in the bathtub, and I want to wash your hair and kiss your wet toes and I know this is pretty soapy . . .

He finished the last one and folded it into an envelope. Addressed and stamped, the letters went into a shoebox shoved onto a closet shelf.

15

THE FOLLOWING MONDAY at work, Austin schedules an afternoon meeting with Julian. As he heads for the conference room to go over figures with the civil engineering team for the library, his office phone rings. All rings seem ominous, and sure enough, it's Shelley.

"Austin, thanks for taking my call. I know you're at work. I just saw my doctor and want to give you a heads-up."

"Shelley, I hope to hell you're okay for both our sakes. What's happening?" Austin looks at the office building across the street, scanning the windows as if to find himself in the crosshairs of a random shooter.

"Well, no good news but nothing drastic either. I'm now in the eighth month, still on the steroids, and I can't tell you how awful they are. There are waves of euphoria, just lovely, when I feel I can accomplish anything, and big surges of energy like I'm eleven years old, but I'm bloated like some World War One dirigible floating over . . ."

"Shelley, please!"

"I am just trying to give you an idea of how it feels."

"I'd rather stick to the medical situation." Austin hardly pays attention to his fury anymore. He's too preoccupied with consequences. Grim, sickening, that he will be tied to her, the tie that binds, for all the foreseeable future. Terrifying, the child. Dara, what? He just wants to know the fate coming toward him. "Let's focus. What does the doctor say?"

"My platelet count is not improving but hasn't plunged either. I'm on watch for that. Constant monitoring. If it happens, I'll have to go to hospital immediately and be induced. So, I will keep you posted. Is it okay to call at work?"

"I'm working, in meetings, it's not easy. Call here if there's an emergency, otherwise, call me at home at night. I'm there, as I have nowhere else to be."

"I catch your drift. My fault that your marriage is gone with the wind. Miss Scarlett has absconded?"

"That's really mean. And it happens to be correct. Look what you've accomplished. You must be pleased." Maybe the fury hasn't subsided. "Listen, someone is waiting for me. Is there anything else I need to know?"

"Someone else has been waiting for you for a long time."

"Shelley, stop it."

"Yes, there is another thing. I've moved. I have provisions for the baby there, if it's a worst-case scenario. Not that it will be. I'm determined to live my big life."

"You mean a crib and all that?" The secretary is waving at him through the glass, motioning toward the conference room. The last thing he wants to hear is about the location of a crib.

"Yes. And I made my will and left some letters for my family."

"Sounds like you're ready for any contingency. Why not let your mother know all this instead of me? I need to go. Now. Let's hope everything resolves in the easiest way possible." He puts down the phone and wants to shout or sob or bang his head on the desk, but he tucks in his shirt, gulps some water, and gets down to business.

Late in the day, when Austin meets with Julian, he doesn't downplay anything, just tells him the facts and timeline.

Julian commiserates. "Deep shit, deep and wide." He spins around and takes a bottle of scotch out of a cabinet. He seems to look down along his lengthy Roman nose as he pours several glugs into two glasses. "My architectural practice saved me when my wife—you met Jennifer at the London office—left me for the yoga instructor. Such an embarrassment. I'm ashamed to say it would have been easier if it had been a professor or an insurance guy." Julian suddenly laughs. "All I can say is let work be your shield." Before he laughs, he snorts a little and it always makes Austin smile. "I worked sixty to seventy hours a week." Snorts again and raises his glass to his high-ceilinged office. "That's why I'm the boss here. Thank you, Mr. Downward Dog." His laugh sounds almost like a bark.

Austin feels the pressure lift. "I'm taking that advice. The big question about work is, and I hope a moot one, is what happens if I am gigantically unlucky and—I hardly can say this—I am raising a kid all of a sudden." This is the first time he has phrased the possibility out loud.

"Ah, cross that shaky bridge over troubled water only if you must. But, Austin, let me tell you, you're our guy. Top of your class at St. John's—and look what you've already done in a short time. I was ahead of you by nine years, and it took me three times as long to get a lead on an assignment like that library. Believe me, your contribution to the design will make your name in this firm and elsewhere. Another thing—it's hush-hush as yet, but there's something significant coming our way. This major investment group is looking into building a whole ideal town in Sussex, houses, retail, schools, the works. It's a game changer, and we will be invited to submit plans. You'll want to be in on that, big time. If we get it, we'll all be scrambling to get back to London. See? We will work this problem out. You won't be exiled to the drawing table or whatever you fear. But, I get it—it's a nasty cock-up. Can you remember what you ever saw in this tricky woman?"

"I was intrigued, I guess, maybe dumbfounded, by her intensity. She's pretty. Smart. Smarter than I, as it turns out. And she was so un-English. That was alluring for a proper boy. I never saw myself with her long term. That town project sounds major. Is it happening?"

"Looks good right now. Man, she sounds crackers to me." Julian offers more. But Austin's glass is still full. He will never again enjoy the taste of scotch. That was what landed him in this office today, pouring out his sordid life story to his boss. Still, he feels chuffed. Julian has affirmed his worth.

Austin and Amit meet for dinner at an Indian restaurant Amit likes. He praises everything on the menu and orders more than they possibly can eat. "You'll take it home and reheat for days," he explains. He orders beer and tears into the garlic naan. "How did it go with Julian?" Amit works under Julian, too, a good guy. He already assumes that Austin will be supported by the firm through whatever happens.

"Couldn't have been nicer. Said he'd explain everything to London and added that the director's daughter had a child 'out of wedlock,' as he put it, and was sure to be sympathetic. With the business expanding so rapidly, he said flexibility is built into our jobs. He kept reiterating that it could happen to anyone." Anyone idiotic, Austin doesn't say.

"Well, that Jennifer of his flew off with some studly guy. Not sure Julian got over that easily. By the way, I read in depth about that platelet condition. Seems like she will be fine, and your life can get back to manageable."

"Except for the strange sense of responsibility this situation comes with. I've never faced a moral dilemma like this. Ha! Horns of a dilemma, they say. Maybe that's why my dad said I should go run with the bulls in Spain."

Amit likes that. "Your dad is a prince of the realm. Hey, how's this biryani?"

"Good, not as good as yours. The second unknown is Dara, Dara, Dara. If she'll ever get around this or through this or over this."

"She's gutted right now. I predict this time next year, you'll be where you want to be and with whom you want."

"You're a prince yourself. Thanks. That's enough about my woes. How's the Hudson Village going?" Talk turns to work. Amit's bound to be pulled back to the London office soon. His landscape practice has more traction there. But right now, he's engrossed in the design of garden space and roof conservatory enclosures of an apartment complex the firm is designing. He's full of permeable paving, recreational transitions, access, rain cisterns.

Austin goes home with the doggie bags. For the first time since his future imploded, he sleeps, dreamless and long.

16

As soon as Dara returns to DC, she begins to think of leaving Washington. When she knew Austin would be at work, she left him a message. "Hey, Austin, it's me. I'm canceling the honeymoon reservations that were on my card and assume you're canceling, or have, the charges you made. I guess we'll be stuck with the airfares unless you know otherwise. My mother has taken on the return of gifts and a lot of other things. Well . . ." long pause ". . . you know who you are to me, and I hope you see that I'll have to figure out this U-turn. Right now, I don't have a direction. Call me back if, only if, there is anything new to say." Lucky, she thinks, that we opted for the free-cancellation hotel rooms. Or was that some omen? They'd gone for the deluxe room with a view at Lake Garda, and for the Grand Canal balcony room in Venice. For an indulgent moment, she imagines them in those rooms, looking out at water views, at their rumpled bed, the discreet room service knock, the scent of jasmine, and bougainvillea cascading from terra-cotta pots on a terrace. Then the familiar knot forms in her stomach, gripping pains that catch her breath.

Dara can see that Bill Dellinger has been organizing the Mann papers they've retrieved on loan from Duke. He's also read some of the boxes Dara brought back from North Carolina and annotated several files. In her absence, Dara sees, he has set up two long folding tables, one in the study and one in the hall. Neat stacks arranged in the chronological order she'd established, the desk cleared for writing, and a bulletin board tacked with notes, arrows to other notes, and a few newspaper photos—he must be poised to launch this book. Dara stands in the doorway, imagining him here, his jovial presence and laser concentration filling the air day after day. Could her plane ticket to Italy be changed? Could she exit this project? Does he need her anymore? She ticks through possible destinations. Where? Italy, no, not alone. Not now. Back home, where I can light until I figure things out? Feels regressive. Certainly not New York. Like many before her who might have run out of options, she thought of California.

She's still in her robe when she hears Bill's key turning the lock. "You're back! Sorry, I didn't know; I should have knocked."

"That's okay. I see that you've gotten super organized. Come in. Want a coffee?"

They sit in the kitchen, and she has once again to repeat the story of the canceled wedding and feature herself as the runaway bride. And to field the usual questions. Must just be too young. Not ready. Don't know where I'm going to law school. Do I even want to go? Do I want to be a speechwriter instead? Turn my HUD internship into a job? Do I even have the guts for politics, even the zeal, which is what fueled Stephen Mann?

Bill looks at her with steady eyes and a somber demeanor. He's someone to talk to but she can't. He just says, "I hear you. You're smart to wait for clarity. Let me help in any way you need. Do you think some therapy might help? Someone to listen?" He, like the family and her friends, picks up right away that she is keeping something back.

"What if I left for a while? You could move into the apartment and work at all hours, as you please, without having to worry about me sniffling around feeling sorry for myself."

"That works, if it's what you need. As you know, I'm living in my parents' garage apartment in Chevy Chase, and that's a commute I'd gladly swap for this fantastic place. Could I bring my cat? And I know you might want to come back at any time."

Then Dara hears herself say, "I think I might go out to California to see my old roommates and to check out Boalt and Stanford law schools. Maybe UCLA."

"That sounds like a plan. A good one. A placeholder while you sort out what comes next. But wouldn't you have to wait a year instead of going this fall? You must apply all over again."

"That's true. But so what? I can delay starting until I hear from those schools. Is that fair? I need to accept Georgetown soon. New York has suddenly lost its appeal." As often, she wishes for a brother. The image of Johnny comes to her. His smile that lifts more on the left than on the right. "Thank you. And the cat is welcome. What's its name?"

"Bingo. She's a green-eyed monster."

"You know Big Mann had a cat for years, Jennyanydots, named after one in a T. S. Eliot poem. She slept on the bed. Mimi doted on that cat, too. She lived to be nineteen, probably because they fed her imported sardines. Now, there's something you didn't know for your book. See, you'll have a hard time without me."

California, what a good idea. The boss at HUD already has me down for honeymoon leave. She dials Courtney and Katie, her would-be bridesmaids in San Francisco. She'd given them the news right away, and luckily, they had not yet booked tickets to North Carolina. Maybe they can take time off from their jobs, since they'd arranged vacation days off for the wedding.

No answer but Dara leaves a message. "Okay if I come to San Francisco? I need to get out of Dodge."

RICH FLIES UP ON WEDNESDAY FOR HIS DREADED INTERVIEW ON THURSday. He has work to do and Dara's place, taken over by Bill's massive paper piles, seems stuffy. He sets up outside at a table on the terrace.

Dara interrupts to bring him a sandwich. "Hey, Dad, I am going to fly out to see Katie and Courtney for a while. I just want a new scene. Maybe new thoughts, new plans. I might even consider going out there for school—Stanford or Boalt instead of Georgetown. Or maybe I'm deciding not to go to law school at all."

"Yeah. I get it. Everything's gone to hell. That's a good idea. How long are you thinking of staying?" He's thinking of the terrific financial package Georgetown offered and the use of Mimi's condo making things oh so easy. And of Dara three thousand miles away. He says nothing about any of this.

"I'm buying a one-way ticket. I'll leave Friday, that's the twelfth. Just reinvent spontaneity. You know, maybe this whole marriage idea wasn't me after all. Settling down . . . I don't know. I'm hopelessly confused."

"Ever heard the old saying, when God made the world, he tipped it at the Rockies and everything loose rolled west?"

Dara smiles. She has heard this. "I'm loose. That's for sure. So, you tell Mom, okay, and I'll be in touch along the way. I hate to miss Mother's Day but I'll have Flower Power deliver, not that you need flowers at Redbud. I'm going out now for a couple of hours. I need to return a few things I bought for the honeymoon . . ." She pauses and takes a deep breath. "Maybe get some new jogging things for the coast. I can pick up groceries. Want to grill hamburgers tonight and maybe ask Bill to stay?"

"Excellent. I just have to think of questions to grill this wombat I'm interviewing."

"What's a wombat? Whatever, you'll charm him into putting his foot in his mouth!"

"Get some guacamole and chips."

17

DARA, USED TO zipping up and down the east coast in her own car, has never rented one before. She stands at the Avis counter at the San Francisco airport with a highlighter marking the map she's been given. Seems easy but she knows the hills are daunting. Up 101, up Van Ness a long way, then out California into the trendy Fillmore Street neighborhood they've told her about. She marks their block on Clay Street at Scott. Easy. Courtney and Katie's place, a third-floor flat in a Victorian, overlooking Alta Plaza Park.

She pulls out the new mobile phone her dad gave her for the trip. He's had one for a couple of months and swears that soon we won't know how we lived without them. It's bulky and has a stiff antenna. Feels like a rock in her handbag, but she'll be driving the coast roads and the phone will be handy in case of trouble. No one has her number except her parents. Austin can't find me, she realizes. Not even Mei. She stuffs the map in her pocket, dials, and Katie picks up.

"Yay! You're here. We are so excited."

"Yes, and I already have the car. I'm calling on my new portable phone Dad gave me. It works!"

"Get in that car and drive—you'll be here in a little over a half hour. You have to park on the street. We will be waiting."

. . .

A ratty, congested entrance to the famed city, but soon Dara turns into their shady Pacific Heights neighborhood of fanciful, well-kept period houses, the park poised a plane higher, and brisk people walking small brisk dogs. Luckily, someone pulls out just half a block away and Dara grabs the space. The rental car looks as if a plainclothes cop might drive it. She parks easily and pulls her roll-on out of the back seat. A root breaking through the sidewalk snags her wheels and the bag turns out of her hand, wrenching her wrist. She rights it and looks around at the appealing neighborhood. Low wrought-iron fences define miniature front gardens, all planted with abundant fuchsia, hydrangeas, and roses trained to climb over garages that dip under the raised houses. She admires gables, spindles, and tall windows where she glimpses modern paintings, book-lined walls, a black cat on a sill, a woman plumping pillows. From a few houses on, Dara sees Katie at a high window, waving. Then there they are, running down the steps, Courtney and Katie, hair flying, arms out.

Skinny houses make living spaces one room wide, with the larger rooms at both ends. Theirs, three flights up, has a back-to-front hallway with rooms off to the right. They show Dara to the small blue guest room with three large windows looking west onto a huge pine treetop. Perfect—a single bed and a watercolor of a sailboat heading under the Golden Gate Bridge. The house next door is small, leaving a backyard garden that Courtney and Katie's apartment looks down into. Their bedroom, in front, has the characteristic bay windows, as does the living room. Edwardian, post–1906 earthquake, they tell her. The kitchen is compact but has a giant stove, black-and-white tile floor, and more windows across the back. Katie grows flowers outside on the back-door stoop, where the stairs plunge down into a tiny garden given over to the first-floor family's two children. "What bribe did you have to give a real estate agent for this?" Dara is dazzled. Her friends have a grown-up, glamorous place in this gorgeous neighborhood. She flashes on living there with Austin, the table set in the big dining room with a view of the distant white city and a slice of the

Bay Bridge. Starting over, if that were possible. Then something darker hits. She thinks, my friends have things figured out better than I have. They hightailed it to California, got their MBAs, and look at them now. The West is more in the future than the East, and they knew that while I languished in DC. Who needs another DC lawyer? I'm not writing the bio. I'm not inching up in HUD. What am I fooling myself for? I fell in love, in love, in love.

I thought we would build our world. Look at them! She notices a purple bruise on the underside of her wrist.

"We lucked out. Someone in Katie's company told us it was coming up and we started pestering the owner right then."

Their front bedroom's vintage lace curtains filter soft light onto their massive king bed, books stacked on either side, and a wicker chaise longue where one of them tosses her clothes. Katie, surely. Courtney always has been impeccably neat, even at Georgetown when they were roommates known as the "lipstick lesbians." They didn't mind at all. They loved clothes, manicures, perfume, heels, and each other. Even as juniors, though, they knew their lives would be easier in the tolerant West. Both were good at math and business and geared their careers toward the buzzing computer science sector, where they would get in on the burgeoning digital/electronics scene. Here they are, smart girls, at twenty-six making six-figure (barely) salaries with nowhere to go but up. "I am so proud of you two. How did you plan ahead like geniuses and just go for it?"

"Well," Courtney smirks, "we are geniuses!"

"Then there's the right place at the right time thing, too," Katie adds.

Dara thinks, then there's the wrong place at the wrong time, Austin.

Katie serves mimosas in the dining room. "Major celebration called for. We thought you'd never make it out here. Guess it took something drastic."

"Drastic is an understatement. My whole life just went off a cliff. It's more complicated than I've told even my parents so just forgive me right up front that I may not lay out the whole . . ." She sips the cold mimosa, imagining that its happy effervescence would transfer into her mind. "The whole gory story."

"Plenty of time. Take it. No rush to justice, or is it judgment?" Courtney, lanky and at ease with her height, flips her flaming red ponytail and pours more bubbly into the three glasses.

The friends have made a salad of little gem lettuces, artichoke hearts, potatoes, and celery. Southerners still, they made a pitcher of iced tea as well. The three reminisce, dip the amazing sourdough bread into the bottom of the salad bowl, talk about careers, empty the iced tea pitcher and the rest of the mimosas.

"You go settle in, take a rest, and we'll clean up and rest a bit, too. Then we have a surprise." Katie cleared the table like the waitress pro she'd been all four years of Georgetown. She's affirmed that she's taken to wearing all black. It looks natural with her curly dark hair and pale skin.

The three-hour time dif makes this a long day. Dara sank for only half an hour, and then heard Courtney and Katie banging around in the kitchen. She emerged in jeans and a sweatshirt. "Perfect," Katie says. "How did you know? Well, you've heard the trite saying, the coldest winter I ever spent was the summer I spent in San Francisco. That's attributed to Mark Twain but really, he never said this. Anyway, you're just right. As always." They're filling a cooler with what looks like shrimp in a jar, sourdough—she's already in love with the local bread—and something that looks swirly and chocolate.

"Let's go. Sunset is the goal. Dara, you are going to be knocked sideways, I guarantee."

They jam into Katie's Honda. Dara sits up front. She's going to be blown away by the views, Katie predicts. Somehow the six feet of Courtney has folded into the driver's seat. She opens the skylight and Katie straps in behind her. "Okay, let's go," she says. "I promise not to sing 'I Left My Heart in San Francisco.'"

"Oh, do," Dara says. "I love it!"

Courtney drives up Broderick Street, turning left and right, zigzagging through the streets of immaculate and gorgeous houses. "Is this where princes and princesses live?" Dara asks on Broadway. She leans out the window to take in the glimpses of water, gasping at the stops on steep inclines, where the hood of the car displaced the view as it reached the top and seemed to fall over the crest. "No one is ever unhappy here, I can tell. They just wake up every day and praise the gods and their bank accounts and whatever luck landed them on Pacific or Broadway." A dainty Chinese woman walking a skeletal whippet looks like a stick drawing on a 45-degree slash of sidewalk. Dara calls out as they pass, "It's your lucky day!" and the dog strains at the leash, rising on back legs, and the woman waves and smiles. "See, she knows it."

Katie leans forward and squeezes Courtney's shoulder. That's the old Dara, she signals. She's thought Dara subdued, and no wonder, since her arrival. Responsive and excited, yes, but without her usual frisson. Along the Marina, Dara wants to get out and stare at the Golden Gate Bridge, the runners along the bay, and looming, sad Alcatraz in the distance. "Can we walk here tomorrow?" And, yes, when they drive down S-curving Lombard Street, Dara is standing on her seat, head out the sunroof. "You two didn't tell me! Why didn't you gag and drag me here sooner? You're keeping this a secret because anyone in their right mind would want to live here."

As they cross the Bay Bridge, Dara looks back at the city. "Why are we leaving? Who'd ever leave?"

"The surprise. Here's where a part of the bridge collapsed in the earthquake of '89. I never cross without thinking of what it must have been like to feel the bridge become insubstantial and you have no option but to keep going." Dara doesn't reply. She looks out at the layers of traffic, slices of water, and the sun bedazzling the left windows. She hasn't felt this way since she first saw Florence. Everything racing by sends her reeling.

Over the bridge, Courtney turns down into a marina and parks.

At the dock entrance, she unlocks a tall metal gate and they walk out to the end. She stops at a sleek wooden sailboat, immaculately varnished, with blue trim. "Here's *The Pilgrim.* We love the name because aren't we all?"

Even nicer in Italian, Dara thinks. Il Pellegrino. "It's beautiful. Is it your boat? If so, this is getting to be surreal."

"No, it belongs to Katie's company, but we can use it. We both got certified."

"That sounds easy but, oh, believe me, sailing this bay is tricky. But we're on it!" Katie opens the hatch door and pulls out blue cushions while Courtney starts the motor and eases out into open water. Sails hoisted, motor off, and they're suddenly quiet, the wind catching quickly, mainsail billowing, and the boat tilting sharply, too sharply. "We're under way!" Courtney's ponytail flies. Dara grips the halyard, trying not to show alarm that they right away are speeding along at this crazy angle. But soon, exhilaration hits her—the water sheened with cloud reflections and the great city zooming past as they head for the Golden Gate. Katie points out Russian Hill, the Marina, Marin County, the headlands. Dara pulls up her knees and rests her chin, letting the beauty in.

Near the bridge, the water becomes choppier, the current stronger. "Tacking!" Courtney calls out. "We usually stay inside the bay. It's a different world on the other side of the bridge—big swells and stronger currents." She shouts to Katie, "Trim the jib. We'll loop around and head over to the leeward side of Angel Island. That's where we love to anchor for boozy picnics."

A different world, Dara repeats to herself. For sure. "The leeward?" she asks.

"The downwind, sheltered side," Courtney explains. "Back behind the island, in the very pretty Alaya Cove. No one lives there now, except for the caretaker."

The wind blocked, Katie drops the anchor and the boat calms. Dara pulls out the cooler from below and opens the wine, spreading the picnic on a cloth over a folding table. Cold marinated shrimp, that sourdough, gooey cheeses. No sound except for a slight jingle in the rigging. Sails down, feet up, a little chilly. Katie brings up plaid throws and they wrap them around their shoulders. "No wine for the captain," Courtney says, "but I'm going to make some tea. Did you see the tiny gimbaled stove? So cute."

In the island's deep shade, the water turns glossy green. Along the shore, a dozen deer have come down to drink from the sprinklers watering the caretaker's small lawn. The stag prances, shaking his rack, obviously reveling in a shower. At the stillness, the peace, the gentle water that seems to breathe, Dara feels a surge of calm and happiness to be with her old friends. They know she's in crisis but are acting as if this were anytime, and Dara, spontaneous and unpredictable Dara, has popped out for a normal visit.

Normal to talk about what has happened to Judd, Elaine, Jimbo, all their crew at Georgetown. Talk about the luck and future of their jobs, what's the scene for young professional lesbians, the cool new restaurants and food emporium on Fillmore, the ease of their Pacific Heights neighborhood. Finally, Katie broaches the present. "Are you going to check out west coast law schools?" She doesn't ask, what's next for you, is the marriage truly off, are you rethinking your public service career, still interested in speechwriting, where is Austin anyway? None of these. She's holding back until Dara opens up.

"Maybe. Being out here, seeing San Fran, driving down the coast or up the coast, wherever you think I should see, seems like the most appealing thing I can think of now. I never expected an American city like this to be possible. It's a dream."

"So, you could be lured to move west? So far from Redbud and DC?"

Dara raises her glass. "Who knows?" But, yes, she could be lured. Hell, she could be lured anywhere at this point.

While Katie and Courtney are at work, Dara walks. She takes the vertiginous hills in sectors, pausing to marvel at the idyllic houses lining the streets. Some of the white, elaborately trimmed Victorians look like pastry shop confections, like wedding cakes, she thinks. She turns onto Sacramento, stopping in chic homeware and jewelry stores and at the upscale and compact supermarket in Laurel Heights. The produce seems more alluring than at home—watermelon radishes, bunches of fresh herbs, tiny carrots in three colors, Asian vegetables she doesn't recognize, gnarly purple potatoes. The salads in the take-away section are tempting and she selects a serving of three. She picks up veal chops and fennel and arugula and goat cheese for supper, which she will have ready when Katie breezes in after six and Courtney at seven. Meanwhile, she takes her salads to the park and finds a bench. Anytime she is still, Austin, Austin, Austin arrives. What if he walked up right now, navy windbreaker open, jeans and white T-shirt, and always pristine white trainers, his characteristic gesture of running his fingers back through his hair that tends to flop forward, his smile that says *I'm totally here;* he just could walk up like that, slide close to her, and say, could I have a bite of that chicken salad, um, it has almonds in it, so good.

18

Mei knows what happened. The secret she wishes had not come to her. And Rich has given her Dara's mobile phone number in California. She wants to call but doesn't. Dara chose not to tell her. How awkward to let her know that Luke unwittingly told her.

At the dinner at Redbud, she and Luke had exchanged some, oh, interested looks across the table, and as the evening broke up, he walked her out to her car. They'd talked for a few minutes. He asked for her number and said he'd be looking forward to the wedding and maybe they could have lunch the day after the newlyweds fled to Italy. When Austin called him to let him know the wedding was off, he told Luke the whole situation. Since he didn't know that Dara had not told anyone the reason, he didn't warn Luke that this horror show was unmentionable.

After absorbing the news, Luke thought of contacting Mei. He has a nonrefundable ticket—Austin offered to pay him, but he might as well use it and get to know this gentle and mysterious woman. When if not now?

When he calls, Mei picks up immediately. "Hey, it's Luke Jackson here, down in Sarasota. How are you?"

His face from across the table swims up in her mind. "Fine, fine, and you?"

"Well, good, apart from the news about Dara and Austin. That was a shock. They seemed on the road to bliss. Crazy how things can go so wrong."

Mei is looking at Dara's unfinished dress hanging on the back of a door, the creamy, lemony silk brought from Thailand, the small white flowers embroidered around the scooped neck. A threaded needle dangles from an unfinished petal. "Yes, everyone here is reeling from that. Her parents have been undoing arrangements and sending back gifts. Now Dara has flown off to California to visit her old roommates."

"I don't know where Austin is at this point, maybe already back in England. I need to check in with Amit. Hey, Mei, I hope this isn't too outlandish, but I was thinking of coming up there on the Saturday anyway. I'd like to take you somewhere great for dinner and maybe you'd show me your workshop. I still have my reservation at the Eno Inn and my car rental at the airport. Does that sound crazy?" He holds his breath. Luke is rather shy, and dialing her number took some courage. Is she going to say she's busy?

Mei is silent only for a moment. She likes him, liked his gentle demeanor, ginger hair, and amused smile at the dinner. "I think that would be lovely. We can redeem something from this awful mess. Imagine how the day should have gone."

"They're in hell. In the long run, who knows what will happen? If they can't get beyond or over this, you know Dara will eventually move on. But Austin, not so easy to maneuver that situation."

Mei isn't so sure Dara will just move on but doesn't want to go into it. "I'm still hoping that they can work something out."

"Me, too. Maybe after the baby."

"Baby?"

Long pause. "Mei, you don't know what happened? Dara didn't tell you?"

"*Baby* is a scary word. Dara isn't pregnant? Surely she hasn't gone to California for an abortion . . . She, I know, doesn't want children until she's finished school and established and . . ."

"Oh, no, not Dara. Look, Austin didn't say it was a secret. I am so sorry. Maybe I shouldn't go on, but I've gotten myself too far in now. Whew. Long story short, he went back to London a few weeks after they first got together. He was partying hard—really unlike him—with some of our Cambridge friends. He literally passed out at his former girlfriend's place. Apparently, she was ready to pounce. You get the picture. But . . . She waited like six months or something before she told him that she is big with child. God, this is screwed—I feel weird being the messenger. Feel free to shoot me!"

"I'm too stunned to make much sense of this. She's keeping the baby and she never told him? What kind of person would do that?"

"She's always been obsessed with him. And now she's caught him by the short hairs. Excuse that, I mean she has made him complicit in her life plan."

"No wonder Dara didn't want her parents to know. How perfectly humiliating for her. And, oh, for Austin. What will he do?"

"My best guess, he'll do the right thing. Figuring out what that is may be the hardest part. Supposedly, she'll take the baby to her family's home in Delhi and live there."

"My heart is way up in my throat. I'm in shock."

"Mei, that's not all. It's more wretched."

"What else could there be?"

"Shelley, that's her name, she's developed some serious blood disorder. It's not sure that she'll make it through. Also, the baby. Here's the part I can't get beyond: She wasn't going to tell Austin, ever, at all, until she found out she had this blood thing. Then she knew he had to be informed in case something happens to her."

Mei looks out the window at King Street, at people going about their business. "Whoa, she was having his child without telling him. That is heavy. Like some fairy tale or Greek myth, the hidden child. Put him in a basket and let him float down the river. This just can't happen to real people in 1995. Luke, I'm going to have to go." Mei slides down onto the floor, leaning against the wall. "This is too much. But do come. I'd like that."

"Bye, Mei. Sorry again. Bye." Luke stares out the window at boats on the bay, then changes into shorts and bounds out for an exhausting run along the water.

Mei grabs her keys and flies downstairs, sandals clattering. She drives through town fast to see her mother.

She is sitting out on her deck, shelling peas and talking to the cat. Mei dashes up the steps and throws her arms around her mom. "What's wrong?" Her mother immediately notices Mei's open mouth and frantic look.

"I know what happened to Dara's wedding."

Slowly, as if she can't believe her next words, she tells her about Luke's phone call. Her mother's eyes are darting back and forth. The tabby spills the bowl, scratching and rolling the peas, then dashing away down to the river's edge. Her mother rocks, then becomes still, reaching for Mei's hand. "My girl. You are not the one to tell Dara that her privacy is broken. You are not to tell the Willcoxes, above all. It's terrible that you're burdened now, but all you can do is keep still. And wait, think that maybe this brings *you* to an opening. You have never really found anyone. Could this Luke be a peculiar serendipity?"

"No, it would have been better if we'd met again under happy stars, not under this horror show."

"Hmmm. Stay clear. Stay open. Austin made the mistake. He must pay."

"That sounds hard. Like something in the Bible."

"No, I'm sorry. I'm sorry, sorry. Just say the ending comes from the beginning."

"Oh, Mom. Maybe this girl, this sick or malevolent or sad girl, will live happily ever after in India."

"I have a feeling she's not made for such happiness. She's a landslide."

“The child, though.”

“Yes, that child. Who knows. Sometimes the unexpected brings news to all.”

“Is that some old wisdom from Shanghai? Something in a fortune cookie?”

“There are no fortune cookies in Shanghai.”

“Let’s hope you’re right, unexpected news to all.”

19

MESSAGE LIGHT BLINKING after a long day of sorting details on the final proportions of doors and windows on the façade of the library. Austin slings his backpack onto the sofa and plops down. Dara's message a few days ago is the last message he's received: Call me back if there's anything new to say. He did call a couple of days later, desperate and without anything new, only to say I miss you like mad, but her own machine had a new answer. "I'm traveling. Leave a message here for Bill Dellinger, and if you're a friend and need to reach me, call my parents, as I am currently unavailable."

He watched his phone blinking its warning light. With a premonition, he pressed the button. Yes, thought so.

"I'm calling from the maternity hospital. It's Wednesday. I'm in room 328 if you will call me back." She gave the number and clicked off. Already close to midnight there. What is going on?

He called Amit. "Are you up for some dinner with a zombie man?"

They met at their usual Italian place with candles in Chianti bottles, old-school menu too, meatballs and thick tomato sauce. Austin stared at the menu, overwhelmed by the long list of choices. Amit said, "Let's just get the carbonara and the mixed grill. Not a night for overthinking, I presume."

"Okay, spilling it—she's in hospital. That's not good. I got the message too late to call so first thing tomorrow I'll find out. A bit early for delivery—two or three weeks—so there must be a problem."

"Better call the airline tonight. And Julian early, too. You're going to be on a plane. We know Julian will be on deck for you. This is all about to play out."

"I'm scared down to the bone marrow, but maybe, maybe relieved that the suspension is going to end. Thanks for putting up with all this. Can't have been easy for you. Shelley is, was, your friend for years and I know she appealed to you at one time, back when she was the smart girl in your high school."

"As it turns out, I'm lucky she didn't reciprocate my crush."

"She was a fireball at St. John's. Why she fixated on me, I'll never understand. I never loved her; she knew that."

"Well, she was more than infatuated right out of the gate. You know quite a few girls were. But she internalized you so you became symbiotic to her. I think you were, and are in some twisted way, her ideal—but more complicated. She wanted to *be* you. She wanted you in her, not just sexually. The baby personifies all that. Not your fault. Nothing is, aside from the last two drinks you took that stupid night."

"Did you miss your calling? Psychoanalysis instead of architecture? What you say all rings true. What if she goddamn dies? Then she's made me her nemesis, at the least. Quite ghoulish, man."

"Just remember, you get to survive. She may not."

"Granted. Not one of the options looks promising, although her going home to her family with her heathy baby has to be the best possibility. Let's talk about you. Enough of my sad-sack life. How's the green project coming along?"

Awake at six, Austin calls Shelley. Eleven on Thursday there. She answers, her voice strong. "Shelley, it's me. I got your message too late to call yesterday. What is happening?"

"They've put me here for observation for preeclampsia. I had a fierce headache that wouldn't go away, then I was seeing blurry spots.

When I went to the nurse, she took a urine sample and it had protein in it; that's a sure indicator of preeclampsia."

"Is that serious? It must be, but I don't know what that is." Could anything else possibly go wrong?

"I didn't know either but there's some blood pressure elevation, and if it gets high enough, they induce immediately. Mine is 140 over 90 right now. It used to be 120 over something. They're treating me—making me eat meat for protein and I think I'm getting magnesium. They're hoping I stabilize. The fear is seizures, you can have seizures that cause stroke, or I think that's what he said."

"Is this part of the platelet issue?"

"I'm not totally sure. It's confusing. I think that it is separate. Seems unfair to have two life-and-death issues. He said this problem stems from the placenta, and that the eclampsia can disappear as soon as the placenta is delivered."

"That's good." Austin tries to sort the hemorrhage problem from the placenta problem, both occurring at the moment of birth. Even the words are hard to speak. *Seizure. Eclampsia.* Plasma transfusions. The cold fact of mortal danger. He closes his eyes and imagines Shelley, her fringed boots, the way she'd lift her long black hair and let it fall. "So that's why they may induce? To get rid of the placenta problem before it gets any worse?" *Placenta* was a word he'd never even said before.

"Exactly, smart boy. Exactly. But first they're on hold to see if it resolves. The doctor makes his rounds about now, so I'll call back and let you know his verdict. My headache is gone, thanks to a lot of aspirin, and I still know I will get through this delivery and get to raise my boy."

"I hope so, too."

"And my mother is on her way here. She arrives this afternoon. She'll be staying at my new place. You'll have to decide if you are coming. But maybe I'll turn this around and my blood pressure will drop and all the chops they're feeding me will up my proteins."

"Call me."

"I will. I love you."

"Shelley . . ."

"I do." Click.

Two hours later, Austin picks up.

"Mr. Clarke, this is Dr. Jason Farthaway, calling from the Chelsea and Westminster Hospital in London about Shelley Suri, who identified you as her partner. Have I reached the right number?"

"Yes, although I am not her partner, I am the biological father to her child. Pending DNA verification."

"Be that as it may. I was asked by her to let you know her medical status. And I can't emphasize enough the gravity of her present situation. Right now, she's stable, she's resting under slight sedation. We are treating her aggressively for preeclampsia and so far with no progress I can report, although the monitors are showing no worsening. Given her previous immune thrombocytopenia diagnosis, this is about as high risk a delivery that I have had in my experience."

"I understand. Okay, what is the course of action?"

"We plan to monitor closely and if there is no change for the better, we're compelled to induce. There are just too many variables at play and how they're interacting with one another is impossible to gauge. I don't know your involvement, but I suggest that you be present, if this is your child. I understand that her mother is arriving today. That's very good for her. Shelley is determined, and that will help. We have every hope of a healthy result but are exercising extreme caution."

"Thank you for all the information."

"No problema. I'll do my job. Best of luck to all of you."

Problema? Seriously?

Austin buys a ticket on the evening flight. When he explains that the trip is a medical emergency, they miraculously allow him to apply his honeymoon ticket to the fare. He won't think that he and Dara should be flying on Saturday night to Rome. He'll be in London by morning. He debates about what suitcase to take, roll-on or the big one. Both, he decides. He packs everything he can stuff into the large one, all his papers in the small one, calls a taxi, and goes to the office for the rest of the day. He meets Amit for a quick sandwich, giving him the key to his apartment. "Big favor. If I can't get back . . . Hope that won't happen. But if, would you take that coffee table we found to your place. Whatever I've left—not much—pack and stuff in the back of a closet, if you have room. I can't pay the rent if I'm stuck at home. I've got my clothes, the essentials. My bag is probably overweight."

"That sounds fun." Amit punches him in the shoulder.

"Will repay quadruple someday."

He calls his dad, who says he's delighted to have him back, even under these dire circumstances. Last task, get a cashier's check for his bank balance. He leaves the account open with a hundred dollars. For the rest of the day, he works. Because of his excellent training, he's able to compartmentalize, at least for now. The project is in good shape. Julian smacks him on the back. "You'll be welcome in the home office, pal, and back here before you know it."

Heathrow Arrivals at dawn is already a madhouse. He clears customs, rushes to the taxi queue, and waits forty minutes. But traffic into the city is light and he's opening the door at home by nine o'clock. Hoisting the unruly bag out of the taxi, he twists his knee and feels a bolt of pain, as if it could just give way any minute.

Michael helps him drag the suitcases up the stairs to his room and settles him at the kitchen table with tea and toast, a cushion under his knee. Austin wills away the pricking rise of tears. He wishes he could just let Dad handle it. Dad will take care of this. Back in his childhood room, the honeyed light from the garden below, his college textbooks still on the shelves, the photo of his mother on the desk, the worn Oriental rug his parents brought back from a long-ago trip to Istanbul. "Dad, I'm going to crash. I'll be getting up in two hours. I probably won't be here when you get home from the shop."

"Where is she?"

"Chelsea and Westminster."

"That's a good hospital. You call me if there's anything I can do. I don't even know her name and she's about to bring my grandson into the world."

Austin flinched. My grandson. "It's Shelley. Shelley Suri."

On the way, Austin stops and buys a mobile phone. He's been meaning to and now he'll probably be running all over the city and it could be handy. At the hospital, he takes the elevator to the third floor, after checking at the desk. Yes, she's in her room. Yes, he can see her.

The door is half open. He knocks and waits. An unfamiliar voice calls, "Come in." If her name were not on the door, he would not know it was Shelley in the bed. Hooked to various drips, she's propped in a half-sitting position, her feet, swollen and red, raised on pillows. He is not prepared; she never emphasized at all the way she looks. He hasn't seen her in over eight months, when she was lithe and poised. Her face is bloated and stretched tight; her previously large dark eyes look lost in her face, her body bulges in the hospital gown, making the basketball mound of her pregnancy incidental to the rest of her distended frame. Next to her, a petite blond woman, not a nurse. Her mother? For a moment, he stands in the doorway, wanting to turn and run.

"Austin!" she shouts. "I knew you'd come. I knew it."

He walks to the end of the bed. Her big smile is the same. "This is my mother, Fiona. Mother, this is Austin."

"I've heard a lot about you," she says inadequately, eyebrows raised.

Austin is speechless. Understatement of the year. He shakes his head, as if to clear what he's seeing. What is wrong here? Shelley looks frightening.

She sees his confusion. "I know I look weird. It's the steroids I've been taking, they've upped the dose. Told you I'm a blimp. This swelling and weight just keep getting worse. I won't look like this forever. They say it melts away after you stop taking the pills."

"I talked to your doctor yesterday. I got here as soon as I could."

"Mother, could you step outside. I need to tell Austin some things."

"All right." Her mother looks at Austin, her eyes dark-circled with worry. "Just please don't get upset, Shelley." She cuts her eyes at Austin as she passes him, meaning don't upset her.

Shelley reaches into the bedside table drawer and hands Austin a thick manila envelope. "This is something you will never need to read. It's the worst-case-scenario packet. Just give it back to me next week without opening it."

Austin nods and takes the envelope. "Shelley, I hope to hell you're going to be okay, more than okay, that the transfusions will work, the placenta delivery will stop the other problem. It's damned unlucky to be double hit like this. And when you're in India, I will of course contribute child support. I'll be an absent father, but we can work out an arrangement so I'm not a stranger. I wouldn't do that to my own child, even if his existence is the shock of my life." No need now to rail about his aborted marriage, his shortchanged life, his howling rage, and his absolute lack of interest in being anyone's father at this point.

"You won't have to worry. That's generous of you. Maybe Miss Scarlett O'Hara will . . ."

"Cut it out. Let's keep focused on getting you through this. When is the doctor deciding?"

"Soon. My blood pressure is up so the preeclampsia danger isn't resolving, the blurry vision is still there, and the platelet issue, of course, is the worst. I can't see you clearly and I really would like to see you clearly. Will you stay when the doctor comes?"

"Yes. I'll be back. I'm going to step out into the waiting area. I'll talk to your mother. What's her name. If you've told me, I've forgotten."

"Fiona. She's Irish, you know."

"You look nothing like her. She's so small and pale."

"She's fierce, though. I got it from her."

Fiona sits in a corner chair, turning the pages of *Country Life*, surely a far cry from her own life in Delhi. Austin isn't sure how to say it, but he needs to be clear. He doesn't know what exactly Shelley has told her. "Mrs. Suri, I just want to say how sorry I am that Shelley has these serious problems. I—"

She interrupts. "You don't have to say anything. I know that you were an unwilling or innocent participant in this choice of hers. When she explained to me what happened, I told her you were being put in an untenable position and that it would be unforgivable. I'm apologizing on behalf of my family for the trouble this is causing with your upcoming marriage."

Austin is silent. He bites his lip and looks at the floor. Finally, he says, "Can I get you anything? Coffee, tea?"

"No, thank you." She pats the chair beside her. "I have to say the unsayable." She has profound blue eyes. Irrationally, Austin wonders if the child also would have blue eyes; his mother had beautiful clear-sky eyes with a darker ring around them.

He waits, not breaking eye contact.

"If Shelley, if Shelley doesn't come through this, I cannot raise the child. I regret this down to my bones, but I cannot. My husband is descending into Parkinson's, life in my India isn't easy, and there is not a possibility that I could do right by a motherless and fatherless child on my own. Shelley's brothers are angry with her, about unprotected sex and her crazy scheme of hiding the child from you. Whether they'll soften . . . I just can't predict or even grasp the consequences if . . .

"But, Austin, I do know there's fate, and if the unthinkable happens, my fate is already written. Yours, I can't speak for. Consequences sometimes catapult out from the original circumstance, and this is one of those. A one-night stand . . ."

"Wait, it wasn't the way that sounds . . ."

"I know the dynamics. But the consequences are the same as if—"

"Let's not torture the subject. My mother used to say, the river crossed, the saint forgotten. Let's hope that will be the situation here."

Fiona looks puzzled.

"It means that when you've come through the difficulty, you forget all the invocations you made to be saved by the saint, and you just go on with your life."

She nods. "Well, there's that. I can help out; I just don't know how that will work and there's not a need to go there today."

Austin rejects her prognosis of what could happen. Having seen the drastic physical transformation in Shelley, caused by what was supposed to cure her, he could in this moment only try to converge all the splintered possibilities into one: her rising from that bed and becoming the mother she wants to be.

The morning drags. The doctor is delayed. Austin remains in the waiting room. Fiona comes out once and tells him that Shelley's blood pressure is up; now there's no longer any doubt of the preeclampsia threat.

Dr. Farthaway arrives with two interns. He's apprised of the blood pressure rise and sends off a nurse to arrange the operating theatre for the afternoon, though, he warns, sometimes labor can take its sweet time.

Not so sweet, Austin thinks. Since the preparations will drag on, he ducks out into the mild spring day where everyone is oblivious to the drama on the third floor, that a young woman's life lies on one half of the balance scale and the skill and luck of the physician on the other. Garbage cans lifted and emptied into the jaws of the truck, the driver squawking, the clatter of lids. The high navy-blue pram of an important baby pushed by a nanny. A woman setting out a pie in a bakery window, her painted red nails digging into the crust. He walks. It's high spring, his wedding day in another life. How far from the meadow at Redbud. He's remembering a poem his father likes, a poem based on a painting. It's about Icarus escaping the labyrinth's monster on wax wings. Giddy with his power to fly, he forgets and flies too close to the sun. His wings melt and he plunges into the sea. Within observing distance, a farmer continues with his plowing, as though nothing happened. Then there's that ugly line in the poem that's otherwise written in elevated language, the line where the poet wants to rub your face in it—" . . . the dog goes on with his doggy life." There are the sky-changing events and there's the unaware life. He's feeling the sorrow all around, especially for Fiona. Her only daughter having made a foolish choice and now paying like this. And it runs through him, the price to pay. I would lay down my life for Dara, he thinks. Dara, off traveling, while here I am in this quagmire.

Inadvertently, Shelley is laying her life on the line for me. Out of whack as she was, it was love that got her here. Snarled love. Having only rage before, he feels a loosening of that noose. Even his knee seems better. Maybe we all will be okay, he thinks. Then with a rush of possible survivor's guilt, he prepends, I am going to be okay so why the hell not think of Shelley and that boy instead?

He turns into a corner flower shop and selects a bunch of pink peonies—the most promising flower on display. He heads back toward the hospital. (He doesn't remember that peonies grow in great swaths along the creek at Redbud and were to have festooned the wedding dinner tables.)

Shelley is alone in the room. "Hi, I'll find someone to get us a vase for these. Where's the doctor?"

She half sits up on one elbow. She's heard the word *us*. "Those are my favorites, did you remember? Thank you!" She falls back, as if tired from such a small effort. "Austin, does this mean you somehow forgive me?"

"That's a big question, big girl. Let's just get you through this and we'll have plenty of time to hash out the ins and outs of our lives. You just concentrate on yourself." He takes her hand and pats it but does not hold on. Forgiveness, he thinks; somehow that just seems irrelevant.

"Dr. Fart-away will be back soon with some gel that is to facilitate things, something that prepares the cervix to soften up."

"You can joke, even if it's cornball, so you must be feeling okay."

"I'm with you."

Austin shakes his head. "You are unbelievable," he says, but not unkindly.

When Fiona comes in from her lunch, she sees the flowers on the bedside table and smiles but doesn't comment. When the nurse arrives with folded linens, she asks them to leave, as she must shave the patient and give her an enema.

They wait outside Shelley's room without talking until the doctor returns and Shelley is wheeled away for the inducement treatment. "This part might take a while; not everyone responds right away," the nurse calls back to them. Austin gets a flower vase from the nurses' station and then tries to acquaint himself with his new mobile phone.

In an hour, Shelley is brought back. The nurse seems to be reading the chart at the same time she explains. "The ripening treatment, basically a loosening of the cervix, then the doctor stripped away the membrane that connects the amniotic sac to the uterus. That should give us action. Might take awhile but if contractions don't begin in two hours, he'll start the oxytocin drip."

"How does that stripping thing work?" asks Fiona.

"The fluids called prostaglandins that are released can stimulate contractions. Normally, we'd wait several hours between these procedures, but with the issues, the doctor wants this labor under way as soon as is possible. We should be seeing some action."

"I don't feel anything yet," Shelley says. "Except for an elbow scraping across my side. Or a foot." Austin balks every time he looks at her. She looks as if she could be punctured like a balloon, shrink, and drift up to the ceiling.

"It's soon yet. Don't worry, this is going to happen. If not soon enough, the doctor has ordered an IV with more of that same fluid the body makes. A synthetic version called oxytocin."

Not knowing what else to ask, the three of them just nod and thank her.

Hospital hours are time that exists inside another time, Austin thinks. An hour is three here. At least. He feels himself aging in place. The young dude who said, "Can I get you a plastic glass of something?" to a pretty girl at an art opening in New York has morphed into a sweating, itchy stooge, hapless and powerless to walk this back or affect the outcome.

After an hour, or ten as it seems, the doctor returns, and the nurse attaches an IV drip. Then time speeds up and the minutes flash by as Shelley begins to thrash and kick away the pillow her feet are resting on. The onset of labor comes startlingly fast and hard. Fiona wipes Shelley's forehead, talking calmly to her daughter. Austin steps out as the gloved hand of the nurse disappears between Shelley's splayed legs.

He hears Shelley say, "You go, too, Mom, I need to concentrate. Don't babble this nonsense about relaxing. Could you relax with a hot poker swinging inside your vagina? Just go now. I'll be fine."

"What's the procedure? I've never been near a delivery room before," he asks Fiona.

"They'll monitor her dilation, keep tabs on her vital signs and the baby's heart. The contractions will get stronger and stronger. She'll be moved to the delivery theatre. The nurse says right now she's only dilated about six centimeters; when it gets to ten, the baby is heading out."

"I do know that can take a long time." He doesn't say that ten centimeters hardly seems enough for a head to squeeze through.

"It was twenty hours for me with my first. The doctor said he may give her a round of platelets before delivery; he doesn't know yet. The big transfusion happens just as the baby crowns."

Austin walks out in the hall and calls his dad at the bookstore. "Just to give an update. She's in labor now, first stages of it. She's feisty—just told her mother to get out. I don't know how long this will go on."

"Could be a long day indeed. It was with your sister. You came a bit faster, already keen to be out in the world."

"This is surreal to me. I keep seeing myself as if from above; I'm witnessing myself in this illusory situation and at the same time I'm in it, a horrible reality."

"So sorry. Birth is drastic. And under these circumstances quite fraught for sure. Men are cowed by birth. Women are powerhouses men can't possibly comprehend. May be why they fear women so much. Well, we'll talk later."

Two hours later, the contractions have become almost nonstop. Shelley's caterwauling reverberates in the little vestibule where Austin and Fiona wait. "Could you, I'm sorry, but could you stop jiggling your knees?" Fiona says. Now and then they exchange frowns. She goes into the room a few times, only to hear Shelley's pants and curses and one "Go, go. I am having this baby for me, not anyone else, so leave me." When she is wheeled by them in a flurry of nurses and orderlies, she doesn't look at either her mother or Austin. Her eyes are closed, her arms clasped around her abdomen.

They follow down the long hall. "May I use your phone? I want to call my son in Manchester. He is coming today and I want to alert him now."

Austin hands Fiona his phone and watches as the double doors swing open to a brightly lit room and Shelley is transferred to a high table. Fiona, he sees, is crying and gesturing a few yards back. He slumps into one of the vinyl chairs lining the corridor. Now it really begins.

The cries continue. They've been told that because of the issues, no one will be allowed in the delivery room, but they can check through the doors' windows. Fiona must stand on tiptoe. The light is icy and there's Shelley, alone with all those strangers, fighting for her child. Fiona can see bags of plasma hoisted and ready. The doctor is leaning down, talking to Shelley. He pushes back her hair that has escaped from the cap, a gentle gesture that brings Fiona to tears again.

At some point there's a visible tension. The blood pressure cuff is removed and the doctor shakes his head. He consults something Fiona can't see and nods to the nurse, then at the door. The nurse slips out to say that they won't be able to give Shelley an epidural because of her platelet count. That the labor will intensify but some numbing gel might allay some of the pain. "The good news is that she's fully dilated, and the fetal heart shows no stress."

Fiona returns to her chair and tells Austin the good news. Austin pats her arm then goes to the men's room and douses his face with cold water. When he returns, his father is there, shaking hands with Fiona. Michael is saying something about the good doctors here, but Fiona quickly turns back to the window. "Austin, the baby, the baby is crowning. Come here! They're starting the plasma."

He can see only a slice of the scene, the crater of her opened body, some blood oozing, and an emerging round thing like a wheel of brie. The doctor crouches in front. "Oh, my god, is . . ." Fiona cries. Suddenly, the whole head crowns, spilling out in a bloodbath and then the rest of the body slips into view, wet and whole, held up to the light, a pink form that disappears behind several backs, a cry, scary and high, then is seen again on Shelley's breasts, her face half eclipsed, radiant and smiling. The doctors are busy again; two appear to be massaging her stomach. They watch for ten, fifteen minutes and the placenta is not appearing. "Is this the platelet problem or the eclampsia?"

Fiona doesn't know. She would burst into the room, but she would be in the way. They see the baby off to the right being bathed in a bowl and wrapped. He's placed on Shelley's breasts.

What happens can't be happening. The placenta delivers abruptly in a torrent of blood. Austin sees the baby quickly removed from Shelley's arms, can't see her face, the room turns into a frenzy of activity, plasma transfusion bags, some beeping noise. The blood is not stanched, it's pouring, pours on the doctor's blue booties, his hands trying to insert something into the volcano. What the doctor briefly mentioned as the outer bank of possibilities: postpartum hemorrhage. He had several treatment options, if given the efficacy of the transfusions. But she's emptying out like an open sluice. There's no stopping it now.

The last view Austin has of Shelley alive—she's trying to sit up, looking around wildly for her baby.

20

AFTER AN ETERNITY, the doctor emerges. "I am very sorry. We did what we could but the transfusions in this case couldn't beat the platelet problem. Her body was overstressed by the eclampsia as well. She had a mild seizure just before delivery. Normally we can stop postpartum bleeding with several methods, but the new plasma didn't kick in and clot. All my interventions were overwhelmed. I am so very sorry for this terrible loss. She'll be back in her room soon and you can see her before she's taken away. There are arrangements that will need to be made. And you can see the boy in two hours. We will run tests, but I think he is just fine—no jaundice and his cord sample looks clear."

He had put on a clean white coat and his shoes were covered by fresh paper boots, but Austin noticed that he had rims of blood under his nails.

They sit down, the three of them, Fiona weeping into her hands, the men stunned silent. Austin presses his forehead to the window. He wants to shatter it with his head. Fiona cries out and falls sideways on the sofa. "I can't tell her father . . . Please, leave me alone. I can't face anyone."

Michael flags a nurse. "Fiona, we're going to take you home in a taxi," he says. "Come on downstairs. When is your son coming?" The nurse sits beside her, covering her hand with her own.

"Soon. Now. I'll wait for him here. I want to see Shelley. You go. I want you to."

"I'm staying," the nurse says, "until her son arrives."

Austin knows he absolutely does not want to see dead Shelley.

"Let's get out for a bit." Michael steers Austin by his elbow.

Austin counts back. He's eaten nothing since leaving New York, except for a slice of toast. How could he be hungry after what has happened? Is he?

"You need to calm. Let's go to Noble Rot. You can come back when it's time to see the baby." His dad shepherds him to the lift, his arm on Austin's elbow, as though he might wander off.

"Thank her god her son is coming. The worst night of her life. Wasn't she a nun, or something? At least she has someone with her tonight. Her boy can drive her to the flat."

"No, she was a nanny to an Indian family."

Austin lets his dad maneuver them to the Bloomsbury restaurant, dark and quiet. Another world from the one they've escaped.

"Drink?" Michael orders a scotch, neat. This day is the last thing he's ever expected in his life.

"Just a glass of some good red. You choose. I'll never touch scotch again."

"Good idea. Let's do what we must do and end this inconceivable day as soon as possible."

The waiter brings two generous glasses and Michael pushes aside the empty one and raises his glass. "The Greeks say, 'To the living.' I think that's what we need to think on now."

Austin calls back the tiny body held up from the enamel basin, dripping, his little fists pulled up to his chest like a pugilist. "Agree." They clink glasses and Michael reaches over and rests his hand on Austin's shoulder. "We'll do what we must. The old saying, press on regardless."

"Fiona is out. She's not taking the baby. She told me. Her husband is sick and going downhill. She seems like a tough sister, but she can't take on raising this kid."

"Bloody hell, what!"

"Really. I literally cannot see beyond today."

"Me either."

"Shelley gave me a big folder I was not supposed to open if she made it through." Austin shifts his backpack to the floor. "I'll look at it tomorrow, maybe when some of this seems true. I'm not up for another revelation tonight."

Michael grimaces. Aiming for a touch of levity, he says, "Let's hope it's stuffed with money. You're welcome at home, of course, but I can't imagine you'll want to be there long. You and a baby in your small room." At his age, or any, he cannot imagine the chaos of an infant entering his sanctuary. Hard to be the parent, obliged to remain upbeat, when you want to lie on the floor and weep.

Austin stares into his glass, suddenly remembering the red wine spilled at Lee and Rich's party and the rims of blood under the doctor's fingernails. A strain of reality slowly twists its way into his brain. "How am I going to figure this out? I have no inclination toward babies, no plan, a life that's derailed. I am legally and morally sucker punched."

"All too true. One step at a time." Not to say I have no idea. Not to say this is an incubus. Not to say once again bloody hell.

At neonatal, the babies are lined up in their cubicles. One is labeled "A. Clarke."

The nurse leads Austin and Michael into an anteroom and brings in the swaddled bundle, placing him on a low table. Austin leans down and looks into the eyes of his new son, squint-eyed and watchful. "Almost all babies have dark blue eyes," the nurse says. "They'll change quickly." Austin sees his little tongue, pushing in and out of his mouth, pursed rosebud lips, his hands raised and jerking as if feeling the new air, the pearly, miniature nails. Austin touches the crinkled pink hand and the baby clutches his forefinger and squeezes, surprisingly strong. By this gesture from this new human, Austin wells up. "Look at that thumb, Dad. He has two. He's on his way."

Michael leans down and says, "Hey, you, we're your good guys."

"Could we see him? Naked? Is that strange?" Austin asks.

"Not at all," the nurse says. She unwraps the baby. "Everyone wants to make sure that everything that should be here is here. Ten fingers and ten toes."

He's longer than expected, his scruffy hair the color of wheat, like Austin's, like Michael's. If Austin had expected anything at all, he would have thought the baby would have Shelley's black hair, her dominant feature. What surprises them, however, is his testicles. "Wow. Those are some cojones," Michael says.

The nurse laughs. "That's a shock, always. They're swollen at birth but go to normal size quickly. You've got a beautiful boy here. Most babies look wizened at first, then like Winston Churchill."

Austin has never seen a newborn before. He keeps feeling the world lurch and right itself. Maybe he's about to pass out. Maybe he is dazzled beyond telling. Maybe he can't believe he's staring at the new body of his son. But yes, he is. He's under fluorescent lights in a small cubicle with a person who has come from the eons of space before anyone is born, who's entered time and now will start life. Nothing could have prepared him for the enormity of, well, of this miracle.

"Normally, he'd go to his mother's room frequently, but in this case . . ." She turns and busies herself at a cabinet. "Don't worry, he'll get lots of attention. He's the only solo baby right now."

Back at the house, Austin takes a hot shower and falls into bed. Scenes from the day sweep through him like a sped-up slideshow, the last one being of his father's head bent over the baby's blond hair. Michael's is the same color, though his is shot through with silver. Something about the span of time hits Austin. Dad, sixty-five now, he thinks, the baby five hours old. I remember being told in Ancient Architectural

Structures that on the day a pharaoh was born, construction began on his tomb. I'm always emerging into life and now, with death, the actual death of Shelley, and the mind-boggling appearance of Austin II, I'm sliding into an unimaginable continuum. A sharp memory comes, of the Milky Way unfurled over the sea in Greece in summer, swath of stars so dense they become a veil. Then he slept like a stone for ten hours.

Michael stayed up. He pulled out a box from cabinets under the bookcases and spent an hour looking at the baby pictures of Annsley, their first, and Austin. This new little one looks like Austin all over again. Déjà vu, he thinks, but that wee boy isn't already seen. He's the new thing in our lives and will change whatever course Austin was on. He stares long at Delia, his lovely wife, her dotted dress akimbo, ecstatically happy cradling open-mouthed Annsley. Another of her in a burgundy jumper, looking proud, holding sturdy Austin three years later. Annsley blowing out the candles on her third birthday cake, her hand squished into the icing. Austin propped on a stack of books at the shop, grinning up at the photographer, who must have been himself. Baby Jesus, he thinks, always an understandable metaphor for what we feel when a child is born: Here's someone to save this world. He carefully returns the photos to the box and puts them away. "Come on, Boss. Nighty-night time." The cat thumps to the floor and precedes Michael to the bedroom, tail erect and swaying, as if leading a marching band.

21

BEFORE HE GETS out of bed, Austin reaches for the folder. Shelley has been thorough. The first envelope Austin pulls out is filled with photographs of her with a note, *show these to him*. He crams them back inside the envelope. As his dad joked, there is an envelope of cash, £10,000. The Shelley-scrawled note under the rubber band says her mother will be sending £10,000 a year for support. "This goes for twenty years. It is not to be refused, as it is the inheritance I would have received and my son deserves this. Upon my parents' deaths, Austin II is to receive whatever inheritance might remain plus my portion of the Delhi house. My brothers have the registered legal documents."

Then there's a letter.

Austin, you're reading this, so I am erased. But not quite, as I have left you a magnificent gift, whether you understand that or not. I'm aware that the baby might not have survived either but that's another story and one for my family to handle, not you. If that happened, just give all this info back to my mother and go your way. My mother knows that I would like my ashes to be scattered in the Cam River.

I don't know whether you were nearby at my end, how you have interacted with my family—I can't know that. I just want to lay out the provisions I have made, in the hope that I can make up to you the strange change in your life that I caused. Believe me, I was naïve not to foresee the possible circumstances that did transpire. I apologize down into eternity. What a proud error I made. I wanted you, something of you. I saw a way and once the deed was done, my mother agreed to help me. Fate is unimaginable.

In brief, and my lawyer has all the official papers, I have a two-bedroom apartment leased for the next year. It is leased in the names of my family and you. After that you can renew, or let my family take over, as my brother Ollie may want it. The address: 10 Lord Ormond Street, WC1, in Holborn. You will be happy to see how close it is to your father's house and to your Calvert & Marlowe Architects. It is near several parks and has a back garden for Austin II on sunny days. I have eliminated all previous furnishings from my old place, in the event that you will be moving into this space with Austin II. I want it to look more you than me. My mother will pack and take the personal things of mine home with her and give the clothing etc. to charity. I cannot imagine you there with our boy, but it is yours, that is, if he survives. After that, you will do what you will. The keys are enclosed.

Everything for Austin II is ready. It was one of the greatest pleasures of my life to arrange his needs, down to the musical bear and the Beatrix Potter books you once told me your mother read to you. Please let him be named Austin. You select the second name.

My life was full of hope. I am gone. I hope he is here for you. If not, may your life revert to normal.

Austin folds the letter and puts it back. He hunches on the side of his bed, head in his hands. This is wrenching information, but the "lay out the provisions," "in the event," and "in brief" reads as though she's leaving instructions for a house sitter while she goes off on holiday. If only. She was probably barely holding on, having to write this.

Stuffed into the folder are the lease, keys, what looks like her will, and a loose photo: Austin and Shelley in shorts, big smiles, punting along the Cam with two brown cows and King's College Chapel in the background. Amit took that, Austin remembers, from the boat behind them. Who else was there, Reggie? Angie, her roommate? Angie, yes, because she brought the picnic, and they pulled up under willows and leapt out. And he recalls lying back in long grass, his back damp, Shelley feeding him cherries, so it must have been June. Idyllic, but he remembers that he did not like to be fed.

Austin doesn't want to talk but knows Amit is waiting to hear something. Hoping for the best, the easiest, the least damaging outcome. As Austin describes yesterday to him, Amit can't speak. He croaks, *Sorry, sorry.*

At the hospital, Fiona is holding baby Austin in the small anteroom. She's red-faced and blotched but she looks up with a slow smile. "He's a good boy. Look at this good boy."

A lanky man stands up and holds out his hand. "Ollie, younger brother." He has Shelley's quick-flashing eyes, her black curls, and a spotty beard. Austin thinks of saying the usual I've heard so much about you, but he doesn't remember Shelley ever talking about her brothers.

"I don't want to interrupt. I'll poke down the hall and see what the situation is. There are papers to fill out." He knows he must sign the birth registry and provide the child's name. Austin, he certainly will honor. Names? His own middle name is Justice. His mother wanted to name him after one of the virtues. But, no, not two identical names. One for his own. He likes Gavin but Austin Gavin isn't good. David? There are so many. Christopher, pretty name but effete and timid. He likes James. It comes back to him that Dara's brother, who did not survive a single day, was named Hawthorn. Could a child be called Hawthorn now? he wonders. Am I seeking a filament of connection? He does not want to call the child Austin. They'd be Big Austin and Little Austin. Awful for both. Hawthorn, I really like that name. It's strong and mythic. Hawthorn Austin Clarke. Then a rogue wave washes over him. He will be tied forever to this newborn he's naming. When will it seem possible? Probably when changing a smelly nappy at 3 A.M.

In the bathroom mirror, Austin sees that he looks the same. Twenty-eight, big career ahead, love beyond measure in his hands and heart, now stalled. Why doesn't it show? he wonders. I look normal. Not even droopy bags under my burning eyes. And Dara saying, just keep those lips against mine, don't kiss, just rest your lips on mine forever. That seems impossible because who he was a month ago now is over.

22

LUKE CHECKS IN at the Eno Inn. Odd to be here, with the wedding off, no Amit and Austin in the bar to greet him, Dara apparently driving around California, and Austin, my god, Austin coping with an infant. Amit let him know this morning the traumatic news about Shelley. Austin had called before he went to the hospital to register the infant's name. Luke cannot imagine that his old lab partner in chemistry is erased from the planet. Smart girl, didn't Amit tell us that she came up with a theory about the discovery, or was it invention, of zero when she was only sixteen? Pity such a brain and beauty fell off the planet, even if she did bugger up several lives, her own most of all.

His room faces the street. He looks out at the row of pastel-chalk-colored shops, orderly and cheerful with bright flowers in window boxes and blowsy small trees in their spring finery. He cranes to see around the corner where Mei lives over the dry cleaner's. He is wondering if he should tell her what has happened. Again, Austin hasn't told Amit to keep this mum, and how could he, since everyone at the office will know why he's taking a month off. The rumor mill at Calvert & Marlowe must be grinding this story to bits. But he doesn't want to put Mei in a bad position. She would, with this development, feel compelled to contact Dara. Isn't it Austin's place to tell Dara, not a thirdhand party? Still, if the situation were reversed and he'd found this out about Dara instead, he'd want to tell Austin. He also hopes this news won't skewer the weekend.

He showers under tepid water but lets it run, washing off the flight and the confusion. He wants to emerge, take a walk with Mei along the river, and have a long, delicious dinner.

❧

LEE PULLS THE TWO PORK ROASTS OUT OF THE OVEN. BRONZED AND crusty, they fill the kitchen with the savory aromas of the garlic, shallot, and thyme she slivered into them. Odd, the wedding day. Charlotte and Bing arrived early in the afternoon. Her mother had called last week and suggested that they have a dinner in the meadow anyway. So much of what was planned could still be used and why not have the local best friends over, officially celebrate moving on? Besides, she wants to introduce them to her sailor, Bing, who will drive them up and they can stay in the guesthouse.

Rich, just back from interviews, feels, as he calls it, like a "salty dog" from so much interaction with politicos. He's been to the river for a cleansing baptism and has set up two adjacent tables, not in the meadow, not there, but under the garden pergola much closer to the kitchen.

Bing comes out of the guesthouse to help with the chairs and shake out cushions while Rich cleans the grill for the peppers, onions, and eggplant he's roasting for dinner. He is relieved to like Bing. With Charlotte you never know what you're going to get. He was engaging at lunch, with stories of sailing in the Caribbean last winter, but not boring anecdotes from the deep past. And he was interested in Redbud's history. Rich has a thing about people who don't ask you questions and always carps to Lee when they've been stuck with blowhards. But Bing is obviously socially alert. He is quite buff for sixty-eight or whatever, with slicked-back steel-gray hair and a tan, probably year-round, from sailing. "I didn't want to bring it up at lunch, but I've of course heard the saga from Charlotte. My college true love dumped me just before my graduation from the Naval Academy. We were getting married, like your girl. We were way too young, but I was crushed. Turned out to be the best thing that ever happened."

When there's a drastic situation, everyone has a story. "Yeah. I hope that's true for Dara. She thought she was too young, but she was swept into the air by this English guy." He waves his arms upward and two pigeons fly out of the rafters, one pooping on the table. "We were—are—crazy about him, too. Everything you'd hope for in a son-in-law. Last of the storyline isn't written. As any writer knows, everything builds toward the last line."

"True. Very true."

The men set the table then Lee comes out to make everything right, bringing two low vases of peonies. She must run into town to pick up the lemon tarts she's ordered.

Outside the bakery, she squints as she sees someone on the corner, familiar but out of place. Luke? The friend of Austin's? What?

He sees her at the same time and raises his hand. "Lee, how great to see you. I came up to visit Mei, just for the night."

"Oh, from Sarasota, how nice! I thought I saw a spark or two fly between you." Pause. "Luke, have you heard from Austin?" She doesn't want to ask what happened. How much goes unsaid, she thinks. Sometimes more than said.

Luke scratches the side of his head and looks over Lee's head then back at her. "No, not from Austin." True but, oh god.

"We worry still but are trying to accept that it was not to be, even though we were so sure of them. They seemed incredibly tight, didn't they?"

"Yes, they were. I know for sure Austin was, *is* wildly in love with Dara. I hope something changes." He swallows hard.

"Why don't you and Mei join us for dinner—we're having some good friends over and we'd love for you to come."

"That's a very nice offer, but I just have this one night and really want to get to know Mei. I hope that's okay."

"Of course. How silly of me." She laughs and gives Luke a hug. "Say hi to Rich."

❧

HE WALKS TOWARD MEI'S. HE WOULD LIKE TO SINK INTO THE SIDEWALK. He feels a flash of anger at having been put in this position, but as he analyzes the players, he can find no fault except Shelley's, and Christ, talk about the ultimate price. Lee and Rich want the whole story, and Dara, he thinks, has every right to her privacy—but the web of truth has spread, and he's the fly caught in the center. Before knocking on Mei's door, he sits down at the outdoor table at a coffee shop and calls Amit. "Man, this is a situation. I'm in Hillston now, haven't seen Mei yet but I just ran into Dara's mom. She's in the dark. She was asking about Austin, naturally enough. I said I had not heard from him, which is technically true but didn't really answer the question she was asking."

Amit commiserated and gave him the number of Austin's dad's house. "But why don't I call him. You go enjoy your brief time with Mei. I'll tell him he needs to contact Dara and let her know. She still hasn't given her family the first round of the events? You've told Mei?"

"No. I've told Mei about the pregnancy, yes, but not about Shelley croaking."

"Luke! That's gross."

"Sorry, but I want to be an innocent bystander in all this."

"Too late, mate. I don't know what to say about filling in Mei with the news. Up to you."

"I don't want to burden her. But she will ask, I know she will, and do I want to lie, say I haven't heard anything further? Not a good way to start off a relationship."

"She probably would be honor-bound as a friend to call Dara. I'm not sure she should have to make that call. At least when everything's out in the open, we can breathe again. Hell, Austin's fate is *accompli.*

Dara needs to know that, and you're right, we don't want to be the messengers."

"I hate to bother Austin right now. He must be in some hot purgatory."

❧

FROM THE WINDOW, MEI HAPPENS TO SEE LEE AND LUKE MEET IN FRONT of the drugstore. Luke looks taller than she remembered. He's smiling down at Lee, but Mei sees some awkwardness in his twitchy shoulder movements. Is he telling Lee about the pregnancy? She hopes he is but sees no astonishment on Lee's face. They part quickly, and she watches Luke turn back to the Coffee Station and take out his phone.

Mei has wildflowers in a jar on her coffee table constructed from big art books. Her cozy living area under the front windows takes in the afternoon light. From the kitchen, she brings in a plate of bite-sized biscuits with country ham, some olives, and a bottle of rosé. Since Luke told her about the pregnancy, she has wanted to call Dara, has resisted, has dreaded running into Lee and Rich in town, has wondered about Austin and feels puzzled sorrow for him. Not good. With Luke, they must, she thinks, explore what there is to talk about other than Dara and Austin. What else do they have in common? She feels attracted to him and he must also be to her. Start somewhere.

❧

DRIVING HOME WITH THE TWO TARTS ON THE CAR FLOOR, LEE RUNS through the dinner she's planned for this now nonfateful May 20. Halfway through the menu, she thinks of the wedding dinner and how it would feel if the wedding were still occurring late today instead of the folding-tables dinner with Fawn and Charles, Eric and Elizabeth, her mother and Bing, a few colleagues, and three friends of her mother and Big Mann who are curious to meet the replacement,

Bing. Something sticks about her chance meeting with Luke. He didn't seem at ease. "He knows something we don't," Lee says out loud. I wonder if Mei knows. Uncomfortable for them, if true. Despite everything, we are going to have a lovely evening, and if Dara's breakup is this convoluted, maybe I can be glad I don't know, at least for tonight.

Dara, last heard from, was planning to drive to Big Sur, just to see the views. Lee imagines her in California, aimlessly traveling, alone, Courtney and Katie waving her off from their idyllic condo while they go to their fabulous jobs, with Dara zigzagging north, south, and east since there's no farther west to go, all the people living there shoved to the last shelf of the country, hanging off, as Lee imagines, the precipitous edge, with *terra incognita* scrawled into the ocean, as on ancient maps. How odd, California seems more incognito than Europe. Lee is only driving from the downtown Hillston bakery back home to Redbud, down a country road where a lone skinny kid shoots baskets in a broken driveway, dreaming of becoming a UNC star like Jerry Stackhouse, and a mangy dog from the cluster of poor houses lunges at the car's tires and howls as it is outdistanced.

Oblivious to her own road, Lee imagines Dara speeding along the coast, hair blown back, the cool Pacific air, the crisp scent of pines and sea air, gnarled trees shaped by the wind silhouetted against the cold cobalt ocean, and has no idea what is going to happen with her daughter. She would like to know what music she's listening to.

23

Dara loved Berkeley, all scruffy and vibrant. The Bay Bridge traffic makes her think she'd never want to live there. You'd want to go to the city; otherwise, you'd feel stuck. Life's too short to bog down on the bridge, especially if there's an earthquake like the one that took out a piece of the bridge a few years ago. So, Berkeley, no, despite its appeal.

She's walking around Stanford this morning, with its Alhambra vibe, the arches spread across the flat campus, the palm trees and arid air. One of her Georgetown profs is now on the law faculty. She searches out his office and knocks. Fred Moretti, appearing not professorial at all in cutoffs and a sweatshirt, opens his door, taken aback by Dara, who looks totally familiar. Where? Yes, daughter of the legendary senator.

"Just to say hi—I'm literally passing through, looking at some law schools kind of out of my territory. I'm Dara Willcox, if you don't remember. I was allowed to audit your torts class my senior year at Georgetown. I'm pretty much slated to go there, but now I'm out here and I thought I'd check other options. I remembered you got kicked up the ladder." She laughs, tilting her head.

"I do indeed remember you, Miss Willcox." He recalls her probing questions, her eyes the color he associates with icy Antarctic waters—ah, not the daughter, the granddaughter of the famous southern senator. Sassy one on the front row. "I'm glad you stopped in. So, you're looking at law schools?"

"I'm looking at everything in California and I am perpetually miffed that it's been kept from me all my life. It is just so staggeringly beautiful. I can't believe San Francisco is in America. And the headlands; I'm stunned; my friends and I went hiking there." She looks out the window at the sandstone arcades. "I had no idea Stanford would look so . . . so Moorish."

Fred, born Federico, is originally from Italy and isn't so impressed by California architecture. "Stanford is quite an anomaly, for anywhere. A bit of the Spanish missions, a dose of Romanesque. The whole original campus was designed in memory of the Stanfords' son who died young. I can show you around. Look, it's almost noon. Let's grab a bite and I can answer any questions you might have. It's good to see someone from Georgetown. This place can seem surreal at times, but"—he needs to retract that—"it's a new world and I'm liking it. It would be a pleasure if you decide to apply here."

Dara is flattered. Stanford is hard, hard to crack. They crossed the quad and came out in front of Memorial Church, covered with mosaics. What would Austin think of this? Would he smile that sideways smile and say *ersatz*, or would he respond to the contemplative mood, the swaying palms, and the rhythms of the arches? "How old was the boy when they lost him?"

"I'm not sure. Fourteen or fifteen, typhoid. All this grandeur for him. If this were Italy it would be for a big-name saint."

"Or the Madonna, who also lost her son." A child lost. What Austin is facing sweeps across her mind. He might know the odds by now.

In the café, they talk about what Dara might want to do with a law degree. She tells him about her work with Bill Dellinger on the Stephen Mann biography, about her HUD work, and the lucky paid internship as speechwriter in the policy group at the White House. Dara catches her reflection in the mirror over Fred's head and thinks, *There's Dara being Dara*. He asks her to send along her transcripts and he'll advise her.

With the wildest luck, could she and Austin ever live here?

She's parked near the train station. The campus, set back from Palo Alto's downtown, has a long buffer. As she recrosses the grounds, she fantasizes that Austin would start his own firm in the booming Silicon Valley, she would attend law school, they would live in a bungalow with a front porch shaded by lemon trees and jasmine. She walks around the humanly scaled town, browses at a bookstore on Emerson, then wanders, liking a town that names its streets Cowper, Addison, Tennyson, Kipling. On her map she also sees Mark Twain, Coleridge, and Chaucer. I must tell Mom, she thinks. Most of the roads around Hillston are named after churches and Bible references: Gilead, Gethsemane, Damascus, Ebenezer Baptist, Resurrection Hill. They should come out here. I love it. Austin would, I know. Then there's the shadow child growing up in India. California dreaming, I must be. As she drives out University toward the freeway, she's singing Joni Mitchell fragments. Lee loves Joni, and Dara grew up knowing all the lyrics. Old and cold and settled in its ways, and I'm comin' home, and will you take me as I am . . . Califorrrnia . . . How disconcerting to be driving toward Big Sur, singing at the top of her lungs.

Her phone rings and she reaches across the seat to dig for it in her bag. By the time she retrieves it, the ringing has stopped. Highway 1 goes from one heart-stopping view to another. Dara wishes she were not driving so she could see more. Precipitous hills spill into the ocean, the road a ribbon unfurling, and, it seems, liable to slide into the churning water. Creeping purple wildflowers splotch the hillsides, with a few late orange poppies flinging themselves down the slopes. Far below, she glimpses empty stretches of beach with waves scrolling foam onto the sand. When she can, she pulls over and takes pictures.

The drive to the Big Sur area is long and often tense because of precipitous drop-offs and narrow climbs and dips. It's late when she arrives at the lodge but she's in time to sit on the porch swing for the big western sunset, dark crimson and streaky pastels, the sun a wobbling orb with the sky above gold-lit, as if an angelic host were about to appear. The waiter brings her a glass of cold white wine. She takes out her phone and sees that she has no signal. It must have been Mom or Dad, she thinks. After dinner, I'll call on the real phone.

Dara doesn't mind eating alone. Mimi taught her to enjoy the idea that she is dining with herself, a chance to slowly enjoy each bite and to think calmly. "Never read the paper or a book. That's just sad," Mimi told her. "And never say 'just one' to the maître d', say firmly, 'One, please.'" So many useful lessons from Mimi. That night at Indigo, Mimi, talking on and on about great marriages, threw out her belief that something is wrong if you have to say "I love him but . . ." The conjunction must be *and*, as in "I love him and . . ." She stabs her fork into the peppery arugula salad with goat cheese and beets, thinking that her future may be in the balance of that dictum. This morning I thought of living with Austin. First time that idea has surfaced since the debacle.

She orders a glass of red, and the waiter recommends one from the central coast. All big and robust, it's just what her tender filet and tiny potatoes need. She concentrates (thank you, Mimi) on slathering the good bread with soft, pale yellow butter, on anticipating the first luscious bite. So good. She imagines the grapes for the wine ripening on a hillside under intense sun. Maybe I came to California, she thinks, to learn something. I've noticed the pervasive present-tense atmosphere. I've been fixated on my future. But the future was never that clear. I hadn't solved my law ambitions and if I really do want that, or if that's the path I've been influenced to follow. And Austin, work permit issues, a family, small like mine, in England, the advantages of the home office versus the New York outpost. We were plunging along blindly. Happily.

It's only seven at home. Dara dials Redbud and Lee picks up immediately. "Mom, I am at Big Sur. It is beyond belief. I know you love the Amalfi coast, but this is as spectacular and has an untamed, untaken, wild quality that I love."

"Why we've never been there, I don't know. Take pictures. Of course, I've seen many photos but it's hard to capture the feeling you are describing in an image. Maybe better in words." She's thinking, why are we chatting about photographs?

"You know, I've never traveled alone very much. This is good for me. I feel like I'm opening to a new place in a new way. My semester in Florence felt that way, too, but in a context of man-made beauty and culture—that truly human miracle of a city. But this is different. Expansive."

"How long do you plan on staying out there?"

"Just playing day by day. I stopped at Stanford and was dazzled by the campus and by Palo Alto. Courtney and Katie are great. They're thriving here. You'd love their Victorian condo. They've made a true home. They're sailing and getting rich and eating at fabulous restaurants and still taking the time to volunteer at a homeless shelter on Saturdays. They have it all figured out."

"Those girls were always on the rise, even at nineteen. Sweetie, you have a package here from John Harrison. Shall I just keep it?"

"What is it? Can you open it?"

"Let me get scissors." Dara can see her mother rummaging in the kitchen drawer for the orange scissors, the phone cradled against her shoulder. She's struck with a desire to be home, talking with her mother at the round table that's usually scattered with books her mother is reading. She hears paper tear and Lee exclaim. "Dara, this is a portrait of you!"

"Oh, Johnny said he was going to try that."

"It's not at all a student work; it's extraordinary. Not big, maybe ten by fourteen, maybe smaller. You're leaning against a low wall, pale sky in the background and a tall palm. Oh, I wish you were here. It's kind of Edward Hopper but sharper, prettier. Quite haunting."

"I hope he made me look better than I felt that day." She had just told him the Austin story and felt gutted.

"It's a beautiful likeness, and what startles is your eyes, not looking at the painter but . . . How to say it? You know your eyes are unusual, but they seem to be looking a thousand miles away. He has a remarkable talent. I'm shocked. Here comes Rich. Darling, I'm talking to Dara. Look at this! John Harrison sent it."

"Hey." He leans into the phone. "We miss you. Oh my god, this is a stunner. You look quite stark. The lone palm seems to echo that."

"Like 'The palm at the end of the mind . . .' " Lee quotes.

"I'll just have to wait. Sounds intriguing. Is there a letter?"

"Yes, shall I open it?"

"No, no thanks. Don't open it. Just let it wait." For sure, John would mention what Dara had confessed to him. I've got to tell them, Dara thinks. But not right now.

"Okay to put this in the living room?" Rich asks. "I'd like to study it more. I always liked the boy. He was smothered by his mother and those bouncy sisters, but he seemed unperturbed and already obsessed with his art supplies."

Lee describes their weekend with Charlotte and the outdoor dinner, glossing over the portentous date. "You'll like Bing. He probably hasn't read Mimi's books and just seems to enjoy her feisty, up-for-anything nature. He's got her interested in sailing."

"I'm not surprised. Does he know he won't be the captain for long? I do want to reread her books when I get home."

Lee mentions running into Luke in Hillston, but not her unease. "I was so surprised that he came up to visit Mei. Did you sense anything of that?" Most might say at this point, what the hell is going on, but Lee and Rich never have tried to force a situation. They let Dara unfurl her own wings.

"That's thrilling. I did not. I'll call her to get the story. I miss you all. I'll be in touch. Love you!"

Dara opens her window for the sound of the waves. The crash and boom, boom seem louder than at Indigo. The Pacific is bigger than the Atlantic and, odd, even from here it looks and sounds bigger. She shivers, feeling its power and ferocious beauty. It's cold. She props up in the window seat and leans back, listening, absorbing the rhythm and momentum. Out the window, she senses the last edge of the continent. Metaphor for her, Lee might call it. What a good place to sit. She pulls up a pillow behind her shoulders. I should always have a window seat for dreaming, for musing. As she reels through the beauty she saw today, all shades of blue and slate, high scudding clouds and the enormous clean sky over the water, silvery light glancing along the cresting waves, she feels her shoulders come down, a constriction in her throat loosen. The thrum, like that of a pylon in a cornfield, vibrates down her spine. Shock, she realizes; I should ask Mimi. I think I've been in a diagnosable shock. And now here's the Pacific slamming the beach, dark as the night. Finally, the panic that started that night in Washington, the panic that settled in her throat, making her always want to gasp for air, the panic that drove out any vision of the future and undermined the vision she possessed, the panic dissolves. How, she's not sure, maybe the beauty and immensity of the big world drives it out.

For once, she's not thinking of the aborted wedding, the future, or of anyone, not even herself.

24

On his lunch break Amit reaches Austin at his dad's house. Five thirty in London. "Just checking on you. How's the situation?"

"Hey, hey, thanks for calling. I'm hanging on to the edge of the world and the world is whirlpooling, that's what. Well, Shelley has been cremated. There was no ceremony; Fiona will have some memorial back in Delhi. So, she's taking the baby in a couple of days to the apartment Shelley has leased and will get him settled in for a week. Then, guess what, I become Poppa."

"That gives me the cold shivers."

"I'll start living there; our home place is too cramped with books, and I wouldn't do that to Dad anyway. Meanwhile, my sister, Annsley, will take some time off to help me, and I'll have to hire a daily nanny asap. I've been at work these last few days, stopping at the hospital afterwards. The baby is damned cute, and he looks at me as if he knows me."

"Sounds like you've got a good start." Amit is rolling his eyes.

Austin tells him about Shelley's will and the unbelievable level of detail she's left for him.

"Controlling to the last," Amit remarks. "But also redeeming, don't you think? That's good news that there's financial backup and a place all set."

"I can't really make any plans. I'm taking this day by day right now."

"Listen, my friend. Sorry to bother you but you need to let Dara know about this deluge. What's happened is that I told Luke about the pregnancy, and he told Mei."

"Mei?"

"Yes, apparently they locked eyes or something at the dinner. He went up to Hillston to see her. Meanwhile, he'd heard from me again, about what happened to Shelley, and he felt between a rock and a hard place about telling Mei the latest. I think he had to, or else get the relationship off to a wonky start. She already knew about the pregnancy. This must seem trivial but it's kind of a mess down there. And then Luke ran into Lee, who knows nothing. Quite the muddle. A pile of secrets. Those southerners are secretive people. Who're they protecting, themselves or others?"

"Probably both. This is nutty and means Dara never told Mei and her parents what happened?"

"Yes, she just fled. Couldn't face the shame. She went to her grandmother's at Indigo Island, now has gone to California. I haven't talked to Luke again."

Austin is sorting the details. "I had no idea no one knew. I feel even worse for Dara now, that she's isolated. It's unlike her—she's so close to her family and friends."

"She's visiting her Georgetown buddies, the lesbian couple who were going to be bridesmaids."

"I'm going to call Dara. How can I reach her? Her message machine says call her parents. That will be fun. Guess I have to."

"I'll come over in a month or so. We can push the pram around Russell Square."

"Get out of here! But come. I'll be needing that."

❧

"RICH, GOOD MORNING. AUSTIN HERE. I KNOW THIS IS A STRANGE CALL, but I need to reach Dara."

"Austin, good to hear your voice. We've been on tenterhooks around here. We don't know what happened between you, but it's clear Dara doesn't want us to know, for whatever reason, and we respect that."

"There are many reasons that she's mute about it. I'm so sorry I can't even say I'm sorry because that's inadequate. And there's more I need to tell her. I wonder if you'll give me her number."

"Well, she's on the run but let me give you Courtney and Kate's San Francisco number, the name of the lodge at Big Sur where she was last night, and her mobile number, although I doubt it will work for transatlantic."

The end of the call is awkward. Rich says, "I hope you find her."

Austin thanks him and says, lamely he thinks, "It is my greatest hope that Dara and I can get back together somehow."

Since Rich doesn't know why they're not together, he simply says, "All the best to you."

AS DARA IS CLICKING SHUT HER ROLL-ON, ABOUT TO CHECK OUT, THE phone rings. "Dara? Dara . . ." Austin. She sits down on the bed, feeling the now familiar sensation of an elevator door closing, leaving her in a small space. She's not sure she can bear it.

"I really want to talk to you. First, how are you?"

"I'm okay. Coming to California was a good idea. Seems like I've been here a month, but it's only been about ten days. What about you? Where are you?"

"London. I came back when Shelley was about to be induced. So much has happened. Just to get the worst out—Shelley died in childbirth. It was horrendous. The baby is fine. He is still on supervision at neonatal, but he can go home tomorrow. Home being the apartment Shelley leased. Her mom will stay only a week."

Dara literally cannot speak. Her eyes track from one corner of the room to the other. "Oh . . ."

"She has totally bailed on taking the baby back to India. She had to. Her husband has Parkinson's. It's a situation with one solution. And that's me."

Dara sinks onto the side of the bed, her mouth gone dry.

"Before I go any further, Luke and Mei and Amit all know this. Your parents are in the dark, but I thought you'd want to know that Mei is in a very uncomfortable position. She and Luke, it seems, are getting together. He's the one who told her."

"I understand. Well, that's one nice thing—Luke and Mei. I need to tell my parents and Mimi. I was blindsided by this incredible drama with Shelley. My entire reaction was *reject*. I wanted to crawl into a cave but, well, there's California. Now there's this. I wasn't able to tell anyone and could hardly think, Austin. I only told Johnny."

"Johnny?"

"Old friend from high school years, that summer I worked down where Mimi lives. I went down to see her and I ran into him at Indigo. I just spilled it."

"Dara, should I tell you more, or is this already too much?"

"She's dead, at what, thirty, you said. Thirty-one? That's hard to fathom. Was it a bad hospital or doctor or what?" She envisions a small bundle alone in a maternity ward, the first thought she's allowed herself of a living baby with no mother and a gobsmacked father.

"No. A rare death. In addition to the platelet problem, she developed something called preeclampsia, which contributed, too. I only went to the hospital when they induced labor. She was strong and I felt so much pity for her that it blotted out my rage against her. Not that I'm remotely okay with the situation, but guess what, looks like I'll have to be. I saw glimpses through the delivery room window. Meant to be for a happy viewing, the windows, but she bled out and it was beyond words."

"How sad. And for her mother. The baby . . . The baby survives. What is his name?" Horrific, what Austin witnessed. He can never unsee it.

"Austin Hawthorn Clarke."

"Hawthorn! Like our Hawthorn?"

"Yes, I hope you won't mind."

"Did you hold him?"

"I did. His hair was still wet. Color of straw. He grabbed hold of my finger and squeezed."

"Austin, I'm knocked over. This is a crisis for you more than for me. I should think more of you than myself, I know. Why can't I say we'll manage and fly right there? But I'm too overwhelmed by this whole situation. A baby. Plus, betrayal. I understand, but I can't get around it."

"I'm sorry. I'm going to be saying 'I'm sorry' for a thousand years."

"I don't want that. I am so very sorry for you having to bear this."

"I don't either, Dara. I'm going to be after a new vision. I have to. Both our lives have been botched and mine now involves this tiny, innocent Hawthorn."

With this, Dara is shaking. She doesn't reply.

"You will do what you must. I'm here. I'm going to be here. Glued. I miss you every minute. Just, please, tell your parents. I can write to them if you want me to. Tell me, though, if you keep our love, if you are putting me in the recycle bin, if there's any chance, if you think of me as much as I think of you."

"Austin, you know I said we're two peas in a pod. I'm not going to 'get over' you. Every beautiful thing I've seen on this trip, I've wanted to share with you. Every new sight and I'm wondering, what would Austin think. I won't ever want anyone as much as I've wanted you. I've been fantasizing that we live in California! But . . ." It hits her—here's the "but" Mimi was talking about. "But raising another woman's child when I don't even want a child—that's been too big and drastic for me. My whole body rejects this possibility. I wanted years and years alone with you. Then, maybe."

"I know. All fault accepted."

"Right now, I'm going to be, I guess, twisting in the wind. And knowing how much harder it is for you." Dara pulls her suitcase off the luggage rack, ready to roll toward the door. "I need to go."

"Dara, just please, keep open to something we can make. Bye, my love."

Austin will not be free to twist or sink or flee or fail. He will do what he is compelled to do.

She shuts the door. She's off on her own.

Hawthorn, the name, always a thorn, a name on a small mossy stone, now it's this living baby's name. Is he to be called Hawthorn? Dara is suppressing tears as she checks out. Deep breath. She fumbles for the car keys.

The desk clerk hands back her credit card and looks at her. "You okay, Miss Willcox?"

"Thank you, yes. Sad to leave!"

She pauses at the top of the parking area and heads the rental car north. She'd intended to drive all the way to Los Angeles, visit UCLA and the County Museum, but now instinctively turns back toward San Francisco. She'd dreaded driving in LA anyway, and after talking to Austin, she's trying to form coherent thoughts but only knows enough to turn around. Turning around and around seems to be what she does best these days. She thinks of her mother always quoting Yeats, *the center cannot hold*.

What's next? she's asking. I can't go back to Washington right now. As one of Mother's best writer friends says, Plan B for southerners is always to return home. Guess I'll go.

25

AUSTIN FINDS 10 LORD ORMOND STREET easily. It's familiar Holburn, close to the Russell Square neighborhood he's known all his life. His father's house and bookstore are not far, and the home office of Calvert & Marlowe on Bury Place within an easy walk. Good homework, Shelley.

He stands outside the enameled blue door, a blue the color of Greek waters, with a lion's head knocker. The street is canopied with sycamore trees meeting overhead. Number 10 has window boxes blooming with pink geraniums, and gleaming big-paned windows. A place he can imagine living with Dara. When they cashed in miles and came to London for a mad spur-of-the-moment weekend, he'd shown her this neighborhood where he grew up. She'd loved the dignified row houses and leafy squares, loved his dad—"Well, I see where Austin got his looks"—and their afternoon in Cambridge, where he showed her where he studied, and they had tea with Annsley in her shop. He'd fantasized then, a place like this, their big life taking place inside. He dreads the finality of lifting that brass knocker. He turns back to Lamb's Conduit Street and strolls, imagining he's on lunch break and checking out the cheese shop, tailors, and pubs. Imagines Dara waiting. But Fiona is waiting.

She took Hawthorn home three days ago and it's now the time for

Austin to get acquainted with where the two of them will be living. She flies out in only four days.

She opens the door, holding Hawthorn. "Welcome home," she says. "The baby is an angel. He's sleeping so well and already is reaching out as if he wants to hold the bottle. Come in, Austin. I know how strange this must seem. Why don't I sit in here," she gestures toward the bright living room, "and you take a look around." If it weren't for me, Austin thinks, her daughter would be alive in another reality entirely. How generous, in the depths of grief, to be so calm and gracious.

Austin expected Shelley's aesthetic, her embroidered scarves and pillows, her maximalist sense of a room. Instead, the flat is spare and white. It smells not of patchouli but of clean air. The front windows have simple linen curtains to pull closed. One jewel-colored rug in the foyer but the hall left bare, presumably so that he can do what he likes. A half bath is tucked under the stairs, and a closet with a stroller, tags still attached. He looks into the large living room, with a graceful, curved fireplace and a marble mantel of the building's late 1800s era. The room looks bright with a soft cream chenille sofa, two sage-green armchairs, and a large octagonal coffee table, low enough for a little one to pull up and reach for one of the children's books she's left there for him. Aside from an inset mirror over the fireplace, the walls are bare. He admires the neutral braided rug over the period parquet.

The kitchen, he sees, has had a wall knocked out; it's combined with the dining area, quite spacious with a contemporary wood-and-steel table, as great for spreading out his drawings as for throwing a dinner for ten. "Fat chance of that," he says aloud. She has found ten bentwood chairs in excellent condition. She remembered that Austin admires the work of Thonet. The back wall is all windows, except for the glass door leading out to a terrace and a splotch of garden. All planted, he notices, with hydrangeas and vines starting to climb over the brick walls. In back, a small swing and slide. Can this be happening to me? he wonders. I have stepped into never-never land. I am going to be pushing a baby in a swing?

The kitchen area is the same blue as the front door. White soapstone counters look recently installed, and the appliances all new. He opens a drawer. Neatly aligned pewter cutlery. In the upper cabinets, simple glassware and white plates. Austin will think about this for a long time. Haunting, he thinks, that in her last weeks on earth, Shelley was making a home that I would like. Where her Austin II would thrive. If she had lived, maybe her colorful block prints and rugs would have been hauled back into use. But, no, she would have left for India, the flat empty except for an occasional visit from Ollie. Or a sublet?

He hears a cat then realizes he hears crying. Fiona is walking the baby, singing something that sounds Irish. From the front hall, Austin goes up the stairs to the two bedrooms. This is where he wants to just sit on the floor and stare. The baby's room looks happy. Shelley has abandoned the pristine blank slate and has painted canary-yellow walls with a band of animals running around the wainscoting: ceremonial elephants with hats, tigers standing on hind legs, a red rooster, polka-dotted crocodiles, pink and purple cobras, furry housecats. Animals she saw growing up, he realizes. A large sheepskin rug on top of yellow carpeting invites snuggling down with Lego or crayons. All the necessities: a crib made up with blue sheets and a soft blanket, changing table, and a closet stacked with nappies and a row of tiny outfits on satin hangers. Enough clothes for two or three babies folded in the chest of drawers. A carrier and a folding cot are still in their boxes. The room looks out at the street, almost at treetop level. Austin rests his forehead against the glass. He practices pursing his lips to distract himself from breaking down. Leaf-sifted light falls into the room, a green-gold cast. This is where the boy's first memories will imprint.

Below the windows, the bookcases already hold a half shelf of books, several stuffed animals, and a ball. The rest are empty, waiting for Austin to bring home *Winnie-the-Pooh*, puzzles of clowns, and counting rings to stack in ascending order.

At the back of the flat, he turns into what is to be his room. It's especially bare, as if she finally had no wish to intrude. The one note of luxury, placed under the two windows, a vintage Eames chair. He remembers that she said her father had one in the house where she grew up. How did she score that? Empty bookshelves line one wall, floor to ceiling. Other than that, the bed, made up now for Fiona, with a luxurious mohair blanket in subtle stripes of tan and cream folded across the foot.

The surprisingly huge closet is hung with Fiona's few clothes but Austin notices that Shelley even has lines of wooden hangers and a built-in shoe rack. Spooky.

He walks back into Hawthorn's room. Not given to prayer, he stands looking out the front window, biting down on the facts, overwhelmed by the flat, almost dizzy with uncertainty, but more ready than he has been. May I . . . May I . . . he doesn't know how to finish his prayer or to whom a prayer might be addressed.

Fiona places the soft-wrapped bundle on Austin's knees. "Let me show you how to give him the bottle. Here, Mr. Baby."

Austin holds the warm glass, almost feeling the suction. "Powerful jaws!" He laughs, smiling at the little oval face.

"If you're happy, probably the baby will be," Fiona says. She's inclined to rave about what a beauty Shelley was but refrains. "How do you like the place?"

"I'm overwhelmed by what Shelley did when she must have been terrified."

"It was a godsend. She was focused. Even though she hoped you never saw it, she was performing some kind of homage and apology to you. I think she did a superhuman job."

"Everything for the baby and me. There's not a speck of her, except for the animals she painted."

"That was the only time she broke down. Imagining her boy waking up to see those joyous creatures."

"Fiona, I will show him her pictures and tell him how smart and beautiful she was. It will be a long time before I need to tell him the whole context of his parents' lives. And will you come back? He needs to know his grandmother. You know my mother isn't with us anymore."

"I want to. And will you sometime come to Delhi? For my husband?"

Hawthorn zonks out, a bubble of milk expanding and popping from his puckered mouth. "I'm exhausted. Come tomorrow. I need to show you many things before I go. Young mothers do this all the time. You can, too. And you can always call me if you need advice."

"My dad and my sister will be on hand. I'm not entirely alone." Yeah, they're thrilled to have landed the no-love child in their midst. Just what they dreamed of.

Back at Michael's, he feels disoriented. Heart pounding against his chest, he throws off his clothes and sinks to the side of the bed. Hard to breathe, he needs to gasp. He places his hands over his knees. Whose body is trembling? He turns on the warm water and slides to the floor of the shower, willing himself to calm, letting the water fall on his face, trying to think of something serene, that day on the North Carolina beach, of holding his mother's hand and walking to the park with bread for swans, looking out at dreamy spires from his mullioned windows at Cambridge, recent late nights with the immensity of the library project at the tip of his pen. But other-Austin looks down into the shower from above, seeing him wheezing and flailing. At last, his pulse slows, he dozes, jerks awake as the hot water runs out and cold douses him.

26

REDBUD, ALWAYS WELCOMING, outdoes itself in late May. The rose garden, profligate, the saucer magnolias throwing out their scent, and the perennial beds of columbine, echinacea, volunteer poppies, ginger lilies, zinnias, miniature butterfly bushes, white and lavender, all outperforming the weeds that Lee and Rich will battle all summer. Dara is home. The turbulent red-eye flight east had just seemed appropriate to her churning insides. She called Mei and her parents from the San Francisco airport and Rich was at RDU to meet her 7 A.M. arrival. At last, they were to learn the truth. However scorching it might be. Rich hardly slept, nor did Lee. She has a final PhD oral to attend early this morning, one of her favorite students, who has followed her into studies of the Irish poets.

Rich suggested that the three of them meet at Crook's Corner for lunch, maybe easier for all than the home turf. He and Dara turn into the driveway just as Lee is leaving. Dara jumps out for a hug and is accosted by Rocco. She waves Lee goodbye and romps around the garden, with Rocco jumping on her, sliding to the ground, barking, rolling in the dew. Rich makes coffee and Dara has some gingerbread with hers, then collapses on the sofa under the portrait of her that John Harrison sent. She sleeps curled in a ball. Rich leans over her, seeing her at eight, at fourteen, this fraught morning he couldn't save her from. Still the same peachy glow, hair prone to tangle, eyelashes that brush her cheeks when her eyes are closed. He covers her with a throw and closes the door, glancing at the portrait where she has the thousand-mile stare.

At Crook's, it seems like old times. Over the years, the family must have dined there a hundred times. The chef always brings over complimentary pimiento cheese and crackers, or desserts, in season the favorite honeysuckle sorbet. "Shall we have the usual?" Rich asked. Unanimous, yes, shrimp and grits. While they wait with sweating glasses of iced tea, Dara launches right in. "I know how hard this must have been the last weeks. I just dumped the bad news and ran. I love you so much and I don't understand yet why I couldn't say what was happening with Austin. I guess I couldn't accept it myself, and to speak it would make it real."

"Sweetie, we understand." Lee puts her hand on Dara's arm. "We are relieved if everything now will be out in the open. We can deal, you know that." Dara did. She won the lottery with such parents. They have never let her down. A few skirmishes in high school when she stayed out too late and smoked pot with sexy Marshall. Not his fault his granddaddy headed the Klan, his mother was known as a famous boozer around town, and his daddy often was just out of jail for forging checks. Not sweet Marshall's fault but her parents were alarmed and said so. They would have been more alarmed if they'd known she lost her virginity in the back of Marshall's daddy's pickup. She almost smiled, remembering the air buzzing beneath them, whooshing out of the camping mattress they'd blown up.

Dara sucks in her cheeks and begins. "When Austin and I were first together, he had to go back to London for a few weeks. While he was there . . ." And the story of the former girlfriend, the party, and the ensuing sex spills out.

Rich leans both elbows on the table and covers his lower face with his hands. Dara recognizes the gesture. He's wary of what he might say. But he says nothing.

"He came back to New York and that's when we became seriously involved; you know our love story. Two humans could not have been happier. Six months after his work trip, in fact, the very time of the dinner at Redbud, she—her name is Shelley—dropped the bomb. She was pregnant. Apparently had not been with anyone else. She knew their thing was over and decided not to tell Austin anything. Couldn't have him, so wanted his child. She'd gone off the pill long ago but told him 'not to worry.' Turns out, she'd fantasized about getting laid by him one last time." Dara spilled everything about that evening in London last fall. "Not to gloss over anything, Austin was stupid drunk. I doubt if he'll ever enjoy a drink again!"

"That's all absurd," Lee says.

"Here's the hardest part. She only let him know because she developed a serious blood condition. She had planned to move home to India and never, ever tell him that he was a father. But then she had to because her family isn't able to take on a child if something dire happened. If she dies, he's the father and he has to face that."

"Extraordinary. Is it leukemia?" Rich is trying to understand the mentality of the woman. Running off to India with a secret child? Enticing someone who'd rejected you? Planning a lifelong secret?

The food is brought but no one lifts a fork.

"Let's just take a breather while you absorb this, because it gets worse. When I canceled the wedding, this was all I knew. It was bad enough."

Lee passed the breadbasket, and they began eating. "I certainly understand how you couldn't speak about it. And the girl's health was in jeopardy, so he was truly under the gun. How sad to make such a goofy mistake."

"Exactly. All that was terrible. But for me, there was the other issue. He slept with his old girlfriend, and even if he was plastered and even if she wanted it to happen, even planned for it—still this happened. It was the last thing I would expect. I was crushed."

Rich is calculating in his head. "You hadn't known him long . . ."

Dara stiffens. "That doesn't matter. He knew we belonged together."

"If she hadn't become pregnant, his, what, his indiscretion could have been just that. A kind of betrayal, but he was utterly plastered—not that he shouldn't have left an hour earlier. This, however . . . it's like in *Tess of the d'Urbervilles*—the note under the mat that was never found, like Othello; so many missed small things change the world." Lee felt flooded with Austin's shame as equally as she felt Dara's outrage and sorrow.

Dara scraped up the last of her shrimp and grits. Nothing wrong with her appetite now, Lee thinks. But Dara looks wan, that characteristic vivaciousness quelled.

Dara puts down her fork and leans her chin on her fists. "Here's the awful upshot. Shelley's platelet condition worsens, and she gets some other serious problem, preeclampsia, so they must induce labor, and Austin flies over because if she dies, he's legally responsible for the child.

"What else can happen I'm sorry to say—the worst. The procedures they had in place to save her, the massive transfusions at the time of birth—did not work. She bled to death."

Lee and Rich, dumbfounded, lean toward Dara and take her hands. "No. This can't be. She's dead? What about the child?" Lee sinks in her chair and grabs for Rich's other hand.

"The little boy is fine. Austin is stupefied. Shelley's mother is there for one week, then Austin is on his own."

"But this is insane. Did he consider putting the child up for adoption?" Rich already knows the answer.

"I know Austin wouldn't do that. Whatever his mistake, he's an upright person. I met his father and sister, you know that. They're not ones to shirk in that family. And Shelley's mother, she's overwhelmed. Not only the loss. But her husband is failing fast."

"Damn hard for him."

"Yep."

The chef brings over a buttery pound cake with a scoop of vanilla ice cream. "Honeysuckle isn't quite ready. You come back in two weeks for the sorbet, I'll have it for you." Rich shakes hands, envying him for his concern over the timing of honeysuckle blossoms, while somewhere in London, Austin is concerned with his life turned inside out. The pound cake, dense and moist, rivals any sorbet. He's trying to remember to taste it as he sees like fast-forward film the first months of Dara's life, the exhaustion, the glory, too, but Lee struggling through the 3 A.M. feedings, the groggy mornings, the lifting, the balky baby carriage, gagging the first time I changed a diaper, yellow poop, the pail smelling of uric acid, the burping. Took a toll for two people, for one it must be staggering. The reward of smiles and seeing her eyes change from cobalt blue to their aqua water blue-green, my father's genetic gift. Now Austin faces that. Alone. Bet he's never picked up an infant more than twice in his life.

Lee simply says, "I feel so sorry for Shelley's mother. I can't imagine losing your daughter and in those circumstances. And going home with her belongings in a suitcase, all that is left. Well, she's left a child, of course."

As they continued talking, neither Lee nor Rich offer opinions about what Dara should do. Though they often suggested options as she grew up, they never pinned down an *ought*. Nor did Mimi. Dara always knows this as respect and admires them for their subtle way of encouraging critical thinking skills. Must work, she realizes. She, through all this, never has said to Austin what he must or should or must not do. At least there's some dignity. And Austin. Hell for him, but he did not shirk. She hurts but feels pride in his reactions. And plenty of white-hot anger.

❧

RICH RIDES BACK TO REDBUD WITH LEE, WHILE DARA DRIVES TO MEI'S. She's meeting Moira there, too. This time no dirty dancing at Randy's, just a bald confession. As she eases onto I-40 toward Hillston, Dara wonders how long it will take for Austin to begin to recede into the distance. Will this be like someone you love dying? She didn't see Big Mann's heart attack on the porch floor, or the ambulance, the bustle and excitement and denial of his death. Just the urn come home and the ensuing absence at the table, the jokes, his stepping outside for a forbidden smoke. Then the stark reality, he is gone, that can't be real. She turns on the radio, classical station, and the music from a far century disturbs the dust motes flying in the AC vent. Big Mann, she sees him, face still bright, rotating among cumulus clouds, scattering, dissolving like the mermaids and lions she spotted as a child. What a loud subtraction he made. She thinks of the unknown, despised, now mourned Shelley, also an amorphous cloud. Those once acute ones, now gone, are not listening now, no smart-ass comment coming. No final letter of instruction on going forward, just low morning fog they dissolve into without a wave and no last look back. While I, still planted on terra firma, drive to visit old friends, pack for the weekend, upright, forthwith, sauntering into the shadow of their absence. May my parents never leave. Our Hawthorn, early to leave the party that had barely begun. He left without one word, not a single glance from his deep-sea eyes. Old losses fall far back in their deadness and hardly survive. Lisa, my adored riding teacher, thrown off Helianthus. Liver crushed; neck snapped. Hawthorn, with no immortality after me. No one else will ever remember. But maybe the same eyes as the new Hawthorn on the block. Big Mann, his pause and twinkle before the punch line, anticipating your delight. Her, that Shelley, her sly half smile, as I imagine it. Yanked, as easily as tongs take the lobster from the boiling water. And you (me, I) who last, lucky you of the gene pool worth swimming in, you get the *lucky me* astonishment as you drive toward home. Those gone before, where are they? I lie in the grasses at night, and they softly tread the Milky Way. Dara experiences a surge of energy. She wonders if others also experience this chemical exaltation. She has always had these physical moments, occasional, when energy rides up like a sneaker wave. Austin isn't, won't pass into fog; no *go, went, gone.* Vibrant life, a strong current to ride. She grips the steering wheel, feeling it anchor her. Otherwise, her power might lift her through the open sunroof.

HER FRIENDS ARE ALREADY WAITING. MEI TAKES DARA'S BAG AND KISSES her cheeks, whispering, "You poor devil. I'm so glad you came home." Her signature biscuits and ham, her orange shortbread cookies already are laid out.

Moira pushes herself up from the sofa and embraces Dara, rocking her back and forth. "We can't imagine what you've been through." She plops back down, reaching for a plate. She takes two of each. "Before we get into the business of the day, I might as well tell you right off, I'm expecting again. It's a surprise and you'd think, with the twins driving me nuts, that I'd be crazy, and I don't know why but it's fine. Carleton is happy and the news seems to have made him notice that I get sidelined constantly in our relationship. He's doing the dinner cleanup and asking me about my schedule. He's been a new man."

"Moira, extra hug, come here!" Dara jumps up and pulls Moira's soft body into an embrace. News of another new baby, this one with a loving pair of parents, shoots tears to her eyes.

"Then I guess you won't drink this rosé. More for us! Congratulations, what sweet news." Mei goes to the kitchen and brings out a pitcher of tea. They toast Moira. "Is it a boy or girl?"

"We don't know. Not sure I want to. With two girls, you can imagine that Carleton would like someone to fish and hunt with. So far, our girls say *eeeww* when they see him come home with a string of fish. One thing—it's not twins, thank God. But that's all my news. Dara, I think you have some."

Dara slides off the banquette to the floor and crosses her legs. "Okay. Here we go. I, first, apologize, truly, for keeping everyone worried and stressed. You know we've always confided in one another, and I've certainly been lucky to have non-judgy parents. The story—which, Mei, you already know—was too harsh for me to absorb. I didn't handle it well. I couldn't talk about it. Feigned the runaway bride myth. I had to go to California to clear my head."

"Wait," Moira says. "You know, Mei? And you didn't tell me?"

"I wasn't supposed to know so I couldn't. Couldn't tell Lee, of course."

"How did you know?"

"Luke. Remember him, Austin's groomsman, at the party? We're seeing each other. It's just happened. Amit, that other groomsman, told him. They didn't know that Dara had not spilled the beans to any of us. Luke—I really like him but let's get back to the story. Go on, Dara."

Dara begins with the cryptic message Shelley left on Austin's phone and ends with her final letter and the child.

"There's a lot in there that I didn't know," Mei says. "Surely not the black-and-white drama I had in mind. What a mysterious decision—knowing you could get pregnant and, well, encouraging the chance. I bet your Mimi would have a lot to say about obsession."

Moira pats the soft swell of her belly. "Beats me. If Carleton had done something like that, I'd have liked Gary Crofton to step right up. He was rich, too."

They all laugh. They knew the story of Gary calling on her wedding day, begging, "Don't go through with it . . ."

Moira wants to say *I think you should hightail it to London* but wisely does not. Not everyone is into sacrificial rites, she thinks. But her heart lurches for Austin and the baby. And surely Dara's does, too, she realizes. "Are your parents okay?" she asks instead.

"They are a bit wobbly on the whole subject but couldn't be more sympathetic to everyone concerned."

"Now, what about you?"

"Yes. I loved California. I don't know. I was thinking about losing people on the way here. Big Mann, and you remember Lisa being thrown. How we idolized her, right, Moira? And there's Shelley, too. Regardless that I'd like to shake her teeth out if she were healthy, she died. So young. Having made a stupid choice once. Maybe she would never be that idiotic again."

"Wait, I have to run to the bathroom." Moira speeds out and Dara and Mei laugh. She comes back, taking two shortbreads from the plate. "Sorry, go ahead, Dara."

Dara throws up her hands, shaking her head. "Well, it's just that everything two months ago seemed so blissful, so innocent. I think I'm just beginning to understand loss, and it's sobering. I'm now hyperaware of how fiercely I want those I love to be alive and picking out the best tomatoes at the farmer's market. I don't want to take anything for granted anymore. Pop the bubble! When I was driving back from Chapel Hill just now, all these feelings were swirling through the car. It felt like a lifetime of emotions all at once." Dara falls silent, sipping the rosé and glancing around Mei's studio—her unfinished wedding dress hanging on the back of a closet door, a mood board of Mexican embroidered blouses, a photo of Coco Chanel with "Nazi sympathizer" scrawled across it, a vase of drooping yellow and white roses. Luke must have brought them. Then, an illumination comes to her, like a searchlight picking out the culprit, the source of her tumultuous thoughts. It pings off Lee's oft-quoted *A pity beyond all telling is hid in the heart of love*. Betrayal, what has plagued her—*betrayal*, that's another word for loss. Loss that flows into all the other losses. I wonder, she thinks, if Mimi already knows that or if I have learned something to tell her.

At Redbud, no one around. Rich sprayed his legs for mosquitoes and took a book down to his chair by the river. Lee's somewhere, doubtless up to her chin in papers. Rocco, splayed flat on the cool floor, doesn't budge. What Dara needs is a nap. No sleep on the flight has caught her. Dara finds a vase of cheery zinnias by her bed, and there's her short stack of mail. Junk, all of it, except an envelope with "J.H." on the back flap, Johnny's note that was enclosed with the portrait. Dara kicks off her shoes and tosses off the covers, drops backwards on the bed, and reads.

Hey Dara,

I hope you like your portrait. I admit I think it's one of my best efforts. My mentor here agrees. If so, it came from the inspiration of your beauty. No kidding—sometimes the subject of a painting emits a force that the painter can absorb. The hard part was your eyes, but I think I got something there. Where you were at that moment but also who you are. Bright star! Enough about my great work of the western world!

I am wondering how and where you are and what has transpired in the meantime. I hope that the sad woman has gone on her way back to India. And that whatever resolution you want is the one you have. If by chance that's not the way it shook down, I have an idea for the meantime until you know what's what.

When I left you, I went home to Charleston for the first time since Christmas. I found that Mama and my sisters, Joy and Bee, have been busy. They didn't want to tell me until something was nailed down, but when I got there, they were very excited. Mama has secured a good loan for the restoration of The Palms, mainly structural stabilization, heating and cooling, that kind of thing. Joy and Bee applied to Preservation South Carolina for a grant, and got historical-status tax credits, state and federal—you may know the place is already on the National Historic Register. Smart girls, indeed. They nailed it. So, my family will be back in the hotel business. Long-term, I can base there, work, and still have a painting life.

My brilliant idea is to invite several artist friends from here to spend a few weeks at the hotel. We'll use their skill and inspiration to paint the rooms and the lobby and dining room with, not frescoes as we have no wet plaster, but our own designs on the walls. Dara! Will you come? You can brainstorm, help with the decisions, shop for stuff we'll need. Like all good southern girls, I know you have excellent taste. It would be memory lane, too. Beach fun. Mama is in charge. Think about it. I'm going down mid-June and will be with my motley entourage bearing paintbrushes. I'm envisioning this hotel to be a work of art itself, certainly not the boring could-be-anywhere décor of most places. You can have your old room or, really, any room you want. Say yes! Call me: 843-711-6207.

Yours, John

Clever John, incredible idea. Exciting. Why not?

Lee orders barbecue for supper. Dara has never admitted to anyone that she doesn't especially like barbecue, for in the South that would be equivalent to saying you don't necessarily believe in the virgin birth. But she's okay with it tonight because Lee included sides of potato salad, slaw, and hush puppies. They eat in the kitchen, all the containers plopped on the table, Rocco circling, hoping for a bite tossed his way.

If Lee and Rich want to probe, they don't. The three of them talk instead about sprinkler problems at Redbud, how low the river is, and Mimi's Bing, whom they liked. Lee is wrapping up the manuscripts for the master's candidates, and eager to devote the summer to finishing her own book. Rich has assignments in Thailand (environmental assessment) and the Dolomites (a rare first-person travel piece, which he enjoys).

"Here's a new development." Dara takes a beer from the fridge for Rich and pours tea for Lee and herself. "That letter from Johnny—he has a wild idea for The Palms." She tells them about the financing and the troupe of artists descending from RISD. "It sounds like a good distraction and a fabulous idea. It will put our Palms on the map. I don't know of anything like it, in the South or anywhere. And for Johnny and his family, a big renewal. I want to tell Mimi."

"Fantastic to hear this." Rich raises his glass. "Good thinking."

"What happened to his father—I don't remember," Lee asks.

"As far as I know he absconded early on. So Biba raised him. She's a force of nature. I think I'll go. My second adventure in the Recovery Annals." Irrationally, she wants to tell Austin about the project. You've got to quit that, she tells herself. Tell yourself.

Propped in bed, Dara reads the third volume of Cazalet Chronicles. As a child in the same bed, eating Ritz crackers with peanut butter and reading Nancy Drew, she realized that this comfort and pleasure was a happiness she could have no matter what. Always books will transport, give inspiration, push new ideas into the open. These chronicles are especially enticing because there are five books—a multigenerational family saga of pre–World War II and on into the latter part of the century—the greatest generation. Reading about the privations and brave suffering, the losses and the indomitable spirit of this complicated family is also doing side work. Dara admires them, especially the women and even the duplicitous husbands. Besides, she can't put them down. The writer is juggling twenty-seven characters. Dara's right there in Sussex in wartime, wanting the best for them. What they're learning, she realizes, is the constancy of change. At 2 A.M., she's still reading *Confusion*. As she reaches to turn out the light, she's thinking of what she said earlier about not taking anything for granted. These characters certainly couldn't. Maybe other people are tougher, she wonders. More used to being slapped down. I have a strong family and I've always felt, what, launched by them. Someone else might be more prepared for upheaval. I'm now understanding. Don't want to but I am.

The marshes are a recurrent dream since childhood. This time she's in the brackish water, smells of iodine and salt, a white sun pulsing, she's floating, eddied over into a backwater while the marsh and sea float her with the tides.

AT NOON, MEI, MOIRA, AND DARA MEET IN TOWN FOR A WALK ALONG the river path. Dara has brought chicken salad sandwiches and potato chips. They wade out, only ankle deep, and step onto a huge flat rock with overhanging shade. Her friends are excited to hear about Johnny's project, but especially pleased that Dara seems enthusiastic. Mei dives in with ideas. "You could make simple curtains out of painters' drop cloth. It's off-white, light-blocking but hangs well. Just think of embroidered or stenciled borders, simple but with the artisan touch."

"Brilliant." (That's one of Austin's words.) "You should come down there. I thought of putting books in every room. What goes together more than beach and books? I bet Mom would donate a boatload. Nice reads like *The Voyage Out* and *To the Lighthouse*."

"*Moby-Dick*," says Moira. "Sometimes whales pass Indigo."

Mei opens her bag and takes out the shortbread left over from yesterday.

"Confession. I never made it through *Moby-Dick*," Dara admits. "Maybe this summer. A seaside book I love is *Break of Day* by Colette. She's trying to give up love because she thinks she's old. I think she was around fifty. She's hard on herself, thinking she's washed up. Meanwhile, she's shagging someone half her age every night. But the best part—where she is, a flowery cottage by the Mediterranean." Dara stands up in the ankle-deep shallows, brushing crumbs off her shorts. "You all must come down. And Moira, you could write about it when it's done. A big article. That is, if it sizzles the way I imagine it will. *Southern Living* would be all over it. The *Washington Post*. Any publication with vision."

"I would love to do that. Now what about Johnny Harrison? Are you going to be shagging him?"

"Ah, shut up, Moira. Idiot girl!" She splashes water on Moira's feet. "Where your imagination goes." Maybe I will.

THEY PART WAYS AT THEIR CARS. DARA TURNS NORTH FOR A SOLITARY drive around some of her favorite countryside roads. She always stops at an abandoned cemetery with leaning wooden crosses, graves decorated with shells and broken colored glass, rotting plastic flowers, moldy teddy bears, and on one grave, a half-full bottle of gin. There's a lily-choked pond bordering the slope where a few headstones have tumbled. She tries to call Johnny. No signal. Could have guessed. She speeds along other well-known roads, admiring a flower bed bordered with tires painted in chartreuse and purple, families lined up in rockers on the porches of brick ranch houses, a mailbox made of an old plow, walkways bordered by geraniums planted in giant tomato cans, Snow White and the Seven Dwarfs surrounding a wishing well, plaster having fallen in chunks from their faces and shoulders, and a new contender for house décor, two toilets on either side of a stoop, used as planters. She laughs and hits the steering wheel with her fist. And that's what I like about the South. Who would do this and why? The scraggly plants are about dead. Could I ever feel at home in California? Or anywhere else? She heads home. Can't wait to tell her parents about the toilets.

On her own front porch, where it's possible to catch a signal, she calls Johnny.

"Johnny's phone," a female voice answers.

"Hi, is he there? It's Dara Willcox."

"Let me find him."

"Hey, Dara. It is really you? How are you?" He sounds breathless.

"Okay. I'm in North Carolina, and Johnny, I love the painting you sent. My parents do, too. They have it in pride of place under the taxidermy deer my grandfather mounted years ago." They laugh. "Seriously, it's good. It's serene but has this nervous vibration."

"That's what I like to hear. So, gorgeous, are you coming to Indigo for the revels?"

"I would love to. It's a fabulous idea. You will put that hotel in a category of one! It's lucky to be grandfathered in via the preservation covenants. Otherwise, you couldn't do all this."

"I know. There's a long story to that inn. By the way, that was Abby who answered. We're in studio now. She's one of the three friends who want to come. Everybody is super excited. We are starting down on the fifteenth, so come whenever you want."

"I'm ready. And, John, I love the idea of books for each room. And Mei, you remember my friend who came down a couple of weekends when I worked there? Anyway, she's a talented fabric designer and I want to rope her in, too."

"I don't remember. But great. We've got a tight budget but we'll make it work. Mama's there now, getting estimates."

"I'll let you know my ETA. Not sure how long I can stay, but I'm in. I'll go up to DC and get my life there in order and pack some summer clothes. Or will we just work in our bathing suits?"

John flashed on a memory of Dara in a green bikini and that dude from Charlotte she dated saying something like *she can shake that bootie*. He almost, at the time, knew what that meant. "Dara, can you say what happened to the pregnant woman and her blood problem?"

"That's a long story for a walk on the beach."

"Gotcha. Okay. I will see you soon."

"Thank you again for the painting. I'll treasure it."

Well, that's settled, Dara thinks. A plan. A good one. She mentally revisits Mimi's remodel a few years back, remembering how strict the rules were. There was a dispute over the size of her sunrise window, and she somehow beat them down on that. There are bound to be new environmental regulations. With my, ha, vast legal experience, I can keep tabs.

She wants to research the native dune flowers, beach roses and plums. Already, she's seeing Mimi, backing a pickup filled with sea oats and beach grasses. She remembers the ghost story always told over and over at The Palms when they sat around a campfire. The Gray Man, who wanders the town, a suitor who was coming to see his true love in the 1700s and drowned in the marsh. Now he gives warnings when hurricanes approach, and generally just performs ghostly duties of being a haint and scaring the wits out of people. Best not to depict him, but maybe his foggy presence might be somehow evoked on the veranda.

Talking about Indigo reminds Dara that she needs to call Mimi. For once, Mimi stays quiet while Dara spills the story. She ends with Austin facing the apartment that Shelley has left for him, furnished down to the vegetable peeler and night-light. She has the wild thought that Shelley would have been good for the Palms project.

Mimi seems at a loss. "Darling, all I can say is to take your time. You've both been knocked out of your orbits. This is not easy to solve, and no one should give you any advice because in such a vulnerable state you might be inclined to take it. That might not go well in the long run." Her mind was erupting with sympathy for the mother, for the sick father waiting in India, for the foolish girl who made a bad choice but redeemed it heroically. "This is a major chapter in your story. Write it slowly."

"I will, Mimi, thank you. California was a good move. I loved it instinctively. Now I have something else to tell you. I am not going to live in the apartment this summer, but Bill is working there and staying in the guest room as well. With his cat. He'll be delirious that he doesn't have to move. That is, if you're not planning to use it. He's paying the utilities and phone."

"That's fine. I can't wait to read the book. I am staying put but still hoping the family can get a vacation in. Rich is busy and Lee is determined to get that book out the door. We'll see. Now, what do you have in mind?"

Dara explains John's project at The Palms.

"Well, of course I knew that Biba and the girls got good financing, but this is grand news. I can't prove it, but I always think boys raised by women, with no man in the picture, turn out to be more creative than boys with fathers."

Dara wonders about boys raised with a father and no mother.

What are they? More vulnerable? But she drops the subject. "I'll be there soon, but don't worry, I won't be crashing on your sofa. I'll be staying at the inn. Maybe I'll need to borrow some mildew spray from you."

Charlotte neglected to mention that she signed on as guarantor for Biba's loan. She thinks for a moment about why she doesn't just share this piece of news—it's a happy thing. Knee-jerk reaction in the South, she thinks: We keep our cards close. The flip side of outrageous hospitality. Dara proves that point, mum for weeks about what transpired, meanwhile flitting to California to escape all those she kept in the dark. Now this—artists running amok in Biba's hotel. But what a cool idea. Sounds original and like a winner. Charlotte thinks of the abused women's home she helps support in Chapel Hill. Oh! Maybe some of the women in the shelter would like jobs on the coast when The Palms reopens. She smiles. See, circles beget other circles. We saw John painting on the beach and now Dara is coming to Indigo.

A few days after Dara visited, the trip when she told Mimi about the canceled wedding, Charlotte ran into Biba at the Shrimp Shack. Biba told her she was determined to bounce back and get the inn running. Charlotte was intrigued; her generation, the one before, and those after, all have nostalgic memories of old Indigo, so many succeeding waves of people loving that place. And The Palms was its heart.

She met Biba on the veranda the next day and Charlotte got a tour. Other than a few dumpster hauls of mattresses and faded chintz chairs, the place needs a lot of rotting wood replaced, new heating and cooling. Kitchen updates. Shouldn't the knotty pine dining room with the mounted swordfish get about ten coats of white, with rattan chairs and potted ferns? Biba had solid plans. Charlotte offered help and Biba demurred, but when the financing complications became real, she called Charlotte and thanked her for the confidence and help.

Charlotte kicks off her shoes and walks out on the beach. The sky looks overcast, but no cool breeze lifts the muggy air. She runs down to the water and walks, sinking her toes into the soft sand. Privately, she is stunned at Dara's story. She'd guessed it was some infidelity, what else could it be, but could not have imagined the stern morality play of obsession being acted out. Dara is young and resilient, primed for a career in law, and everyone will say she'll be fine. Well, I hope so.

Charlotte will be contemplating and analyzing for weeks, from this angle and that. How much has been given up, how much lost? She tries to picture a squirming little baby in a crib—your eyes still unfocused, the ceiling a blur, and the face leaning down to pick you up, the face coming close, your father. And the young father—who can say what he is feeling?

27

WHAT WOULD I do without Annsley? She won't take the bed; she insists that she prefers the sofa. She's a brick. The first ten days have lasted a month. What I've learned is how attuned your ear becomes to the least sound of wakefulness, hunger, distress, and how utterly helpless a new human is. All he has is his loud cry. I guess in a mother those signs pull forth milk. I don't have any, but I have an endless rotation of bottles that must be just the right temperature, I suppose the temperature of the mother's milk. What is paramount: There is no mother. But Annsley has shuttered her bookshop. "Closed Temporarily" the sign says, implying a spring break somewhere warm, but this is light-years from any form of relaxation.

After so much time away, I'm going into work every morning. Then I bring home my work. Not much gets accomplished. I'm sleepwalking. Annsley naps in the afternoon, works on her correspondence. I take Hawthorn out for a neighborhood stroll, then we have a makeshift dinner. Hawthorn joins us in his infant seat. He is surprisingly here. I expected weeks of him in his own universe but no, he's a lively little lad, his head turning back and forth, as if he is following our conversation. He wakes up in the night but holding him in the dark while he slurps is quite nice. Peaceful. I take the night shift, but Annsley has been bathing him and putting him down. She winds up a musical bear and he falls asleep listening to "Hey, Jude, don't be afraid . . ."

Hawthorn has fallen asleep. We speak softly while we eat. What luck, the beef pie I picked up at Sainsbury is savory, with a nice crust. Annsley has tossed together a celery root remoulade. She is, I'm finding out, quite a good cook when pressed. "Hey, we make a good team." I pour her red wine and slice a loaf of bread. "I must say, this place is perfect. I haven't lived anywhere nearly this cool since I left Dad's eccentric manse. If Shelley had put her stamp on it, I don't think I could bear living here."

"I didn't know her, of course, but she had good taste. Ha! In men, as well. Or a man. Giving you this beautiful place plus a tremendous responsibility. Much to ponder in that equation. What does it equal?"

"Equals more than the sum of its parts. Those old maps you and Dad love, there's always a dragon creature in the choppy waters where the known world ends. That's where I am swimming."

It's been years since they have spent more than a couple of nights in the same house. After dinners and holidays at Michael's, she usually takes the train back to Cambridge. She and Michael share their passion for fine editions, first editions, letterpress, broadsides, the whole esoteric world of early prints and engravings. Their two bookstores maintain a clientele list that includes everyone from scholars and book lovers in the UK to Arab sheiks and coffee plantation owners in Brazil. Collections of eighteenth-century botanicals, Greek fragments, editions of Dante, medieval books of hours, original Bodoni typeface samples, and hundreds of other elusive items connect Michael and Annsley. When a query arrives, mad searches ensue. Those have occupied both of them to the exclusion of romantic partners. But Annsley seems to take to the maternal mission, Austin thinks. It's a pity if she does want a child and doesn't make room in her life for that to happen. "You seem to have a knack for this new adventure. Do you mind it, or have you just the natural instinct?"

Annsley considers. "I want to help. And I'm loving being with you. We were so close after Mama died, clinging to the same log in the raging river. Dad was half mad, but he perfectly embodies that Kazantzakis quote: 'To be English is to be all on fire but let out no smoke.' Then you went off to Canterbury, then I'm at uni, then you enrolled—we've just drifted. I'm finding my brother again, in weird circumstances, but I'll take it. I'm surprised—I'm quite enjoying Hawthorn. The innocence and dependence are overwhelming. As is his ability to produce a smell! To feel this needed . . . I'm not used to that. My clients need what they need but there's nothing primordial about that."

"Ever want to have a few wee bairns scuttling about the bookshelves?"

Annsley laughs. "Never. Did you?"

"I didn't get to choose, did I? But, yes, I assumed in good time we'd have a couple. We talked about making that decision someday. But I can see how miraculous, to create a human being out of love." He looks at Hawthorn. "Or even out of blind fate."

"I'm thirty-one, never met anyone who inspired me more than books do. That sounds pathetic but it's true."

"It's certainly not too late." Shelley was thirty-one.

"Yes, it is. I'm perfectly content."

"And Dad? He's never gone out with anyone since, as far as I know."

"Dad has us. And Boss, and a stack of books up to his knees by the fireplace. He's okay."

"He's at the shop all day with people. Maybe that's enough. But I would think going home alone would get old. Sorry, that was crude. You say you're happy and I believe you."

After dinner, Annsley changes into her bathrobe, a scruffy terry cloth thing she must have had since college. She finds an old movie on the telly. Soon after Austin sinks into the sofa with a sheaf of papers, he's out. Annsley sits cross-legged, watching Barbra Streisand and Robert Redford not figure each other out in *The Way We Were*. She mutters aloud, "And they think they have troubles . . ." She looks over at Austin, vulnerable in sleep, and young. She doesn't realize how attractive she is because Austin was always the one people noticed. Lips like on the preclassical statues. Cheekbones also finely honed. Head back and turned into the pillow, he still looks like the boy she looked after when their mother died. How bereft they were, all three of them, but Austin seemed the most damaged. Now this. Annsley senses that Austin makes a major effort to accept the child because he lost his own mother.

She unfolds from the soft sofa and walks over to the mirror. Hair swept up in an untidy coil, ugly scrunchie, pale, unruly eyebrows, uneven fingernails, and the ghastly bathrobe. Wouldn't hurt to get a trim, she thinks. Barbra is singing *has time rewritten every line . . . and we simply choose to forget*. Annsley wonders what Shelley looked like. Dara, met only once, seemed all glow and polish. A manicure, I think so. Everything's changing, I might as well, too. She didn't ever tell Austin about her senior-year crush on her Greek professor, married with four children. He'd walked her through the college rose garden, commenting on her Thucydides paper. It was nothing. Against the rules, he picked a dark red rose, tucked it behind her ear, and lifted her hair. His face came near, and she turned away. It was absolutely nothing. She's ashamed to remember that she still has the disintegrating red corpse between the yellowed pages of Thucydides's funeral oration. But that was it—all the classes, the blur of boys her own age, no one else. She heard after graduation, that Dr. Mitchell had divorced.

A thin wail from upstairs. Annsley lets Austin sleep. She warms the bottle and dashes to Hawthorn's room. He looks wide awake, as if he'd like to talk. She scoops him up and settles into the comfortable chair. "Would you like to hear a lullaby, sweetie?" He's guzzling away. Annsley rocks him slowly, singing her best version of "The Way We Were."

28

June 1995

It's all right if you grow your wings
on the way down.

—ROBERT BLY

JOHN HAS SHIPPED two large cartons of art supplies to his mom. Still, the two Hondas are jammed to the gills. He's driving his car with Abby. Silvie and Ben in the other. They've been through RISD together and bonded at the first freshman icebreaker social. Abby hopes that summer will give her a real relationship with John. Providence to Indigo: fourteen hours on the road. They'll overnight somewhere in Virginia (nine hours max for one day) and push on to South Carolina the next day. Biba has promised a low-country boil to celebrate their arrival. None of his friends ever has been to the South. Silvie is from Boston, Ben from up east in Portland, Abby from Duluth. They're slightly apprehensive, especially Silvie, who's Black, but John has joked, told them that Biba will protect them. "No one messes with Biba's guests," he explains. "She hires the best person for the job and treats everyone like her family—that is: work your tail off, party hard, and turn up on time. Not that this applies to you. You are the saviors, arriving with your talents to transform us." He didn't explain what a low-country boil is. After two days of gross fast food on the way, let them be stunned!

John has a letter in his back pocket. He is too astounded to talk about it to anyone. Abby was nominated, too, and hasn't mentioned hearing any result. He has been selected for a fellowship at the American Academy in Rome, beginning in the fall. When his mentor proposed nominating him, John thought sure, let's see how quickly that flops. Now he's going. Meanwhile, summer at Indigo and the excitement of friends working together, transforming the place he loves. Where he first knew he was always going to paint. Where his mother and sisters loved him to pieces and made sure he was given every bit of attention that a fatherless boy needed. Where the beauty of the coast and marshes seemed like an extension, somehow, of himself, that identification that the great southern writers call a sense of place, the concept of where you are is who you are. Never felt that in Providence, a nice enough town. But maybe . . . Who knows, maybe in Rome.

They're on the road by nine. Silvie tries to keep John's white Honda in sight, but he drives fast and she sticks to the speed limit.

❧

DARA BROUGHT HOME SUMMER CLOTHES FROM WASHINGTON BUT DEcides to pack only one medium bag for Indigo. Shorts and T-shirts, beach things, and a couple of sundresses and sandals. She lines the suitcase with the last two volumes of the thick Cazalet Chronicles, along with several novels Lee recommends. Her parents will be down to visit in a month. Dara predicts that Rich will join in the work. He's learned a lot from his time with Habitat for Humanity. Before that he always hit his finger when he drove in a nail. Lee will bring a trove of books.

Lee feels like she's sending Dara off to camp. She's packed a double recipe of brownies, sunscreen, Bug Off, and a brimmed hat Dara probably never will wear. Rich kind of wishes he were going. A hands-on project that will enhance one of his favorite places, feisty Biba giving the orders, a chance to sail with Bing. But he's got to go sweat it out in Thailand for two weeks, during which he hopes Lee gets a lot done on her last chapters. Four years of work. Enough of Yeats. Rich suspects he was a narcissist.

❧

BIBA'S CREW HAS ACCOMPLISHED MIRACLES IN THREE WEEKS. SHE'S sublimely happy to be back in her downstairs back room with its small private porch in the dunes. Best rooms are reserved for guests, but she likes this one, reached through the kitchen, for its privacy. She's not updating the décor here. The blue-and-white mattress ticking couch and the maple bed with a tree-of-life quilt are much to her liking.

Most of the cooling and heating work takes place in an outbuilding. The dining room remains in its original state, a disaster, but the cypress floors in the guest rooms have been refinished to a grayish white, a cooling color, and the walls painted soft cream—John's suggestion, so that they're blank canvases for the artists. Charlotte Mann, her fairy godmother, offered to help with furniture choices and trips up to the manufacturers in High Point. Everyone pitching in. Joy and Bee, Biba's girls, are still in Charleston. Bee, a ceramicist, is working on dinner plates for the inn, which Biba finds ridiculous because of the rate of breakage. But Bee wants designs of the local sea creatures painted on each, and, she insists, John's not the only artist in the family. She has her template for crab, flounder, lobster, crayfish, shrimp. Skip the alligator. Joy will come for weekends with her husband, Carlo, but right now she works five days as a nurse practitioner. Hope we don't need her services.

Biba sees meal preparation as the biggest obstacle she faces. Divide into teams of three, she decides, and take turns shopping and cooking dinner. Tacos, spaghetti, grilled corn, okra and rice, tomato sandwiches, hamburgers, all that. Watermelon for dessert. Next, I will make my chicken bog. Wonder if anyone bakes. Tomorrow, we feast. These kids will be starving. How pretty that Dara Willcox turned out to be, at least she is in John's portrait of her. Shame her wedding was canceled. Charlotte was vague, and Dara certainly doesn't seem like a girl someone would bail on. Poised and smart.

Oh, but, she muses, neither was I the sort to abandon, but he did. Funny, I hardly think of Aaron Harrison anymore. His exit when John was one, no, fourteen months, defined my life in every way possible. And why, I never knew. We were happy. But obviously we were not. Jerk.

29

EVERYONE ARRIVES AT ONCE. The four artists, looking as if they need showers, then Dara. Biba points John to his childhood space at the end of the stairway, the three others to ocean-view rooms. Dara to an end room with views of the ocean on two sides. They disappear to wash away the freeway ordeal and unpack. Dara checks her phone but there are no messages. She looks in the mirror above the scuffed maple chest. Who's this? she thinks. Is this a step back or a step forward?

Biba has shopped and prepped all day. Low-country boil is her culinary crown of glory. Simple, really, just cook everything you like in a big kettle of seasoned boiling water. The trick is the orchestration—the potatoes go in first, and before they're done, add the sliced onions and sausage. When they're just right, the shrimp and corn. Crabs and crawfish, too, if you have them. Ladle everything out onto butcher paper (never newspaper) in the middle of the table. Pour melted butter with lemon juice over and invite everyone to dig in. She's sure these artists have never tasted anything like it.

Everyone gathers on the veranda and John pours. Beer and wine, iced tea for no one. The pitcher sits sweating at the end of the serving table. On an outdoor burner, Biba's elixir bubbles—he wonders if she shucked all that corn. Dara knows the drill—pile your plate—but the others dip into the savory pile over and over, awestruck. Silvie holds up a crawfish. "Is this a cicada?"

Biba passes dishes of crackers with pimiento cheese and brings out a skillet of fried okra. She retires to a wooden lounge chair, awaiting service of copious refills of white wine. Thankfully, she's hired a local woman to help serve and clean up.

At seventeen, Dara didn't particularly notice Biba's age. Now she sees that Biba still looks young. She's slim, lightly freckled, with a wide smile and short bronzy hair brushed back on the sides. Tonight, she's wearing a pink linen shirt with the collar turned up, white pants, and striped espadrilles. She must have had her children when she was quite young; she can't be more than fifty, fifty-five tops. Dara jumps up and helps pass the cornbread.

Dara likes John's friends. They seem properly goofy and spontaneous. Obviously, they're talented or John wouldn't have hauled them down here. Not that long since she was a senior, but university is a rite of passage, and after graduation, Dara experienced a sadness. "Of course you're sad," Lee had said. "You spend your teens looking toward college, building it up in your mind as a utopia. Then it passes so quickly—and possibly without the big reveal of who you are to be."

Dara remembered the finality of leaving the ceremony, proud of her honors but with the stark sense: That was then. The artist friends are at that portal. Maybe this summer will lead them, all of us, to something unexpected.

In the morning, Biba calls a meeting. Everyone brings their coffee mugs out on the veranda. She welcomes each person by name, then outlines the scope of the decorative work, hands out schedules of dinner rotation, explains the other projects in progress by contractors, and briefly tells the history of Indigo since it was settled. After, she takes them on tour. "Claim what rooms you want to work on besides the one you're in. Have you talked about any ways to keep it cohesive, subject matter or color palette?"

John speaks up. "Everybody's got ideas, but don't settle too quickly until you get to know the place. I'm thinking we should wait till the end for the lobby and restaurant so they can bring the whole project together. Since we're on a limited time frame, we might think of keeping most of the designs simple, even repeating the best ones in several rooms. We've all done research so let's share some initial plans. I've mentioned the local vernacular in subject and color. Let's see where we can go with that. Dara, I'm hoping you can be the overseer, help with lists we'll keep for needed supplies, et cetera. Of course, you might want to try your hand with a room or two."

"Happy to do all that. I might pick up a brush, even if it's only to make wide yellow stripes, or a border of stylized waves. I can't wait to see this place transformed. Another thing I can do is make lunch. You geniuses shouldn't have to. Believe me, it will be simple." She toasts them with her mug. "This morning feels momentous!"

"Anyone have comments?" Biba is passing the coffeepot.

"You threw out wide stripes, Dara. I think that's cool. Maybe especially in the bathrooms. They could be vertical or horizonal. Cantaloupe and cream, blue and white."

Silvie says, "I'm dying to do an oversize white flower on one wall, then keep the fabrics very simple. Outline the flower subtly so that it seems barely there. Poetic, elegant."

Biba laughs, recalling raucous two-year-old guests bouncing on the bed.

Dara closes her eyes—the junior-year semester in Italy, hot, hot trip to Pompeii, where almost all the walls had been decoratively painted, the gardens outside re-created inside, plants and birds so precise that they are identifiable. "Let's bring the flora and fauna in, the colors of the sea and sky, I'm seeing these rooms lavished with moss-draped cypresses, waving sea oats, sculpted-by-the-wind pines."

Ben adds, "Agree. This landscape is new to me, but after less than a day here, I'm tuning in to its power. The designs we've mentioned, the stripes and borders are simple compared with what Dara's talking about. The figurative designs must be awfully good. Otherwise, kitsch sets in."

A discussion ensues about figurative and abstract approaches, Silvie pointing out that the oversized white flower, for example, is abstracted by its size. Abby joking, "Ribbons and wreaths, swags and branches of twiggy blossoms are officially banned."

John moves to the low wall where Dara is sitting. "How's this going for you? I am beyond happy that you came." She looks not that different than she did at seventeen, thinner maybe, her face more defined, same luminous skin. Odd, at fourteen, he'd been startled every time he saw her, as if suddenly awakened by a noise. When he ran into her at the coffee shop in April, he had the same reaction. By then, he hadn't seen her in years. He hoped she couldn't tell that she flummoxed him. Ben notices. At dinner, when Dara is listening intently to something Abby is saying, John is watching her. The way she cocks her chin at an angle before she laughs, the way she slowly looks down then up before speaking. Ben leans over and elbows him in the ribs. "Got a little something going for Dara?"

❧

DARA HALF-TURNED, LOOKING TOWARD THE LAYERS OF BLUE AND INdigo ocean. "I'm glad you invited me. This hotel is going to hit every travel magazine in the country. I feel like we've all landed at some combined art seminar and dream adult camp. Soon we'll be toasting marshmallows! We need to catch up, but basically I am doing well most of the time. Some explosive things have happened. Things completely out of my control. I've always been in charge of my life and expected to be. It's a time to learn and relearn things I thought I knew. Have you ever experienced your life going completely out of your hands?"

"That's intriguing. Let's talk. Can you take a walk on the beach? I think Biba is cooking again before she lets us loose in her kitchen. When my dad left, I was only one, so I didn't know my little life had imploded. Biba, though, she's told me how she had to reinvent herself. With the three of us, that was huge."

"Exactly. And she did it. She is a warrior. A sweet one. Have you always called her Biba?"

"Sure. Her name's Barbara, you know. I think I was three when she told me 'Mama' was reductive."

They leave their shoes at the top of the dune and run down to the water's edge. Far out, the boats look like floating beetles. A sailboat tacks toward Myrtle Beach, and Dara wonders if Mimi and Bing are aboard. "When last seen," John begins, "you were in limbo and your fiancé was in hell."

Dara can laugh. "The plot went haywire, John. Strange as it may seem to you, I told no one else what was going on. My parents, Mimi, and my best friends were in the dark, and hurt, I'm sure, that I didn't confide the reasons that I was a runner from the wedding. It's made me think about why we hold on to secrets. One secret covers over another. Or, as in this sequence of crazy events, keeping a secret makes the next event even more extreme. I was withholding from everyone I love most the secret of Austin's betrayal and the secret behind that of the woman's duplicity and her mental issues."

"I think I'm following."

"When I ran into you, I was unable to keep it locked inside my body any longer. I spilled out to you, innocent bystander! But, John, what happened is light-years worse than the situation that day. Then, there were possible solutions. She'd go back to India, and Austin could be responsible. Maybe she'd marry someone else. Other possibilities. But, John, she died as the baby was born. Bled uncontrollably while Austin and her mother watched from the waiting room."

"That's unreal. Bloodcurdling—oh, no, sorry, terrible word. And the child?"

"Fine. Healthy. I'll spare you the entire saga. Short version: The mother couldn't take on raising her daughter's out-of-the-blue baby. The girl, woman I should say, left Austin an apartment in London for a year, and some money. He is now a single daddy, and I am on Indigo reviving a hotel. End of story."

"Seems like closure?"

"It does. Doesn't feel like closure is possible but I guess it is. Biba must have waited for your dad to just reappear and things to right themselves."

"For over a year. One day she picked herself up and sold everything. Took all they had in the bank, the money from the house sale, and bought this place." He gestures toward the inn in the dunes, the sun spangling behind the roof. "No doubt you'll do something equally mad." John laughs and throws his arm around Dara, squeezing her close and inhaling the warm sun scent of her hair.

"Where's he now, your father? Did you ever look for him?"

"No trace. Maybe he's the island's Gray Man. I had fantasies for years that he would check in as a guest, not knowing we ran the place."

"But do you feel that someday you'll meet him?" Dara can't think that she won't see Austin ever again.

"Yeah, he'll arrive in a tux to my first show at the Museum of Modern Art!" John runs out knee-deep into the shallow waves, bending to pick up a scallop shell. "I wonder for how many there is that one who got away." Austin is gone, he thinks, and she's fragile as a newborn bird. Must feel like a cameo role in someone else's drama. He hands Dara the shell. "These shells are symbols of those who take the pilgrimage walk in Spain, the long walk to Compostela, where the remains of Saint James have been drawing people since the ninth century. Also, you know *The Birth of Venus*—she's riding the waters on a scallop shell—early surfer. But I like it that the pilgrims identified themselves this way. You should have a symbol. Showing you're on a quest. What would it be?"

"I'll have to think about that. A battered, skinny palm? A scrambled egg, a flattened Coke can?" Right now, she's thinking about how attractive John is. How if her wings were not scorched, she might fly near. "Dad wrote this article about the Alaska spill. In my own little world, I'm one of those gulls with oil-soaked wings. Sorry, poor me!"

"You can't help but feel humiliated, and that's not your line of work."

"It will get easier, I tell myself. It will. I'm deciding soon about law school, and Georgetown is looking best. Wonder why, suddenly, New York has lost its appeal? Big Mann's work was mainly in voting rights and housing—two basics that draw me, too. I'm finding this project at The Palms reminding me of his drive not only for urban construction but for building places that will mean something. I want to, I can, throw myself into projects." She stops and looks at John. At that moment, Dara makes a decision. Georgetown, yes. To go to Stanford, she'd have to wait to apply and delay by a year. Not worth it, when DC is where hands-on impact is made. But California. Maybe someday.

"I like the idea of quest as a way forward. I'm going to be on one this fall. Dara, I haven't even told Biba yet. Through some latter-day miracle, I've been invited to the American Academy in Rome."

"Huh! That is beyond fabulous. Have you been to Rome? What a huge honor! I'm thrilled, thrilled for you." She kisses him on both cheeks.

"Never. I've never been farther than New York."

"Well, look who's riding the scallop shell! You'll whoosh up into heaven like the Virgin in all those paintings."

30

Jade McCracken came into Austin's life like a winged creature alighting on earth. The first and second nannies the posh agency sent were harrowing. The first lasted two days. Austin came home to a messy kitchen, the stove crusty with boiled-over formula, a red-faced Hawthorn, and a wet towel. Nanny had obviously taken a shower. At the end of work on the second day, he found cigarette butts in a coffee cup on the windowsill. Not only was she slovenly, he thought, she didn't have the sense to cover her lapses. That was more alarming than the crusty burner or the towel thrown over the shower door.

The agency wasn't apologetic. The secretary seemed to blame him somehow, but since they "weren't a proper match," someone else was sent the next day. She looked promising, broad-faced and smiling. Hawthorn seemed content in her arms and Austin went off to work. He popped back at lunch to check, and all seemed well. Hawthorn was lying in his infant seat surrounded by bears, a musical clown nestled close. Nanny sat on the floor beside him, watching a cooking show on the telly. Austin went back to work feeling relief. She seemed to be doing what a mother might.

When he came home, she was waiting by the door. "He's sleeping. I need to go. See you on Monday." And she was gone. When Austin opened the fridge, he noticed that the wine bottle he opened last night was in a different place. He poured himself a glass. Watery. He poured the remains down the sink and sat at the table, running his fingers through his hair.

Nanny 2 is fired. Why would anyone risk a job for a couple of glasses of mediocre wine?

Annsley now comes down for Sundays. While she's there, he catches up at work—the office is quiet, phones silent. On Saturdays he can stay home. Out strolling with the baby in the late Saturday afternoon, he stopped at a coffee bar. With Hawthorn bound in his snuggly, he ordered a pastry and his coffee to go, planning to walk to Russell Square and sit on a bench. On his way out, he stopped at the message board, glancing at the notices. One read:

SCOTTISH GIRL NEEDS A FULL-TIME POSITION. CHILD CARE OR ELDERLY. TAKING GAP YEAR. CAN START IMMEDIATELY. DEPENDABLE. REFERENCES.

He tore off her number and slipped it into his pocket.

Annsley arrives Saturday night for her Sunday with Hawthorn. Austin notices that she's had that everlasting ponytail cut off. A chic short cut emphasizes her great cheekbones and the delicate arches of her groomed eyebrows. Michael brings over ingredients for pasta with three cheeses. "Who's this glamour girl?" He parks the grocery bags on the counter.

"I thought it was time for a change." She had felt humiliated having her eyebrows shaped and tinted but liked the result. While Annsley grills sausages and Austin tosses a green salad, he relates the week's nanny ordeal. He feels for the thousandth time his inadequacy, not to mention the constant burying of his unwillingness, which is at this point forever moot. No offense, little guy. I just was not ready for you.

After years of laser focus on becoming an architect, obtaining a position, and scrambling to succeed in the job, Austin enjoys the easy pleasure of being with his dad, sister, and, yes, unexpected, unwanted, unknown son. The thoughtfully furnished flat begins to feel comfortable. Michael must be happy to have Austin's room cleared out. Finally, college term papers and exams, worn textbooks, and old clothes have been tossed. He's moved his books, a watercolor his mother painted of their back garden, the plaster reproduction of Hermes he brought home from Greece when he was sixteen, and his lacrosse ribbons from high school and uni, though he stuffs them in the back of a drawer. His studio in New York never was personal. He hardly noticed it, geared only to designs on paper and the overwhelming newness of New York the whole time he was there.

Annsley brought over a potted orchid that he has managed not to kill. He's not minding giving things a dusting and running the vacuum around—but only when Hawthorn is at the park with Annsley; he starts to wail immediately when it's turned on.

Tonight, Hawthorn sucks his fist at the table, looking at, it seems, his nose. They marvel at his tiny shrimpy ears and long fingers. Austin fleetingly thinks of Fiona back in India. He likes her and hopes that she comes back to spend time with Hawthorn. One of the many surprises; he'd never expected to bond with Shelley's mother. Michael spears a sausage onto Austin's plate. "Eat. You need protein. You need to keep up your strength." He thinks Austin has lost weight, at least a stone.

"I could get the mad cow disease that's spreading everywhere. What I need is a glass of that red; please pass."

"This sausage is from a proper pig." Annsley gets up, comes around the table, pours the wine, and kisses her brother's forehead. They talk about O. J. Simpson on trial for offing his wife. A dropped glove is in evidence. "Probably planted," Michael says. "A good mystery writer wouldn't use that clue. Too obvious."

They move on to the latest government sex scandals and how long the American astronaut stayed in space. Eighty-four days. Floating in space. Austin feels a weird kinship. Notable: They no longer discuss the injustice, the levels of betrayal, the death and erasure of Shelley.

In the new, they're finding fresh ground. In the casual day-to-day conversation about faraway events, the activities of the bookstores, they're grounding themselves on this unfamiliar terrain.

No dessert. Michael rises and embraces his two children. "I must say this turn of circumstance has a serendipitous side. I haven't seen the two of you this much in years. I hadn't realized that I've been lonely. The shop is consuming, never enough time. I enjoy my evenings. But this is a major pleasure at the weekends." He pats Hawthorn on the head. "I quite fancy this young mate. Certainly made a cheeky entrance into our insular world."

Jade McCracken arrives for the interview on Sunday at teatime. If Annsley hoped for a ditzy Mary Poppins, she did not get her wish. If Austin hoped for a strapping dynamo, neither did he. They got Jade. She stands at the door with a dripping umbrella, which she shakes onto the walkway and props beside the door. With copper ringlets, freckles, a round face, round brown eyes, and pursed lips, she looks as if she's walked straight from a bucolic farm. Her smile reveals a gap between her front teeth. "I'm Jade," she says forthrightly, holding out her damp hand. Her print dress reaches to her ankles, skimming the top of large orange trainers. She shakes their hands and walks straight to Hawthorn, lying on his blanket and pillows in the living room. "Hello, pet. What's your name?" She sits down on the floor, hoisting her dress away from her shoes. "Thank you for calling me. What can I tell you about myself?" A take-charge girl. She hands Austin an envelope. "Please call my references—my teachers. I haven't worked yet, except at home and there was plenty to do there. I'm nineteen last March. You'll find that I am truly good." Her Glaswegian accent, soft and clipped, sounds soothing.

"So, I'm taking a year out to explore what I want to study. Maybe I want to be a singer. Maybe I'm too shy for that. Maybe a teacher, or work in the travel industry. I just don't know. I like kids and I have three younger brothers I helped raise from the time I was four. They're right lads." She tells them that she came down from Glasgow and lives with her father's sister in the Islington district.

Over scones and tea, Annsley and Austin both find Jade down to earth; in fact, blunt. She has questions of her own and cocks her head and narrows her eyes when she learns that Annsley is the aunt and Austin is a single dad. He explains that Hawthorn's mother died in childbirth. Jade says simply, "I can't even imagine." They talk about hours and salary. She seems pleased, and Austin silently thanks Shelley for leaving the yearly support. Otherwise, he would be living with his dad or in a cramped apartment, certainly nowhere near work.

"Is there any way you can start tomorrow?"

"I was hoping to."

"Okay! Thank you. That's super. I'll call your references because I should, but I think this is going to work out fine."

"I'll be the best. I promise."

Austin picks up Hawthorn. "Hey, buddy, this is Jade. She's going to take care of you when I go to work. Let's show her where you sleep and eat."

As they tour the flat, Austin explains the formula and laundry and where the supplies are. She opens kitchen drawers, peers in the loo, looks out back, delighted at the garden space. "I really like being here. Mr. Hawthorn and I will have a ball."

"I'll see you in the morning. Anything special you fancy for lunches?"

"I eat anything. Not at all picky. Wait, I don't eat rabbit. Peter Rabbit, you know."

"Easy enough to avoid. I'll give you our work phone numbers tomorrow. I'm nearby and can dash home if you need me." Home, he said.

Annsley walks her to the door. "Don't forget your umbrella."

"I would never forget my umbrella." She waves goodbye. The rain has stopped and sunlight through the trees gives the air a watery transparency. Annsley watches as Jade walks away. She starts to skip.

31

August 1995

Most of the major construction work on The Palms finishes in early August, although the kitchen work, new elevator, window repairs, and ten thousand other maintenance issues will run on into the fall. Biba hopes for a holiday opening. She's envisioning all the tables in the dining room set end to end, with pink poinsettias down the center—and a grand celebratory feast. She dreads surprise delays and racing even for a spring opening.

The biggest visual transformation came when the exterior changed from weathered wood to white with shutters of sea green. For the porch that runs the length of the hotel, Mei made cushions for the refurbished white wicker chairs and the long banquette. She sewed them from painters' canvas drop cloths and embroidered a palm tree on each one. She even taught Dara the easy stitches for the trunks, though Dara has a hard time sitting still for long. The biggest physical transformation was in mid-July when the air-conditioning installation was completed. In the bedrooms where they worked, when the heat reached easily into the nineties, they had felt they were wading through the humidity. Suddenly, the artists were comfortable. The men working outside doused themselves in the outdoor shower and drank gallons of water and iced tea. From 12 to 1:30, they lounged under umbrellas, avoiding going back into the bright reflections from the paint and the muggy, suffocating air. Everyone cheered when the last lick of paint went on. Biba passed around cold beers. Maybe only Dara noticed that Biba favored Ethan, the boss of the construction crew. After he made his inspections, he sat with Biba in the kitchen, and Dara, passing through, sensed a connection. There was a pile of bills between them but there was electricity, too.

Dara loves the project, especially after working on stacks of Big Mann's closely written papers and in the bureaucracy-embroiled HUD office, where much seems one step forward and two back. They all feel both empowered and that they're at the coolest possible camp for grown-ups. Not that they always behave as grown-ups. Frisbee, card games, body surfing, pitchers of mojito, sunburn, late-night confessional talks, oversleeping—but sustained exuberant work, spiraling ideas at the lunch table, praise for a new idea. Only Abby seems . . . not crabby but sometimes aloof.

Every sunny, light-filled room is unique. There's the work, then all the ideas around the work—art connections, books, speculation. A few tantrums, quickly dissolved. Biba constantly encouraging and admiring. When Abby asked Mei if Dara was interested in John, she told her that Dara is a long way from being over Austin. John is like someone possessed with his projects. Obsession runs in the family. John's sister Bee, back in Charleston, has worked on her dinner plates all summer. They're painted with bold fish designs. Everyone pretends to like them but privately even Biba finds them garish. Joy and Carlo both roll their eyes when she displays the new ones, but no one is blunt enough to say, *tone it down*. Joy just wants to enjoy the beach after long shifts at the hospital, but when they come for weekends, she and Carlo love to take over the cooking. On the new grill Carlo bought to replace Biba's rusted one, he turns out dozens of ears of nicely charred corn, mahi-mahi, and skewers of shrimp.

Each of the four geniuses, as Dara calls them, deserve all the accolades they're going to be getting from the newspapers and magazines who've visited and interviewed all of them. Moira, growing big with child, stayed overnight and wrote a proposal that landed her an article for *Southern Living,* scheduled to come out in April, perfect timing for spring and summer reservations.

Dara did paint her simple wide stripes in her space, the peaches-and-cream room. After that, she finds lobby furniture and accessories, down to the water glasses for the bathrooms and hangers for the closets. One of Mimi's former patients owns a High Point furniture company and, forever grateful to Mimi for getting his marriage back on track, he lets Dara and Mimi roam his warehouse of overstock, remainders, and accessories used in staging the annual Furniture Mart. Great finds! Tall glass vases, baskets, candlesticks, and fabric table runners, as well as a round coffee table, matching rose linen sofas, two peacock chairs, and rattan desks to go under the windows in the lobby. Biba can't believe their luck; she'd expected the lobby to be a major expense, but this benefactor has given a deep discount. Dara always left any décor decisions up to Lee and Mimi. Now she can't wait to design her own spaces and continue this conversation she's started with empty rooms. One of her touches: In a dusty corner of the warehouse, she spots a large easel, meant to display a signboard or wall décor at the Mart. It's now at the entrance to the dining room, holding one of John's marsh landscapes. She envisions it always holding something beautiful. She and Mimi haul in palms in white pots, also a bargain at the end of summer. The lobby now draws them on rainy days, everyone researching design motifs, writing in journals, sketching, sipping tea. No one minds if feet are up on the coffee table.

The others' rooms are more elaborated than Dara's stripes. Abby's are the most charming. She sprinkles the walls with wildflowers—chicory, morning glories, buttercups, vines. She's not remote at all when everyone lavishes praise on her designs. Dara senses that Abby is in love with John. Her antenna is sensitive enough to see that John practically jumps up when she comes near, that he stands close to her, but that he's all too aware of her runaway bride story and won't make a move unless she invites one. Which she won't.

Silvie's walls are also floral but hers are widely focused single blooms or fern fronds blown up large on one wall, the rest of the room painted a lighter, faded color of the flower. Ben's designs are the most dramatic. He installed wainscoting and above the paneling, painted lozenges, diamonds, geometric optical illusions in various fresco colors. His inspiration came from the marble tile designs of floors in European cathedrals. The walls below the wainscoting echo one of the fresco colors.

John's rooms are Dara's favorites. Subtle murals of the marshes and dunes over the beds, a corner room painted with squares like paint samples of every shade of blue tacked on a sand background. In one, a love poem running around the middle of the walls, and another room he wallpapered with the pages of an old book of Biba's with yellowed pages and Gothic type. He's taken on eight, but of those, one is left creamy white with no distractions. This he kept bare for a residency of an artist or writer. He was elated when he asked Biba about an artist-in-residence, and she twirled in a little dance. She pointed out that on old southern farms, there was always a rustic room outside, "for the stranger," maybe just a corner of a shed, or space just beyond the chute into the basement. But she adds, "Of course, we can rent it when there's no artist."

Because of costs, the stolid wooden tables and chairs in the dining room have simply been given a few coats of matte white paint, the walls the same faded sage as the outdoor shutters. One wall of windows faces the ocean. On the other walls are grouped trompe l'oeil paintings, reproducing the botanical illustrations in William Bartram's books. Each image is identically painted inside a gold surround like a simple frame.

Flipping through Biba's battered old copy of *Bartram's Travels* one night, Silvie came up with the idea. From the start, John wanted the downstairs to reflect the spirit of the place, the beauty of the powerful landscape of the South. Everyone agreed. They decided on groups of six re-creations of flora and fauna copied from Bartram's drawings, with the identification calligraphed beneath, just as Bartram did when he wandered the Southeast in the eighteenth century.

Each of the three artists has taken a wall. John works the window wall that connects to the lobby. He has a broken space around the door, but he continues the Bartram scheme—a fantasy mural of native trees. Ben took the birds—owl, purple martin, crested heron, purple finch, ruby-throated hummingbird, and wild swan. Abby focused on fauna: tortoise, several charming snails, a great bat, alligators, and rattlesnakes. Silvie has done all the calligraphy and the flora. She frequently calls out "I'm the luckiest!" as she lavishes her care on Bartram's delicate swamp canna, evening primrose, gentian, oakleaf hydrangea, and *Franklinia alatamaha,* a delicate white flower with a tufted gold center.

When Biba walks through, she's ecstatic, having never imagined her Palms could look this exquisite. John sees her passing through with the contractor, their heads close. Could they be having an affair? He mentions it to Dara. "Thought you'd never notice." She laughed.

Everyone can't wait till the last night, when six of them, Charlotte and Bing, and John's sisters and Carlo, will have their final supper in the finished room. They all know it's a hit. Everyone has swooned over the serene and elegant dining room, and it has been the easiest to accomplish. Just takes a good idea. And talent. And rising early for the light, wandering in at midnight to marvel.

Dara thinks no one here this summer ever will forget the joy of creating together something so lyrical and exhilarating. The synergy among them purely sparked. Abby is super talented and doesn't know it. She's blown back by not getting the Rome fellowship, but she'll shine in grad school at RISD. Ben has a way of seeming steady and sensible, like no one is going to knock him off his perch. That's enforced when you see the beautiful control he has over color and design. Silvie is all strong whimsey, her lyrical touch probably produced the rooms that guests will like best. Everywhere at once, John is enthusiastic for everyone's work. In addition to juggling the inn project, he's trying to put together his own outline of what he hopes to accomplish in Rome. Shifting focus seems surreal—from Indigo to ancient Rome. Biba soon will be alone. Maybe her budding romance will flourish. Once the artists depart, the nitty-gritty restoration work will continue, with the soft opening planned for December, but perhaps more realistically, March.

Although Dara was not holding a paintbrush, she felt involved with every accomplishment. Her own work with furnishings makes a huge impact, and her bringing in Mei, who roped her into some embroidery, added that special artisan touch to the simple curtains in every room.

For Mei, the project changed her. She's always working independently, taking inspiration from history and art. She bonded right away with Abby, who became more interested in fabrics at the same time. Now Mei is eager to collaborate with Abby, even if it takes her outside her beloved studio. She confides, here at the end of August, to Dara about Luke. They've seen each other over the summer, and Mei has been to Sarasota, which she did not expect to like. "The light is brighter there," she tells Dara as they slide the linen curtain onto the rod. "I was too embarrassed to use an umbrella among all those tanned, shiny people. Luke seems as at home on the Gulf as on land. As native as an alligator! He missed home when he was at Cambridge. I'm not sure what future we could have, unless I were willing to leave. He'd pine away in North Carolina."

"Well, the coast is only two hours away. He could keep a boat. He could start his own firm." Dara is never without solutions, except for herself.

"Let's just slow down. You're always ready to leap and I'm always making lists of pro and con."

"Oh, just follow your instincts—does he set your body on fire," she jokes.

Dara is shocked that Mei is already moving in such a serious direction. How odd that a romance sprang from the dinner at Redbud. And Moira has told her she thinks that was the night she got pregnant.

Dara remembers seeing Austin alone out on the terrace, very late, and sensing that something was possibly amiss.

Mei is balancing on a ladder, trying to hook on to the rod. "Con: But it's colder here. In Florida, he's out all year. Pro: He's smart. He gets me. Oh, we shall see. I've only known him four months. Let's go to the rest of the rooms." She has a pile of the panels stacked on the bed, each one's decoration inspired by the way the artist has painted the room.

She's been with Luke barely three months, Dara thinks. When I knew Austin for three months, I was shouting from the rooftops: Forever. "Let's finish here and hang my window. I love the cantaloupe stripes and can't wait to see what you've done with the linen. I wish I could keep the room forever." His laugh thrilled me. His beauty that turns heads, yes, but the laugh! I wanted to know every centimeter of his body. I did.

For Dara's room, Mei has embroidered a trailing vine of moonflowers down each panel, very quiet but recalling a memory of summer nights at home when they were young and stealing watermelons at night along country roads. The fences they climbed were draped in the white blooms that, strangely, opened in the deep evening light and shone in the moonlight.

"Mei, how magical. Now I really don't want anyone renting my room!"

"Abby says the same. I think all the rooms have become personal to the artist."

All summer, anytime Dara starts to take a dive into her problems, someone is there to distract her. John, even in his obsession with painting, is always attentive. He's waiting for something, it's palpable. She's not there for him romantically, though she thinks she could be if she didn't feel like a package dropped off a speeding truck.

John is aware that Abby might feel awkward—sex a couple of times after studio parties at the end of the term—but he's never misled her or led her at all. He'd probably have fallen in with her over the summer but with Dara around, even though she has this untouchable aura around her, she seems to block out his interest in anyone else.

Charlotte drops by often, always bringing a cake or buns or a few bottles of wine. She's watchful, too, relieved to see Dara so busy she hardly has time to brood. It's only been four months but to the young four months is long. Rich and Lee came down to Charlotte's twice and the family gathered for dinners. Dara is charmed by Bing—how suave and fun he is—who returns the admiration, calling her Miss Peaches. Sunday sails on his boat and dinner at Mimi's Banana Republic are great breaks in the action for the artists. On blustery days, Bing raises the big genoa, and the giant sail puffs out, sending them skidding along the water.

When Lee and Rich see the rooms, their enthusiasm thrills Biba and the artists. Rich hauls in boxes of books from his trunk. "Hardly made a dent in our library," he says. "Glad to bring more." It's hard for Lee to part with books.

Meanwhile, Lee rummages through a stack and takes two back. "I'll bring these next time. I've never read them." She is already thinking of driving down for weekends, staying here rather than on her mother's sofa. She loves the room John papered with the pages of *Middlemarch*. She'll have to bring a copy of the novel for the bedside table. Poor, brave Dorothea, she thinks. Not a great marriage, not at all.

Dara wants a special object for every room. This one papered in yellowed pages has a taxidermy owl. Lee finds this spooky, but otherwise what a perfect place to read. Rich agrees. He's already set up on the porch with his portable computer, trying to concentrate on pollution in Thailand. Lee feels buoyant; her book is in the last throes and she sees the end. Next semester, she'll be eligible for sabbatical, and she and Rich, always inundated by research, are planning a sentimental trip to Ireland, kind of a farewell to Yeats.

Over several beach walks Dara has told the artists and Biba the brief outline of her miscarried marriage. Reactions ranged from Abby's "He was so out of line," to Ben's "Almost happened to me right out of high school. She didn't want me to leave for college. It was a horror show for two months, then she miscarried. Changed sex for me forever. Man, it's fraught, unless you're married." Laughs. "Maybe even then." Biba: "You walked through a field of land mines." Silvie: "I probably would have married him anyway and not known what hit me. Imagine suddenly being mom to someone else's kid." Silvie shook her head and hugged Dara hard.

Dara is buoyed by their support, and their astonishment at the turn of events. As it should, sympathy veers toward Shelley, with the collateral damage fully acknowledged. Now that the news is out to everyone, Dara experiences huge relief; the trauma directs outward, what next, what now, instead of churning in her guts. Lying in bed before falling asleep, she's able to remember joy with Austin, and not to dwell on images of him at Shelley's place, drunk and dumb, or on images she only imagines—him looking through a small window at the bloodbath that took a life and gave one. She reads late, often until the book falls to the floor and she jerks awake.

The inn seems to sleep, Dara muses, no noise except the billow, roll, swell, and fall of waves. She lets herself relive the best times with Austin, the afternoon at Willowbend, the beach at Ocracoke, chopping vegetables together, with Rachmaninoff turned up loud, in bed at Austin's studio, after making love. Eyes closed, she meanders over the long Saturday afternoons, thinking, I loved playing on his body—tickling the inside of his ear with my tongue, nuzzling my head under his arm, tapping his knees to test his reflexes, propping his penis upright, and inventing stories about a Frenchman named Pierre. Crazy with love. How Austin laughed. His big laugh. "Be quiet," I said, "I'm writing *I love you* on your back with my breath. Over and over." There were stories about each toe, and marches with two fingers up his spine. His collarbone with the bump, where it was broken in a punting accident. His incredible legs, smooth as satinwood. How he raised them, with my pelvis on his feet, lifting me, arms out as if to fly. Ensconced among pillows, sipping wine, he would say, "Tell me something you've never told me before." Then again the falling, over and over, into each other, two bodies, wet clay spinning, thumbs molding the curves, when the knife strikes open the apple and five seeds tumble out, when the plane nose plunges down into clouds, pulls sharply up into blue, when the silence goes fathoms deep where a gold coin shines in the sand and you dive and dive, a tilt, a whirl, stopped on top of the Ferris wheel, chair swinging, how the radiant bodies scatter, a meteor shower. Those times, she thinks, those hours on one side of the balance scale will outweigh anything counter that ever comes my way. Then she falls asleep.

Through the sequence of Austin to Amit to Luke to Mei to her, she knows that he employs a nanny, his sister helps on weekends, he is working full-time. She can picture him in Bloomsbury. During a trip to England when she was twelve, Lee took her on a search for the house where a blue plaque identified where William Butler Yeats once lived. Austin must live on one of those streets lined with dignified row houses. White with black trim? Dark red brick? Dara would like to hover over the scene of Austin's flat. Beyond the few sentences from Mei, she knows only that new babies cry during the night. Moira was a wreck when her twins were born. She imagines him leaping from bed, dazed with sleep, tending to a yowling infant. The picture is too far from how she knows him to have reality; it's as if he would try to imagine her piloting a spacecraft, opening a door and stepping out on the moon.

Who he is in this foreign circumstance makes her realize how much we know of the person we love and how little we know their capacity to change. Flip side, she thinks, he might be puzzled that she has spent these last months painting walls, embroidering crabs on pillows, grilling burgers, body surfing, and loving campfire closeness with new friends.

The grapevine goes the other way, too, from Mei to Luke to Amit to Austin. Maybe he pictures everything. Dara on a ladder, paint on her forehead. Speeding back from High Point, her car loaded with pendant lamps, cachepots, and decorative finds for the rooms—an old globe, a ship in a bottle, some frames that can be used for mirrors. Dara on her sunrise walk, writing words in sand at low tide, lying flat, arms out, where the foam spreads. But he could not picture her one night near the end of the long summer, the moon wavering behind clouds, listening to the retreating sluice of low tide and a cassette of Spanish guitar music, lying on the washed-over sand with John Harrison, when she rolls sideways and places her lips on his in a long, giving kiss, a kiss that seals a bond, a kiss with their mouths in an O, a communion kiss that does not turn to passion but is preciously intimate, that means at another time maybe, that lingers as they exchange breaths, liminal kiss, at once like a first kiss and a kiss saying goodbye, goodbye, mutual scent of salt, tongues barely touching, soft as the rain that started, and neither wanted to end this kiss or end the summer of sun, moon, spinning stars, end the good work, end living close by the wash of tides.

32

Amit lugs four boxes of cleaning and laundry supplies, vacuum cleaner, towels, a bedside lamp, and clanging pots and pans down to the curb. The studio has been empty for over two months. The landlord has been nasty, thinking he can charge a higher rent as soon as Austin's abandoned stuff is gone. He is especially enraged that he found a window left partially open and pigeon shit on the sill. "Who opens windows when there's air-conditioning? There could be hundreds of pigeons in here," he spits at Amit. He has the face of a snowman, pallid white with coal chips for eyes.

Finally, Amit has a Saturday to finish Austin's clean-out. Earlier, he'd arrived at Austin's studio, which looked surprisingly inhabited—the unmade bed, the Moka pot and a cup in the sink, a takeout menu on the dining table. All Austin's fastidious clothes gone. Only a pair of slippers half under the bed remained of his sharp wardrobe. In the closet he found the box of letters addressed to Dara. He packed up the bed linens and debated about wineglasses, plates, and cutlery, finally deciding to store them at his apartment, along with the Noguchi-style coffee table that Austin and Dara found on the street back when he moved in. It feels weird, as if Austin has died or disappeared into thin air. All that's left is for the landlord to inspect and refund Austin's deposit. Amit expects there will be a nice long delay for that. "So, Austin, New York is over," he says aloud. Finding a can of beer in the fridge, Amit thinks *why not,* pours himself a glass, and sits down to recover. Moving out, even a minor move like this, is sobering. Distressing in some primitive way. He pulls up a stool to the kitchen bar. A damn good friend, he thinks, to move someone out, and raises the can, here's to me.

Even sweeping out someone else's kitchen cannot dampen Amit's euphoria. He's completed his design for the Hudson project and the developers are impressed, even with his over-budget additions. His team has smacked him on the back, raised a few glasses, shaken his hand, and Julian has called him in for exuberant congratulations. He's happy with the ways he found to get around a generic, corporate layout, practical and soulless. He's ticked the boxes—made the requisite paths for bikes and strolling, yes, but with deviations to follow into private, copse-like gardens, a large allotment area for gardeners, a blue-bottomed pool that looks natural and inviting, a colorful playground that makes even adults want to swing, and three times the number of trees originally in the budget. As he planned the mix of trees, he once again walked through the Ooty Botanical Garden, where his school traveled in sixth grade. And at Cambridge, all those courses in English landscape theory, that tramping through the gardens of Humphry Repton, Vita Sackville-West, Rosemary Verey, Capability Brown, on and on, subtly channeled through his head as he sketched basic sight lines and dreamed of making the formidable apartment complex a place someone would be thrilled to come home to. The venerable garden designers gave him permissions and cautions and one priceless lesson—establish the boundaries, then you create your world. While designing, he felt a desire to revisit the other great gardens of India he was shown as a child, terraced extravaganzas, temples, reflecting pools and water features, but always back to the botanical gardens, too, where at eleven he first dreamed of laying out a habitat for tigers. Home. What might he accomplish there?

Tonight, he flies to London. Work. What's next? There's the continuing talk of the ideal village in Sussex. On again, off again, the massive idea gets shot down by the locals, praised by the locals, a yin yang that must be settled in the chambers of the authorities. I'd love to hop onto that scheme, he thinks. Especially if it means leaving New York and getting back to England. The Cupertino start-up possibility offers little to the landscape architect. Sure to be boring—corporate shrubs and a meaningless sculpture. New York has been a constant adrenaline rush, a sense of fabulous opportunity, now realized. If I hadn't grown up in India, he thinks, I probably would not see this city as a monochromatic hive. He's remembering the jumble of sensations—godlings in turbans, animal cults, decorated elephants in farm plots, painted caves with mysterious echoes, holy rivers. America (is this true?) lives on the surface. The thought of home in Delhi brings a blaze of colors—cinnamon, saffron, curry, the elegant aqua, gold, rose of the saris swishing down the lanes. On their vacation trip, his parents gently brought up the name of the Bhatt family's daughter, which he has blocked out. His parents won't force the issue, but he knows the four parents have discussed marriage. What a chance to take. I want what Austin has with Dara. Look what happened there. When I think of a Western woman, I go blank. I don't know if they are trustworthy. They are far from my own culture. But then there was Shelley. Statistically, my father tells me, arranged marriages go as well as any. Thank the gods they never suggested Shelley. What a minx. Whatever havoc she caused, she didn't deserve her fate.

Anyway, no hurry. I'm homesick. Is this a place to anchor my life? I think I've answered my own question. Tomorrow I will see Austin where he must anchor his life for now.

33

THE FIRST WEEKS of Hawthorn at home seem a blur to Annsley. Her commute on Sundays felt hard after the week at the bookstore. Usually, her free days were for catching up on mail, getting her clothes ready for the next week, a long walk along the Backs, and maybe tea with a friend. Although the shop is closed on Monday, she's there, relishing the quiet among the books. Often, she's paying bills, placing orders, and reshelving. When she volunteered to give Austin a break on Sundays, she was more concerned about him than about the baby. From the sofa downstairs late at night, she hears him upstairs, thrashing, unintelligible words, sometimes falling off the bed, making agonizing noises. He puts it down to bad dreams, but she's read about night terrors and suspects he is having a bigger struggle than he acknowledges. She's proud—he's doing the right thing, but at an unacknowledged cost. Shocking her is Hawthorn. At eleven weeks, propped up in a red hat and soft, striped blue pajamas, he's already a person. He smiles broadly, as if to say *I know you.* He kicks and grins and makes eye contact. To a soft yellow duck, he's entirely partial. Stunning—he's already making choices. She finds that she's anticipating Sunday. Her assumption always has been that she has no interest in children. In the shop, she keeps her eyes on their sticky fingers, their tendency to tear a page when turning it. Hers are vintage books for children, meant to be cherished by sentimental older readers or collectors seeking to fill out a first editions shelf.

Hawthorn bobs his head when shown A is for Apple, tries to bat the image, and Annsley finds herself laughing. On walks, she's assumed to be his mother and she doesn't bother to correct. During the week, she calls Jade and Austin to check on what he's up to.

Walking toward Austin's flat tonight, arms full of groceries, she has an almost out-of-body realization. She wishes she were Hawthorn's mother. Well, that's creepy, she thinks, since Austin is his father. What if I adopted him? Austin could go back to Plan A, if Dara consented. The faster she walks, the more this begins to seem like a feasible solution. For quite a while, he could go to work with her, Annsley continues, and the small inventory room could double as a quiet place for naps. Austin could come to her on Sundays, along with Michael. All this could wait a year, until the flat's lease is up. She is stunned at her turnaround, resolves to say nothing until good sense possibly returns her to her former reasonable self.

❧

AUSTIN'S SUNDAY IS A BREAK FROM RESPONSIBILITIES BUT NOT FROM work. With the proposals for the massive Sussex development in progress, he loves the empty office and the chance for solitude. He loves his drawing table, the smell of graphite, the scrolls of paper, the metal drawing utensils.

After melon and coffee with Annsley, a half hour of pushing Hawthorn in his back-garden swing—he gasps and smiles as he's pushed—Austin can go. He's learning the efficacy of generating drawings on the computer but craves the tactical feel of real tools. Annsley has brought a strawberry cake. For Amit's arrival, Austin will grill steaks American style. He remembers Rich once producing a platter of slightly charred vegetables and decides to do the same. There's good bread and farmer's market tomatoes in the fridge. But now, his empty worktable, tilted toward the light, awaits.

He's thinking, what a grand responsibility, a village ready-made. A Utopia? Schools, hospital, shops, parks. How to give it soul, a reason to exist beyond the practical. And concomitantly, Hawthorn, also a grand responsibility. He's landed here complete with the assumption that he has every right to his large life. Austin smiles, thinking of Hawthorn propped at the table, his eyes following Austin's bites of what he is not yet eating, as if he's priming himself, imagining, *Soon I will eat pasta. You will give it to me.* In a week or two, he will roll over on his quilt. Jade says he has the foot motion down; he's ready to pivot over. Crawling, up, walking, running. Austin wants to see it all. As for the night terrors, as Annsley labels them, he has become too reasonable. The power within him that was waylaid takes the middle of the night to assert itself. When he crawls back into bed, it's Dara who soothes him. Ebullient, playful Dara. He lies still, staring at the dark ceiling, holding on to the sides of the mattress as she plays her songs and stories upon his body.

WHERE TO BEGIN WITH A NEW TOWN? WHERE DO PEOPLE WANT TO gather? That's a place to start. He imagines an Italian piazza, not grand—humanly scaled, ringed with trees, perhaps with a lake along one side of the piazza, like in Lago d'Orta, where they were to have spent part of their honeymoon. Is there water on the property? He doesn't know. I need to get up there, he thinks. Rent a car, maybe take Hawt, as they've fallen into calling him, on his first trip. He's sketching fast. Will the partners agree?

He's by no stretch the lead architect. That would be Fred Marlowe, head of the firm. Amit must be brought on board; he'll be ideal on this. After the basic siting, the landscaping will mean everything. He thinks of Dara's flare-ups over her job at HUD, furious at delays and inefficiency, her passion for fair housing, influenced by Big Mann's life commitment to urban planning, farm subsidies, and rent control. Influenced, too, by the hands-on dedication of Rich to Habitat, and Charlotte, in her quiet support of abused women. A shared family trait. He'd never put it all together like that. His own family devoted to books, preservation of the word, living their quiet lives that don't feel quiet to them, a medieval psalter being far more exciting than a Maserati. According to Amit via Luke via Mei, Dara's been zealous at the hotel renovation, bossy, he says, and herding everyone to exceed whatever they thought possible. He refrained from asking about John, whom Dara had described as a friend. Thrown together in the sultry, florid South with a wild project between them . . . Austin doesn't want any images to form in his mind. He doesn't even know what this John looks like. Scrawny and pockmarked and bowlegged, he hopes. Dumb. But he can't be that.

Amit appears at seven, bearing an armful of lilies, two bottles of wine, and a grandly wrapped gift. An easy flight—he slept four hours—a walk around Chelsea, and an indulgent spree at Sloane Square to buy some fall clothes. Spend all that bonus in the same place, why not. London is easy. Hop on and off the Underground. He stopped at Harrods to buy a Paddington Bear for Hawthorn. He almost wanted it for himself, the sad hat, little coat, and the vulnerable black bead eyes. On second thought, he bought the books, too, although Hawthorn is years away from loving them.

Austin hugs Amit hard. "Man, I have missed you. Thanks for the dirty deed of cleaning up the studio. Embarrassing!" Austin points the direction to Hawthorn's bouncy chair. "Look who's here, Hawt. My best friend." Hawthorn duly stares at Amit.

"He looks like you. That hair." He stares at Austin, then the baby. "Lucky guy!"

Amit had expected a Shelley replica. Why, he didn't know, except that irrationally he thought Shelley had so totally caused this that the boy must be all from her DNA. "Looks like you are all doing well here. Great flat, my god!" This is so weird, he thought.

Annsley hasn't seen Amit since the boys were at St. John's. She's thrilled with the Paddington books, even though they're new. She has a good collection of first editions.

"This was the first book I ever read in English," Amit tells her. "I've adored the refugee from 'darkest Peru.'" They begin to speculate on the bear's origins, quote their favorite parts.

"You know," Annsley says, "the 'take care of this bear' sign he arrived with was inspired by someone who witnessed the Kindertransport and wrote the book."

"What's that?"

"The ten thousand children shipped out of Nazi Germany to the UK by parents desperate to save them."

"That's heavy. I thought it just a charming story."

"Well, it is a charming story."

Austin gets wine poured, picks up Hawthorn, and settles beside Amit on the sofa. He's clearly infatuated, Amit notices. He's astonished, expecting Austin to be edgy and resigned. Expecting Annsley to be plain and quiet. She's, what, only three years older, a fourth year at Clare when they were first year. She does have an upright bearing that reminds him of his regal mother, that's a good thing. Her hands, like Austin's, are sculptural, and her hazel eyes, also like his, light up with intelligent humor.

Austin relaxes. He's as happy as he's been since Shelley dropped her A-bomb on his life. Annsley takes Hawthorn up to his room for his bottle. Once in the crib, she always reads him a story, whether he can understand anything or not.

Austin starts the grill. Opens another red. There's no vase for the lilies. "Shame on you, Shelley, nothing for flowers," Amit jokes.

Austin combs through the cabinets and finds a water pitcher. "Apologies, Shelley, here's the perfect vase."

They laugh and clink glasses. Austin says, "Maybe she can become more normal now."

Annsley slips onto her chair at the table. "Out like a light. He is so ready to sleep on Sunday nights. I think it must be because I amuse him too much during the day. He is such a good boy." Again, she flashes on her idea of adopting him. That's crazy, she thinks. "Amit, have you noticed, Austin is smitten, too. Exhausted but smitten. The responsibility has to be hard for him."

"Don't talk about me in the third person. Let's talk about the impossibility of all that's happened. The way Shelley laid out the future with the flat and the money. Hawthorn's blood tests, all normal." Austin pours water, pushing away the sudden vision of blood squirting through the doctor's hands and onto the floor. He gets up and steps outside.

"He has nightmares," Annsley tells Amit. "But it's going to be all right. It's like that Goya drawing of the monsters rising out of the sleeping man's head, *The Sleep of Reason Produces Monsters*. He's had to be incredibly reasonable in a situation that seemed insane."

"Makes sense." Amit passes the bread, his hand grazing Annsley's.

Austin comes in, running his fingers through his hair. He sits back down. "Sorry. Now and then, I get a rush of images I can't shake. But it's over. I know I can't expect to forget that ordeal. Sometimes it smacks me."

"How could it not?" Amit reaches for the salad bowl, tosses the lettuces, and passes it around.

"What I really want to talk about is the unbelievable Sussex project. Could you see leaving New York?" Austin explains his ideas for the piazza concept, grabs a pad, and he and Amit start brainstorming. Annsley runs up to check on the baby.

"All quiet on the western front," she calls from the kitchen. She brings out her dessert and the drawings are shoved aside. Amit says he wants to see Cambridge, he misses it still. If he comes, could Annsley take a walk with him to the old spots? And he'd love to see her Paddington collection. They linger at the table until the wax pools and the candles gutter.

Austin walks up the street with Amit, jostles his arm. "Hey, you hitting on my sister?"

"You noticed? No, no. Well, you know I'm terrified of most women. She seems gentle."

"Annsley is the least terrifying person on earth. You know, she's never been interested in children, and I think she's fallen in love with Hawt. Maybe we are all changing; sometimes I feel like a different person than four months ago. Who *was* that lucky guy?"

They hug, smack each other on the back, and wave as Amit walks toward their friend Reggie's flat, where he is staying. "Hey," Austin calls, "be at the office early. We've got work to do."

Austin sleeps soundly. Annsley sleeps lightly, like the mother she is not. Hawthorn, for the first time, sleeps through the night.

34

Bill has cleared out of the town house. He's returning to his bolt-hole at his parents', but at least he won't need folding tables and kitchen counters anymore. Most of the files are boxed in the hall and ready to go back to the Duke archives. This is the best summer of his life. He has accomplished more than he expected, and with efficiency and pleasure. There are holes in his research on Senator Mann, but he knows how to fill them. The biography, he feels sure, does justice to a great American. Not that it's finished; he'll be lucky to be done by this time next year. Somehow, it feels intact. He just has to prioritize and work to create a sense of the whole man. He remembers James Agee saying he'd like to glue an old boot on the page to give the reader a sense of a tenant farmer's life. He'd be hard-pressed to find one thing to glue, if he could. A favorite image is of the senator in a tuxedo, leaving a fancy ambassador dinner, exiting the marble foyer and leaping onto his battered bicycle hidden from the valet in the bushes. He rode off into the dark. That about says it, more than the saber-tipped arguments before the Supreme Court in his professor days, or even his late-night impersonations of Little Richard.

More interviews to come, some with Charlotte, and others with colleagues, but certainly none with that raging co-senator, Jesse Helms, or the new one. God forbid. Bill smiles, twirls around, running a feather duster over—hallelujah—now-empty shelves in the study. "Dara, slide those new law books right in." What a gift to have stayed in a great place. At his parents' apartment, he would have felt stifled. His bags and boxes are already loaded in his car. He wants Dara to come home to a clean, empty house. Now, where's the cat?

LEAVING INDIGO IS WRENCHING. JOHN WILL STAY ON WITH BIBA TO wrap up some ends, and everyone else scatters over the weekend. "Keep in touch," they say a hundred times, Ben, Silvie, and Abby stuffing duffels, portfolios, boxes into every crevice of Ben's car. Dara hugs Biba, hugs John the longest. "Come see me in Rome," he whispers.

"You! 'Come see me in Rome,' what a slick pick-up line."

"Yeah, but I'm serious."

"I know. Maybe I will." She's headed to DC. Him, soon flying out of Atlanta into another entire world.

Dara spends the last Indigo night with Mimi. They drive down to the boat for a quick drink with Bing, who is leaving tomorrow to visit his sons. He brings up from below deck a wrapped gift. "I was in Charleston last week and I thought you might like this. It's a serious thing."

Dara unwraps Julia Child's *Mastering the Art of French Cooking.* "Wonderful! I can't promise much, but if you and Mimi come to Washington, I'll cook the entire dinner from this." Touched that he thought of her, she feels a buoyant surge of something like joy over the summer she's had, and her luck to be surrounded by Mimi, her parents, now Bing. Fit and handsome guy. Could they possibly still . . .

Charlotte stands up, as if sensing Dara's drift. "Right now, we're picking up shrimp burgers and glad of it," she says.

At her house, they eat on the deck. Last night with waves, the eternal this-then-that of the tides. The slight salt-tinged breeze feels like heaven. Hard to leave, but Redbud will be a buffer before the reality of DC. "Well, sweetie, how's the fall looking to you?"

"Good question. Looks like I'm on my own—everybody is scattering. I am in a better place than I was earlier this summer. I felt disoriented in California, kind of unmoored but thrilled. I'll have the house back. Bill says he's got a grip on the biography and he's moving out. I'm looking forward to classes. I start out with constitutional law, like Big Mann, and I have requirements—torts and civil procedure. I might prefer *tarts* now that I have that cookbook. I want to learn more about public policy and legislation of federal law. This summer—you know I organized this venture? It was satisfying. Juggling personalities and supplies, sequencing and scheduling, budget. Everything new. I was good at it. Something just mine, nothing traceable back to family influence or impulse. Then there's my work at HUD—these make me think I ultimately want to do something in public housing, housing in general. How exciting if I could make a difference, like you-know-who. Cause low-income projects to be livable. Beauty. The Palms—we did it! It's not hard. It takes vision."

"Nothing more important than the roof over your head. And personally?"

"That's the question!"

"Do you want to see Austin?"

"Of course. But I also don't want to. I think I need to figure out my own life before I can face his."

"Good girl." Charlotte passes her the fries and refills her beer. She pushes back her chair. "Look—" The faintest glow of the rising moon appears on the horizon. "Watch how fast it rises!" Dara turns around. Out in the dark east, the rim of the dome springs up gold as if glowing from within, not reflecting a shard of faraway sun.

"My Lee would quote Yeats."

"At length." Dara laughs. But she remembered the line *I sought to love you in the old high way of love . . .*

"*Fringe of a fingernail held to the candle,* that's one of hers. Hopkins? A bit out of scale, I always thought."

"I'm so glad she's finished the book. Dad is, too. I hated adding to her stress level these last months. Mimi, this whole ordeal has been a nightmare. I'm coming around to see that although I could have done without all this anxiety, I have changed. Gotta be some upside, no? I seem to have taken a few core samples in California and at Indigo. Like, what's really going on here? I never thought about my independence that much—I've always had such freedom within my family, and my life unfolded in a way that let me think I was in charge. Then I wasn't. Now I'm groping toward being in charge in a different way. Make sense?"

"Indeed. You're going to make good decisions. And Dara, what you just said . . . Have you thought, see if you think this is off-the-wall, but can you imagine," she continues slowly because she's thinking as she speaks, "this bubble you've been blowing, this bubble that also has you inside it, this bubble finally bursts and you're open again, with a vision for your own life that you recognize as crucial," Charlotte pauses and pushes back her plate, "with your law skills and god-given drive, that something amazing could happen and you *don't* fall into a life not of your making. All this you're opening into, this creativity and consciousness around housing, this could be dynamite fused with Austin's architectural career?"

Dara stares at her grandmother. She stands up and steps around the table to throw her arms around her.

"Mimi, you've always given me everything I need. Now you give me a new idea. Remember all those donkey piñatas you brought to my birthday parties? How you said, 'Beat it with a stick till the gifts fall out'?"

Charlotte doubles over with laughter. "What a good motto. Do that."

❧

AT REDBUD, DARA MADE DINNER FOR RICH AND LEE, SHOWING OFF HER summer cooking skills with a tomato tart in a purchased pie crust.

Rich spreads a map, marking the places they will stay on their upcoming trip. Mei drops in for coffee and a stroll in the late light along the river path. Rocco finds his spot to wade in then come shaking out to roll in the dirt. "Hose bath for you," Rich scolds.

Up in her room, Dara pulls out her old backpack from college, packs away her Indigo clothes, and selects a few sweaters and pants for wearing to class. Rich and Lee will follow to DC in a few days, staying with her before they fly out to celebrate in Ireland. They'll meet Charlotte later in London, after her time in Bath, where she'll be giving a lecture and teaching a three-day seminar. She's thrilled for Lee—her manuscript at last done, she is floating in the joyful limbo between finishing the work and hearing the comments of the editor. She's not worried; she knows Yeats like she knows the body of her husband. But handing over your work to another is always a bit like donning the gown, mounting that papered table, and fitting your feet in the stirrups.

Mei's coming soon to DC, Moira probably not. But at least a shred of the long-lost girls' weekend.

Dara made good time from Redbud to DC. Now what? Seriously inventing the future, that's all.

35

September 1995

LEE HAS NOT been in London for ten years, at least. She and Rich traveled to Italy when Dara took her semester abroad in Florence, then they'd stayed in Rome and Venice, like all tourists. She'd always remember the gondola ride through the dark canals late at night, the glimpses into the open windows of palazzi, colors of wavery light reflected on the water, the ceiling frescoes and grand chandeliers, high rooms where unimaginable lives have taken place for centuries. Rich arranged the gondola. He had also arranged prosecco and glasses. Touristy, they were aware, but nothing ever has been more romantic.

They've been on many other trips, a previous research trip to Ireland, Provence, others to Australia and Singapore associated with Rich's work, but somehow not back to England in too long. Ireland is a culmination—six years of work on the Yeats book. Having lived through the whole saga, Rich also wants to visit the poet's grave and tower, where apparently Yeats had been miserable every year when the river rose and the place flooded. First stop, the dismal, to Rich's eyes, famous stone tower. Lee wants Rich to see the poem Yeats had carved on the place where he labored.

I, the poet William Yeats,
With old millboards and sea-green slates

And smithy work from the Gort forge,
Restored this tower for my wife George.
And may these characters remain
When all is ruin once again.

"The last line, what a punch," she says to Rich. "You don't see it coming."

"Call me literal-minded, but it's not true. This heap might collapse but any wider metaphorical significance, no. His tower, his books—your book on his work! Those last."

"But maybe that's what he meant by 'may these characters remain.'"

"Okay, point taken. Right now, let's bask in the prospect for you of fresh fields and pastures new."

Lee grimaces. She can't resist correcting him. "The cliché is a misquote from Milton, who wrote 'fresh woods.'"

He pulls her close and surrounds her with his arms. "You English professors. I prefer the cliché; nice grazing cows come to mind in grassy meadows."

They sit on a mossy rock, kissing, and Lee cries a little, there at the end of a major lifework herself. She will never forget the library at Trinity, the woods of Yeats's mentor, Lady Gregory, the bleak grave carved with the epitaph *Cast a cold Eye / On life, on Death. / Horseman, pass by.* "I think I'll always love the world because of the creative geniuses that spring forth now and then."

"You're saying goodbye," Rich says. "Bittersweet. No more chasing references to obscure myths. No more peer review. What's next, my love?"

"Certainly out of the Irish twilight. I'm thinking travel literature. That's an underappreciated genre, and imagine all the trips we'd take for research. I have a better idea. Let's go back to the hotel."

A pelting rain begins and they dash to the car. "Bet ol' Yeats really hated to see the rain."

CHARLOTTE JOINS THEM IN LONDON. IN BATH, HER SESSION ON DOMESTIC abuse trauma went well. The practical programs she'd initiated with the director of the shelter in Chapel Hill proved efficacious. Sometimes basic first steps—taking a course, learning a skill—open the way faster to deeper therapy. Start with a possibility. Lead to a solution. Many of the women suffered childhood abuse, usually from relatives or boyfriends of the mother. That's never going to be forgotten. She stayed for the second and third days, catching up with colleagues and meeting a few whose work she knew. Mostly she walked around Bath, wondering how civilized a town could get. That famous Royal Crescent—living in one of those dignified houses must make you stand up straight and do the right thing.

The three meet at the Dunham, a small hotel in South Kensington. Near an Underground station and possessing a small Italian restaurant just under street level, the hotel is perfect.

As they walk toward the Natural History Museum, Charlotte whispers to Lee, "Are you scanning every face for Austin?" Lee admits that she is. They are on a small mission for Dara. The drawings of William Bartram ended up here, and Dara wants any books they might have on his work, a gift for the lobby at The Palms. Biba's copy of *Bartram's Travels* is a precious old one; Dara wants one that can be handled. They decide they'll get this done on their first afternoon and have an early dinner at the hotel.

Suddenly Rich says, "Wonder where Austin lives?" It seems to him that they are fated to meet Austin here. He has a wild vision of him across the room in a restaurant, or knocking on his door, or bumping into him on the Underground. And saying what?

"Dara says he lives near his father in Bloomsbury. Let's just forget about that and enjoy this short time." Lee is looking forward to the Tate, the National Portrait Gallery, the British Museum, two plays, and the all-new part of the trip, a week in Scotland.

Charlotte says, "Only several million people, why shouldn't we bump into Austin."

They are able to see some of Bartram's pen-and-ink drawing, but the gift shop keeps no copies of the book and no scholarly work on him.

"Mission aborted, but seeing the originals makes me realize how talented those artists were at The Palms." Charlotte has looked forward all day to the moment for scones and tea. She leads them into a corner pastry shop and orders the cream tea, nicely spoiling dinner for all of them.

For Lee, a favorite part of travel is the interim between when the day is done, and dinner is still two or three hours away. A long soaking bath with lime salts, then she props herself up in bed—Rich is out walking—reading her guidebooks, then an Elizabeth Bowen novel. She suddenly misses Dara. It's one in DC. She reaches for the phone.

Dara's message: "This is Dara. I'm not here. Please leave . . ." She picks up.

"Hey, it's me. In London. We wish you were with us. It is so great to be here."

"You sound close. I know that makes me sound like a hick, but, wonderful, wonderful that you called. How was Ireland? How's Mimi, Dad?"

Lee updates her and asks about classes.

"Going well. I'm in the usual One-L regime. More choice later but right now the lectures are terrific, and I am lapping it up. I bought a computer and I have Big Mann's office to work in, and a place to have my study group—they form quickly—over for takeout and long talks about the classes. Bill Dellinger has cleared everything away."

"Good! We'll call from Edinburgh. I won't keep you. I know you're swamped this, what? Second week? Just want to say, we went to the Natural History Museum but they had nothing for sale on William Bartram. This is a strange idea, maybe, but I wanted to run it by you. I'm looking for a variorum edition of Yeats's complete poems, published after his death in 1939. No luck in Dublin. The special thing is that he signed pages before he died that were tipped into the edition, and I've always wanted a copy."

Dara isn't one to miss a nuance. She laughs. "You want to go to Austin's father's bookstore to look for it."

"Yes, and for your Bartram, too, of course. Would you object? If so, there are more antiquarian bookstores I can try. And I won't go stalking Austin, I promise. I do not want to do this without your permission."

Dara rather liked the idea of her mother meeting Austin's gentle, scholarly father. She knows her mother will be discreet. "Fine. It's fine. I'm okay with it. But maybe not overwhelm him with the three of you. Especially Mimi. I am afraid she'd be unable to resist the questions that are burning for her."

"I may or may not go through with this. I'll see what my nerve is tomorrow. We have tons of plans. I wish you were with us, but I am so excited for you. Law school! At last. We're proud, especially under the circumstance."

"I'm going to be so busy I won't have time to think. That's good."

Lee and Rich meet Charlotte downstairs for breakfast in the book-lined restaurant with its chic leopard-print carpet and good espresso. The hotel serves the full English breakfast, which Charlotte pushes aside, those skinny sausages and pallid grilled tomato. "All I want is scones. I must learn how to make them."

Rich has calls to make and a quick meeting with an editor friend. Charlotte had the concierge make a hair appointment for her. They're fine when Lee says, "Can I meet you all at noon at the British Museum? In the courtyard? I want to run a couple of book errands I'll tell you about later." Just now, she doesn't want to hear opinions.

"Can't wait," Charlotte quips. "Suitcases getting heavier, Rich."

. . .

Lee exits the Underground at Russell Square, looks at her map, and glances around, feeling that odd sense of knowing her way, although she does not. Mrs. Dalloway might be opening the door to go out to buy flowers (that famous opening line), Dickens covering page after page, the words flying over us all, her Yeats could be ambling along the sidewalk muttering about feeling Innisfree in the deep heart's core. Graham Greene! The world of English literature walks these streets and Lee feels at home among the memories. Lucky Austin, growing up here.

Near Bedford Square, there's the storefront, MA Clarke Ltd. Rare Books and Manuscripts. Like several other buildings in the area, this one's first floor is royal-blue high-gloss enamel with gleaming brass hardware. Some of the books in the window are covered by protective fabric and others have bindings and titles that let you know just how specialized the works inside might be.

A low bell rings as Lee steps inside. Looks like no one's home, as she takes in the dark bookcases and spacious wooden tables spread with enticing volumes. You could step on rickety ladders that allow you access to the higher shelves, pulling wheels with a thick velvet cord along the books. She so wanted to do that, to ascend almost to the ceiling and find herself among early editions of Coleridge and Blake and Keats. How exhilarating to ride the ladder. How fortunate to spend your days among the greats. She spots the man she knows to be the father of Austin. Leaning over a table of books, he is a slender man in a gold cardigan, probably a few years older than she, with a thatch of blond-gray hair. No doubt, Austin's father. He looks up from the folio he's paging through. "Let me know if I can be of help."

Lee feels a twinge of uncertainty. What am I doing? She asks, "Could you direct me to poetry?"

He gestures toward the windows. "All along that wall." Spontaneously, Lee laughs. "Seriously! In most shops poetry has half a foot of space. This is heaven."

American, Michael thinks. So enthusiastic. He goes back to the vellum pages, making notes on his new computer as he inspects.

Lee does not find the Yeats volume. She finds many books she can't resist holding and inhaling the lovely smell of old pages and the sensation of many others having gazed at the fonts, the line lengths, sometime the ex libris bookplate with the name of the long-gone owner. Summoning a bit of nerve, she crosses to the table and Michael looks up. "I'm Lee Willcox, the mother of Dara, your son Austin's former fiancée. I came here to look for a book, I did, but also to introduce myself and say how much we care for Austin through all this."

Michael reaches for her hand and takes it in both of his. "Mrs. Willcox, this is a pleasure for me. How kind of you to stop in."

"Lee, please. May I call you Michael? How is everything going for Austin now? And the baby?"

Michael tells her of the arrangements. "We are all pitching in. The shock seems over, and Austin is working normal hours. He thrives there and I think he is doing quite well, given the circumstances. The bizarre circumstances." He raises his eyebrows.

"Please give him our best. We're at the Dunham in case he wants to get in touch. I doubt if he does but . . ."

"He's fond of you and your husband—and the grandmother as well. Needless to say, he's deeply shamed by—"

"No, no, please. It is a massive . . ." She's missing the right word, helplessly gestures to the folio on the table. "Typo." They both laugh.

"Book in the wrong binding. The boy, though, you look at him and it's hard to think of mistakes. He's here with us, wherever he came from."

Lee's eyes fill with tears.

"Sorry," Michael says. "I didn't mean to upset you."

"No worry. I agree with you, truly." She had thought of the fleeting moment she'd held her own Hawthorn, a moment hardly longer than a wobbly bubble popped in clear air. "Now, maybe you can help me. I am looking for a special variorum edition of Yeats's poems."

As she described the book, Michael nodded and led her to another section in the back. Autographed copies, and there it was. The heavy volume looked not so special in its faded buckram binding, but Lee turned to the first page and there was the scrawny minuscule signature, *W B Yeats.* She was elated. Only 825 copies exist. The price printed on the insert was not as high as she expected. She asked, too, after *Bartram's Travels*, but Michael shook his head, adding that he probably could find one. "Ring me at the Dunham if you can locate one before we leave."

Michael wrapped Yeats in the same bright blue paper as the color of the store. "This is going to a good home in America." He smiled, handing back her credit card. "Please, this is a gift. I'll charge you exorbitantly for the Bartram, don't worry." He pushes back her card again. "Absolutely not."

"This is too much. This is an absolute treasure." She tells him that she's just completed a book on the poet, after years of research, about her classes, papers she's written, abiding love for the work.

"Then I'm doubly happy to have you own this." They part at the door, Michael touched by her grace, Lee moved by his generosity, and sad again for the way things turned out. How marvelous it would have been to have Michael in the family.

As she walks to the corner, she has a fantasy of a long holiday table, a line of candles, Dara and Austin laughing as they had last April, Michael and Bing chatting, Charlotte holding forth—Rich carving, holly twined in the chandelier, the whole scene seeming so vivid that she does not realize as she steps off the curb and looks left that, of course, the traffic is coming from the right, and at that instant a gray Renault rounding the corner strikes her sideways, lifting her over the curve of the hood and throwing her into oncoming traffic on the other side. A driver swerves, missing her, hitting another car, and then Lee hears a loud silence fill her ears. Everyone at the scene scrambles toward her, shouting, *Call an ambulance.* The pale woman on the pavement lies on her side, as if sleeping.

Someone takes charge, covering her with his coat, the someone finds her—thank god—pulse and shouts others back. Half a block away Rich and Charlotte, a few minutes late, are entering the British Museum courtyard, expecting to see Lee waiting. Soon the sirens approach and the someone whispers you are fine, you will be fine, the crumpled body is secured with straps and loaded by a bevy of paramedics, the siren screeching off through the placid day. The someone, dazed, shakes out his coat and sees a bag on the ground imprinted with MA Clarke Ltd. He knows the store and walks back there. Michael is at the door, having peered out to see what the confusion was up the street. "A lady was just hit by a car. Here's something she got here. Must have just been in the store before it happened. Maybe she'll come back for it, if she lives."

"Wait—what happened, where is she?"

"I guess she looked the wrong way. I don't know what hospital they took her to, probably closest. She looked like a goner. I didn't see blood except out of her nose. She was alive, for sure."

"Come back here, get some water. Sit down. You were right there. You must be shaken. I'm Michael Clarke."

"Paul Stone." He sits down, takes a few sips, then puts his head down on the table and weeps.

❧

WHEN RICH AND CHARLOTTE HAVE WAITED OVER AN HOUR, THEY DEcide to go have lunch. "This isn't like Lee. What could she be doing?" Rich is looking at his mobile phone but already knows there's no service here from their American carriers to her phone.

"Why don't we phone the Dunham? Maybe she's left a message there."

This call works. When Rich identifies himself to the desk, the clerk quickly says, "Oh, Mr. Willcox, just a moment." She calls over the manager.

"Mr. Willcox, I am so sorry. There has been an accident with your wife. The hospital called when they found her hotel receipt and passport in her handbag."

"NO," Rich shouts. "Is she okay?"

"I don't have any information, but she is at the Royal National Orthopaedic Hospital. I am so sorry. And wait, a Mr. Michael Clarke also called about Mrs. Willcox."

The latter information barely registers with Rich. He is in the street hailing a taxi, explaining the little he knows to Charlotte.

❧

LEE IS FAINTLY CONSCIOUS. "WHAT IS YOUR LEVEL OF PAIN, SCALE OF ten?" A nurse is jabbing her arm, hooking up an IV.

The room is bright, too bright. She can't feel anything except a grinding ache in her lower half. "I have to meet my husband."

"That's not happening, my friend. You were hit by a car. You are lucky."

"Lucky?" How is that lucky?

"Just try to relax. You're fine now, or you're going to be."

The nurse wheels her down a flickering fluorescent corridor to another bright room. When she is shifted to the X-ray table, she feels horrific pain. "Eight. Nine." But the nurse has forgotten the question.

There's a doctor peering down. Magnified eyes. "Young lady, we are going to fix you right up. We may have to wait a few hours. We're backed up."

I hate it when they call you "young lady" when you're not, Lee thinks. So condescending. She glares at the doctor. "I need to see my family. We are going to the British Museum." She turns her head, struggles to sit up, and retches onto her gown. The nurse gently eases her into a clean one. Yes, there's pain, sharp and hard. "My leg? What happened?" She glimpses her right foot, scraped up to her shin. Under the gown, she can't see where it ends.

"It's not your leg, your leg is just raw from the landing you took after a car rolled you over. It's your pelvis. I'm afraid it's broken, luv, and we're going to fix it. A CT scan is next up. And we're watching for concussion. You had quite a bad hit."

Now it's "luv" he's calling me? This does not seem right or real. "How can I reach my husband?"

"He's been notified. We found your contact info from your purse. American, aren't you? He is probably on his way here now."

Taken back to another room, Lee falls asleep, wakes to a bank of monitors, Nurse Ratched scurrying around adjusting blinds and moving screens. She's moving easily, with no broken pelvis. With no broken pelvis you can move anywhere you like. Lee thinks they must have given her medication; she feels nothing except a large confusion and the beginning of a pounding headache. "You rest, pet. You'll have a long wait, and you need rest. You can't eat now but you can have sips of water." Maybe she's not Nurse Ratched.

"Am I going to die? Is this my last day on Earth?"

"Not if I can help it, pet."

Charlotte and Rich are able to see Lee but only briefly. She's lucid but confused and now in deep pain, like wedges of iron spikes are hammering into her lower body. She's cogent enough to ask if this is a good hospital, is the doctor reputable, what the hell happened? She remembers feeling wonderful as she walked toward the British Museum, then nothing.

"Rich, didn't you say the hotel also said that Austin's father somehow knew and called?" Charlotte asks.

"I went to M. A. Clarke to buy a book. He wouldn't let me pay. He is so nice."

"This happened just after you went there?" Rich is relieved that she's following the conversation.

"Must have." Must have, she says to herself, what odd words, must have, must have. She remembers her blue package. "Where's my Yeats book?"

"It's not here. Missing in action." The last thing Rich cares about right now is a damn book. Damn Yeats. He thinks his head might implode.

"Maybe he saw something," Charlotte says. "Go call him, please, Rich. And ask about the hospital, too. We have no information."

Charlotte pulls a chair close to Lee's bed and takes her hand only to place it carefully on the sheet when she feels her lacerated palm. Instead, she gives Lee a spoon of crushed ice and wipes her forehead as she did when Lee was a child with a fever.

"Okay. I have two good colleagues I can check with, too." Rich steps out.

❧

ON FIRST RING: "M. A. CLARKE."

"Good afternoon, it's Rich Willcox. My wife is Lee—she was there earlier today. I know you called the hotel. Thank you."

"Rich, may I? How is Lee?"

"Escaped something worse but she's in rough shape with a broken pelvis, and she's pretty skinned up, and definitely out of it. They're operating late today, and I wanted to ask you about the Royal National Orthopaedic Hospital. Am I right to leave her?"

"They were smart to take her there—its specialty is orthopedics, of course, and the place is known for good docs. She was hit just three or four minutes after she left here. I heard ambulances and horns, quite a cacophony, but of course I had no idea what had just transpired. The man who helped her, wrapped her in his coat and talked to her, found her package and came in right after she was taken away. He saw the accident, said she was smiling as she stepped off the curb, just a step and this Renault came around the corner." The scene replays in Rich's head.

"I called the hotel—she'd said earlier to call if another book she wanted could be found. I'm glad you got the message. Let us help any way we can."

"You are very kind. I'll let you know. Thanks for telling me what happened. Please give my best to Austin."

Rich called his colleagues and they, too, affirmed Michael's opinion of the hospital. Rich feels reassured; navigating another hospital with Lee in bad shape seems overwhelming. He stands in a stall in the men's room rubbing his temples. His shoulders shake. He hasn't cried in years. Lee.

The doctor is writing on a clipboard in the hall outside Lee's room. Rich introduces himself and asks for an assessment. "The hip socket is broken front and back. We're looking for internal bleeding." He is pointing to marks on a drawing of the pelvis. "Small incision here." He points. "Insertion of screws, another long incision, a plate, examine for tears in ligaments," and he goes on, Rich trying to hold on to the idea that this is Lee he's talking about, her beautiful body. "Should go well. She's in great physical condition," he's continuing, "and she's been checked for nerve injury—she's able to feel sensation in her feet. So far, she can't move her right ankle but let's not worry now. It's not broken."

"Dr. . . ." Rich looks at the name on the pocket. "Dr. Ware, I don't know you. We're in a foreign country with no backup. I'm sorry, but how can I know if you are the right person for this operation?"

"Fair question, quite fair. I'm going to have you pop upstairs and discuss this with the head of the department. I want you to be secure."

Even with that, Rich feels better. If the guy got defensive, he would have suspected a weakness. He skips the elevator and takes the steps up to the office two at a time. He wants to hurry back to Lee.

He returns to Lee's room with a great sense of relief. They're in the right place. He wants to do something for the ambulance crew who made a lightning assessment. He's assured that Dr. Ware is a top surgeon. Luck so far, though Lee is rejecting the idea that we should call any of this luck. "Luck was finding the book, not getting lifted into the air and tossed aside by a rickety Renault," she complains. She's getting exhausted by the pain and stress. "Let's don't call Dara until afterwards. I don't want her agonizing when there is nothing she can do, nothing. And don't ever tell her I looked the wrong way. I'll never live that down."

"Let's let her know when there's good news to tell. It's three here, Wednesday—she has classes today—probably she's just off to campus now." Charlotte is stricken with fear but not revealing anything but a let's-get-this-done-and-move-on attitude. It's sinking in that there will be months, not weeks, of recovery. She and Rich must get busy right now planning for difficult days ahead.

Since it's going to be a long afternoon and night, Charlotte walks out to buy lunch. It seems impossible that the normal London day is still in action, she tells herself, their reserved table at the restaurant given away, the traffic rolling. Please god look the correct way, she tells herself. She crosses the street. Bright world moving on, as though nothing at all had happened to Lee Willcox. No matter who you are, world keeps on keeping on. Right away she finds a bakery with croissant sandwiches.

Rich has been given a pile of paperwork—insurance, medical history, credit card info, and the do-not-resuscitate for Lee to sign. The not-so-gentle reminder of what could go wrong. "Hey, I'm going to do all this while you're in surgery. Sign this one form and let's just sit together."

"I would like to sleep, but I'm too nervous." She hands back the form. She has crossed out "not" in Do Not Resuscitate.

There being no clear place he could touch her without causing pain, Rich pulls his chair close and cups his hand around the top of her head, gently pushing back her hair. "It'll be over. You'll be here only three or four days. What Mimi and I will do in the meantime is find a flat to rent until we can go home."

"Sounds expensive."

"Not the time to worry about that." If only they could get back to Redbud. To friends and familiarity and Rocco and the prettiest fall coming on, Dara popping down for weekends full of stories about her new classes. "We'll find someplace easy, and I'll read Dickens to you, long, complicated chapters about the Artful Dodger and David Copperfield and Scrooge. Mimi will learn to make scones and what's that absurd dessert?"

Lee manages a laugh. "Spotted dick."

"Sounds like a sexually transmitted problem." He leans in, kissing her lips softly. The upcoming surgery scares him down to the soles of his shoes. Anesthesia is something to fear. No one really knows how it works, only that it does work. He's been told by the director, three months until she can walk without crutches, a full year to heal completely. He can't even ask how long till they can fly home.

Charlotte returns with lunch—the croissants, brownies, chips, Cokes. "What a load of calories. Sorry, darling, you're not allowed to eat. Should we go outside?"

"I don't even want anything at all, except to get this over with. Go right ahead." Lee tries not to let them know what excruciating pain she's in.

"I brought you some magazines, *World of Interiors, Country Life*, and for when you can concentrate, the *London Review of Books*. I hope your book will be in there this time next year." And that we will read it in North Carolina, she doesn't say.

"Save them for tomorrow. I'm just going to close my eyes for a few minutes." She falls asleep. The nurse comes in and wakes her; they're watching for concussion. After eating, Rich nods off in the one comfortable chair, and Charlotte tries not to pace, looks at the street below, still persisting in going on with its day.

When they come for Lee, Rich follows the gurney toward the operating theatre, as they call it. His hand rests on Lee's arm, he's smiling at her, giving every indication that all is well. Only twice before has he done this walk, both toward the delivery room at Duke Hospital. Full of holy dread and anticipation both times. Right one time. Immense joy, as if the sky opened and joy rained down on their lives. The other, unfathomable sadness. What is the harder part, he wonders, Lee reduced to the word *patient*, feeling totally alone, about to give over her life to the hands of strangers, or me, left to wait, helpless to help the person I love?

Four hours later, Lee is in recovery. Dr. Ware shakes Rich's hand. "All went according to plan. She's got some metal in her pelvis, a couple of screws can come out when she's healed a year. The hip socket was broken in such a way that I had to make an incision of about thirty centimeters. We'll have her on heavy narcotics as long as she needs them. Those cut muscles smart a bit. I'm going to keep her here for four or five days. The recovery is the long part, but for the moment, relax, take a walk. She's in good hands, and you can see her in a bit."

Charlotte decides to take a quick trip to the Dunham and pack a few things for Lee. She'll stop somewhere to buy a robe and practical gown. She knows Lee didn't pack one—she and Rich sleep naked.

Rich sits down in the waiting room with his head in his hands, trying not to hyperventilate. A thin woman in a sari cries at the window, and he does not want to know what she's waiting for. Eerily, he thinks of Shelley's mother, who probably doesn't wear a sari. He walks down the hall to the phone booth.

"There's no need to come. You're in school and everything is going well here now." Rich has reached Dara just as she heads to the library. He'd started the conversation with immediate assurance that Lee is doing well, she's had an accident but not to worry, then backed up with the blow-by-blow of the day. He feels immensely tired. He forgot to mention that Lee had been leaving Austin's father's bookstore when it happened.

"Evening flight—I'm on it. Get me a room at your hotel. I'm coming. Wait, what's the hospital. What's the hotel?"

Dara hangs up, already flinging clothes from her closet as she mentally rearranges her weekend plans, books her ticket—only the last row available—and races to make the evening flight. Her mother has never had anything worse than flu. Her mother is invincible. Her mother has had major surgery a million miles away.

36

THE CALL COMES from Michael while Austin and Amit, with two other associates from the firm, are driving back to London from the Sussex site visit. In the back seat, Amit is whacked out because, as the others were assessing and photographing the land proposed for housing and shops, he trudged over the entire holding's terrain, some of which is muddy. He found a swiftly running stream, which gave him full impetus for designing sylvan nature walks and pocket gardens similar to his apartment project in the States. Because his work has just been nominated for the Green Sphere award for contribution to urban living space, he's confidently sketching ambitious ideas for this utopian concept. (He wonders if it ever will be built.) His expensive trainers are probably ruined. He's nodding off when he hears Austin answer, "Hey, Dad, everything okay?"

Michael fills him in on what has happened to Lee Willcox. Driving in stop-and-go traffic, Austin barely can concentrate. Lee? Here? Hit? By a car. She visited Michael? Dara sent her? But no, it was about a book. Austin knows of Lee's academic interests but, still, this is beyond strange. Even if she thought she was there about a book, wasn't she still an emissary from Dara? Maybe, maybe not.

They decide that Austin will contact Michael as soon as he's back in London. When she's better, Michael wants to go to the hospital with flowers or chocolates, and the famous book that caused all this.

Austin swerves slightly, knocking Amit on his knee through the gap in the seats to rouse him. Amit immediately leaps to conclusions. "You're going to see Dara, man, she's going to be at that hospital if I know Dara. Yes, she'll be coming here, even if she has to fly hanging on to the wheel." The thought already had occurred to Austin. He smiles, imagining Dara hanging by one hand from the plane over the Atlantic. That's my girl, he thinks.

Amit is heading for Cambridge tonight. He's reserved at the University Arms, where his parents used to stay when they visited him. Now he's an adult, returning to a place of memory. It seems impossible that he and Austin, Reggie, Luke, the whole crew have been out in the real world for six years. He has invited Annsley to join him for dinner. He's been concentrating all day. Now he can get nervous.

37

Dara goes straight to the hospital from Heathrow. Lee's bed is raised to half sitting and she's looking normal, her hair brushed, sipping tea, and wearing a pink fluffy kind of shawl thing Dara knows Mimi must have bought. Dara feels so relieved to see her looking herself that she jokes as she comes into the room, "I cannot believe you looked the wrong way! Dad has already confessed." Closer, she sees that Lee is pale and has circles under her eyes, pale purple, really, so probably black eyes, not fatigue circles. "Oh, are you really okay?"

"Hick from Hicksville!" Lee opens her arms then winces. Any sudden movement provokes a stabbing pain sharp as a stiletto wound. "You came! You shouldn't have. I'm going to be fine. It's been no fun so far but now it looks as if we will have an extended vacation in London. I've always wanted time here." She turns back the sheet. "But not like this." She's ensconced in bandages. She gestures to the morphine pump attached to the IV. "This is allowed. When the pain starts to crest, I can give myself a hit."

Dara, exhausted from the ordeal of getting here, feels like crawling onto the bed, curling up, and falling asleep for days, holding on to her mother until she can walk out of here.

Rich offers a bag of warm buns. "Sweetheart!" He hugs her hard. "I'm going to find you a coffee. You must be about flattened. You're going to need to crash. Mimi is back at the hotel, but she'll be here soon. We'll be here in relays."

Although she's heard the story, she listens to Lee repeat what happened. She will never forget her mother hit, tossed over the car hood, crumpled and at the mercy of strangers. She can hear the crash, the shrieks, the siren. But she only says, "Oh, you did see Michael. Isn't he just the nicest? But if you hadn't gone, this would not have happened."

"You can't start with ifs. If I hadn't gone to the Georgetown dance, I wouldn't have met Rich, and you wouldn't be here in London on a mercy mission."

"Yeah, but a book. Just a book. Admit it, you really just wanted to meet Michael?"

"Just because we were here, and we'd almost had a very close family connection. Yes, I did want to say hello. I told you I might stop by."

"Well, go ahead and tell me—did he say anything about Austin? Is he okay?"

"Nothing personal. Briefly, he's working hard, has a nanny, his sister helps on weekends."

"Okay. Enough of all that. What is your doctor saying?"

Lee has tired herself with the excitement of seeing Dara. "Ask Rich. I think I'd like to rest."

"Okay. We'll keep quiet."

Rich brings in a foam cup of battery acid. Mind-curdling, but the cinnamon rolls are plump and rich. Dara sinks into the chair where Rich slept, feeling that everything has upended. "How could this happen?" she whispers.

Rich reassures her. "The doctor is pleased. The concussion is mild. That's amazing. She is on pain medication and although everything's clear to her, she says she feels as if she's somehow at a distance from reality. The doctor says that, in a way, is protective. She needs rest and calm. She needs to stay well hydrated, hence these tubes. How long can you stay?"

Dara calculates that if all goes well, she probably will stay only through the weekend, missing one day of classes. "Ha! Dad, I can't even be here but I am. These first weeks are crucial in establishing a presence in class. The professor needs to know the students he can count on."

After Charlotte arrives, loaded with bags, Dara and Rich take a taxi back to the hotel for a break. After lunch, they'll spell her so that someone is with Lee at all times.

❧

SEVERAL CALLS TO REAL ESTATE AGENTS PRODUCE ZERO POSSIBILITIES for a place to go when Lee is released. The hotel recommends a business temporary-lease accommodation, but the photos look like a sad motel. Rich now has a promising lead on a house with only four steps up to the front door. She can be taken there by ambulance and settled inside until she can maneuver. Later, he can carry Lee, if necessary. His colleague Spencer, at the *Financial Times*, phoned him. Someone on senior staff is going away for a month and his arrangements with a neighbor have fallen through. He would like someone to stay at his place to feed his two caged African gray parrots. Rich doesn't much fancy birds in cages, but this sounds good—a place in Richmond, a bit far out, but he knows it's an area of London that's like a village. On nice days he could take Lee to Kew Gardens and on slow strolls along the Thames as she recovers.

❧

DARA SLEEPS.

Rich showers, scarfs a quick lunch downstairs, and takes the Underground out to Richmond. The key left under the mat, that kind of neighborhood. The cottage is bigger and nicer than he expected. He walks through three bedrooms, utilitarian kitchen, and quite pleasant living areas. The *Financial Times* guy, Finley something, is fastidious, Rich can see that. Lee is going to like his old-family taste, rooms for the sort of people who don't buy furniture, they have furniture. Under the front window, a library table is stacked with art books; unctuous damask overstuffed chairs semicircle the fireplace. Swaggy silk curtains full of soft light, a silver tea service standing ready in the dining room, high ceilings. In back, a view over a flagstone terrace and a grassy meadow invites taking that tea outside. The two offending birds have their own small back room and presumably keep each other company. After the owner departs tomorrow, Charlotte and Rich can stock the kitchen, bring in armfuls of flowers, and make the place a haven for Lee's recovery.

When Dara wakes up it's almost four. A note under the door says that Rich will be ready to go back to the hospital at five and to ring him. Charlotte will be leaving for the evening and feels secure enough to use one of their theater tickets tonight. Before she and Rich left the hospital this afternoon, she heard him saying to Lee, "We'll have fun. We'll watch cooking shows and I'll learn to make stupendous dinners. I'll play our favorites, Joni, Haydn, Thelonious. The Thames out there is like a bucolic painting. You can try watercolors, and we can read—who do you want to read? Some pastoral poets? You rest."

A flush of anger at Austin washes into sadness. That's what marriage should be. Rich is not just taking care; he's putting his imagination into Lee's recovery. Not just *got your back* but a natural commitment to constant enhancement.

Lying in bed after deep jet-lag sleep, Dara thinks of the many ways her parents take exquisite care of each other. She's witnessed the same with Mimi and Big Mann. They were a pair. From her family's marriages, she always has been able to tell, meeting any couple for the first time, whether they have that kind of connection she's blithely witnessed her whole life. There's something invisible but sensed in such a match, as if you could wave your hand through ions circulating between them. Remembering how soothed her mother was by his words, Dara thinks, that's what Mimi knows. And I thought until that night in Washington that all our juice and joy would just continue for Austin and me. Now here's Dad, madly inventing not just Mom's recovery but her happiness. Are most failed marriages, as Mimi says, due to a failure of imagination? I want to be the one who does my dead level best day after day to make the other happy. Otherwise, what's the point? All that, yes, Mimi. But that extra—that recitation of all the fun he'd invent—that's my revelation of the day.

It strikes her that possibly her unequivocal reaction to Austin's folly with Shelley comes from what she knows about her parents and grandparents. If they'd been ones who took compromise for granted in their relationships, maybe she would have, too. Bears thinking about. But who knows what they were like with others when they were young? Mimi did divorce. Dara pulls the pillow over her face. Where is my imagination in my own crash? Let this stalling pass, let this anger pass, let me pass over into clarity.

She throws off the covers and jumps in the hot shower. She knows Rich will insist on sleeping in Lee's room tonight. He's wearing himself out. She makes a decision. When it's time for her to leave the hospital, she will go to Austin's flat and knock on the door. During the summer, he'd sent his new contact information with a brief note that he hoped she was loving Indigo, missed her, that's it. She hasn't seen him since the night in Washington when he flew in to confess.

38

NOT A NATURAL NURSE, Charlotte is solicitous. Ice chips in a spoon. Cool cloth on Lee's forehead. Checking on pain and comfort. The second full day seems rougher than the first; the pain is severe, even with whatever knock-out drops they're giving her. She doesn't want TV. She would really like everyone to leave for a few hours. She doesn't feel as if she has had time to reflect. That's not going to happen for a long time; she's under close surveillance. "Mama, go for a walk. This room must be oppressive. I am fine and really would like just to be totally quiet for a little while. You could get me some baby oil for my feet. They feel so dry."

Charlotte agrees. "All right. I'll just pop out for a few."

Preoccupied as she is with her harrowing experience, Lee is also thinking of Dara and Austin, that night at Redbud in April, when the future looked brilliant. I'm returning to the party over and over, she thinks, like an old home video seen many times, each viewing setting the participants into facsimiles of themselves until any reality is replaced by only mysterious semblances of ourselves. In the summer, a friend in Maine had sent a newspaper clipping, a photo of officials breaking ground on the college library Austin's team designed. With a wallop of real pain, she imagines all the family there, proud and thrilled when the building is complete. His team steps up to say thanks. Dara bursting with joy. Not to be. Did Dara see the article?

We talk about anything else other than Austin. I wonder always about his life, who he is now and how he was spun, shaped like a clay bowl, by what happened to him. Let's be frank. What happened because of him. Because of the woman. Because of because.

By now, I should have long since stopped fantasizing about Dara and Austin, the two as one. Better to visualize the tiny yellow crocuses coming up around the stone ruins of the springhouse. I have planted two hundred hyacinths along a stone path. They're pushing down their pale roots, preparing to dazzle us in March. Me, my mother, my grandmother—all the garden work, adding, subtracting, endlessly dividing those iris and dahlia roots. It's left for Dara to break the chain. Or not.

I should think of what gives me joy. What is way far from this chilly room painted the color of throat lozenges. My rose garden, always a gargantuan pain, also gives great joy. Teaching. But I do not miss my students, especially the ones in the three-hour night classes, coming in smelling of fast food and unwashed sweatshirts—though I love their eager questions, their willing struggles to understand Milton, all the kind notes at the end of the semester. Joy. Dara and Rich. My mother. She sleeps again, under a haze of rolling pain, pain in riptide waves that threaten to pull her out to sea. When she wakes, Charlotte has four vases of flowers around the room. At first, they were not allowed. Now they are; Lee is out of intensive care.

❧

RICH HAS THE HOTEL RESTAURANT BOX UP DINNER FOR HIMSELF AND Dara. "May we slip in some biscuits and an excellent wine for Madame's recovery?" the maître d' asks. The staff is so solicitous that Rich feels his throat constrict. Charlotte, about to leave for the theater since that's what London is all about, will get a bite alone afterward. She enjoys dining alone. "I'm excellent company," she always maintains.

"I'm happy that someone is wrenching a bit of enjoyment out of the situation," Lee says. Rich notices that Dara is not eating her veal piccata, which is quite good. He has brought in the contraband—two half bottles of red wine. Dara takes only a few sips.

Rich gets rid of the debris down the hall so Lee doesn't have to smell old food in her room. She has only picked at her own tray of food, all in shades of white. Rich has looked up a movie for them, showing at eight.

"Don't be shocked. I'm going to leave you all and see you tomorrow. Don't get all in a knot, but I am going to Austin's place. He doesn't know I'm coming. He may not be there on a Saturday night, but I'll see."

"What are you going to say?"

"I'll know when I say it."

A BLUE DOOR. HOW APPROACHABLE. LAMPLIGHT BEHIND THIN CURTAINS throws out a faint shine onto the hedge under the window. Dara walks by slowly. To the end of the block. Crosses the street. Walks back. She stands half hidden behind a tree across the street. Where Austin lives. Where Austin came to lick his wounds. Where he has had to carve out a new day. Where there is someone new, perhaps in the upstairs room where a faint glow must mean a night-light. Where if he looked out, he would see a person half hidden, half in darkness. Where, if she lifts the knocker, she gives up her immunity.

Austin is at the dining room table with a drawing pad and a book on Leonardo da Vinci. He is sketching for pleasure, the pure delight of visiting the mind and genius of his old friend Leonardo. He first saw the originals as a boy on a class trip. He remembers noticing a face profile, with lines, many of them, drawn to show how light strikes the face at angles. At fourteen, his mind blasted open with the discovery that Leonardo's genius was grounded in geometry, proportion, and optics. His practice as an architect became an endless education into these three basics. Always, wanting inspiration, he can spend an hour on one messy, notated page of Leonardo's drawings of clouds, a blade of grass, a horse half rearing, two trees—one bare, one with leaves. Drawing clearly is a way of understanding the world for Leonardo. Such evenings, full of silence and astonishment, these are sacred space.

The single bang of the doorknocker. Austin, barefooted, looks out the window in the door. The face framed, eyes wide. He flings open the door.

"Dara!"

"That's right."

"Are you real? I can't believe you're here. I heard about Lee. I thought you'd be coming to see her. You look . . ."

"You, too." They stand in the hallway, door still open.

"It's been almost five months."

"Seems like five years."

He takes her jacket. She steps into the living room. "This is lovely, Austin. It looks like a home. Not at all like your studio."

"Yes, but it's missing our coffee table we found on the street. Never be home without that."

"Were you busy?"

"I was just visiting a bit with my old friend Leonardo. Now I have these long nights, formerly would be out with mates but now I'm here. Obviously." He gestures to the upstairs. "Little guy up there. How could you forget? Let's get something to drink."

Dara leans over the open book of drawings. "Isn't it miraculous when someone is an artist *and* a scientist? Look at that profile with all the lines showing the angles of light hitting the face. To be able to analyze all the layers of light and then to absorb all that into a drawing. Look at this skull in cross section! Is that why he could paint such faces? He knew the structure underneath?"

"Yes. Funny you should turn to that drawing. It was what first drew me to him. What's been knocking me out tonight is that our Leo was studying the skull in slices. It's an architectural drawing in sections—the way he learns to understand the skull. That's the way any architect worth his salt designs and understands space."

They look at each other and laugh. "We haven't seen each other in almost half a year and here we leap into talking, talking, talking. Like always." Dara throws her arms around him and they stand still, holding on.

"My love."

"Yes. It seems so." She pulls away, her eyes on his. "I just want to look at you, see if you are who you were."

"Let's sit. Not here with this mess."

"Well, we certainly know how to make a mess!"

"Correction. I did."

"I'm not blameless. I turned tail and took off."

"You had every right."

"That's true, but wasn't I selfish?"

"Look, women need to be. Throughout time they've been swept along in men's desires and schemes. Look where it landed them most of the time." Austin lights a candle on the coffee table. He sits down beside her on the sofa, takes in her new shorter hair, her luminous skin, and always the aquatic eyes. Mermaid, he'd once called her. She takes his hand.

"Dara, are you back, or is this a courtesy call on an old boyfriend. Just need to know before my heart explodes."

Dara leans closer and kisses his wet lips. "Hello, old boyfriend. I've looked for something new in California, I've tried to erase you all summer at Indigo, I've thrown myself into law school, which I'm really liking, now I've come to London because my mother was crushed. It's been dramatic." She outlines his lips with her fingertip. "I love your lips. I'm back for your lips. And Leonardo. You're my favorite person to talk to. I think we met somewhere long ago, maybe in Leonardo's atelier. You were grinding the lapis lazuli for his blue robe on the Madonna. I was probably sweeping the floor."

"No, you were the model for the angel in *Madonna of the Rocks*."

"You're off your rocker!"

"For you, yes. Always have been."

For a couple of hours, Austin tells her about his life, the new project his firm might get. The surprising news that Amit is seeing his sister, how Jade makes his days possible. "She likes ironing, making sticky toffee pudding, and sings to Thor."

"Thor?"

"Jade and Annsley call him Thor. Sometimes I call him Hawt. He's little for a big name like Hawthorn but eventually he'll grow into it. Will you come up and see him?"

In his crib, Paddington Bear stationed at one end and a soft monkey at the other, the baby Thor, Hawt, Hawthorn sleeps on his back, both arms raised as if he's giving a cheer. Puckered mouth, chipmunk cheeks. Dara sees a tiny Austin. Same straw-blond hair and brows like children's drawings of birds in the sky. She absorbs the beneficent look on Austin's face as he adjusts the blanket. When they tiptoe out of the room, she notices the border of fanciful painted animals and she's hit with a visceral ache for the mother who didn't live to see the new person she delivered to the world. The admiration she has for Austin's unshrinking choices is overtaking the anger she has carried. "I'm sorry you've been alone. I let you down."

"Probably character-developing. Let's not get into blaming or extolling anyone. I let you down more. Let me say, but you know, I'm always yours, ever since that night you insisted we get wet in the rain, then you ate all the fries, and I had an inkling that I'd met the you that one hopes is out there somewhere but seldom finds."

Back downstairs, Dara says, "Do you have anything to eat? I don't think I ate anything today but a cinnamon bun."

"I can make a cheese omelette. And I have Jade's Scottish pudding."

"Both, please. Let me help." Dara fills the glasses, beats the eggs, and finds the cheese in the fridge. Austin pushes Leonardo to the side and sets places for them. "At the beginning of this evening, I never would have imagined that it would include us discussing Leonardo's cross sections of skulls."

Over Austin's quite fluffy omelette, they talk about Mei and Luke's dilemma about where they'll locate if they continue their romance, Dara's classes, and the progress of the biography. Austin tells her about his night terrors and how he has grown closer to his sister, as in childhood. He describes walking into the flat for the first time, the sense that fate had flattened him like a frog under a tire. Like a coin on a rail track. Dara laughs. "Now, which is it?" But she takes in the huge loneliness he experienced for months. "I'd better go soon. This has been the best night of my life since May."

"Can I see you tomorrow night? There's another half of this conversation waiting. Annsley will be here. We could have dinner out. I know Dad wants to call on Lee. He has the famous book that triggered the whole episode. Is she allowed outside visitors yet?"

"I think she is. I'm just here until Monday. On Tuesday or Wednesday they're moving her out to a place Dad found in Richmond. If it's convenient, come to the hospital. We can go from there. Dad, of course, sleeps in her room. Mimi is leaving for Scotland when they transfer to Richmond. She thinks she'd be in the way. As you know, there's always a high-energy field around her."

"You're going on Monday. No!"

"Maybe I will get back before my parents come home. Expensive jaunt, but I can tap into my Mimi funds for school."

"Clear I won't be going anywhere for a while. But, Dara, I am shocked that I have not only adjusted to this life with an infant, but I have the sense that I'm enlarged somehow. Ever had one of those dreams where you find a room in your house that you didn't know was there? He's already a person. I know him."

"You'll be great, as great as Rich and your dad. I should go." Dara takes her jacket off the chair. But she does not go. She gently kisses him good night and the kiss won't stop. How could it stop? A kiss holistic and never-ending, with the longing of months for Austin, with sorrow and surges of joy for Dara, a beginning not an ending, for Austin a vacant-lot fire started by children, for Dara, for each, flushes of adrenaline and strength, the waterfall at Resurrection Creek, a hot, deep need for Austin.

The sudden shrill cry from Hawthorn reverberates down the stairs. Startled, they separate, then begin to laugh.

"See you tomorrow, my love."

Dara walks up the street toward the lights. From the corner of her eye, she sees a slight movement in the shrubbery ahead, just off the sidewalk. A small fox emerges, walks toward her. It holds her stare for a moment, then slinks back into the bushes. A fox in London. There is wildness in everything.

39

Lee has had a better day. Getting up was tough but the effort did give her a vision of recovery. She and Rich both feel encouraged after the constant fluctuations of pain, constant nurses, the whole hospital atmosphere, which makes escape a pressing desire.

When someone knocks, Rich is expecting Dara, but there's Michael and . . . Austin—smiling, holding a bunch of roses. Michael introduces himself to Rich. Austin goes to Lee. "I never expected to meet you next like this."

She reaches to take his hand. "So sweet to see you, anywhere, even here. Oh, Michael, what a beautiful boy you have."

"He'll do." Michael holds up the Yeats volume, still wrapped in blue paper, now scuffed and partially torn. Michael thought Lee might like to see how it survived.

"Ah, the book. I will never, ever pick it up without remembering it tossed through the air."

Michael opens his case and takes out another book. "I was able to find this."

Lee takes *Bartram's Travels* from him. "Well, I won't say all this was worth it just to hold this, but thank you. This will be a treasure at Indigo. I know it must have been trouble."

"It's not, of course, a first edition but it's a good binding in excellent shape. Makes you wonder if anyone ever read it. I never had but I found it fascinating, not only for the flora and fauna drawings, but text. He was there in the South in the 1700s—a memoir of someone bringing form to wilderness."

"Sorry, I was in traffic for so long." Dara comes in. "Oh, Michael, wonderful to see you." She lightly hugs him, kisses Lee, slips her arm around Austin. Rich and Lee have heard earlier today that Dara and Austin had an easy time together, and that meeting Hawthorn didn't seem as cataclysmic as she expected.

Dara sees the bouquet Austin brought and raises the lush pink blooms to her face. Feeling awkward, Austin says, "I'll get a vase from the nurses' station." He's thrust back to the maternity hospital, finding a vase for the peonies he brought Shelley. At any trigger, the memories, not that long ago, slam him with force.

Filling the vase in the bathroom, walking back, he's able to push aside the drastic delivery room images, to anticipate the lively faces waiting in Lee's room. He finds his dad in deep conversation with Lee. They've moved on to finding Bartram seeking order in nature and living in the chaos of uncertain food supply and encountering wild animals.

Lee reaches for her notebook in the drawer beside her, wincing but straightening her shoulders. "I came across an interview when I was researching Samuel Beckett for a class. Beckett's responses struck me as a modern idea but maybe it's not. Maybe we're always floundering . . . okay, just let me read a bit gleaned from my notes:

> *We cannot listen to a conversation for five minutes without being acutely aware of the confusion. It is all around us and our only chance now is to let it in. The only chance of renovation is to open our eyes and see the mess. It is not a mess you can make sense of.*

> *He goes on to say It—meaning the mess—invades our experience at every moment. It is there and it must be allowed in . . .*

Austin and Dara look at each other. Is this about Bartram in the wilds or Austin and Dara in a mess and finding accommodation in a new way?

Michael nods, yes. "What makes the quotes ring is the word *mess,* so unliterary that it empowers the sense of mess." Clearly, Michael and Lee have much to discuss.

Charlotte quietly entered as Lee began quoting. Half soaked from sudden rain, she's running her fingers through her damp curls. "You're Michael, I can tell, and oh, Austin, you are a sight for sore eyes." Arms wide, she takes him in. "Sweet boy, big mess!" They both laugh their huge laughs.

"So, now we're laughing?" Dara raises her shoulders. "Not sure I'm ready for that."

"Mama, you're just in time for one of my lectures! You're late to class." Lee turns several pages in her notebook and reads more:

> *What I am saying does not mean that there will henceforth be no form in art. It only means that there will be new form, and that this form will be of such a type that it admits the chaos and does not try to say that the chaos is really something else . . . To find a form that accommodates the mess, that is the task of the artists now.*

"I'm getting a message here, are you, Austin?"

"It's to the point. I guess we have to thank Mr. Bartram."

"Chaos certainly entered our lives when that car flipped you, my sweet girl. Seems like—who are you quoting?—this writer is surprised. Chaos is only a misstep away, and accommodating it is no choice." Charlotte always has a sideways response that skewers and acknowledges at the same time.

"Beckett."

"He's right, but we adapt to mess all the time. Michael's right, the best thing about the quote is the word *mess. Chaos* sounds grand, but what we usually step in is a sticky mess."

Lee thumbs through her notebook again, not willing to relinquish the last word. "You probably all know this. Keats. His negative capability principle. He wrote to his brothers that Man, or I assume anyone, needs to be 'capable of *being* in uncertainties, Mysteries, doubts, without any irritable reaching after fact & reason.' I think he and Beckett are on the same page. He's talking about mess, too."

"The good word there is *irritable.*" Michael has always loved the Keats quote. He's seeing in everything he knows about Lee a woman he would give the world to find. Lucky Rich—and he seems to know it, leaning in the doorway with an acknowledging smile.

"Sweetheart, are you exhausting yourself? Are you missing your classes?" Rich asks.

"No. Yes, probably, but for the first time since I was hit, I'm myself again, not a whining, inert patient on narcotics."

Charlotte is still thinking. "I agree that *irritable* is the key word. A word, that, if it's always working on pinning down facts, keeps life sour. Your Keats seems more open to possibilities."

"We can talk more. I think Dara and Austin have a dinner reservation," Rich says.

Michael says he, too, must go but he hopes to see them while they're in Richmond. "I'll bring out my unfamous roast lemon chicken." He likes Dara's family. He wonders why he's remained too long alone, except for his books, his children, who have been off in their own lives. There's a customer who comes in quite often, shy and delicate, an occasional collector of botanicals. Maybe she would like William Bartram. Or Keats.

"We'd like that. Anything, as long as it's not bubble and squeak," Rich jokes.

Austin takes Dara's raincoat off the hook and holds it open for her, grabs his own. Goodbye is not easy. Dara nestles her face beside her mother's, whispers, "Love you so. I'll be back before you know it. I'll be in touch every day, now that we have the magic email. Dad's going to spoil you as usual and Mimi is always spoiling you. Please don't push yourself."

"I'm off to Scotland. But, yes, I will be back very soon," Charlotte says. She knows Lee will need a period of complete calm after she's moved.

"Where will you be?" Michael asks.

"In Edinburgh, first. Not sure after that."

"You must ring my sister. She would be delighted to meet you." Michael writes on a business card and gives it to Charlotte. "She's Sarah Rankin."

"Thank you. I will call her."

Dara hugs everyone, aware of their acute interest in what the next few hours hold for the errant couple.

❧

"I HOPE WE HIT IT OFF AS WELL AS OUR FAMILIES DID," DARA REMARKS as they exit the hospital. "That was quite a literary salon going on." Austin hails a taxi and takes them to a conservatory restaurant full of orange trees. It's too chilly for outside, but they're seated by a large window overlooking the garden. "Is everything cooked with oranges? Duck à l'orange. Pork in sour orange. Orange juice cocktail?"

"I think you'll find not." Austin doesn't care what he eats. He only wants to luxuriate in the company of Dara. The waiter brings coupes of champagne, crisp and cold. They touch glasses, holding each other's gaze as they drink. "Early tomorrow you will rise off the tarmac and disappear into the clouds. I will be back in my quite ordered 'mess.'"

"Now we can keep in touch. Both of us are swamped. Maybe if we still have our heads above water, you could come to Redbud for Christmas."

"Ah, nice idea, but I'll have this by-then-crawling-around Hawthorn."

Dara sips her champagne. "Um, yes, you do. This doesn't sound good." She points to the menu. "Lamb rump." She orders the duck, but not with orange, the one with Armagnac and roasted onions. Austin agrees it's the best choice.

"Dara, what do you think? Can we go to your hotel after dinner? Annsley is at my place tonight. I desperately want to make love with you. Would you?"

"Yes. I'd already thought of that. I don't think they'll blink at the hotel. We won't be the first lovers they've encountered. And I have the key. We don't have to ask for it at the desk."

They skipped dessert.

No one was even at the hotel desk when they walked to the elevator. Dara had packed earlier. The flight leaves at 8:00; she must leave the room at 5:30. "You can have the chocolate on the pillow." She pulls closed the draperies.

"No chocolate. Only you."

Austin feels thinner, his shoulders bony through his shirt, and Dara, sad again for his troubles, wants her hands over every inch of him, the bump where he broke his collarbone, his smooth knees, the small of his back. They fall onto the bed, kissing with their whole bodies. His arms tight around her, his thigh over her leg. They stand up only to strip and fall back, wanting to binge on each other, to begin, to begin again, to fuse, hinge, to call back lost time. Sex always, more than sex, finding the nimbus around the moon, the perfect circle Giotto drew in the sand, the soul, whatever soul is, twinning. This time it's Dara who cries, slow racking sobs, with Austin still inside her, and he rubs her hair, rolls them sideways, and starts to sing low, *hush, little baby, don't say a word . . .*

"You're making me laugh."

"I want to make you laugh. Always."

"I want to cry. I've only cried a few times."

"Then cry a river. I've done a bit myself."

Dara hated to think of that. "Will this time we've lost ever tip over into a story?" She slips away and props the pillows so she can lie along his side.

"Lee might title it 'The Mess.' Not a story I'd want to tell anyone. Can I say how delicious you are?"

"Maybe every time we tell it something new will be revealed. You, you're still you."

"Parts of all this I would like to obliterate. Better if Hawthorn had been left for me in a basket on the doorstep."

"In a way, he was."

But Austin knows the searing memories will never become colorful origin stories. "The wrenching part is that I am grateful for him. I think you will see when you know him."

Dara slept on and off. Austin deeply, the best sleep in months. The alarm sounded too soon and the desk called. Car already waiting.

40

DARA EXPECTED CLASSES to be a blur after the long flight, but she is surprisingly focused. By afternoon, beginning to fade, she skips her HUD hours and drives home. A vase of out-of-season anemones waits on the steps, with a card that reads, *You, you, I will always love you.* She sits down smiling and again weeps more tears held in for months. Frankly, she is exhausted after the scare of her mother's accident, the ensuing family gatherings, and the charged reunion with Austin. She keeps zooming in on the brief view of the tiny child sleeping so snugly in his sweet room, alternating the still-puzzling vision with the visceral reconnection with Austin.

In the flurry of mail she hasn't brought in for a week, she sees Italian stamps. She drops her books and satchel on Big Mann's desk. The study has been further cleared by Bill and it seems spacious and inviting, plenty of room to spread out papers, plop down a plate and glass, spend the evenings learning every smidgen she can about the constitution's ramifications. Going through mail, just the sight of the tissue-thin blue paper and the four huge stamps brings back memories of her semester abroad. Italy. How she immersed herself in art. John!

Dear girl! The minute I stepped off the airport bus, I said *I'm home*! Being here is a revelation. The Academy, oh god, what luck. I have a glass studio pierced with light from above. I am resisting painting the ruins. I wander, and I don't know what is seeping into my psyche, but something is. I'm mystified by this place—the depth, the endlessness. Something large to take the place of my longing for you, which you must have felt this summer. I knew it was hopeless, but I hoped. I will always remember that night on the beach. My desire was similar to my passion to paint something valuable. Deep and wide. But, I knew. Oddly, I have met someone named Ginerva. She's from Naples but is a 100 percent Renaissance girl. I can't stop painting her. So don't worry about me. I know you do.

An article about my fellowship here appeared in the Charleston paper before I left. What a shock—I got a letter from my father, who all these years has lived just down the road in Savannah. He said he would like to meet. Said he had no explanation for his abandonment, but that he always loved my sisters and me. (Shove it! What's love like that worth?) Could we meet? I thought about it for about five minutes and tore his letter into shreds and flushed it. Biba approved. What an asshole, was all she said. That was a great moment, liberating me in a big way. So—I came to Roma on winged heels. Biba reigns over Indigo and she's happy that my sister Bee is moving there. She's going to manage the dining room and make ugly plates in her spare time. Our crew seems well settled, both Silvie and Abby back at RISD, Ben curating at a gallery in SoHo. They loved working with you.

Dara, keep in touch. I hope we can celebrate at Indigo. All's well there. Per sempre, John

In a brown envelope she finds photos of her California trip from Courtney and Kate. She thought she was doing well there, but in each shot she's frowning or biting her lip or slumped. Courtney and Kate look wildly alive and vibrant. One photo is of a spotted dog, a mutt. Their note says, *Come back to California! We're negotiating our semiconductor/data management start-up. Our datura bush is in full bloom.*

Meet Bill, a rescue. He's named for Bill Clinton because your grandmother said President Clinton is "a hard dog to keep on the porch." Priceless. Miss you. K & C.

Email from Mei:

Hey! Send me news. I heard about Lee's terrible accident. How frightening. So hope she is recovering. When can she come home? I know you are starting classes. What phase are the constellations and the moon in that so much craziness reigns? My "romance" with Luke bumps along. It feels important but the hurdles are high. Saw Moira and she got some more new work, thanks to Indigo. She's huge already. I'm in touch with Abby and Silvie. We are tossing around ideas for a project together. Would love to come up for a weekend as soon as you have time. Call me when you can. Xoxo Mei

Dara spends hours studying but makes time for turning the condo into a home, not just Mimi's pied-à-terre for family convenience. A tall ficus, rose velvet pillows, old candlesticks, a soft mohair throw, her books on Big Mann's study shelves. She and Austin zip emails to each other. He sends photos of Hawthorn, which Dara studies. A bold-looking little guy. She is surprised that he has blue eyes. He looks older than four months. Maybe he's an old soul.

Mimi writes that she extended her stay in Scotland because she found Michael's sister simpatico. *Sarah is also a psychologist,* she wrote, *but merry and droll. She knits. Quaint. We went to her stony little place on the Firth of Forth and took what she called "bracing" walks. I am inviting her to visit Indigo next year during the long winter when everyone here must grow mushrooms out of their ears. We have had innumerable cups of milky tea. I had to introduce her to bourbon on the rocks. Soon back to London. Lee is progressing, and who wouldn't with Rich fawning over every move?*

❦

RICH ORDERS A LOAD OF WOOD. WHAT IMPECCABLY CUT LOGS. HE STACKS it neatly. Late September has turned chilly, and Lee loves a fire. She reads aloud to Rich, and he's content to follow the murmur of her voice, which sometimes takes him back to the river at home. His work is on hold and he misses it. He brainstorms ideas for articles he would like to research and begins an essay on what the American medical world could learn from Britain and Europe. Hard to find parameters with the vast subject. Lee's hip pain continues. She feels her bones grinding together with each step, and the slow strolls in the meadow exhaust her. The path is level, but coming back she starts to have the pulsating pain so intensely that blue sparks flash behind her eyes. By the time she reaches her fireside chair, she's shaking. The two-week checkup trip to the doctor was excruciating even though the news was positive. Her relief is that her editor's comments are few and helpful. Years of work, a deeply rewarding time. The book will come out as scheduled.

Charlotte is back from Scotland, raving over the heathery colors, placid lochs, and her new friend. She has brought jams and a lumpy yellow scarf she knitted herself at her friend's cottage. Her verve cheers Lee, and as if to please her mother, she begins to gain momentum. By mid-October, they will be home. One morning, mincing along the path with a rolling walker, Lee regains a memory. Just before she stepped off the curb, she remembers, I had been imagining Christmas, or was it New Year's? Could it happen? Will I be normal again, ever?

41

Lord byron said comedies end with a wedding, Lee thinks, tragedies with death. This year has felt anything but comedic. And the death bit was almost mine. She has pulled a plum silk dress out of the closet and holds it in front of her slim naked body. At least something good came of the accident; I am at my ideal weight. In the mirror she glimpses the foot-long scar, the pink of raw shrimp. She rubs it with olive oil like the Italians do with stretch marks, and Rich has kissed the length of it many times. It startles her every time she sees or touches the slick skin. The dress is pretty and will be perfect for holidays.

We're home. Strange, she thinks, how I miss the house in Richmond with the two weirdo birds. She smiles. They were raucous. Once they'd lived in an auto repair shop, and instead of having learned words, they imitated the sounds of engines gunning and sputtering, and dropped wrenches, and tires squealing. She sees herself filling the seed tray, trying to teach them a line from Yeats, *I will arise and go now, and go to Innisfree.* But they weren't interested, responding only with car horn beeps.

The house was solace. In another life I would have liked to live there. In the first weeks at home, friends drop off cookies, flowers, casseroles, books, CDs. Charlotte stays and orders a professional cleaning service to clear the dust Carol, the housekeeper, has missed over the weeks they were gone. She keeps flowers in every room and makes sure dinner is delicious, whether she cooks it or not.

Dara arrives their first weekend back, laden with notebooks, and studies half the night. Lee is walking well by herself, occasionally with a crutch. Redbud is home, deeply home, Lee thinks, and what a miracle. We will share it with our English almost relatives. When Michael came to dinner one night in Richmond, Lee brought up the visit, explaining Redbud Farm and its history. An escape, she proposed, from the English winter.

Michael has only ever been to New York and Philadelphia for book business. If Austin and Dara are making progress together, he is all in for the trip.

Charlotte and Lee scour the attic for a baby bed, last used by Dara and never by the first Hawthorn. They find a playpen, too, but Charlotte says they are cages and barbarian. "He will love a blanket in the meadow," she maintained. "He can roll in the crocuses." They buy a new mattress and crib sheets, borrow a few toys, and a high chair from Moira, whose twins have outgrown it. Lee is all set to welcome Hawthorn. Dara seems remote on the project, but perhaps she is trying to figure out a way forward.

The guesthouse's alcove off the bedroom becomes a nursery. Dara may be wondering if she'll be in that bed with Austin, ten feet away from a sleeping baby. Too cold for the Willowbend possibility. Michael will have the extra bedroom in the house, Charlotte will be in her own room (her Bing visiting his own kids), and Annsley and Amit must stay at the inn. Dara and Austin were stunned to learn that they have quietly continued seeing each other and that Annsley will be spending a week in New York before she goes home.

Austin, Hawthorn, Annsley, and Michael arrive at RDU on December 23. Dara and Rich wait for them in baggage claim amid the clamoring holiday crowd. There's Austin in the throng, the top of his blond hair shining, big grin, the baby wide-eyed and dazzled by the hubbub. They collide with Dara in a hug, the first hug with the three of them. And then Dara says, "Let me hold him while you grab the bags." She holds out her hands to Hawthorn and he leans willingly toward her.

They've brought two cars to the airport. Both are loaded with luggage and baby paraphernalia as they caravan back to Hillston. Amit is already at the Eno Inn, where he was surprised to spot Luke in the bar with Mei.

A lot of clapping on the back, brief hugs, Mei hopping up to greet Amit. "This may be déjà vu," Luke says. He grabs a chair from a nearby table for Amit to sit down. They were devouring hamburgers, a taste Amit has never acquired.

"Does Austin know you're here?"

"Dara and her parents do," Mei says. "We're surprising him tomorrow night for the Christmas Eve dinner."

"Well, hold on to your seat because I'm here with Austin's sister, Annsley. Remember her, Luke? She was at Clare, ahead of us."

"I don't think I've met her."

"We sort of bonded over Austin's situation when I was in London this fall. She's quite formidable."

"That's an odd word for a new girlfriend." But Luke thinks Mei is formidable and Dara, too.

"She's independent. Has her own business, a rare bookshop like their dad's. I think she's been a bit of a loner. They're dropping her off here from the airport." Amit has reserved adjoining rooms in case they're not ready for total proximity.

"Well, don't overwhelm us with info," Luke jokes.

"You'll see. I've told my parents I'll meet the person they expect me to marry, but they have to agree to meet Annsley first. Not that we're marching to the altar. What else? Her specialty is children's books, and that's her whimsical, playful side. We've visited many of the great gardens, so we have that in common, too. I'm helping her with her garden. She has one of those really charming row houses on Orchard Street near Christ's Pieces. Mei, that's a park in Cambridge, no matter how it sounds. The first time I went to her house she made dinner and afterwards we read original Pippi Longstocking books."

The next morning they'd read some early Kipling editions and Amit was plummeted back to childhood.

"You lost me there, man. What the hell is Pippi Longstocking?"

Rich has swagged lights along Redbud's porch and lined the path from the driveway. The splotched bark of the sycamores catches the glow all the way up to the bare branches. Dark now by five, the white lights of the tree in the library window blink, and the front door is hung with the holly wreath made by Lee and Charlotte. Thus it has ever been for Dara, and she's wondering, as they swing into the driveway, how the reserved English are taking in such a vigorous display. Lee is at the top of the steps, not venturing down but waving her arms as if she's guiding the plane to the gate. She's thrilled. This, the vision before the accident, is truly happening.

Everyone settled into their rooms, Annsley left at the inn, Hawthorn naps briefly. It's time for Rich to build a fire by the tree in the library and for Lee to start the oven for the roast. Dinner at home. She's stirring leek soup; Dara made the family's favorite potatoes dauphinois, bought yeast rolls at the farmer's market, and picked up the standby lemon tarts at the bakery. Charlotte serves her pimiento cheese wafers and toasted almonds in the library.

Hawthorn, looking surprised at himself, has pulled up by grabbing Austin's pants. He edges with sideways steps along the sofa. He has never seen this many people in a room at once. Their applause—he seems to realize it's for him—emboldens him to take bigger side steps. Even though his eyes want to blink closed, he rallies with each smiling encounter with the strangers. Michael peruses the library shelves, picking out *Middlemarch* to take upstairs tonight. If ever there was an ill-sorted marriage, it's in those pages.

Austin brings in a warmed bottle and places a cushion near the tree. Resistant at first, Hawthorn allows himself to settle beside Austin, who's sitting cross-legged on the floor. Hawthorn grabs the bottle and soon succumbs to his own warm-milk solitude, falling asleep with a wooly reindeer clutched in his free hand, the bottle slipping and rolling away. Rocco, wary of the baby and keeping his distance, inches toward the bottle and licks the nipple. He's ushered to the kitchen.

Rich leaves to pick up Amit and Annsley. Charlotte goes upstairs to change. Dara and Austin hustle in the kitchen, getting the food organized so nothing will be served cold, while Lee opens wine bottles and lines them up on the sideboard. Left to relax, Michael nods off on the sofa near his grandson, thinking vaguely that of all the results of Austin's freakish folly, he couldn't imagine it would come to this—leaving London, where the December clouds are looking like clumps of dryer lint, taking all his long-distressed family, depositing all of us in a farmhouse in North Carolina, Christmas lights blinking, smell of roast starting to waft through the room, and generous hosts whose every gesture affirms a saving grace.

After dinner, Dara and Rich cleared. Annsley and Amit drove Dara's car back to town, where they were meeting at Mei's. She's promised to take them to Randy's bar. She thinks Annsley and these Cambridge guys need to learn a little dirty dancing. Annsley had a two-hour nap in the afternoon and feels strangely energized to be in this quaint and foreign place. Amit, seeing her open, smiling face in candlelight, bringing out the same charms of her father and brother, feels more smitten than ever. These are all, he realizes, special people.

Lee first, then Charlotte and Michael drift upstairs. Austin lifts Hawthorn from his cushion and takes him to the guesthouse.

All quiet. As it often is, the holiday weather feels unseasonably warm. Dara sits on the front porch, a late-night habit of her family for her whole life. When the kitchen is gleaming clean, candles blown, linens piled in the laundry room, they usually retreat to the porch for an immersion in the big night.

Lee had them eating early because of jet lag and a full tomorrow—a visit to Montrose, an idiosyncratic and fascinating garden that Amit will adore, a walk in Duke Gardens, lunch at Crook's, and a stop at the arboretum in Chapel Hill. Lee will probably be reading on a bench for much of this touring, but she wants the guests to have a meaningful introduction to the area.

For Christmas Eve dinner, they'll gather for the buffet at the inn, where carolers stroll through. Austin will be surprised that Luke is there. Mei has described to Dara a sage velvet dress she designed for the occasion. Rich thinks the inn's entertainment is likely to be hokey but Lee says everyone loves a good "O, Holy Night."

The blinking lights have gone off, leaving the deep country sky to its darkness. Dara has always felt the luck of living where she sees the whole panoply of the night sky. Two owls call back and forth, who, who, who WHOO. Often, the resident albino skunk prowls the buddleias and whoever sits on the porch stays very still. Tonight, nothing moves.

Dara is giving Austin time to settle in before she joins him on the back terrace of the guesthouse. The night is heavenly clear and almost balmy. Austin says he's not tired, but after crossing the Atlantic with an active baby, he must be.

"Finally!" Dara spreads a blanket over a chaise longue, and they squeeze on together. "Is he comfortable in there?"

"He's in never-never land, blissful. I read him the alphabet book and he loved that. He's down for the count."

There are so many things to talk about that neither knows where to begin. They begin with classes, professors, work, Lee's progress. "There's Orion." Dara points. "Many things we don't know about each other. Do you know I took astronomy to get out of math? Big Dipper. My favorites, the Pleiades—seven sisters. Austin, I have a drastic idea. Are you ready?"

"I love your drastic ideas. Remember when we ran into the cold water on the Outer Banks?"

"This is more drastic than that. Listen . . ."

Austin can't stop laughing. Dara will always surprise him. Isn't that reason enough to plan a life together? By then, his hand is under her skirt. Her cool thighs and the feel of a bit of lace. "Shall we go in?"

Dara isn't ready for making love in the vicinity of Hawthorn. "Let's just let the stars watch us." Adroitly, she lifts the lever and flattens the chaise longue with a bang. "It's wide enough for one. You on top, then me."

"That's a plan. If we don't wrench our backs."

Around three, as the dew gathers, they wake up cold and scramble naked into the guest bed, falling immediately asleep. Later, when Dara gets up to go to the bathroom, she peers into the alcove where Hawthorn is sleeping. Behind his lids, she sees his eyes roving. Mysterious that someone this new is already subject to dreams. When will I love you? she wonders. She pauses, waiting to see if her feelings clarify. So long resistant to the idea of his existence and the origins of it, she's waiting for replacement emotions in the face of his actual, startling reality, his excited, hand-waving smile, his innocence, his capture of Austin's love, and his way of spreading wide his fingers, as if about to count to five. She remembers the cross-section nautilus shell on Lee's desk, how the chambers seal off as the living creature moves on in time. A metaphor but is it a good one? How to go on, she thinks, accommodate "mess," but remain alert to the past versus closing a wall and simply adapting to the new? Or maybe, just stop analyzing, justifying. Try to know the little boy on his own terms, not the circumstances that landed him in this windowed alcove at Redbud. What I would have preferred is moot. Maybe at some point, what I preferred isn't what I prefer at all.

42

THE DAY BEGINS with garden touring at Montrose, which Dara and Austin skip. They have errands to run, and Annsley and Lee are happy to take care of Hawthorn. Everyone meets for the sampling of hoppin' John, shrimp and grits, and buttermilk pie at Crook's, and in the evening the groaning-board buffet at the inn. Lee had hired Carol for the afternoon to amuse Hawthorn. She took him on a long stroll through town to see the lights and to meet Santa on the courthouse lawn. In the Polaroid, Carol balances him on Santa's knee and he looks startled and not amused. Austin is home to feed Hawthorn his carrots and peas, then Carol remains for their long evening out, which begins with a buffo performance of *A Christmas Carol* at St. Mary's.

Mei continues the evening festivities at her place, with hors d'oeuvres and a toast. Austin is chuffed to see Luke. Mei taps her glass and announces the news that Moira deserves the first toast as she is in labor right now at Duke Hospital. A few weeks early but nothing to worry about. Austin takes a hard breath and stares down at his shoes. Nothing to worry about, she said. What amazing words.

Charlotte hands around fake tiaras for the women. "There's something about a tiara . . ." she insists. In her black velvet, she looks queenly with hers. At the inn, Michael is astonished to see the gargantuan American turkey ringed with garlands of cranberry. He's not enchanted with the hard cider but Rich assures the free flow of syrah. The carolers prove sweet, their pure, high voices silencing the rowdy group. Everyone does, as it turns out, love a good "O, Holy Night." At the end of the memorable Christmas Eve feast, the group photo of the whole party shows them with eyes wide open, tiaras sparkling, arms linked. Outside, the O, holy night stars are brightly shining . . .

IN BED, LATE AND SATIATED WITH CHEER AND EXHAUSTED FROM THE physical effort, Lee curves around Rich's back. "I think we should change our lives," she says.

"What?"

"My sabbatical was a near-death experience, and my recovery is still going on. I know it's a cliché when a close call becomes a wake-up call. Hello, hello, your life is sifting through your fingers. And I never did not appreciate my one precious life. Do you think I could convert my lost sabbatical to medical leave, since I had no chance to inspire my work?"

"Seems reasonable."

"If I could get next semester off, or fall if it's too late for this year, we could think of a challenge. Restore a preservation house. Write a book on gardens in Marrakech. Take a course at Le Cordon Bleu. Learn French or at least how to pronounce *l'oeuf*. All the above. Or a big trip. Something outside the box. A lot of my clothes are fifteen to twenty years old! I think we need to shake it up. Travel and write. I loved our little outpost in London with those crazy birds and the meadow."

"You liked having me at your mercy." Rich turns over and pulls her gently close, as close as they've come in months. She still gasps as she goes up or down steps. "Let's do that. I want to do anything you want."

"Why don't we each spin out two viable ideas. It would be fun to plan. Hiking is out."

"I'm portable. I couldn't take off work for a semester but I can work anywhere. Donate all those sweaters of mine while you're at it. Some have moth holes the size of my fist."

"They do not!" Lee starts thinking of places she wants to see during her time on this small blue marble traveling through space. Egypt. India . . . she could reach out to Hawthorn's grandmother. How must she bear what happened? She moves on over the map. Japan, the serene, poetic gardens.

43

And what did you want?
To call myself beloved, to feel myself
beloved on the earth.

—RAYMOND CARVER

DARA RISES FIRST. It's Christmas. Already the solstice has passed and the earth is again turning toward the light. She has things to do. Austin sleeps. She sees Hawthorn snuffling in the alcove, not crying but amusing himself with the wooly reindeer. She picks him up, grabs his diaper bag and clothes, and takes him to the house. In her bathroom, she runs a warm bath and Hawthorn willingly sits. She laughs as he aims the bar of soap toward his mouth, then grimaces. "What a good boy," she tries. With a dab of shampoo, she washes his hair, rinsing with a plastic cup. He takes the cup and tries to rinse. And he laughs as water pours over his face. "Gla," he says in his own language. "Gla."

Dressed in a red sweatshirt Annsley has bought him, he sits in the high chair banging the spoon on the tray and opening his mouth for cereal. Austin comes in the back door, pausing to see Dara making funny faces and zooming the spoon like a bee toward Hawthorn's mouth.

Lee heats two quiches, pours juice. No hurry to the tree, no Santa mysteries. Charlotte and Michael appear, then Annsley and Amit knock at the back door. Michael hugs her. "My Christmas angel," he says. She looks radiant. Rich oversees the bacon, as Rocco is given two slices every Christmas. He gobbles it fast, expecting more, and looks quite disappointed until Dara slips him another half piece.

Lee gives sweaters for Christmas. Always sweaters. A rainbow of colors, cardigans for girls, V-necks for boys. Rich groans, holding up a navy one. Charlotte gives money to the family but odd things, too—everyone unwraps something unlikely, a birdseed wreath, harmonica, firecrackers, sparklers, blank book, chocolates, Big Mann's cuff links and money clip. She saves the practical items for the residents of the abused women's shelter. Rich, bringing down stuff from the attic a few days ago, found a large box of children's books, Charlotte's from childhood. She's happy to part with them and he's wrapped the box for Annsley, promising to ship to London whatever she wants. Annsley lifts out early copies of *The Boxcar Children*, *The Secret Garden*, *Rebecca of Sunnybrook Farm*, and *Anne of Green Gables.* She kisses Charlotte on both cheeks. "Are you sure? I love them. Look, Hawthorn, you'll get to hear all of these."

Christmas day provides a lull. Reading, river walk, naps, low music playing in the living room. Forget white Christmas. Better the white camellias pushing their faces against the wavy glass, the sun, the sweet benison of sun to shine on their river walk.

Everyone, after the gifts, goes off on their desired paths. Dara and Austin disappear for a few hours, but no one notices. Amit dominates the kitchen while he makes a chutney he thinks will be perfect with the dinner. Annsley sits at the kitchen table engrossed in *The Boxcar Children.* Lee and Charlotte perform their rituals—setting the long table for the feast. Garland of greens down the center, studded with candles. Charlotte's mother's Queen Victoria Herend china, taken out only twice a year, and the chandelier hung with holly. There will be on the sideboard ambrosia, country ham, wild rice, squash casserole, biscuits. The English have brought shiny green crackers to pull so everyone will have a paper hat. Rich and Michael watch some loud game on TV until Michael quietly retires to the library with *Middlemarch.*

Dara takes Austin to the stable where she boarded her horse. She always has visited on Christmas, though she no longer mixes the grains for the horses' breakfast. Other small girls perform that service. The thoroughbreds are already out in the pasture, placidly grazing, but two wander to the fence, seeming to recognize Dara. They pop by Moira's to drop off cheese straws and roasted pecans, and to meet tiny Amelia Mei. Moira is nursing in a big rocker. She's wan but thrilled. Dara is touched that she's selected her middle name for the baby. Amelia was her great-grandmother, Charlotte's mother, whom she never knew. Austin is eager to go. Childbirth may always be a fraught situation for him. Dara bends to kiss Moira's cheek as they leave. She whispers something in her ear. Next stop, Mei's to exchange small gifts.

At the dinner table, Michael toasts his hosts. "I have a whole new vision of American life, if I can judge it by our splendid time at your charming Redbud. Thank you for welcoming my family, for being large-minded, for this dinner that speaks eloquently of your region, for everything!" Charlotte raises her glass. "To my Stephen. He loved this house at holidays, and I wish he had met all of you." Austin: "I can't even say how happy I am. Here's to you exceptional people, especially to Lee, who exemplifies grace under pressure." Then Luke, who has been quiet, stands. "Just want to remember for a moment. In April, many of us were at this table. This stupendous table. Austin and Dara were on a brink but not the one they expected. The wine spilled. But look around." He turns to Mei and raises his glass, then to Hawthorn, and at Amit and Annsley. "So much happened. Maybe too much!" Everyone laughs. "Here's to all you revelers. Let's have a calmer next year."

The party moves to the living room for dessert and, if Charlotte prevails, charades. Hawthorn, having had a long afternoon nap, is still awake. He's dressed up in a red plaid outfit with a white ruffled collar. Rocco, used to him now, lets him lie back on his fluffy body and flail around, grabbing handfuls of his fur. Rich stokes the fire that isn't needed, except for the primitive joy and comfort it affords. He looks for a long moment at the portrait John Harrison painted of Dara last spring. Propped on the mantel, she looks out at the vibrant room full of her family and her love as she leans against a tabby wall, palm trees clattering behind her in the early May breeze. Where is Dara? He looks down the hall. He hears clatter in the kitchen. She's probably helping Carol with the dessert. Mei? She must be in the bathroom. Austin stands with his back to the room, looking out the window as car lights turn into the driveway. "Hey, Lee, are you expecting anyone?"

Lee is setting out the dessert forks on the sunporch table. Across the room she sees Rich open the door and greet Robert Wilson. Is someone dead? He's never stopped by on a holiday. "I want to make sure my favorite parishioners are having a great Christmas." He greets everyone and walks to the fireplace just as Austin pushes in a CD and turns up the volume on Monteverdi's joyous trumpet toccata played long ago at the marriage of Michael and Delia, music that glorifies everyone listening. Dara whoops from the top of the stairs and begins to descend in the breathtaking pale yellow dress Mei made, and she's carrying a pink rose, plucked from the hall arrangement, and a worn leather volume of Keats's poems that her mother carried when she married Rich. Mei following in blue, is laughing, Dara crying and laughing, stumbling once, and Reverend Wilson shouts out, "Dearly Beloved, we are gathered . . . " and the room erupts, clapping and exclaiming as Dara descends, makes her way to Austin, who barely can open his eyes to the vision of his girl, his arms out for her certain embrace, but she touches the rose to his lips, then presses her lips to his, as sweet as being gets.

"We have before us these two souls whose journey to this moment has not been easy." Reverend Wilson holds out his arms as if to embrace everyone gathered.

"Understatement," Dara says loudly.

"I'm here to bless them, though they are already blessed. Blessed by everyone in this room, blessed with fortitude and love and will. Let us attend to what they have to say to each other."

The vows written earlier this year were forgotten. The new ones may have been improvised but as Austin and Dara speak, Charlotte feels her whole career soar: Their solemn promises seem inspired, directly or by osmosis, by the last chapter in *The Good Marriage*, the chapter entitled "The Great Marriage." She starts to cry and Lee moves close.

Austin takes Dara's hands. "I will love you more than myself."

She responds, "You will always come first."

"I will worship you with my body."

"I'll do a lot of the cooking."

"I'll let you drive sometimes."

"I'll protect your dreams."

"I'll dream us out of any mess." Austin breaks up laughing.

"I'll push you to do your best."

"You will be my home."

"In myself, I will always be looking for you."

"I, you."

Austin takes the ring Dara once left beside the note when she fled Washington. His mother's ring. Mei hands Dara the gold band engraved *forever.* The reverend joyously pronounces them married.

Rich breaks open more champagne and it spills over, drizzling over his fingers. Dara hands Austin the knife to cut the cake. Only Mei, Reverend Wilson, and Carol were in on the secret wedding. Carol retrieved the frozen layers of wedding cake, frosted them at home, and all afternoon kept the cake stored in the trunk of her car. Lacking pastry skill, she decorated it with sugared violets, and just before she brought it aloft into the sunroom, plopped a ring of pink camellias around the base. Charlotte starts to dance with Michael, but he raises his arms in surrender, hopelessly struck by the Monteverdi memory. Everyone laughs as Charlotte continues her version of "Night Fever" alone. Amit and Luke are in deep conversation on the sofa. Hawthorn finally begins to give up. Annsley takes him to the guesthouse, where he thrashes before settling down. I'm mystified, she thinks, that Amit and I didn't see this wedding coming. Maybe this is where I begin to know Dara. It's the most romantic one I've ever attended. And Dara's going to do her best for my little darling. She didn't know Michael had given Austin their mother's engagement ring. He has given her the wedding ring. She looks at her bare fingers and wonders if she will ever use it. She kisses Hawthorn good night. "I'll aways be checking on you," she whispers.

Done with dessert, everyone fading. Dara curls beside Austin in the big armchair by the fire. Rich lounges on the floor, his back against Lee's chair. Long, they talk. What are your plans, how long can you be gone from London, when will you meet again, how hard will this be, on and on. Dara answers that they are "being in uncertainty," as Keats recommended. "I may transfer to Stanford if Austin can work something out. I may take a year off in London until he can get back to New York. Who knows! The mess, remember?" Charlotte drains the last sips of her cognac, all nods and smiles.

"We got married because we had to." Austin leans down to clink his empty glass to Charlotte's. "Otherwise, life makes no sense. Whatever the circumstances, we'll roll with it. It's not as if our trajectories were ever that clear." Rich gets up to poke the fire.

The blaze turns to coals, and soon everyone is saying *good night, good night*. Starting tomorrow, they scatter. Luke and Mei road-tripping to Sarasota; Michael, Annsley, and Amit flying to New York, where Michael will stay, via Rich's membership, at the civilized University Club. He has appointments at the Morgan Library and the Public Library to look at specific editions. On Thursday—it will take till then to get the house back in order—Lee and Rich will caravan with Charlotte to Indigo. Biba has invited them for New Year's Eve, and Charlotte plans an oyster roast to welcome Bing home. Austin, Hawthorn, and Dara will drive to Washington.

The house finally gone quiet, Austin and Dara make love in the chair. "Not the Italian honeymoon we planned," he whispers.

"Better," she says.

THE MINI IS PACKED TO THE GILLS. AUSTIN WHISTLES THAT HIGH WHIS-tle of his as he carts out bags. Lee and Rich help stuff the trunk and wedge Hawthorn into his seat. "Drive very carefully," Lee says. "Darling, I am so happy, that was the craziest, best wedding, much better than the meadow would have been." Though they've said their farewells last night, Charlotte steps out on the porch in her bathrobe. "Not coming out. Love you, love you. Proud as can be!"

Dara holds both parents close. "Come up to DC for Valentine's. I'll be practicing my cooking skills, which are nil. I probably won't go to London until spring break. Don't worry. I am in heaven. For now." The "for now" being superstition that the gods smite those who think they're in control.

Hawthorn looks fixedly at Lee and Rich. "Say bye-bye," Austin tells him. Hawthorn imitates his father, raising his fist and slowly uncurling his fingers.

"You're amazing," Austin tells Lee and Rich. "Thank you for raising this beautiful girl. I hope we can do half as well, at that Hawthorn will be a prince."

Austin pulls away from Redbud, Dara waving out the window until they are out of sight.

At last, let loose into their lives.

Acknowledgments

I HAVE THE PLEASURE and luck to work with such brilliant people at Ballantine Books. Hilary Teeman, my editor, combines force and grace so well. My great thanks to her and to the team: Caroline Weishuhn, Chelsea Woodward, Allison Schuster, Vanessa Duque, Pamela Alders, Sandra Sjursen, Cindy Berman, John McGhee, Elizabeth Rendfleisch, Jennifer Hershey, Kim Hovey, and Kara Welsh. To Elena Giavaldi, *grazie mille* for the cover design. I love it! Peter Ginsberg of Curtis Brown Ltd., friend and agent for thirty years: words are inadequate. Sending warm thanks also to Nikki Christer of Penguin Random House, Australia, and to Fiona Inglis of Curtis Brown Ltd., also in Oz. Thanks always to The Steven Barclay Agency for sending me on fantastic jaunts. For sharing their intimate knowledge of London, I'm grateful to Nancy McEnerney, Steven Rothfeld, Susan Swan, and Debbie Travis, and to fellow members of the Cortona Traveling Book Club: Susie and Rowan Russell, Coco Pante, and Jean and Aziz Cami. John Beerman and Nancy Demorest passed on their love of Pawleys Island to me. (And Nancy once danced on the table.) To Hampton Dellinger, my thanks for law school information. My husband, Ed, and my daughter, Ashley King, are always my first readers. No matter what, they're completely enthusiastic, which is just what a writer needs. *Baci* to them.

Notes

p. 27 *The Wind in the Willows* by Kenneth Grahame

p. 49 "I want to do with you . . ." from Pablo Neruda's poem "Every Day You Play . . ."

p. 49 "Delia's Gone . . ." Traditional Georgia ballad recorded many times in the 1960s folk revival movement

p. 55 ". . . wolf on the fold" from "The Destruction of Sennacherib" by Lord Byron

p. 72 excerpted from "Adam's Curse" by W. B. Yeats

p. 130 Reference to the poem "Musée des Beaux Arts" by W. H. Auden

p. 150 Jerry Stackhouse, University of North Carolina basketball star of that era

p. 156 "The palm at the end of the mind . . ." from "Of Mere Being" by Wallace Stevens

p. 163 Plan B for Southerners comes from a 27 Views podcast with Allan Gurganus

p. 163 "the center cannot hold" from "The Second Coming" by W. B. Yeats

p. 172 *Tess of the d'Urbervilles* by Thomas Hardy

p. 180 Cazalet Chronicles by Elizabeth Jane Howard

p. 233 Verse carved on stone at the Irish castle tower Thoor Ballylee, lived in by W. B. Yeats

p. 265 Excerpts from "Beckett by the Madeleine," Tom Driver's interview with Samuel Beckett published in the Columbia University Forum, 4, in summer, 1961

p. 279 Montrose is a garden in Hillsborough, North Carolina

p. 282 *A Christmas Carol by Charles Dickens* was for many years energetically performed by the writers Allan Gurganus and Michael Malone at Saint Mary's Episcopal Church in Hillsborough, North Carolina

p. 288 Giorgio Monteverdi's "Toccata from *L'Orfeo*"

Hillston is inspired by Hillsborough, North Carolina. The name repeats that of the town in the also Hillsborough-inspired novels of Michael Malone. Indigo Island is inspired by Pawleys Island, South Carolina.

The character of Senator Stephen Mann is inspired by the life of a great American and friend, Walter Dellinger.

About the Author

Frances Mayes is the author of the classic *Under the Tuscan Sun,* which was a *New York Times* bestseller for more than two and a half years and became a movie starring Diane Lane. Her other international bestsellers include *Bella Tuscany, Every Day in Tuscany, A Year in the World, See You in the Piazza,* and the illustrated books *Bringing Tuscany Home, The Tuscan Sun Cookbook,* and *In Tuscany.* Mayes is also the author of two novels, *Swan and Women in Sunlight.* Her most recent books are *A Place in the World, Pasta Veloce,* and *Always Italy.* Her books are translated into more than fifty languages.

Instagram: @francesemayes

About the Type

This book was set in Fournier, a typeface named for Pierre-Simon Fournier (1712–68), the youngest son of a French printing family. He started out engraving woodblocks and large capitals, then moved on to fonts of type. In 1736 he began his own foundry and made several important contributions in the field of type design; he is said to have cut 147 alphabets of his own creation. Fournier is probably best remembered as the designer of St. Augustine Ordinaire, a face that served as the model for the Monotype Corporation's Fournier, which was released in 1925.